War With Elves:

For Profit and Amusement

Book 1 of The Elixir of Power Trilogy

Timothy S Currey

TIMOTHY S CURREY

For Leah, obviously. Who else could it be?

No man is an island,
Entire of itself;
Every man is a piece of the continent,
A part of the main.

If a clod be washed away by the sea,
Europe is the less,
As well as if a promontory were:
As well as if a manor of thy friend's
Or of thine own were.

Any man's death diminishes me,
Because I am involved in mankind.
And therefore never send to know for whom the bell tolls;
It tolls for thee.

John Donne

WAR WITH ELVES: FOR PROFIT AND AMUSEMENT

Chapter 1

I'm off to fight the enemy
Before he kills me first.
Whate'er I might do to him,
He's already done worse.

'Fight the Enemy,' First Stanza

From the vantage of the hill he had conquered, Fentor aimed his spyglass toward hostile territory, silently daring the enemy to appear. The hill was his castle, with sandbag ramparts and a mud-brown, midge-infested moat. A month had passed since he had claimed it from the enemy. The day of that triumphant charge rang in his ears still, with the clear notes of trumpets, the crack of muskets, and the shouting of soldiers who had become, for a glorious hour, immortal. The problem with taking land from the enemy was the effervescent taste of glory that lingered in one's mouth, that sip of destiny's champagne. One always craved more.

That craving had gone unfulfilled for an entire month. Such a long wait between battles rendered the otherwise lovely war quite tedious.

Then, as if conjured by his thoughts, a barrage of gunfire began—but nowhere near Fentor or his hill. The skirmish erupted in the west, far along the lumpy expanse of trenches and sandbags. The elves, hidden in dense forest, exchanged fire with Angsley's cohort.

Seen from such a distance, the elves' glowing red arrows rose and fell in graceful arcs, and the blue clouds of spent gunpowder swelled, as did the sound of rifles. Thus, the battle seemed to play out, volley after volley, crack after crack, between two deeply antagonistic hills. One spat red, the other coughed blue. It was almost peaceful to watch, a part of nature, like leaves falling from a tree, or waves caressing the shore. One was forced to think morbidly like that. The longer and drearier the war, the stranger one's thoughts became.

"Hess?" Fentor called, taking his eye from the spyglass.

Looking down at the terraced sandbags below, he saw every tricorne-bearing head turned toward the unfolding battle. They held their muskets loosely, leaning on sandbags for a better view. Fentor could just imagine the slack-jawed, vacant expressions on their faces.

"Wake up, you loafers! This isn't the bloody theatre!" Fentor bellowed. "And fetch me Lancer Hess at once!"

With a flutter of tricornes and a flash of bayonets, his soldiers tore their eyes from the distant battle and busied themselves. It was a wonder that the very same soldiers had been able to beat back the elves just a month ago. They looked hardly able to conquer so much as an ant-hill. It served as proof that an especially capable leader can erase the failings of lackluster troops.

In that stretch of the ever-shifting front, affectionately called the Gutter Trench, there were two constants: mist and midges. As arrows fell in sheets on Angsley's cohort, Fentor was under an attack of a different sort. He swatted and slapped the midges as they landed on him, bit him, buzzed in his ear, but no matter his efforts the swarm returned, redoubling their assault. A swarm of elves would be preferable.

"Confound it, where is Hess?" Fentor roared.

Below, a fresh-faced soldier turned and called up, "She's coming soon, sir! Scouts are giving their report to her now."

Fentor drummed his fingers on his spyglass. The scouts might have spotted something among the trees—a pointed ear, a footprint, a lock of silver hair. That offered a slim thread of hope, at least. Failing that, certain guests would be arriving soon, who could probably break the monotony well enough.

He turned his magnified eye back to the distant battle.

"You were looking for me, sir?"

Fentor turned to see a saluting Lancer Hess. The tip of her tricorne pointed jauntily upward over a freckled, open, bright face, and an expression which teetered dangerously close to mirth.

"Yes, I was, Lancer," Fentor said. "Where have you been?"

"Why, I was receiving the report from the scouts, of course." She let her salute drop, and eased her stance — without explicit permission, Fentor noted.

"What did they report, then, *Lancer*?" Fentor said, raising his brows on the final word. Sometimes, with old friends, a new difference in rank bore repeating.

Hess, however, chose to ignore the reminder. She took off her tricorne, waved a cloud of midges away, then approached him. "Have you noticed what the elves are doing?" She pointed across at the unfolding attack on Angsley's cohort. As Fentor turned, they ended up standing so close that their shoulders brushed.

He glanced over his shoulder. They were alone at the top of the hill. Still, even without witnesses, he could feel her casual air eroding his authority.

Fentor scrutinized the elven position through his spyglass, and caught the distinctive red sheen of a transparent, curved barrier between the trees — an aegis. A shield conjured by the elves, a membrane to block bullets without impeding their own magical munitions. It looked like an enormous crimson soap-bubble. Tiny ripples broke out along its surface as musket balls struck it, protecting the elves, drawing out the battle, wasting ammunition, and rendering the spectacle of battle tedious. The Madeans would shelter behind their sandbags, and the Elarím behind their aegis.

Aegis, from Old Madean, meaning 'shield.' It ought to have been called *tedious*, from present-day Madean, meaning 'dreary, dull.'

"The bullets won't break it any time soon." He sighed. "A stalemate, then."

"Indeed, it is. Fortunately, the scout's report is more promising," she said, leaning in and lowering her voice.

Fentor lowered the spyglass and found Hess' face close to his. He swallowed down a flutter that had come up his throat.

"Look, Hess. Lancer. Remember your place and I'll remember mine," he said.

"Come on, now! My 'place?' "

"Yes! You must treat me as a superior. I'm a Capilet now, for Temlin's sake," Fentor said gruffly. He took her by the shoulders and marched her three paces away from him. "You mustn't stand so close. And call me 'sir,' for Providence's sake!"

"That Capilet patch on your shoulder — are you wearing it, or is it wearing you? Which is it, Fenny?" she said.

"Don't call me Fenny." He looked around frantically, as though the King of Madea might have arrived just in time to hear the pet name. "I am to be addressed as 'sir' or 'Capilet Lonochy.' "

"What about in the city? You'd let me call you Fenny there, wouldn't you, Fenny?"

"We can be friends in the city, if only because I'm powerless to stop you there," Fentor said. "All I ask is that you at least *pretend* I'm your superior while we're on the front. I'm trying to make something of myself — of my cohort. The links in the chain of command rust awfully fast without the lacquer of respect."

"Your point is both poetic and clear, sir," Hess said, with sincerity, although her 'sir' had been ever-so-slightly drawn out.

"Good. Now…what was the report?"

"There's a saying among the scouts, sir: if you spot one elf, there are a dozen more that you didn't."

"Charming adage," Fentor said. "But what bearing does it have on our situation?"

"Well, sir, our scouts saw about fifty elves in the vicinity. Though none seem to be headed this way," Hess said.

"That's quite a number," Fentor said. "Is Angsley's cohort in danger of being overwhelmed?"

"Can't be sure, *sir*. But we're keeping an eye on it, *sir*," Hess said. Her voice had become so monotone, her stance so absurdly rigid, that it was now clear she was mocking him.

"Is there anything else you can tell me?" Fentor said.

"About what, sir?" Hess said, the corner of her mouth twitching slightly.

Fentor pursed his lips. A dozen ironic and mocking answers sprang to mind, but he suppressed them all. He would rather be drawn into an Elarím ambush than into plebeian banter with an inferior officer. "About the fifty or so elves that were spotted."

"They were all armed, and they came and went in small groups, sir," she said.

"Nothing else? Nothing definitive?"

"There is one more thing, sir. A message arrived for you," Hess said.

"What is it?"

"It's a sensitive message, sir," Hess said quietly, beckoning him close. "Best not relay it too loudly."

Her usually bright face took on the earnest sincerity of a pall-bearer. Could it be a secret communique from Grand

Toque Talentus? Fentor looked over Hess' freckled face, and found no twinkle in her eye, no twitch in her lip.

He leaned in so that she could whisper in his ear.

"It's a kiss from your Auntie!" she hissed.

Before he could stop her, she pressed her lips to his cheek, then darted away. While Fentor fumed in paralytic silence, she was consumed by laughter. It was a laugh unique to her, with hiccups and quiet snorts. Only Hess could play such a vulgar trick on him and get away with it. Her snuffling laugh was half the reason.

"Capilet Fentor, sir?" A timid young man appeared nearby, his eyes averted and his cheeks flushed. An air of polite embarrassment seemed to blow in with him.

Fentor cleared his throat loudly and shot Hess a severe look. "Thank you, Lancer Hess. Keep me apprised of the … scouting. You are dismissed."

"Aye, sir," Hess said, her cheeks still glowing, then left.

The new arrival, Junior Lancer Thorassa, came a pace closer and cast up a salute, showing fingers stained blue by gunpowder. He was young, blond, fair, and rather rabbit-like in the rigid, twitching way he stood. The tuft of pale hairs covering his lip, too, only drew attention to large front teeth that prevented full closure of his lips. It did not help that his eyes were rather small and wet-looking, and that the tip of his nose was pink.

"What is it, Thorassa?" Fentor said, with his hands on his hips, and a commanding note in his voice that might overwrite any lingering image of Hess kissing his cheek.

"A wagon full of, er … 'guests' have arrived, sir," Thorassa said. "Though I'm not sure who. The soldiers would only tell me that they were guests."

8

Fentor smiled slightly. That was term given to elven prisoners of war by the rank-and-file. "Have you dealt with guests before, Lancer?"

"No, sir, I have not," Thorassa said. His eyes darted one way and then another, then he said, "Are we to … prepare a tent for them to lodge in?"

Fentor smiled again, this time with the paternal smile of a patient headmaster addressing a student.

"Come along, Thorassa, and we shall greet our guests," Fentor said.

"Aye, sir," the Lancer said.

Fentor led the twitchy young officer down through the sloping mud paths, around the back of the hill.

"You come from a good family, Thorassa. A great store of potential glories and triumphs dwell within you. Why, I think my father may have known yours," Fentor said.

"Indeed, sir?"

"Well, I assume he did. My father knew everyone worth knowing," Fentor said. "But never mind that. How much do you know about keeping elves as prisoners?"

"Not a great deal, sir. I rather thought we'd spend more time fighting them than jailing them."

"Ah, but there's the trick of the question. We *don't* jail them," Fentor said.

They rounded a rocky corner and continued along a ledge that overlooked a long, snaking road that curled between the hills. A wagon holding two dozen chained elves sat there, like a livestock pen on wheels that some bizarre farmer might take to market.

Pale elves with silvery hair and dirty faces looked out at their surroundings with malice, despair, frustration, resignation.

A column of Bluefingers lined the road beside the wagon, each of them resting muskets in the crooks of their arms. Thorassa's eyes flickered across the scene below. Fentor could almost hear the watch-springs winding up in the Lancer's mind.

"Sir, if we don't jail them ..." Thorassa began.

"I trust you are familiar with the Common Power — elven magic," Fentor said.

"I am, sir."

"You know the Common Power as the source of their little tricks of warfare — the whistlers, the aegis. One must always keep in mind what the Common Power actually *is*."

"I believe it's how they share their magic, sir. They share it all together as one ... thing," Thorassa said.

They came to the bottom of the path and started toward the waiting line of Bluefingers, who saluted at Fentor's approach.

"Well, dear boy, you're not entirely wrong. The Elarím, as one big nation, share a single, great store of magical energy. Many say it's the reason this bloody war has dragged on so long. Can you think of a reason why it means we can't keep them prisoner?"

Junior Lancer Thorassa tried valiantly to offer a guess, his brows squeezing down on his eyes as though they could extract more thought from his brain. His lips even moved for a moment, but they made no sound.

Fentor continued, "Because any time you get any significant number of elves together, they have a tendency to use the Common Power to break out. They can't even be trusted to stay in the same building! The only way we *could* keep them locked up would be to give each one a one-cell prison all their own, far, far away from any of their kinsmen. And the King can hardly be expected to cover such an expense, can he?"

"No, he can't, sir," Thorassa said.

"And that brings us here." Fentor turned to the Bluefingers. "Line them up! Ready weapons!"

Four musket-men opened up the wagon, and pulled on the chains that bound their elven 'guests.' The prisoners were soon arranged in a line on the road, facing a parallel line of Bluefingers. Powder and shot were loaded into the muzzle of every gun.

"You give the order, Lancer," Fentor said quietly to Thorassa.

Thorassa's pale eyelashes quivered as he looked across at the line of chained elves. "Me?"

"Yes, you," Fentor said, and he gripped the young man's shoulder bracingly. "Stiff back, clear voice. Show them who's in charge."

The young Lancer cleared his throat, stood straighter, and turned to the Bluefingers with a hard glint in his eye.

The Bluefingers and elves, arranged in neat lines opposite from one another, looked like pieces in a sadist's game of chess. Every eye was turned to Thorassa, who drew a breath and squeezed knotted fingers behind his back so hard that they turned white.

"Fire."

****

The elves assaulting Angsley's cohort had, at last, retreated. A runner later informed Fentor that minimal casualties had been inflicted, that nothing had really been gained or lost. Thus, the battle, if one saw fit to call it that, had been little more than something to look at — a show of fireworks.

At that point, Fentor had traded his tricorne for a bath-flannel, his gun for a cigar, and his sabre for a stout glass of brandy.

True, the glass was chipped, the cigar dry, and the rusted bath far too small. But with an effort of will and imagination, he could believe he was luxuriating in a porcelain lagoon, fine crystal goblet in hand, veiled in a heady cloud of the finest tobacco-smoke. The hot water soaking into his bones and the whisper of brandy in his ear sustained the illusion, deepened it. Soon he was the richest man in Madea, free from all obligations except having to accept awards and medals from time to time. He was a Grand Toque, a war-hero, an innovator, and conqueror. By his hand alone, the elves were defeated, and Madea, fair and mighty, reigned supreme.

Such was the bliss that Junior Lancer Thorassa intruded upon.

A cold evening wind shattered Fentor's visions with all the grace of a pug toppling a stack of crockery. Peeling the bath-flannel from his face, he glared at the young officer, who seemed unable to meet Fentor's eyes.

"What is it, Lancer?"

"Beg pardon, sir. The scouts are due back shortly,"
Thorassa said, leaning half-into the tent and addressing
the ground under Fentor's bath. "Lancer Hess asked me to
… to make sure you'll be ready."

"She asked you that, did she? In those words?"

"She said something I'd rather not repeat, sir. About you
covering certain … she, er, mentioned a hat hanging off
a—"

"That's enough. I would expect no better from her. Very
well, tell the Lancer I shall be dressed and decent in time
for the report."

"Sir," Thorassa said. He then aimed a salute at a point
above Fentor's head, and withdrew.

Fentor dried and dressed quickly, cigar still between his
teeth. His shaving mirror revealed ragged edges on his
moustache, and the threat of incoming stubble upon his
olive cheeks. When he brushed his dark hair out of the
way, it revealed the line where his forehead had been
advancing year after year into his hairline. The day would
soon come when common decency would force him to
shave it all off. For the moment, all he could do was neaten
the hair on his face.

In Madea, a man's moustache was more than a
moustache. Madean Land Corps mandated them, of
course, but few men grasped their true meaning.

Fentor's father had once said, "Less fortunate souls
cannot afford to spend time on the frivolous. A proper
moustache *is* frivolous. That is its purpose: it takes time to
groom. Time that only important men have to spare.
Decent scissors, combs, oils, and tonics are not cheap,

either. A well-maintained moustache will say to the world, 'I am your better.' "

Fentor's aim, as in everything, was to say to the world, 'I am the *best*.'

So, with tiny pair of silver scissors, a dab of grooming oil, and a deft hand, Fentor snipped the ragged edges of his moustache and straightened it. Before long, it looked so straight and sharp that a carpenter might have used it as a chisel.

As he finished his cigar and brandy, he poked idly among the recovered elven weapons he kept on his table. One, the sabre-spear, was something like a collapsible brass curtain rod topped with a blade. The handle could supposedly be lengthened or shortened as needed, transforming from pike to sword with the click of a switch. Fentor turned its little brass gears experimentally, but it remained a curtain rod.

The other weapon, one of their ghastly bows, had interlocking brass gears and switches all along its length. Aside from a little notch where an arrow could rest, no Madean had ever discerned the proper use of its various bells and whistles. Fentor saw little point puzzling over it in earnest. Little could ever be known about the inscrutable ways of elves. The best thing to do was shoot them.

Then his hands drifted by the bust of his father, Baron Jontain Lonochy. The stern marble face looked down from its stand at the cluttered table with a disapproving sneer. Father had looked at everything that way, Fentor supposed. Some men had been raised by doting, supportive fathers. Fathers who praised their sons, hugged them, eased their fears. Fentor had the good fortune of being raised in the opposite way.

A tiny square of folded paper was wedged in the statue's mouth—Jontain's last letter to his son. Reading it was never wise, and yet it had the repulsive allure of picking at a scabbed wound. He had read it countless times before, and would read it again. He shouldn't, but he would. The brandy in his hand all but guaranteed it. He reached for the letter.

The tent opened, and Hess' face appeared. "We're ready for you, sir."

Fentor quickly withdrew from the bust, drained the last of his brandy and extinguished the cigar in the glass.

"Come in, then," he said.

Hess and Thorassa entered the tent, followed by the cohort Alchemist, Lancer Crauford. He was a young, dark-skinned Thambrian, who had renounced an unfathomably large inheritance to come to Madea. Providence alone knew why. Everywhere he went, he squinted at the world through tiny spectacles, speaking with soft curiosity, often lost in the foggy moors of his own thoughts. Fentor had the impression that Crauford's obsessive studies of the arcane and abstract had gone on too long, and rendered flesh-and-blood reality too dull to deserve much notice.

Of course, in times of battle, Crauford's grip on reality was perfectly adequate.

Fentor took a seat at the table, moved aside the elven weapons, and invited the others to sit across from him.

"What is the latest report, Lancer Hess?" he asked.

"Scouts have marked out sightings of the enemy in a rough semi-circle around our position. Some of our lads were spotted, and there were brief exchanges of fire. No casualties, though. They noticed a lot of elves waiting about, like they're expecting orders. Seems like an attack is now coming our way, sir," Hess said.

"What kind of numbers are we facing?"

"With respect, sir, enough that we ought to start sewing some white sheets together to make a flag," Hess said.

"Out of the question. I'll not give up a hill that I've only just claimed," Fentor said.

"The surrender part was a joke, sir, but the imminent attack was not. We may not have a say in the matter of keeping the hill," Hess said.

"We still have a say, so long as I'm in charge. What we need is a new idea, a fresh tactic. Crauford, what have you cooked up lately?"

"In terms of alchemy, a vial of Malcolm's Elixir of Hardskin. In terms of ideas, I'm afraid nothing new, sir," Crauford said softly, pushing his spectacles up the bridge of his nose.

"That's good. That's not nothing," Fentor said. "But — only one vial?"

"It's a time-consuming concoction. Most of my time has gone to optimizing the potency of our ash of tri-kryside, sir."

"What's that?" Thorassa asked Crauford quietly.

"It's just Crauford's overeducated term for blue gunpowder — as opposed to ordinary black powder," Hess whispered, loud enough for all to hear.

"How are we for blue powder, then?" Fentor asked.

"We have plenty, sir."

"That's good news, but without extra guns to shoot it all, powder alone won't repel the enemy. *Think*, people! There must be something that can be done," Fentor said.

"We can either pull back now, or fight them until they force a retreat. The only difference is how much Madean blood will run down the hill first," Hess said heatedly. The others looked at her. She then added, "Sir."

" 'True visionaries see not a fork in the road, but a chance to forge a third way through the unknown,' " Fentor said.

"Saint Temlin's words, I believe," Crauford said.

Hess folded her arms.

"Sir, what about the Lady's Great Bombard?" Thorassa said, raising his hand. "We could ask her to fire on the enemy."

Hess let out a laugh and then snapped a hand over her mouth, as though she had seized the escaping noise and put it back in. Fentor didn't know whether to join in with Hess' laughter or groan in frustration.

"Do you have *any* idea how much a single shot of the Bombard costs?" Fentor asked.

Thorassa's little eyes fluttered and his mouth formed an 'o.' One could almost see the little watermill turning and turning in the Junior Lancer's mind.

Crauford, in contrast, wore a chin-stroking expression that hinted at a more productive mode of thought.

"Suppose we *could* convince Lady Talentus to fire it," Crauford said.

"They say that each time the Bombard is loaded, the king's treasury doubles its deficit. She will never approve it for our little cohort," Hess said. "She would tell us to pull back."

"Now, now. Let's not dismiss this just yet. Go on, Crauford," Fentor said.

"Timing would be everything," Crauford said. Instead of elaborating, he traced his finger through the air, perhaps performing complex sums on a chalkboard only he could see.

"It's just that you said we have plenty of gunpower but not enough guns, sir, so I thought—" Thorassa said.

"Quiet, Thorassa. Let the man think," Fentor said.

Something in the invisible sums apparently clicked into place, because Crauford nodded. "Think back to conventional cannons. Fine on an open field, but useless against the elves. Between the aegis and the trees keeping the elves hidden and protected, cannon shots are wasted, continuous musket fire with blue powder is more efficient."

"Go on," Fentor said.

"Enter the Lady's Bombard. It obliterates the aegis, strips the land of trees. But there's a problem: cost," Crauford said.

"Crauford, they'll never let us—" Hess began.

Fentor held up a finger to her, cautioned her with a glance. Crauford seemed not to have noticed the interruption.

"But when you compare the cost—the *real* cost—of a Bombard round with the cost of losing ground, then fighting to win it back … the Lady will actually save money. *If*"—Crauford cleaned his spectacles briefly—"if, we are able to catch enough elves in the blast. That is why timing is critical."

"How many elves is 'enough'?" Fentor asked.

"Perhaps eight hundred, or at most, a thousand."

"In one blast?"

"They rarely attack in groups that large," Hess said.

"Rarely. Not never," Crauford said, lowering his already soft voice further. "Based on your own scouts' reports, if we extrapolate with data from past battles—"

"Give me a moment to think," Fentor said.

He got up and paced about the tent, giving little heed to the whispered conversation that broke out between Hess and Crauford.

Hess would have him be sensible, he knew, but biographies of sensible men gather dust on the shelf. Bold action alone sets the extraordinary apart, makes for a life worth reading. Every one of the Grand Toques and Saints of history endured criticism and doubt. They even welcomed it! Who was Fentor to deny the beckoning hand of triumph when it reached out to him?

"I've got it!" he announced.

He explained the plan, and part they each had to play. First Hess, then Crauford were dismissed to their duties, leaving Thorassa alone at the table.

Fentor felt incandescent with the promise of victory. Thorassa, though, looked like jelly melting in the sun.

"You understand your role, of course?" Fentor asked.

"Yes, sir, of course."

"Imagine the view we'll have from the next hill! Think of the promotions, the parades, the medals! Think of how very *daring* it is to turn retreat into victory! Doesn't that just fill you with vitality?"

"Very much, sir, it does," Thorassa said. A pinched look came to Thorassa's pale face, which now seemed empty of vitality.

Fentor took the young officer by the shoulders, and looked him in the eye. Conviction rolled off Fentor in waves. The mere presence of such contagious confidence, surely, would infect Thorassa's mind with daring, like a fever of faith.

"All you have to do is drink Crauford's elixir, cross a little stretch of no-man's land, and have a chat with Grand Toque Talentus. After that … glory," he said.

The sound of Thorassa's reply was drowned out by a chorus of high, piercing shrieks. Whistlers were raining down from above with an unmistakable din, like the cry of a hundred diving hawks. The shrieks grew louder and louder, discordant enough to chill the bone.

With moments left before impact, Fentor seized Thorassa by the collar and pulled him under the table.

Chapter 2

A dozen shrieking arrows pierced the tent, filling it for one instant with ruddy light, before burying their glowing heads in every surface. One particularly auspicious arrow penetrated the table, its tip stopping only a hair's breadth from Fentor's nose. He looked at it, eyes crossed. There was a brief moment of silence. Then, the hill resounded with the brassy din of trumpets.

Fentor extracted himself from under the table, and threw the tent's entrance open.

In the waning evening light, the indistinct Bluefingers below swarmed like ants from a disturbed nest. The forested hill opposite winked with tiny red stars—more whistlers, ready to fire.

"Find cover and stick to it!" Fentor roared. "Between the volleys, fire at will!"

Drummers and buglers sounded out the rhythms that relayed the order down the hill. Like a twelve-piece orchestra unites the motion of dancers, the battle song gradually brought order to the Bluefingers' steps. The disparate and panicked soldiers soon became a tidy and disciplined troupe. They filed in columns among the sandbag battlements, passed guns, shot and powder down the lines, and then wedged themselves into cover. As one, the hill held its breath and waited for the next screaming flock of arrows to take flight.

Less than three hundred little red whistlers glimmered among the trees opposite. Fentor doubted the number would stay that low for long—the nectar of destiny had made the evening air too sweet for that. Triumph would soon come.

Back in his tent, with the fletching of arrows sprouting all over the ground like some bizarre daisy garden, Thorassa still trembled under the table.

"On your feet, Lancer!" Fentor bellowed.

Thorassa made no reply.

"Confound it, man, this is no time to cower!" Fentor upended the table, exposing the young officer like a beetle from under a stone.

"I can't do it." Thorassa rocked back and forth, damp eyes staring. "I wanted to be a banker! Father forced me into the military!"

"Good Providence above," Fentor spat. "Get going at once! You're the bloody centerpiece of the plan!"

"Imeldra said she'd wait for me," Thorassa choked, unwilling or unable to meet Fentor's eye. Providence alone knew who he was addressing. "I begged her to hide me, but she said some war might do me good. Then I said, 'Who bought you that broach?' and she said, 'Why, you did, silly.' And I said, 'I never bought you *that* broach. Is someone else buying you broaches?' And she—"

Fentor dragged the Lancer upright by his lapels, slapped him, shook him, and then slapped him once more for good measure. Few things compared to a good lapel-shaking and a couple of slaps.

"Get a hold of yourself!" Fentor said. "Good men will die if you don't go now—me among them!"

"I want to go home. I want to go home …" Thorassa moaned.

A host of shrill whines in the distance announced the launch of a new volley. Fentor, still gripping Thorassa's coat, turned and caught a glimpse of the swiftly rising constellation of glowing red arrowheads.

"Get going, or they'll have to mail you home piece by piece!"

Thorassa's legs went limp. The only thing holding him up was Fentor's grip on his lapels. The whistlers' distant whines soon become shrieks, an off-key choir under the hand of history's most appalling conductor. In mere moments, the arrows would puncture every exposed thing in the tent. Fentor was determined not to be one of them.

Cursing, Fentor dragged the Lancer to the still-full bathtub, planted his foot on its rusted side, and threw all his weight against it until it tipped over. He dropped with Thorassa onto the now sodden ground, took hold of the bath, and pulled it over their heads.

In the cramped, muffled darkness, they waited for the impact. The few seconds spent cringing in their shelter seemed to last an hour.

Then the arrows struck.

One missile hit the bath, and it rang like a colossal church bell. It was so piercingly, deafeningly loud that Fentor forgot where he was. Clutching both hands over his ears, he stood and shouldered the bath out of the way.

So many arrows jutted from the ground that soon, there would be nowhere to stand.

Fentor, ears still ringing, plucked one of the shafts from the earth, and held it out to Thorassa.

"Take it," he said.

Thorassa stared at the arrow, perplexed.

"Take it and stick it in your leg. If they discharge you for cowardice, you'll be a nobody, with nothing to your name but shame and disgrace. Stick this in your leg, tell them you were wounded, and you might just claw back some respect back home," Fentor said. "You might become a banker, after all."

The young Lancer took the arrow carefully with both hands, as though it were a snake that might suddenly twist and bite him.

"Well now, *someone* has to leg it to the Lady's Great Bombard." Fentor straightened his tricorne and patted the hilt of his sabre. "It seems fate has decreed that I am that someone."

"How am I supposed to stick an arrow into my own leg?" Thorassa said, his already pale face utterly drained of color.

"Grasp it firmly, grit your teeth, and imagine the cool autumn streets of home," Fentor said, already turning away. Then, over his shoulder, he added, "And try not to go too deep, dear boy. Nick an artery, and you really *will* go home in a box."

Junior Lancer Thorassa sat frozen among thickets of arrows, in the shadow of the bathtub. He blinked rapidly and shook his head at the arrow, as though refusing some silent command it had given him. Fentor had no time to stay and watch.

He stepped out from the wreckage of his tent, and into the roars, crackles, and screams of the unfolding battle.

The hills reverberated with the crack and hiss of musket fire. Clouds of acrid, metallic smoke from the Bluefingers' guns drifted up the hill and into Fentor's wrinkled nose. Part of him preferred the honest, raucous crack of black powder to the anaemic hissing noise of blue powder. Black powder stank of musty sulphur, but it was an earthy, honest stench. Blue powder, with its timid, sour smell, struck him as artificial, sterile, frivolous. It betrayed its origin as something born in a laboratory, to Mother Science and Father Treasury.

Still, one could not dispute that it was effective.

As yet, no further whistlers had flared into light. The vast scarlet membrane of an aegis, however, shone among the trees, sheltering any number of lurking elves. Its surface cast out ripples with every musket ball that struck it, like a pond under heavy rain.

He needed the Elixir of Hardskin, and the pause between volleys presented an ideal time to retrieve it.

Fentor cupped both hands around his mouth and called, "Crauford!"

He could not spot the Thambrian anywhere below. Between the blaring of trumpets and the snapping of snares, the gunfire, and the shouting, making himself heard seemed unlikely.

There was nothing else to do but search the hill on foot.

As Fentor charged down the hill, the Bluefingers called out to him. They seemed to have made the incorrect assumption that he was bravely rushing forward to lend his gun to the battle.

"Good to have you with us, sir!"

"There's true leadership! A Capilet fighting in the mud with the rest of us!"

"Teach those ruddy elves a lesson, sir!"

He waved graciously at them all. There was no reason to tell them the truth—that he was merely fetching a potion so he could be on his way. All inspiration, even when based on false impressions, had value too great to waste.

All across the dark spaces between the trees across from them began to light up with tiny red dots. As Fentor paused to watch, more and more whistlers were kindled, until the hill was so full of them that it looked ablaze.

"Crauford! Crauford!" He bellowed over the fizz-crack of musket fire.

There was no sign of his alchemist. All around him, Bluefingers were hastily shooting and reloading their weapons, raising obscuring clouds of blue-grey smoke. Between the smog and the impending darkness, visibility was rapidly dwindling. Only the fiercely glowing whistlers and intermittent blue flashes of the muskets were easily discernible.

"Coming, sir!" Crauford's usually quiet voice rang out from somewhere down the hill.

"Hurry!"

Fentor saw nothing but the grey specters of soldiers in the haze. Usually, a lack of visibility did little to hamper the progress of a battle. The Elarím obligingly betrayed their position with the glow of their aegis and whistlers. A Bluefinger had only to shoot in the vague direction of red-colored things, and hope that no red-colored things shot them back. The urgency of Fentor's mission now made the haze a terrible nuisance.

"Where are you, Lancer?" Fentor called.

Behind him, farther up the hill, Crauford called, "Here, sir. Where are *you*?"

They had missed each other in the dark. Fentor's curse coincided with the wail of incoming whistlers. Hundreds of red lights rose high above, outshining the early evening stars. The glowing arrows swarmed so thickly that they looked like one continuous sheet of flame. Fentor's cohort, the sandbags, the mud, and the smoke were all stained red by the rapidly descending barrage.

In the ruddy light, Fentor spotted Crauford standing above him on a lumpy bastion of sandbags.

"Crauford! Do you have it?"

The Thambrian nodded, holding up a glass vial.

"Throw it to me!"

Crauford turned upward, spectacles glinting like rubies, then crouched behind the nearest pillar of sandbags.

"Take cover, sir! There's no time!"

A thousand howling wolves could not have compared to the din that was descending on Fentor's head. Still, it was only with great reluctance that he dove for cover. The fizz-crack of muskets ceased, and the cacophony reached its peak.

The hail of arrows struck. There was pure, breathless silence for a fraction of an instant. Then came the cries of the injured, and the continued fizz-crack of muskets.

Fentor emerged from his sandbag shelter. The arrows stuck in the ground at his feet had nearly hit him. Some nearby Bluefingers had been less fortunate, and now resembled overfilled pin cushions. The sight proved hard to look away from.

"Crauford! Throw me the elixir!"

"I would prefer to bring it down to you. The vial is too valuable to risk dropping, sir," Crauford said.

"Blast it, Crauford, I'm going to start loading my gun. If that vial isn't in my hands by the time I'm finished …"

"Loud and clear, sir. Incoming."

The Thambrian, now a silhouette against the darkening sky, drew back his arm then lobbed a glinting object through the air. Fentor fumbled with it, dropped to both knees, and caught it in his fingertips an inch above the ground.

Malcolm's Elixir of Hardskin was in a handsome, ornate vessel, with a sealed stopper of twisted glass. The liquid itself, however, had the viscosity and color of snail slime. Fentor pulled the top off and drank as quickly as his gagging throat would allow. In terms of its taste, appearances were not at all deceiving. A real snail sliding down his throat may have been more agreeable.

"The cohort is yours, Crauford. Do try and keep them from getting killed, won't you?"

"Aye, sir!" Crauford raised an immaculate salute, then turned, raised his rifle, and fired at the enemy.

Gripping the hilt of his sabre, Fentor cut eastward across the hill, hopping over sandbags and bodies alike. His skin crawled with pins and needles, then hardened, as though iron bands had been hammered all over him. The elixir had begun to take hold. With it, came the familiar, intoxicating aura of looming glory.

No alchemy was needed for that fervor. It was all his own.

New whistlers flared into light, sparsely at first, but soon spreading farther along the hill than before. Fentor couldn't help but perceive encouraging shapes between the bright spots, as one might trace constellations in the heavens. There was a gun! There was a sabre! There was a crown! There was a mansion, with gardens and balconies! Perhaps the shapes sprang from an overly excitable imagination. Or, perhaps they were signs of things to come.

At the easternmost bulwark of his mud-and-sandbag castle, there was a sheer drop to boggy ground. Farther along, there was a hill of massive, lumpy boulders that fit together, loosely, as though some giant had left them in a slapdash pile. The quickest path to the Grand Toque's camp cut through the boulders, though in the dark it would not be easy to navigate. The night air possessed such a rousing freshness that even that gruelling path to the Lady's Bombard seemed as carefree as a springtime stroll.

Fentor stood at the edge with one hand on his sabre hilt and the other on his tricorne. With his back straight, his eyes forward, and his upper lip stiff, he swung one foot over the precipice and brought it down on the empty air with great confidence.

The momentum of the motion sent him tumbling head over tail into the wind, giving him the acute feeling that his stomach had migrated up to his throat and back down again.

A moment later, he crashed to the ground with force that, under normal circumstances, would have broken his legs into kindling.

Malcolm's Elixir of Hardskin could protect hair, flesh, bones, and sinew from most serious injuries. The worst Fentor expected was a few bruises. What it could not protect him from, however, was the vertigo of long drops and sudden stops. He staggered forward, leaning hard to the left and right as the world tilted like a ship in a storm. Tangles of reeds and pockets of mud conspired to snare his feet, but he conquered them all. At last, his head stopped spinning and his churning stomach calmed.

An ear-splitting shriek startled him. He turned just in time to catch a glimpse of the whistler. A streak of fierce, red light burned into his eyes, and the arrow struck his chest. The elixir protected him from the brunt of the blow, but the punch it gave only felt like the best effort of a scrawny junior boxer.

The enemy position had become flooded with clusters of glowing whistlers. One little constellation had broken from the rest, and was keeping pace with Fentor as he continued to thrash through the reeds toward the path.

"Blast it!" he grunted.

His new followers launched the next volley. The shafts raced a long a shallower arc, converging on him with a discordant scream. Some pummelled his torso and limbs, while the rest fell among the mud and reeds like incandescent hail. Fentor cemented his teeth together and redoubled his pace. He reached dry ground at last, and began the ascent up the rocky hill.

He had not been greatly injured by the fall or the arrows — yet. Malcolm's Elixir could not last forever.

The next curtain of whistlers stained the sky red, blaring like steam-klaxons. Fentor kept his eyes forward, refusing to pay them any heed. Timing was everything. He needed time to reach the Grand Toque, time to convince her, time for the Bombard to be loaded and fired. Even an instant spent gawking at incoming arrows had the potential to spoil the plan.

The arrows struck. One whistler took him in the jaw, rattling his teeth and scattering hot sparks of pain through his skull. He was knocked slightly off-course, but continued on.

The path mostly ran over the monolithic stones. In some places, the stone's surface had been chiselled away, forming man-sized grooves that acted as open-faced tunnels. Thus, Fentor ran over, between, under, and through the hill's massive boulders. Under their cover, there was a brief reprieve from the arrows. He also paused to light a small hand-lantern, judging that his time was better spent lighting the way than stumbling over rocks in the dark.

Fentor used the quiet to reflect on the elves who were to blame for carving the makeshift path back when the

31

land was theirs. If they'd wanted a path, why in Providence hadn't they tunnelled through the hill properly?

He came to an exposed part of the hill and spied a flock of whistlers overhead. They streaked across the sky, unerring and tightly spaced, toward an unseen spot far ahead of him. It made no sense. The Elarím did not miss — not by such a wide margin. Then, when the arrows approached their target, the goal became clear.

There was a curtain of rock ahead that Fentor would have to pass under to reach his destination. In the brief moment before impact, the whistlers illuminated the craggy surface. Then, with a great shower of splinters and dust, the arrows struck the rock, went dark. The next whistlers flared into life on the hill opposite.

Fentor cursed. He spat strings of harsh words with passion and virtuosity, a poet of the profane. If the elves broke the overhang before he reached it, he'd be cut off. There would be no hope of reaching the Bombard in time. No hope for his cohort. No praise, glory, or victory.

He had already been hurtling along the path at top speed. He tried to force his body to accelerate. But no threat, assurance, or pledge he made to his legs could convince them to move faster. His own limits had been reached.

Only the divine forces of Providence could help him now. He begged them to hold the rock together, pledging to give at least *some* of his forthcoming wealth to the church.

With his lungs burning and another volley screeching overhead, it almost seemed like failure was not impossible.

Almost.

More and more screaming missiles struck the overhanging rock, gouging an ever-deepening cut. Fentor raced along the uneven path, drawing closer with every step.

The overhang was two hundred paces away, then one hundred, then a few dozen. Fentor's body had never ached so acutely. His legs threatened to detach and roll down the hill. His lungs threatened to leap out of his throat with a great cough and flop away, never to be seen again.

The next shower of whistlers soared high above, singing together with teeth-grinding disharmony. Fentor was within reach. He was almost in the shadow of the overhang.

The very moment he passed under the vast curtain of rock, the arrows struck with a sharp, many-toothed snap. Rasping, cracking, grinding noises filled his ears from all directions. A deep, bone-shuddering groan issued from the depths of the hill.

Fentor was halfway along when the hill began to collapse. Rocks of all sizes broke free of the hill and tumbled thunderously to the earth below.

Fentor bent double, scrambling on hands and feet, fighting to make it to the end before he was entombed forever. Blood pounded in his head. The edges of his vision darkened. The avalanche was behind him, above him, ahead of him.

At last, he made it through, into the open air. The rockslide continued behind him, until it eventually slowed from a cascade to a trickle.

"Ha ha!" he cried out in triumph, his fists high in the air.

He had not seen the volley headed for him until that moment. Now the arrows were bearing down on him, their red tips blazing. Utterly spent of the energy or willpower to do anything else, Fentor stood tall with his arms wide, inviting them to him.

What was a few more bruises?

Chapter 3

The war camp of Her Excellency, the Grand Toque Lady
Elatea Talentus was as extravagant as her name. It was a
veritable palace of timber, canvas, and pressed dirt, lit by
neat rows of lanterns. The paths between tents were so
firmly packed and well-swept that they looked like earth-
colored carpet.

The deep-sea blue tents were spotless, naturally,
trimmed with tassels and reinforced with sandbag walls.
Not a single weed dared to show so much as a leaf. Even
the two Bluefinger guards barring the way into the camp
were brushed, washed, and in all regards pristine.

Fentor, with holes in his coat, rock-dust on his face, and
mud squelching in his shoes, staggered up toward the
camp with a winning smile. The guards looked at him as
though he was a toad fresh from the swamp. Then, at the
sight of his Capilet insignia — a horned rabbit in profile —
their crossed muskets swiftly parted. Even the Lady's
Bluefingers acted like guards in some castle of yore.

The elves had ceased their pursuit as Fentor had neared the camp. Even the largest groups seldom attacked it. Walking the circuit to the top, under high-flying flags and past row after row of Bluefingers standing at perfect attention, Fentor could easily see why.

At the top of the hill, Her Excellency Lady Talentus was watching the battle through a spyglass. She had her back to him, so she did not appear to notice his arrival.

The rest of the space was dominated by the Lady's Great Bombard. Its barrel was as long as a mature pine, its diameter so great that three large adults could fit snugly in the bore. The tangled masses of gears, pulleys, levers, and switches made it look like the innards of the world's largest clock. The Bombard now faced due north — some forty degrees away from where Fentor needed it to face.

He was about to clear his throat, but the elf Dídac did it first.

"Ahem," he coughed into his fist loudly, with a pompous air.

Lancer Dídac, a silver-haired, pale, sour-faced ex-Elarím, had pledged his life to the Lady. Apparently, against all laws, logic, and decency, doing so meant he was allowed to serve directly under her. His reflective grey eyes watched Fentor like a cat watches an unappetizing mouse. One could almost picture a tail twitching under his coat.

"My Lady, a *guest* has arrived," Dídac continued.

Dídac had the smarmiest tone imaginable, and it never failed to grate on Fentor's ears. The simple word 'guest' had turned into a bitter curse upon the elf's thin lips. Fentor had never understood how so many loathsome manners and habits had been able to squeeze into a space as small as Dídac's mind.

Fentor shot an acid glare at the elf the moment before Lady Talentus turned to look at him. After a brief, appraising look at Fentor, she returned her eye to the telescope. Out across the darkening hills, the glowing arrows and flashing guns stood out brightly — a shower of sparks from a fire, a flicker of thunder behind thick clouds. At that distance, the Elarím whistlers sounded as gentle as a birdsong.

"You look somewhat worse for wear, Capilet," she said distractedly. "Was that rockslide your doing?"

"It was, my Lady — in a way," Fentor said. He spoke lightly and approached gradually, hoping not to seem overeager. As jarring as it was to put on his best manners after running a near-death marathon, refined behavior remained his best chance.

The Lady then turned fully to Fentor, lowering the spyglass. He stood tall and doffed his hat. When a small trickle of gravel fell from the brim of his tricorne, he pretended not to notice. Dídac, however, tutted and lifted his eyes to the sky.

The Lady was a handsome young woman with a thin, pale face. Not a strand of her short blonde hair was ever out of place. Her standard-issue coat, bearing only the plumed bird insignia of a Grand Toque, was otherwise unadorned. Some speculated that if she wore all the badges, ranks, and titles she'd earned, it would have weighed the coat down too much. Fentor knew better — she simply had no need of displaying them. One look at the way she carried herself told more than any glittering coat ever could.

When she moved, it was with grace fit for the Royal Ballet. When she was still, she struck a pose with gravitas that no sculptor could capture. When she looked at someone, her clear blue eyes seemed to pierce skin, flesh, and bones to see one's hidden worth.

As she frowned at Fentor's tattered and bruised exterior, he could only hope that she saw beyond to his true value.

"Do I dare hope that you have a legitimate reason for coming here?" she asked.

"I do, my Lady. I have a request that is … quite urgent," Fentor said. Volley after volley of whistlers rained on his cohort's heads, rendering the phrase 'quite urgent' an ironic understatement.

"By all means, request it, then," the Lady said.

"I beg Your Excellency for permission to fire the Great Bombard. If I could launch but one round at the enemy position, my cohort could take the—"

"Dídac, have a look and tell our guest what you see," she said.

Dídac took the offered spyglass and aimed it at the crimson whistlers floating above the hills. "Perhaps … seven hundred Elarím."

"Seven hundred," Lady Talentus said.

"Aye, my Lady. That is my *generous* estimate."

"Thank you, Dídac." When Lady Talentus turned to Fentor, her expression seemed neutral, yet somehow, it still wilted Fentor's spirit like cabbage in a furnace. "Seven hundred."

In the ensuing silence, cold wind probed at Fentor's exposed skin through tears in his clothes. He did his best not to shiver.

"More will come soon. I'm sure of it," Fentor said.

"You're sure," she said — not in question. She turned to face the battle, then back to Fentor, smoothly and with perfect posture. It gave the impression that she was a mannequin on a well-oiled turning platform. "I, however, am *not* sure."

"My scouts reported great numbers of elves converging on the position, my Lady. Soon, there'll be so many whistlers in the air we'll all get sunburn," Fentor said.

"You trust your scout's reports?" Lady Talentus said.

"With my life."

"That's a noble sentiment. Forgive me, Fentor, when I say that your scouts inspire less confidence in me. I will not wager the expense of a Bombard round on their word alone. I would not wager a barrel of cheap ale on their word. Every pinch of the ultra-enriched ash of kryside that powers this weapon costs the treasury dearly. I won the approval of the good King Philliby only by assuring him that I could make each shot worthwhile. Seven hundred elves I see, and seven hundred is not enough."

"I am *certain* that a narrow window for victory will present itself, my Lady. We cannot afford delay. The Bombard takes time to load, turn, and sight properly. A sudden influx of Elarím could overwhelm my cohort before the order to load it leaves your lips. Please, my Lady, prepare the Bombard to fire. You will catch no less than one thousand elves in the blast. I stake my reputation on it."

Dídac raised a pale, thin hand, and smirked behind it.

There was a pause filled with the sound of distant whistles and cracks. Lady Talentus studied Fentor, her shoulders lit from behind in alternating hues of red and blue.

"Your reputation? Isn't it customary to stake things of *high* value?" she asked.

Fentor could have stuffed bees up his nostrils and felt less stung. As much as he winced inwardly at her words, he maintained a stalwart expression.

"Fentor, you are a good Capilet. You may not be a visionary, or a natural leader—"

"But you are," Fentor said. Heat had risen to his neck, and like a pot boiling over he had let the words spill without meaning to.

Lady Talentus raised her eyebrows by a fraction of an inch: an expression of dire warning. Since she appeared to have been stunned into silence, Fentor forged ahead.

"A visionary sees what must be done, and acts. That is what you have always done. It is what I aspire to do," Fentor said. "I cannot help but measure myself against your greatness, however short I may fall."

"That was bald flattery, Fentor, and you won't catch me blushing at it," the Lady said.

"I would not expect you to. You are the most accomplished Grand Toque of the Madean Land Corps, and if anyone stands a chance of winning this war, it's you," Fentor said.

"One more word in my favor, Capilet, and I'll have that silver tongue of yours cut out."

"You won battle after battle by seizing every opportunity you could. As a wise woman once said, 'She who chances nothing and loses deserves it. She who risks it all, yet still loses, has earned it.' "

Lady Talentus' lip twitched. Or rather, the corner of her mouth relaxed for one brief instant. It had been a quotation from her own memoir, *Making War with Elves: For Profit and Amusement*.

"How terribly clever of you, Capilet. Your efforts to flatter and harangue me will get you nowhere. This is not a question of taking a risk. It is a question of why you came here at all. You should be with your cohort, ordering a retreat. Instead, you have come here to request artillery, based on the word of some scouts and a mistaken belief that you can conjure a thousand elves out of the sheer desire to be seen defeating them."

"The count of arrows is still no more than seven hundred, my Lady," Dídac said, unasked. "Might I add that Capilet Fentor only seems to take risks at the expense of others, and never himself."

Fentor briefly indulged in a fantasy of tearing the spyglass from the elf's hands and stuffing it into his smirking mouth.

"Thank you, Dídac," Lady Talentus said.

Fentor suddenly felt exhausted. He had been a ship coursing along with the fair winds of destiny, but now his sails hung slack. Perhaps the elixir had worn off, or perhaps all that running had taken its toll. Whatever the cause, a curious and unfamiliar feeling of impending failure came over him.

His cohort was still under fire. Seven hundred elves were firing on five hundred of *his* soldiers. He had given Hess and Crauford the order to stand ground no matter what happened. As he stood, transfixed, hundreds of glowing whistlers rose and fell on his hill, his castle. They lit up the night sky as they flew, bathing the ground in ruddy light before burying themselves in their targets. Sandbag, mud, timber, and flesh — all would be pierced by the hails of arrows. How many wagons would they need to cart away all the dead and wounded?

Fentor was no longer a war hero charging to victory. Now he was merely a man with holes in his clothes and a clear view of his soldiers' destruction.

Her Excellency, the Grand Toque Lady Elatea Talentus, stood facing him with perfect, neutral poise. All Dídac's snickering and sneering had done nothing to rattle Fentor's resolve. But the Lady, whose face betrayed less emotion than a porcelain mask, brought Fentor to the brink of despair with one long, searching look.

He searched her eyes for any chance that she would relent, that she would save his soldiers with the Bombard, but there was nothing at all.

Just as all hope seemed lost, he was struck by an idea that erased all his doubts as quickly as they had come. Once more, the evening air was as sweet as the sparkling wines of Norimand.

"My Lady, I pledge to pay the full cost if the shot fails," Fentor said.

His words had the expected effect.

Dídac's grip on the spyglass slackened, and he almost dropped it. Lady Talentus tilted her head one degree, her

eyes flashing in the lantern light. A modicum of tension
crossed her face—no more than a crease between her
brows and a slight tightening of her mouth. A moment
later, she returned to her usual inscrutable expression.

Fentor liked to think he could read faces well. In that
moment, though, he couldn't tell whether the Lady had
been considering his offer, or picturing him boiling in a
pot.

"Dídac?" she said, her voice as gentle as a wind chime.

"My Lady?"

"What are you waiting for? Prepare the Bombard."

For a moment, Dídac looked like a child whose toy had
been snatched away. Though he restrained his pout, his
trembling voice still betrayed great depths of turmoil. "My
Lady ... I doubt he could afford to pay for—"

"Nonsense. I am well acquainted with the finances of
my officers. Fentor will be ruined, of course. Even the most
destitute beggar in Madea City will pity him. That is,
unless his gambit pays off." She turned to Fentor, a slender
finger stroking her chin. "There is no losing scenario for
me. Either the Elarím will be dealt a devastating blow, or
one of my over-eager Capilets will be taught a lesson. I
expect it will be the type of lesson that is not soon
forgotten."

"Every moment spent under your leadership is an
invaluable lesson in greatness, my Lady," Fentor said.

Dídac, lurking outside the Lady's view, scowled so
deeply at Fentor that his pale cheeks and pointed ears
flushed pink.

Lady Talentus raised a hand and flicked away Fentor's simpering comment, as though it was a fly. He didn't care. Dídac's reaction had been the real goal.

"Dídac. I am not one to repeat orders," Lady Talentus said, her voice delicate and cold, like a thin sheath of ice on a winter pond.

The elf saluted, then hurried away. As he called out a barrage of orders, swarms of engineers poured out from surrounding tents, and converged on the Lady's Great Bombard.

"Forty-two degrees westward! Double haste!" Dídac shouted in his reedy voice, his hands crowded with a sextant, compass, and other brass contraptions used for the aiming of artillery.

The Bluefinger engineers took hold of levers, cranks, pulleys, and wheels, and with great effort, slowly coaxed the enormous Bombard to begin turning. For every minute spent pulling, cranking, and spinning, the massive barrel turned one degree. For every degree it turned, Fentor's insides tied another knot.

Providence alone could deliver victory now. There was nothing he could do but watch.

Lady Talentus stood beside him, hands clasped behind her back, and watched as well.

"I admire your pluck, Fentor. I know what it takes to challenge a superior. To gall and provoke them, at times. If I didn't, the Lady's Great Bombard would not exist," the Lady said.

"Thank you, my Lady."

"Let me finish—you may wish you had saved those thanks. It takes more than pluck to succeed, Fentor. It takes a cunning, shrewd, keen mind."

The Great Bombard continued its lethargic twirl as sweat dripped from the Engineers' noses. Hails of whistlers continued to fall on his cohort's heads. Dídac continued to shout, "Double haste! Quickly, now!" Fentor's gut continued to twist and tangle.

It may have been his own wishful imagination, but there seemed to be more arrows soaring through the darkness. The pitch of their whistles had increased too, like an awful singer wailing a note above an already unreachable note. He hoped desperately that the blast would catch enough elves.

If it didn't, he would have to sell his home and everything in it.

"I fear that your reach exceeds your grasp," Lady Talentus continued. "You wish to be the greatest of the great, and I sympathise with that. But your ambition needs tempering. Not all of us are destined to—"

She fell silent as a massive, crimson wave of whistlers emerged from the distant trees. They burned so brightly that even Lady Talentus' camp was illuminated. The number of arrows in each volley had doubled.

Fentor was torn. He had been proved right. Sweet as that vindication was, it turned bitter in his mouth as the arrows stuck the hillside. The sound of musket-fire in return was feeble, scattered.

However many soldiers remained, they had little time.

Lady Talentus strode toward the engineers and roared, "Load the Bombard as it turns! Triple check the angles!"

The enormous cannon had only turned halfway at that point. Under the Lady's urging, the engineers quickened their pace, baring their teeth at the strain on their muscles.

A huge timber crane raised a calf-sized package of enriched bluepowder up to the bore of the Bombard. Straining ropes swung back and forth, as shouting engineers on ladders struggled to prod the powder into the opening. Just when they seemed ready to place the powder into the cannon, it turned and pushed the package aside.

"My Lady, we cannot load her while she turns!" one engineer calls.

"You'll do it or I'll load *you* into the Bombard!" she roared.

Fentor dashed forward and took a wooden pole from a nearby stack. With that in hand, he pushed his way onto a ladder, hooked his feet into the top rungs, and joined the engineers in their effort to load the powder. The wooden pole was too unwieldy to get good purchase on the canvas package. The crane's ropes swung to and fro, and the other engineers' prodding competed with Fentor's own efforts. The result was a jolting, dancing package bouncing on the lip of the cannon.

"Stop! You're all making it swing," Fentor bellowed. "Turn the crane — bring the package over *there*, put it in the path of where the Bombard will be."

The engineers manning the ropes and pulleys of the crane obeyed. The package now hung suspended a few degrees ahead of the cannon's present position.

"Now, keep it steady. When the bore lines up with it, we all push at once. In that moment, disengage the crane. Understood?" Fentor shouted.

"Aye, sir!" came the engineers' chorus.

While they waited, Fentor caught a brief glance of Lady Talentus standing below, looking up at him. Her head was tilted once more, with an expression like someone holding an evasive, obscure word on the tip of their tongue.

At last, the gaping mouth of the bombard lined up with the bluepowder package.

"Push!" Fentor roared.

Half a dozen wooden poles pressed against the package. The ropes holding it groaned. Inch by inch, it went up and then inside the bore. In the next moment, the crane ropes released, and the package fell with a heavy thump to the base of the weapon.

The Great Bombard had now turned thirty degrees, with twelve more to go.

The whistlers still fell on his cohort in massive sheets. The clouds above and mist below glowed crimson, giving the gruesome impression that the blood of his dying soldiers had sprayed out into the atmosphere. The feeble cracking of musket fire had almost ceased.

Following the same procedure, Fentor and the engineers loaded the barrel-sized Bombard shell, and cloth wadding large enough to cover two king's beds. Finally, the crane hoisted a stout rod of timber, then swung it into the bore like a battering ram, packing the munitions tightly.

At last, the Great Bombard turned its final degree, with a conclusive metallic click.

"Ready to —" Fentor began.

"Bombard is ready, my Lady!" Dídac shouted louder, cutting him off.

"Get to cover! Prepare the fuse!" Lady Talentus called.

"Clear the Bombard! Get to cover one and all!" Dídac cupped both hands over his mouth and called the order down the hill for the rest of the cohort.

Fentor and the engineers scrambled down the ladders, and hurried away from the Bombard. They ran down the hill, out of sight of the now-deserted weapon, and came to a thick wall of sandbags reinforced with long timber beams. The last engineer to come was carefully unspooling a length of rope that sparkled with blue krysite powder. They handed the fuse gingerly to Lady Talentus.

"Fentor, if you would do the honors," she said, offering him the fuse between forefinger and thumb, as though they were at luncheon and she was handing him tea.

Fentor took the fuse, willing his hands to stop trembling. He took a small flint from his pocket, and scraped it quickly along the fuse's krysite-encrusted surface.

It sparked at once, and sent a spitting blue flame up the length of the rope so fast that it was out of sight before Fentor realised it had burned his fingers.

"Well, Capilet," Lady Talentus said to Fentor, as Dídac and the others covered their ears. "I suppose you were right, after all."

She and Fentor covered their ears.

Then, the Great Bombard fired.

A thousand thunderclaps could not have split the air with such fury. The ground beneath their feet shook like a dog trying to shake off fleas. For one cataclysmic moment,

Fentor thought the entire hill would roll out from under their feet. Some of the sandbags they sheltered under had split, pouring trickles of fine sand on their shoulders.

The echoes persisted for so long that Fentor wondered if his ears would ring with them forever. Gradually, they died away, and the rumbling earth stilled.

Lady Talentus faced Fentor, nodded to him, and her lips took on an infinitesimal upward turn.

He took that to mean that she had honored him with a broad, appreciative grin.

Chapter 4

*Our first connection is the umbilical. We
are born and it is cut. From then on, our
connections multiply for the same vital
purpose.*
Sage Nyendí

In Slee's garden, distant gunfire pattered like rain. She
never paid it any mind. She didn't need to, as long as it
stayed distant. The garden came first. It needed her care,
and in return, it cared for her. The world beyond could
burn to ashes, and she would continue to harvest, water,
trim, pluck and plant.

The síana plants which formed a thick hedge around her
garden needed the most care. Their role was more crucial

than even the berries and tubers that fed her. Síanas, when cared for properly, could make a garden like hers invisible.

Living in secret on a hillside between human and elven lands, she needed to be invisible. Soldiers marching by, once a rare event, was becoming all too common.

The sun had set, and her animals were bedding down. Still, Slee worked hard on the síanas by the light of luminous beards of lichen. With a short, well-worn knife, she combed through the leaves to find buds, flowers, and berries, and cut them off. Síana leaves grew densely, and were roughly the size and shape of fingernails. Emerging buds, especially in the dim violet glow of the lichen, were hard to spot. It was best to do it by feel.

Her deft, calloused fingers flowed across the leaves like a harpist. She cut the buds, and placed them in the large pouch sewn in the front of her coarse muslin smock. Her knees and her back ached. Rest would have been lovely. But the day was not done until she made sure she had cut every bud.

The síanas had no benefit as food or dyes or anything else. The fruits had little flesh or juice, and filled the mouth with coarse seeds. The white flowers had no scent, little nectar, and no flavor. But if she let the síanas bloom and bear fruit, they wouldn't keep her home invisible to outsiders. Living beings could only expend so much energy. As a result, usefulness and reproduction were incompatible.

Slee was now twenty-four, had lived alone for years, but the words of her human Papa and elven Mama still echoed in her ears: *All life cares for all life.* It was not a command, but a statement of truth. They might as well have said 'Water flows downhill, and the sun rises in the morning.' Normal circumstances made words like that blend into the fabric of unconscious thought.

The war between humans and elves ensured that circumstances remained abnormal.

The distant spitting sound of muskets was a constant reminder of murder. Otherwise rational beings crafted ever more cunning weapons, to propel ever deadlier missiles into an increasingly hated enemy, who did more of the same in turn. Slee had never seen what they gained from it. Perhaps 'All life cares for all life' *should* have been a command. Perhaps someone had to shout it into every ear, whether pointed or round. Whoever that task fell to, though, it was certainly not her.

Just then, some voices called out in the Elarím language. She froze, knife in hand, and listened.

Her garden was nestled on the side of a hill, and overlooked a path often taken by the elves. From the phrases that drifted up and through the hedge, Slee gathered that a small group of Elarím were leading human prisoners north. They say that once a human enters Elarím lands, they are never seen again. That much her human father had said. Mama, though, had been reluctant to speak of it at all.

It was no mystery what humans did with their elven prisoners: shot them dead. For all Slee cared, the elves could do the same. Only the faintest thread of curiosity pulled at the corner of her mind. After all, what could be so bad that even Mama would not speak of it?

WAR WITH ELVES: FOR PROFIT AND AMUSEMENT

Slee put down her knife, and gently pushed her way through the síana hedge. The leaves were soft, but dense and noisy. Navigating the branches with relative quiet was an art in itself. The elven part of her made the process easier. She timed her movements with the gentle flicker of wind, and at last pushed far enough that she could see through to the strangers below.

Indistinct figures bearing lanterns that cast ruby-red light led a small procession of rope-bound prisoners. The elves' fair hair flashed like silverfish scales, and the humans' tricorne hats flapped in the wind like bat's wings. Little else could be seen clearly.

Slee's own hair was a muted tawny brown, her skin light brown, her build a little stout, and her features a mixture of delicate and sturdy. But for her pointed ears, there was little about her to clearly mark her as elf-kind. As far as she was concerned, the elves marching by were as different from her as hawks are from robins.

They drifted along the dark path below. None of them looked up toward Slee, but she watched them regardless. There was no rational reason for them to leave the path and climb the rocky incline to her hidden home. But then, they were not fully rational beings. Who knew what whims might suddenly take them?

As the party passed Slee's home and continued north, she let out a long-suspended breath. Soon, all that could be seen were the small, red lantern lights bobbing in the dark. Then the lanterns shone through a thin lattice of branches, and she knew they had entered the high wall of thorny brambles that served as a barrier to the Elarím lands. They were gone.

Relief swept over her. Every time soldiers went past, her chances of being discovered were slim. Still, the threat could not be ignored. Moving her home to avoid being found had become increasingly difficult. So few pockets of land remained secluded.

She pulled herself back out of the hedge, suddenly weary. The síana hedge would have to wait until morning.

As she walked the winding path to her door between curtains of glowing lichen, a distant booming sound startled her. The earth beneath her bare feet hummed.

A few seconds later, there was another echoing blast, and then a sharp ache in Slee's heart. The subtle web that connects all life shuddered and recoiled. The blast had no doubt been caused by the humans' oversized cannon, and it had killed many. The pain in Slee's chest was an echo of their deaths.

Life is like air, Sílandra. When it is all around, you take no notice, but a sudden absence is hard to ignore.

Mama had said those words as she taught Slee the art of telethymia. Elves learn the ability to sense and share *animus*, or life energy, like a fish learns to swim. Slee, born half-human, had struggled to learn it, but only at first.

She sank to her knees with a hand pressed to her chest. It felt as though her insides had been bruised. Though her body was unharmed, the pain in her soul made her gasp.

The only remedy to death was life.

She eased her fingers into the nearby soil. Tiny beings like living motes of dust brushed against her palms. Motelings, she called them. Those she touched linked with others, forming a growing circle. The web touched roots, stems, leaves, worms, beetles, petals, branches, and trunks. It expanded from end to end of the síana hedge, and then beyond, to the entire forest.

Each new thread of the web was a balm to her heart, just as her hands and bare feet soothed the other creatures. No animus was extracted to aid her healing. She was no parasite, drawing life like blood from the land. To connect was to share, to share was to heal. *All life cares for all life.*

At last, the land and her heart were whole again.

Morning came with the distinctive sound of rustling in the síana hedge.

Slee burst from her hut, shovel in hand, ready to fend off intruders. Weaving between the stalks and branches of her crops, she rushed to the source of the noise. She emerged and came face to face, not with an intruder, but with her colossal tortoise, Slowjaw.

He had parked his carriage-sized shell by the hedge, and was plucking bucked-sized mouthfuls of síana leaves from it.

"Slowjaw! Stop that!" she shouted.

Slowjaw groaned, swung his leathery neck round, a large bushel protruding from his mouth. His amber eyes blinked slowly at her.

"You know we need those to keep us hidden! Very naughty!" She advanced at him with a finger raised high. "Bad Slowjaw!"

Despite her being less than a tenth his size, Slowjaw retreated. He tucked his huge, reptilian head back into his shell, and shuffled backward on tree-trunk-sized legs. A deep groan bubbled in his throat. His fear leaked into the telethymic web like a pool of spilled ink.

Slee probed the síanas. No great harm had been done. They grew thickly enough that even Slowjaw's enormous mouth had made little impact.

Slee crouched before the cavernous opening to Slowjaw's shell, and addressed the gleaming yellow saucers of his eyes.

"I'm sorry. I shouldn't have yelled like that. Here," she pulled a handful of fan-shaped leaves from a nearby solan plant. "You can eat as many of these as you like. Just not the hedge, please."

Slowjaw blinked, then shuffled forward. Tenderly, as though handling a kitten, he stretched out his neck and spat out the síana leaves on the damaged hedge. Many of them had been mashed to slurry, but still Slee appreciated it.

"Here, my love. I'm sorry I scared you," Slee said, holding out the solan leaves.

Slowjaw took them in his beak and chewed slowly. Slee stroked his head and scratched his chin. He leaned into her touch, humming contentedly. Telethymia gave Slee an impression of his thoughts and feelings, in the ill-defined way of animals that lack language. She was familiar enough with the mind of her colossal tortoise to translate his thoughts into words.

Sorry I did bad. I forgot I wasn't supposed to eat it, Slowjaw thought.

"You're forgiven. Just remember: we need this hedge so we can stay hidden!" She sketched an image in her mind, of a hedge being like a shell that could hide them all. When she passed the thought along their bond, Slowjaw hummed in agreement.

WAR WITH ELVES: FOR PROFIT AND AMUSEMENT

The commotion had woken the peaducks. The tawny females waddled in the wake of their gaudily plumed leader, Felheim. As with most peadrakes, his head was crowned with long feathers of indigo, orange, and green. He quacked commands at the others, leading his flock through the dense crops in search of slugs and beetles. They devoured the pests with ruthless efficiency, thereby protecting the leaves and stems of the crops.

Slowjaw turned and shuffled away, stepping carefully between the crops.

The morning hours passed steadily as Slee worked alongside her animals. Crops of all kinds grew closely packed in a rough circle around her hut. Even her hut was overgrown with broad-leaf climbing beans with tendrils that curled like pigs' tails. Wherever she stepped, something was blooming, fruiting, sprouting, drying, wilting, or growing tubers beneath the earth. Except for the dirt paths, every inch of ground was covered by something green. Nut trees and hordem stalks towered above Slee's head, berry bushes brushed her hips, and spreading creepers matted the ground.

In most places she could see only as far as the reach of her arm. Immersed in such a dense web of life, it was easy enough to sense her way.

She ate her breakfast and collected dinner as she patrolled. For every berry, leaf, nut, and grain she took, she made sure to propagate three more plants, by seeds and cuttings. Every plant had its role, and she had hers. By nurturing as much life as she could, she strengthened the telethymic web binding the garden together. The garden took care of the rest.

By the third hour of the morning, her belly and pockets were full. She left the hordem grains she had gathered in a pot of water to soak. These she would boil and mash for porridge later.

She took a brief rest. When she was younger, she had rarely needed to do so. But lately, her knees had been creaking and her back had found new places to ache. With her feet up on a stool by the fire, she watched Slowjaw and the peaducks explore the garden with a glowing heart. No other place in the world could compare to her garden.

In a perfect world, her days' labor would be done. But her hidden garden needed a hedge, and her hedge required constant attention.

With her pruning knife in hand, she patrolled the garden's border, running her hands over the síana leaves. Every inch of the hedge appeared lush green and healthy. Still, bitter experience had taught her that real problems flourish out of sight. Only her inner sense could be trusted to check the síana's health.

Distant voices drifted up the hill. Slee stopped, straining her sensitive ears. Felheim quacked loudly nearby, and she hissed at him to be quiet. With a little shake, he fluffed and re-folded his wings, raising his head imperiously so that his wobbling plumes stood out. Despite the indignation that filtered through the telethymic bond, he fell silent.

The voices spoke the Elarím tongue.

"More of them?" Slee breathed. "Soon they'll be passing by every day ..."

At first, she could not hear what was said. Then, one elf shouted, "Look up there! What's that?"

"What?"

"Those shrubs and trees. See them?"

Panic shot through her heart.

The tremor that ran through her spread outward, through Felheim's feathers and Slowjaw's leathery neck. One by one, everything in the garden began to quiver under a hazy aura of ink-black fear. It seemed, to Slee's inner eye, that a cloud of smoke was spreading.

She ran through the garden as fast as her feet could carry her, then climbed up to the roof of her hut, using the dense vines like a ladder.

From the highest point on her roof, she stared hard through leaves and branches. At last, she could discern the group of elves below. They seemed to be carrying their dead or wounded. Two elves had started up the hill toward her home. One of them pointed directly at Slee.

"There! A woman!"

Slee scrambled down from the roof so quickly that she nearly fell.

How were they able to see her?

The síana hedge was supposed to be invisible, as was everything within its border. Even the trees taller than the hedge were usually concealed.

The only possibility was that something had gone wrong with the hedge.

The elves' voices drew closer as they climbed the hill.

"Who's there? Reveal yourself!" they shouted.

Slee rushed to the part of the hedge that Slowjaw had eaten. The peaducks followed close at her heels, alarmed by the danger without fully understanding it. All that mattered to them, Slowjaw, and Felheim, was that *Slee* felt afraid. The smog of fear continued to spread, choking the air.

The hedge was missing leaves, but to Slee's senses, it was healthy and intact. The problem was elsewhere.

"Help me find what's wrong with the hedge!" Slee whispered to the peaducks. "Quickly!"

Together with her animals, she searched the síana bushes high and low for any sign of ill health.

The elves bickered with one another, coming closer every moment.

"I saw nobody. It's a stand of síanas, nothing more."

"There was a woman, I'm sure of it."

"Between battle and lack of sleep, your eyes must have conjured her."

Hardly able to contain her panic, Slee grabbed fistfuls of síana leaves, willing her senses to reveal some sign of what had gone wrong. The peaducks milled around the hedge, wings splayed, pecking randomly at the leaves. Slee was unsure if they had fully understood what she asked them. Perhaps the spreading fear had simply taken hold of them.

Slowjaw, who might cower at a stern word, was stoic in a crisis. Twenty paces to Slee's left, he probed at the hedge. His massive round foot, the diameter of a cart-wheel, swept aside a swathe of síana branches and revealed a tangle of dark brown spines. Patches of leaves had browned around them.

An Elarím bramble had sprouted in her hedge, and was choking the life out of it. Elven magic had corrupted an otherwise normal thornbush. Now the hideous, leafless bush invaded the surrounding lands, sprouting barbs the size of iron nails. Young shoots were easy to miss, and they matured with unnatural speed.

Slee hurried to her colossal tortoise's side, as a mixture of gratitude and dismay washed over her heart.

"Well done, Slowjaw," Slee whispered in his ear.

The dark thorns growing in the hedge were too numerous and dense for Slee's bare hands. Even with chainmail gloves and special tools, it might have taken her all day to extract the noxious growth. Slowjaw's hard beak and rough tongue, though, were well suited to the task.

"Pull it up, quickly," Slee urged.

Slowjaw opened his mouth wide, revealing fleshy, pink ridges, and closed it on the thickest snarl of thorns. Sharp points pricked the roof of his mouth, and Slee's own mouth twinged in sympathy. Despite the discomfort, Slowjaw dug his enormous feet into the ground, and wrenched his head backward.

The bramble came free, throwing up clods of dirt.

Slee threw her arms around his neck, and kissed his scaly head. "You magnificent creature! Good, Slowjaw! Very good!"

The colossal tortoise rumbled a happy note, like a trumpet with too much oil in its valves. Chewing very gingerly, he pulverised the bramble plant, thorns and all, then swallowed it.

"When did you last see síanas growing so closely together? And in such an unlikely place?" one of the approaching elves said.

The danger had not passed yet.

The damaged síana bush was a broken link in a chain. Without something to mend the gap, her garden would be discovered in moments.

Slee held the branches of the struggling síana. It was parched and weak. It struggled to even stay alive, let alone lend its power to concealing the garden. The telethymic web that bound her garden would be strong enough to heal it, but not quickly enough.

"Whoever is hiding here, reveal yourself!" the elf called.

"No one is hiding. I was looking right where you were, and I saw nothing," their companion said.

"I'll show you when I drag them out! Help me up this ledge, we're nearly there."

With her hands still holding the brittle leaves of the ailing síana, Slee bowed her head and gave it some of her own animus. A thin trickle of life flowed between her fingers, warm and faint, like threads of spider silk woven from the palest dawn.

Slowjaw hummed, and leaned his heavy head on her shoulder. Felheim and the peaducks waddled to her, and lay down around her ankles. Quiet and subtle as a moth's wing, fluttering threads of life passed between them all, then through Slee's fingers to the síana.

The parched leaves became lush and full, and new leaves sprouted on the twigs that had been stripped bare.

Every creature in the garden gave what it could across the unseen web that bound them all. Slee healed the síana, leaf by leaf, guiding the energy with telethymia. Within moments, the damaged part of the hedge was as healthy as the rest.

Slee released the plant and sank to her knees, breathing hard. Slowjaw and the peaducks did the same, slumping to the ground. Rapid telethymic healing was taxing. All the other plants in the garden sagged slightly, as though sighing with relief after the exertion.

The elves were still approaching. Slee did not know exactly what she would do if they tried to drag her away. She only knew that they would regret setting foot in her garden.

With the síanas healed, the garden should have been invisible once more. If the elves looked right at her garden, they would see only a few boulders, a patch of dirt, and some shrubs. The síanas could not stop the garden from being solid, though. The intruders had only to reach out and feel the leaves.

Slee stood, head swimming a little, and went to the part of the hedge the Elarím had been approaching. Carefully, hardly daring to breathe, she parted the leaves until she could see through to the other side.

Down the hill, thirty paces away, two elves stood facing her.

They each had a longbow, a quiver of arrows, and a spear strapped to their backs. They wore shirts of brass-colored chainmail, red capes, and boots made of overlapping cloth strips. One was shorter and had a more pointed chin, but otherwise they could have been brothers.

"Where did they go?" the short one said.

"There's nothing here. The others need us, come," the tall one said.

"I *swear* on Crann Arborím that I saw a woman looking at us."

"Your eyes have tricked you, that is all. It is not easy to go through any battle, let alone one where the humans have used that thunder-cannon. None would blame you for—"

"You think I've gone mad! I know what I saw! There are Madean spies in these hills, hiding in …. hiding in the bushes, watching us," the short elf strode about with great agitation, circling the area, like a hound searching for an elusive scent. At one point, he came close enough that Slee could have touched him. As he spoke, he deflated, seeming to lose confidence in his own words.

The taller elf, half patient and half weary, slowly caught up to his companion and took hold of his shoulders.

"Manisár, look at me," the tall one said. "Madean spies in bushes? To what end? What is more likely: a Madean plot to hide women in vanishing shrubbery, or a strained mind mistaking what it has seen?"

"You saw the síanas too!"

"Well … I thought I did. I'm in little better condition than you. At times like this the eyes see what they believe they see," the taller one said. His soothing voice rose and fell, almost like a lullaby.

"I … I …" the shorter elf took his companions arms, trembling. A moment later, he sank to his knees, leaning all his weight on the taller elf, who held him.

Despite herself, Slee caught a flicker of the grief and shock that had overcome the elf. The sight of a massive explosion tearing bodies apart, the sounds of screaming, the long, trudging hours of hauling the dead and dying afterward. Loathing for the peasant humans who picked valuables from corpses like magpies. Those impressions brushed against Slee's heart, like a chilling gust of wind. She could not have blocked them out if she wanted to. Telethymia makes one equally sensitive to strong emotions and death.

"Come. We have strayed from the Common Power. You need *aínan, telethían*," the taller one said. "We came too far away from the others — that's why you were overwhelmed."

The shorter one nodded, wiping tears from his flushed face. The two elves descended the hill as quickly as they had come, supporting each other the whole way down.

Relief coursed through Slee's heart.

Her garden was safe for another day. Slowjaw hummed and shuffled slowly around the garden to express his joy. Felheim and his peaducks quacked happily, waddling in circles and shaking their feathers.

Slee headed back to her hut, brushing leaves from her smock. Perhaps in future, she would check the hedge first thing each the morning and tend the crops later. Those awful brambles were sprouting faster every season.

Chapter 5

You see a stranger crying, and you comfort them. You see a butterfly caught in a web, and you free it. No one taught you these things. No one had to. Nature gave each of us the same gift: an aversion to the suffering of others. This law is written in no book, but every child knows it. Adults, too often, seem to forget it.

Life and Suffering, Sage Muanan.

Everything roared in The Crown Upon a Crown: the rain on the windows, the laughter of the patrons, and the fires in the hearths. Officers of all kinds downed steins of ale, packed together on long tables like pigs at their troughs. It was the largest and oldest tavern in Madea City; it was a fixture, a monument, a hallowed place. Oil paintings of bygone Grand Toques covered the walls, overlooking a sea of black tricornes, blue jackets, brass buttons, and waxed moustaches. A rousing tenor could be heard in snatches as the Thambrian singer Pernicus Thrace fought to rise above the ebb and flow of conversation.

It was warm, crowded, loud, and smelled like it was haunted by the ghost of every ale ever spilled. For Fentor, it was a second home.

With his third ale in hand, the unpleasant memory of recent events had begun to dissolve like a lump of sugar in tea.

He still had his money and his home, Providence be thanked. The shell fired by the Lady's Great Bombard had fallen like a burning star from heaven on the heads of one thousand, three hundred and twenty-two elves. How such a precise number was ascertained from the ash-filled crater gouged into the earth, Fentor did not know. All he knew was that receiving the body count had unclenched parts of his body he did not know were capable of clenching.

What should have followed was a parade in Fentor's honor, a shiny medal or two, and a firm, sincere handshake from King Philliby est Wellendorf. Instead, Her Excellency had seen fit to give him a mere, "Well done."

The scouts that returned a while later reported other, less encouraging things. Things that reflected poorly on Fentor. Things that were the reason he was pursuing blissful, ale-induced amnesia.

After said things had been reported, the Lady had given him a stern lecture about the consequences of his actions, and sent him back to Madea City with little chance of ever returning to the front.

It was that stubborn, sugar lump of a memory Fentor was trying to drown in his ale. He might even have succeeded, if Angsley's question hadn't brought the memory out onto the table, like a soggy brown lump for all to see.

"What did Lady Ironhands *do* to you, old boy? You look like she rolled up the business pages and hit you on the nose for leaving a mess on the rug," Angsley boomed over his ale. His bushy moustache had picked up so much foam that is looked like a well-loaded painter's brush.

"Angsley, you've got …" Hess wiped her upper lip meaningfully.

Angsley gracelessly sucked on the foam with his bottom lip.

"Actually, it was the evening news. And it wasn't my nose she hit," Fentor said.

The broad double doors of the tavern swung wide, letting in wind, rain, and a dozen bandaged veterans. The newcomers began a slow circuit of the tavern, aided by wheels, crutches and canes, and their collected alms in frayed hats.

"Crumb from the table? May I have a crumb from the table, good sir?" they would say cheerily to each patron they passed. Handfuls of bronzers and bits clinked as they fell into the proffered hats, to which the wounded soldiers would brightly say, "I thank you for your crumb, my Lord!"

"Come on, purses out, the lot of you," Hess said sternly to the men. "I don't want to see anyone throwing bits in among the bronzers to look more generous, either."

"Now, who would do that?" Angsley said.

"You did, last time we were here!"

"How am I to know which coins I've gotten? I scoop them out and hand them over without looking. If I counted them out, I'd look like a miser. If it's more bits than bronzers, then it's by mistake."

"Don't fret, Angsley dear boy, your 'mistake' happens so often that you couldn't possibly look like *more* of a miser," Hess said, mimicking Angsley's gruff voice.

Crauford covered his mouth and laughed through his nose. Angsley, already red-faced from the ale, seemed to swell up like an overripe apple. After draining his ale and ordering another from a passing barmaid, he waved a thick-knuckled hand in Fentor's direction.

"If not for the timely intervention of Providence, our Fentor here might have been the one begging for a crumb," Angsley said.

"Nonsense. I'd have had no need to beg, work ethic like mine. Two weeks shining boots and I'd be back to where I am now, titles and all," Fentor said, flashing his broadest, least sincere smile.

"Actually, if the average bootblack worked every day, it would take … eight or nine thousand years to earn what you have," Crauford said, having flicked his eyes to the timber beams above as he calculated.

"Did you miss the joke again, Crauford?" Hess said.

"No. I didn't miss it," he sniffed. "Jokes are funnier when the numbers add up properly, you know."

"Not all of us have an abacus for a brain, Mr … Abacus-For-Brains," Angsley said, stalling at first, but visibly satisfied with his destination.

The group passed barbs of wit from one to another, and Fentor's trouble with the Great Bombard was forgotten. If he could keep them distracted, he might finally succeed in distracting himself as well. He could forget all about Lady Talentus' lecture on 'teaching him, at long last, a modicum of responsibility.' Angsley could jab and thrust with questions all he wanted, but Fentor had long ago mastered the parry and riposte.

A trio of veterans was slowly approaching their table, asking everyone they passed, "A crumb from the table, good sir?"

"I always thought it strange that Madeans say that, given the origin of the phrase," Crauford said, tapping his fingers on the edge of his stein. " 'A crumb from the table …' "

"Why is it strange? Saint Temlin said, 'A table heaped with bread aplenty rains crumbs upon us all.' " Hess said. A strand of her auburn hair had come loose, and was dancing close to the rim of her cup.

"That's not the real origin. It was an Elarím saying first," Crauford said.

"Shh-shh!" Angsley flapped his hands in front of Crauford's nose, as though to clear his words from the air.

"No one's listening, Angsley. What saying?" Hess said, leaning across the table to better hear Crauford.

The Thambrian licked his lips, glanced at Angsley, then said softly, "The elven Sage Nyendí said, 'For humans, charity is not a gift, but a reminder. Here, Poor One, from my table laden with much bread, I bestow a crumb upon you. Just remember: you may have a crumb from the table, but not a seat at it.' "

"What in blasted … Providence above, man!" Angsley spluttered. His thick neck strained against his collar as he twisted one way and then the other, as though surrounded by eavesdroppers. "You can't talk like that in public. Sages and elves, indeed!"

"I'm saying what *she* said, not that I agree with it," Crauford said.

"Is there a difference?"

"Pardon me, sirs and madam. May I have a crumb from the table?" A middle-aged woman supported by a crutch emerged into their midst from the crowd. Angsley jerked, surprised by her sudden appearance.

"It's alright, I don't bite!" she said cheerily.

She had a friendly, careworn face, with rosy cheeks, and eyes bordered with laugh lines. Her coat had faded and frayed at the sleeves and shoulders, but was otherwise spotlessly clean. Fentor imagined she may have had it cleaned for the occasion of coming to the tavern. No, not 'had' it cleaned — she'd have cleaned it *herself*.

One of her legs ended at the thigh, where her trousers had been folded and pinned.

Hess reached over and deposited a fistful of bronze-colored coins into the veteran's upturned hat. "May the Saints watch over you," she said.

"And you, love! Thank you kindly!"

Crauford and Angsley made their contributions in turn. When she turned to Fentor, her eyebrows leapt up. "Oh, my Lord Fentor! It's you!"

Fentor froze with a handful of coins half-extended toward her. "You know me?"

She had recognized him, but he had no clue who she was. Great fame had always been inevitable. He had just not expected to be well-known and adored so quickly, especially with the secrecy surrounding his latest triumph. Word must have leaked, and the pamphlet presses must have been passing around tales of it stamped with an image of his likeness.

He tried not to smile too broadly. It was best to appear humble.

"Of course! You're my landlord, sir," the woman said. "Charlotte Wixler, tenement thirty on Cobblebone Lane."

"Ah," Fentor said. "Of course."

"Don't fret—you wouldn't know me, my Lord. I'm nobody. For you, I must be just a name on a list of tenants …"

"Not at all! I distinctly remember you," Fentor lied. "Tell me, how are things in the tenement?"

"Oh, well …" Her rosy smile remained where it was, but lost its warmth. "Times are hard in the city. I'm luckier than most, though. I carry on as best I can."

"Good for you! The war brings hard times for us all," Fentor said. "Why, I had to let two chambermaids go. Now I must make do with only four!"

Charlotte rubbed her eyebrow and glanced at the floor. "Yes, my Lord, times are indeed hard for all."

It wasn't true—Fentor still had a full house staff. Still, it seemed important to offer the woman something in the way of commiseration.

"Well, Mrs Wixler, it has been a pleasure. May the Saints bless and keep—"

As Fentor reached out to place coins in her hat, she pulled it away. "Oh, no, my Lord. You provide the roof over my head. That kindness is enough."

"Are you sure? I'm happy to give a few coins …"

"No, I couldn't …" Her faced flushed deeper shades of red as she clutched her hat to her body. "Truly, my Lord, I couldn't take a single—"

"I insist," Fentor said, just about ready to force the bronzers into her increasingly well-guarded hat.

"Forgive me, Lord Lonochy, I'll leave you to your drinks." Charlotte bowed her head and retreated into the crowd.

"Wait! Accept my generosity, woman!" Fentor called after her, but she was gone.

He returned to his seat, baffled. Angsley passed him a full stein.

"What was *that* about?" Fentor asked.

"Only the Saints in Providence above can know," Angsley said sagely. "Half the people wounded by war are addled in ways you can neither see nor understand, you know. I read all about it."

" 'A crumb from the table,' " Crauford said, twisting the needle-point end of his moustache. "I wonder …"

Angsley struck the table with his stein. "Keep your wondering to yourself! You give people headaches when you talk like that."

"I didn't mean anything by it," Crauford said.

"Baldershite! You know what you meant!"

"People like money. People *need* money. How could she refuse my bronzers?" Fentor asked, still stunned.

"Look, Fenny, my family never had much money growing up. It's just ... hard to accept charity sometimes," Hess said, leaning over the table and holding his arm. All of a sudden, he could see every one of her freckles, and feel her warm breath on his face.

"But why? Doesn't she need it? Providence knows I don't let her live in that tenement for free ..."

"Well, that might be it." She leaned closer, and Fentor leaned closer to her. Their cheeks brushed as she spoke in his ear. "Don't let Angsley hear this ... An elf may have said that thing about crumbs from the table, but to a little part of me, it rang true. The part of me that grew up with holes in my second-hand frocks, eating cold cabbage stew..."

"You couldn't have used a bit of help?"

"When we couldn't make ends meet, we would get meals at the Church of Providence. But it was *embarrassing*. Like we weren't good enough. My mother kept her head high, but she wasn't hiding her tears as well as she thought. I can't explain it, it just felt like all we got was ..." Hess withdrew a little from his ear, her bright eyes looking into his.

"Crumbs from the table?" Fentor said.

She shrugged and spread her hands. They went back to their drinks, as Angsley continued to berate Crauford. The soft-spoken Thambrian could not hope to compete with Angsley in terms of stature, rank, moustache size, or sheer bluster. Still, Crauford seemed mostly unperturbed by

Angsley's veiled — and unveiled — accusations of
sympathy for the Elarím.

Fentor briefly considered rescuing his Lancer from the
onslaught, but thought better of it. The longer Crauford
was drawing fire, the longer Fentor could avoid it. The
question of the Great Bombard probably still lurked
somewhere behind Angsley's broomlike moustache,
waiting for an opportunity to spring out.

Hess had withdrawn from the conversation, and was
twirling a loose strand of hair around her finger. She
stared vacantly down at her stein. From the look on her
face, images of her childhood might have been swirling in
the bottom of her drink, and she didn't seem able to look
away. No alchemist's brew could compete with the wistful
spell her ale had cast.

Fentor spotted Charlotte across the room. She was going
from table to table, smiling brightly, giving thanks for the
coins she was given. For some reason Fentor could not
place, her smiles and bows now seemed like a
performance. Her embarrassed retreat from his coins,
however, had struck him as genuine.

He finished his ale in one long gulp.

She wasn't being rational. Feelings were feelings, but
coin was coin. Why take everyone else's charity, and not
his? He could be more generous than the rest of them put
together. This time, he would not be refused.

He stood, straightening his tricorne and his moustache,
checking the heft of his purse. Then, he waved to a passing
barmaid who was carrying a dozen steins of ale.

"Bring me some paper and something to write with,"
Fentor said.

The young woman, shifted the tray on her hip, looked down at Hess' slumped shoulders, and raised her pale eyebrows at Fentor. "It might take more'n a nice letter to make things right with your lady, milord," she said in a theatrical whisper. "She looks orful downhearted."

"What? No, you've got it wrong. Her woes weren't my doing."

"Of *course* they weren't. They never are, are they?" the barmaid said, pursing her pale lips sternly.

"Just get my blasted things, will you?" Fentor said. He put a fat, gold coin into her hand. "Here, that should be enough to purchase paper, a functioning pen, some ale, and a little respect."

The barmaid straightened her shoulders, curtsied quite capably despite her laden tray, and said, "Very well, milord. I shall procure the items you requested promptly."

As she disappeared into the crowd, Fentor muttered about disgraces and social degeneration. Had he been wearing the plumed bird insignia of a Grand Toque, the items would probably be in his hands already.

"Where are you going?" Angsley called over the din.

"That's between me, my bladder, and the commode," Fentor said, then slipped into the crowd.

After picking his way through the narrow gaps that opened and closed between sitting, standing, and swaying bodies, he came close enough to Charlotte to call out to her.

"Mrs Wixler!"

She looked around, seeming unsure of which part of the crowd her name had sprung from.

"Mrs Wixler! May I have a word?" Fentor said, squeezing through a small fissure between the large backs of two boulder-like Capilets.

"Of course!" she said.

"Let's find a more private corner, shall we?"

"Yes, my Lord," Charlotte said. Her brow tightened, as though perturbed by Fentor's request.

He led her through the throng to a small table by a window, where a jumble of empty steins stood like chess pieces abandoned halfway through a match. Fentor pulled out a chair for her, but she took the other one, leaning on her crutch as she swung into the seat.

"Is something wrong, my Lord?" Charlotte said. She smiled brightly, but was pulling at the sleeves of her jacket.

"Not at all, Mrs Wixler. I only wanted to know more about you," Fentor said.

"More about me? There's not much to tell, I'm afraid…"

"What about your family? Surely you have one of those things?"

"Yes, my Lord, the Saints blessed me with five healthy children, and three more I've looked after since my sister passed last autumn," she said, her voice as warm and proud as a well-tuned cello.

"Good gracious, eight of the creatures? Providence has cursed you with blessings. That tenement of yours must not be adequately … spacious," Fentor said. He watched her with the same keen eye he'd use to study enemy movements. Perhaps some would judge his words as rude, but they got a reaction, and that was the point.

Charlotte's face fell briefly, and Fentor saw a flash of something in her eyes — anger, hurt, shame, or perhaps all three. Then she recovered her rosy grin, and was once more performing. "Well, we *are* packed in there like sardines in a can," she said, with a laugh. "But I wouldn't trade away any one of them, not for the whole world."

"What does your husband do?"

"He … passed, two summers back," Charlotte said quietly. Her smile had slipped bit by bit, despite her efforts to prop it up, as though its weight was becoming too heavy to bear.

The barmaid came with a fountain pen and a small stack of paper, then cleared the steins away. Charlotte used the distraction of her presence to dab her eyes with the backs of her hands.

"I'm sorry to hear that. Times are hard — that's no lie. Shouldn't you accept every bit of help that's offered to you?" Fentor said.

"I'm dreadfully sorry, Lord Fentor. I ought to have accepted your gift with grace. I was - I was overwhelmed, I suppose," Charlotte said.

"How much do you pay me each week to live in that little box on Cobblebone?" Fentor said. He wrote as he spoke. To the barmaid's credit, the fountain pen worked well.

Charlotte froze and did not answer. She watched his pen gliding and looping across the page.

"Well?" Fentor said.

"Four bronzers and twenty bits a week, my Lord," Charlotte said.

"What you have in your hat there — how far will that get you? Eight mouths to feed, eight backs to clothe …"

"My Lord, I get by well enough. Please, I beg you — whatever you're writing — "

"Are you too good to take help when it's offered to you?" Fentor said heatedly. He looked up from the paper and saw Charlotte shrinking into her seat, her face reddening. The woman was acting like he was drafting her death sentence. Fentor shook his head, cleared his throat, and proceeded with honey to ease the sting of all the vinegar. "Mrs Wixler. Charlotte. Pride is a great virtue, and you have it in abundance. I applaud that. However, it has become clear that in order to help you, I will have to make pride irrelevant. If you have no choice in the matter, if you *can't* refuse, then there can be no shame in accepting. Do you see my brilliance in that?"

"I'm sorry, Lord Fentor, I don't follow," Charlotte said.

"Sign this, and take these," Fentor said. He turned the page around to face her, handed her the pen, and slid five fat, gold crowns across the table. She blinked at the coins in front of her, her face as pale as the paper in her hands. "If you do not accept, then I shall have to terminate your lease."

Fentor leaned back into his chair, basking in his victory like a cat stretching in a sunbeam. It was a small victory, true, but the feeling was the same. How Mrs Wixler thought she could ever best him in a contest of wills, he would never know. Not everyone was perceptive enough to recognize that he was destined for greatness. But sooner or later, every opponent he faced, large or small, would know defeat.

Perhaps the ale had a hand in conjuring the image he saw before him, but he indulged in it all the same. It was a scene of a parade in golden sunshine, with Fentor standing on an open carriage, throwing fistfuls of crowns at the adoring crowd of dirty-faced peasants. They chanted his name and kissed his hands. They loved him. One day soon, the scene would come true. It was inevitable.

He sighed with deep contentment.

"My Lord … this says I don't have to pay rent for a year," Charlotte said, looking up from the page.

"Precisely."

"I don't understand, sir," Charlotte said. "Why?"

"It's a simple arrangement, Charlotte. You won't willingly accept charity from me, so I'm forcing it on you. Either accept these coins along with my offer to waive all rent payments for a year, or find somewhere else to live," Fentor said, gracing her with a grin of irrepressible charm.

"I don't know what to say," Charlotte said.

"Then don't say. Sign."

"My Lord, five crowns … I've never had that much," she said.

A single crown was worth four hundred bronzers, which in turn was worth two hundred bits. Why the treasury had elected to mint coins with such ludicrous differences in value, Fentor would never know. But since he knew that one bronzer could buy a week's worth of bread, cabbage, and turnips, Fentor had a vague idea of the potency of the wonderment Charlotte must have been feeling.

"Don't spend it all at once, then."

"You'll really turn me out of my home if I don't sign?"

"I won't even hesitate," Fentor said, beaming.

With the slow, tentative movements of one packing gunpowder in a room filled with lit candles, Charlotte signed her name on the page. She looked relieved, worried, overwhelmed, and sad all at once. Fentor knew that deep down, she must have been ecstatic. Poor people simply weren't used to feeling good feelings, and she was sure to brighten up with practice.

"May the Saints bless and keep you, my Lord," Charlotte said in a flat voice. She swept the crowns into her hat, then held it tightly in both arms like a newborn.

"Fenny, there you are!"

Hess burst from the crowd and clapped his shoulder. She had evidently lost her hat, and her freckled cheeks were as ruddy as an overcast sunset.

"I must be going," Charlotte said, knocking the table in her haste to stand. She kept her eyes down, seeming to avoid showing her face to Hess. "I cannot thank you enough, my Lord."

In moments, she dissolved into the sea of blue jackets, still cradling her coin-filled tricorne close to her chest.

Hess took the recently vacated seat, and fixed Fentor with a stern glare over the rim of her froth-topped stein.

"What did you do to that poor woman?" She spoke a little louder than was necessary to be heard, even with the din all around them.

"I gave her five crowns, and a rent-free year in my tenement," Fentor said.

Hess scoffed. "Don't feed me bollocks and call them dumplings. I'm not quite as dense as you think I am, dear Fenny."

"I swear on Saint Temlin's socks, it's true."

"The look on her face as she made her escape tells a different story."

"Good thing that I have it in writing, then," Fentor said. He handed the signed agreement to her with a theatrical flourish.

Hess raised her cup, read a few lines, then lowered it slowly to the table. Her expression moved through stages, from confusion, to disbelief, to shock, and finally resting on a muted mixture of the three.

"Why'd you do this?"

"What do you mean, why? She's got eight little mouths to feed, you know. She needs the help."

"But what do *you* get out of it?"

"Nothing," Fentor said. "Nothing but the satisfaction of giving to the less fortunate."

"All because, what, she wouldn't take your money earlier?" Hess said. Her expression, with brow raised, eyes sharp, and mouth ajar, was still too cluttered to read. She would either berate him, praise him, or burst out laughing.

"What you said made me think. She refused my money out of pride. I simply made sure that her pride was no longer part of the equation," Fentor said.

"But … that was a *lot* of money," Hess said. "Bluefingers are paid one crown a year!"

"Business is booming at the gunsmith Father left to me," Fentor said. "Five crowns? Hardly a drop in the bucket."

"Hardly a drop! To you, maybe!" Hess said. She leaned toward him across the table, fighting a grin. The air between them seemed to warm rapidly in her presence. "I see people who have much more give away much less. Her life is going to change."

"As well it should. She seemed like a good sort."

"Maybe I was wrong about you. You didn't bully her into taking the offer? You didn't accept *anything* in return?"

"I just made her see reason," Fentor said. "They don't call me Fentor of the Silver Tongue for nothing."

"Oh, they do *not* call you that!" Hess swatted his arm, and the grin she had been suppressing began to break free.

"It's going to catch on. Just wait."

Hess sighed, shaking her head slowly, and at last one clear expression emerged: she was impressed with him. The same rosy glow that colored her cheeks settled into Fentor's chest. All the racket of the pounding rain and the boisterous crowd fell away, and he was alone with her. Their little table became its own private little world, where either one of them could say or do anything at all.

"You did a great thing, Fenny."

"Now, now, let's not diminish the meaning of the word 'great.' Kings and Saints do great things. They shape history, change many lives all at once. I just gave a woman a handful of coins," Fentor said.

"Well, it was great to me, in the full sense of the word," Hess said, holding the front of his jacket. "Sometimes I feel like there's two Fentors. One Fentor is forever stuck on top of that hill, searching and searching through that spyglass for something he'll never find. Then there's the other

Fentor, who keeps his eyes on more important things. I just wish he would see …"

She trailed off, blushing. The twinkle in her eye made Fentor forget where he was for a moment. He felt as though he had been suspended in warm treacle, and the world became lazy, hushed, slow. The touch of her hands on his jacket seemed to be the only thing happening in the entire cosmos.

They drifted toward each other, closer and closer until, at last, their lips met.

Then, everything happened at once. She went back with him to his bed, and then they were wed and she bore his child, and all the other nobles in the city shunned him and sneered at him for marrying a *common* girl, and his military career stalled. But he was happy, happy with Hess and their four little brats with his chin and her freckles, happy to have responded to the call of destiny with a cordial: 'No, thank you.' He was happy to be unremarkable, ordinary, forgotten by history, common; to have become everything Father had ever warned against.

He blinked, shook his head, and dispelled the dream.

The roar of the rain and the stirring choruses of Pernicus Thrace crowded back into his ears. Hess still had a hold on the front of his jacket. He looked down at her hand, up to her lips, then to her eyes. They had never kissed, and they never would.

He cleared his throat quietly, and she let go of him as though he was scalding hot.

The air between them became as thick and cold as old custard. Fentor almost blurted out an apology, but bit it back in time. At that point, saying sorry would have been an admission that he had perceived what passed between them. Instead, the two of them tacitly agreed to pretend it had never happened: she didn't apologize either.

"Well, we'd better get back to the others," Hess said. "Angsley was on the verge of tearing Crauford's 'elf-loving head off' when I left them."

The pair navigated the labyrinth of close-packed bodies and returned to their friends.

Far from ripping his head off, Angsley was in fact sobbing on Crauford's shoulder.

"I'm sorry I said such rotten, awful things!" Angsley bawled.

"There, there, you great big walrus. Let it all out," Hess said, patting Angsley's broad back.

Crauford endured Angsley's outpour with as much dignity as he could under the circumstances. With one hand keeping his spectacles in place, and the other awkwardly bent by the embrace, he tried to resist swaying too much as Angsley put all his weight on him.

"I forgive you," Crauford gasped. "All is well, my friend."

Fentor sat across from them and rapped the table. "Another round is in order, I'd say!"

"Fentor, dear boy, you're back," Angsley said between sniffs. He relinquished his grasp on Crauford, wiped his eyes, and blinked rapidly. "Another round would be splendid. I'll buy, if only to atone for my shameful display."

Shortly after, four steins arrived. For a while as they drank, no one spoke.

"Junior Lancer Thorassa's body was not recovered after the battle," Fentor said. He hadn't planned to speak. Like a belch, the ale had sent the words up his throat without warning. Like a belch, it hung in the air, and he even found himself wrinkling his nose.

"You mean …" Hess said.

"As it happens, Her Excellency's scouts reported seeing someone running. A weedy young man in a Lancer's uniform. He ran away from the fighting … and into the trees," Fentor said, trying unsuccessfully to turn his pained grimace into a glib smile. The ale blurred the already subtle line between them, and he probably ended up looking like a gargoyle in the attempt.

"He might not have realized where he was going," Hess said. "He wasn't the brightest …"

"There was no hint of sympathies for the Elarím in anything he said," Crauford said. "Hess is right. The shock of battle — "

"Well, he's gone now. Never to be seen again. The darling son of the House of Thorassa vanished under *my* watch," Fentor said. "Of course, his family will be told that he bravely charged the enemy, and then was bravely slain."

"Lady Ironhands can hardly blame you. You weren't the one who gave the boy dandelion fluff instead of brains," Angsley said.

"She can, and has, blamed me."

"Have you been … disciplined?" Hess said.

"They can't punish him! He burnt a thousand elves to a crisp, he should get a medal!" Angsley said.

"I'm not being *publicly* disciplined. Between my little wager and the loss of young Thorassa, the Lady deemed it best if I was dealt with discreetly."

"What's she doing to you?" Hess asked.

"I'm not allowed back to the front. I'm to meet with her and be punished in a manner that she deems fitting. No idea what it'll be," Fentor said.

His friends murmured their condolences and sympathies. Fentor had been successfully burying those words deep in his chest all evening, but like seeds, they had sprouted and bloomed in their own time. Awful as his circumstances were, speaking them aloud and commiserating with friends had brought an unexpected feeling of relief.

"Hess and Crauford, you'll be going back to the front under Angsley. That new stretch of the Gutter Trench I won had better not fall back into elven hands while I'm gone," Fentor said.

"We'll defend it to the death, Capilet Lonochy," Hess said, with a small smile and a salute.

"It's a shame you can't be with us," Crauford said softly.

Just then, Pernicus Thrace sang such a bold, vibrant note that the whole tavern held its breath. Then the singer unleashed the first lines of the song *Oh! Lady Ironhands!* Every hand lifted a drink, and every voice lifted the song.

Thrace had written the tune and the words himself the previous year, and already it was whistled on every street corner in Madea. Every line praised Lady Talentus: her beauty, her grace, and her tactical genius.

In the midst of all the din, Fentor spotted the wounded veterans huddled by the door. They pushed it open together, and as one bowed their heads against the pouring rain and stepped out onto the street. If Charlotte was among them, he couldn't see her.

They would most likely head to one of the poorhouses down the street as a group. There, Fentor had heard, the custom was to pool the night's earnings on the floor, and give out the coins equally, down to the last bit. He hoped Charlotte would keep the crowns for herself. Such a prize was too good to be shared.

Chapter 6

Distant gunfire echoed around the hills as Slee harvested supper. The shots only rang out sporadically, as lonely snaps, and not as the constant crackling of a cohort firing at will. After checking through a gap in the síana hedge, and seeing no movement in the woods, she returned to the garden. She hoped the sound of guns would intrude on the tranquil symphony of birdsong and nothing more.

Finches smaller than her fist flitted among the hordems and síanas, ravens croaked upon the vines that enmeshed her hut, and a dozen blue jays tittered as they made a circuit on the top of a dozing Slowjaw's shell. Each of these visitors pecked up grains, berries, beans, and more from her garden. She didn't mind. Why should she? There was plenty of food to spare, and besides, the birds ate weevils and spiders as well. A gardener welcomes feathered visitors. It's farmers who chase them off. Mama had always said so.

A farmer shuts himself in and shuts nature out. He thinks a fence gives him claim over the earth and sky, but those things are not his to keep.

Slee entered the thickest part of her garden, scattering finches as she disturbed their perches. The tangled tanberry bushes caught on the edges of her clothes, but by moving carefully she kept it from tearing. As she moved through, she picked early and ripe berries, keeping the former in her pocket and eating the latter directly. Some dropped to the ground as she moved, but she left them. In the leaf litter, some would be eaten, and some of their seeds would sprout.

All the while, finches flitted around her, taking their share and chittering cheerfully. One of the ravens, watching her with its clever eyes, let out a call that sounded like an old man's groan.

In amongst the tanberries, there were also a few hordem stalks, some solans, alums, climbing beans, beards of glowing lichen, and more besides. Like everything in her garden, all was intertwined. The branches of one plant snaked among the leaves of another, each plant shading the one below it, cooling the ground and keeping in moisture year-round. She took a little from those who had a little to spare, keeping it all in her front pocket.

The faint *snap* of gunfire became slightly louder *cracks*, and their echoes persisted for longer. The humans were getting closer.

She hurried to the síana hedge. Felheim emerged from
the dense tanberry bushes and waddled along behind her
ankles. Through the gap in the hedge, Slee could still not
see anything. The sun was high and the wind was faint.
The only movement in the surrounding woods was the
lazy flicker of leaves. If they came anywhere near her
garden, she would see them.

She eased the branches of the síana back into place, and
turned to find the rest of the garden watching, and
waiting. Three ravens stood like proud statues on the top
ridge of her roof. The little finches and jays had stopped
darting and chirruping, and were instead perched in rows
along high branches. Even Slowjaw had stopped dozing
and was holding his head high.

"We're not in any danger yet," Slee said. "They may not
even come this way."

The ravens looked at her, heads tilted. If Slee didn't
know better, she would have said they each wore a
skeptical frown.

"Let's just carry on," Slee said.

The birds couldn't understand her, of course. They
continued their silent vigil. It made Slee's skin crawl. Papa
had always said that birds could perceive things that
humans and elves couldn't. What did the ravens and
finches know that she didn't?

She ignored the increasingly tense atmosphere in her
garden and continued harvesting. No strong fears clouded
the air of the garden, but the glow of contentment was
absent also. It was like all the subtle threads between the
creatures had become slightly tauter. Perhaps Slee's

alertness, her constant checking through the hedge, had leaked through to the rest of the garden.

In between the shots, there was the sound of shouting. And then, the steam-whistle scream of Elarím arrows.

Every bird in the garden took flight. Except, of course, for Felheim and the peaducks.

Slee watched as the ravens, finches and jays scattered into the surrounding woods or shot up into the sky. Her garden, now emptier and quieter, felt slightly less *alive*.

She rushed into her hut and dumped the crops on the floor.

Back outside, the shouting was louder, closer, and more urgent. Elves called orders, co-ordinated their assault. The humans bellowed, "Get those bloody elves!"

Felheim had corralled the peaducks under the shadow of Slowjaw's shell. He now stood with his wings splayed and his head-feathers erect, as though his small body alone could shield his whole flock and Slowjaw, too. Slee's heart glowed with affection as she passed. If Felheim's stature equalled his courage, he would tower over them all.

Slee hurried to the hedge and eased herself between the leaves. Distant figures could now be seen, as well as blue-grey smoke gushing from their guns, and red darts leaping from their bows. The leaves around her quivered as her grip on the branches tightened. They were heading directly toward her garden.

Two humans, stumbling in their haste to get to cover, had begun to climb the hillside directly below. They sheltered side by side behind a boulder, then loaded their guns. The strange weapons seemed to require a great deal of poking, prodding, patting, and fiddling before they were ready. The humans' fear stymied the delicate process, a black aura of fear that surrounded them, made their fingers tremble, and wafted uninvited across the forest to Slee.

Four elves emerged from the trees farther down the path, and crept up the slope towards the human's refuge. Slee almost called out in warning. Calling out would risk the garden, Slowjaw, Felheim, and the others. It was not a choice she was free to make.

She was frozen in place as she watched the elves nock arrows and close in on the humans. The fate of the humans was nothing to her. It was the rising cloud of fear, black and wispy like the smoke of a spent candle, that quickened her breath and kept her from looking away. It was *their* fear she felt, not her own.

The humans crouched back-to-back, holding their guns ready. The elves crept toward them unseen, arrows nocked and half-drawn. A hush fell over the hillside, as though it knew what was about to happen.

The Elarím sprang around the corner. Two fizz-crack shots rang out, and the scene was engulfed in gunpowder smoke. Slee held her breath as red-tipped arrows streaked through the veil of smoke, and human sabres clashed with elven spears. Bodies fell, and a tide of pain and death washed over the soil, chilling her toes.

The aura, cold as a grave under snow, rippled through her garden. Leaves curled, blooms closed, and Slowjaw moaned with concern. He raised his head as high as he could to see, but he seemed reluctant leave the protective shelter of Felheim's small wings.

"It will be over soon," Slee said quietly over her shoulder. "There's nothing we can do for them. We just have to wait for it to end. Do you understand?"

Slowjaw's enormous amber eyes met hers, and he sighed so hard that his breath nearly threw Felheim to the floor. The peadrake quacked indignantly, preening his ruffled feathers back into place. The colossal tortoise shrank partway back into his shell, eyes closed, his enormous heart leaking sorrow and confusion.

Slee wished she could make him understand. His instincts only told him that great pain was nearby. When something was hurt in the garden, they always helped, without fail. There was no way to make Slowjaw understand that this time, keeping the garden hidden was more important than nature's law — *All life cares for all life.* So long as humans waged war on elves, nature's law would never come first.

Another life was lost, and the garden gasped and recoiled as one from death's ice-cold aura.

The sounds of battle ended. Quiet returned to the hillside, but not peace. It was the uneasy silence of extinguished life. Even the ravens high above remained silent, somber witnesses of death.

Slee eased herself into the hedge and peered through the gap. Amid swirling eddies of smoke, the two humans stood over ashen-faced elven corpses. A stabbing pain surged through the telethymic web, and Slee winced. A moment later, the smoke cleared a little, and she saw the fletching of an elven arrow poking from the belly of one of the humans.

His companion supported his weight, and together they stumbled across the hillside like a pair of newborn fawns. The uninjured one still held his sabre, aiming it at every tree and rock they passed, as though a host of enemies lurked behind every shadow. They came at last to a sheltered depression in the hill not far from Slee's garden. It was like a basin carved into stone — birds often drank and washed there when the rains filled it. Trees covered in ivy leaned over the spot, like curious old women in shawls, so it was well-hidden from the road below. Slee, moving along the síanas to a better spot, could just barely see the humans between the ivy. The injured one was sweating, pale, breathing hard. His companion stroked his forehead, then kissed it.

Slee withdrew from the hedge to find her animals crowding around her. Felheim's head-feathers were drooping, Slowjaw's eyes were wet. A slow, mournful rumble gurgled up the tortoise's throat as he looked over the hedge. The humans wouldn't hear him while the síana's magic held, but Slee worried that Slowjaw's instinct to help would overcome him. She envisioned him charging through the hedge to help only to be shot. The vision came far too easily to be discounted.

"Slowjaw, my love, you know we must stay here," Slee said. She stroked the coarse folds of his neck, and he looked down at her. "They're *humans*. Their guns can hurt you."

Slee closed her eyes, and projected an image of demonic figures shooting Slowjaw with thunderbolts and piercing him with five-foot long bayonets. The tortoise gasped and murmured, then withdrew his head into his shell. She hated exaggerating the vision, but he would not understand otherwise.

The arrow-wound in the human's belly throbbed sharply, and as his blood leaked into the soil, so did his pain. Myriad creatures from the smallest mite to the tallest tree beat along to the rhythm of the injury. It passed along the roots and the fibres of fungi and colonies of ants until all the soil around Slee's feet was pulsing, warm, and tinged with crimson. The longer the pain persisted, the deeper it pierced Slee's belly, until it felt like her own flesh had suffered the wound.

Only those with the gift of telethymia could sense the suffering. Of all the places to die in agony, why there? Why just beside her garden? He ought to have died among his own kind, where suffering doesn't bother others. The cynical part of Slee almost believed the human had somehow done it on purpose, and intruded upon the tranquillity of her home as an insult.

She turned to see Slowjaw's timid eyes shining from inside his shell, and her annoyance at the humans softened. Despite his fear of their weapons, Slowjaw was still longing to help the humans. Bright silky threads of animus waved in the air about him, hardly perceptible, but strong. Some reached into Slee, and the great wellspring of Slowjaw's life force joined with hers, eased her pain and calmed her fears. She put her hand on the end of his nose, and shared her strength in kind. Soon Felheim and the ducks joined in, and the air between them was thick with wavering threads like spider silk caught in sunlight. Working together, sharing their burdens, their fears and pains were eased, but not erased.

A pale, wavering line rose up from Slowjaw's shell, over the síana bushes, and down the hill toward the humans. Slee knelt and leaned into the shadow under Slowjaw's shell.

"The kindness of your heart knows no limits. But they don't know how to use what you are offering," Slee said. "They are only humans."

Slowjaw offered it all the same: the thread snaked down the hill, through the ivy, where it brushed the human's shoulders and cheeks. They could not sense the telethymic web, nor its auras, nor the richness of life-force all around them. When they did not accept Slowjaw's offer of aid, he became confused. The effort of sending the thread so far became too much, and he withdrew it.

His large head tilted one way and then the other. *They need help. Why don't they take it?* he thought.

"There is nothing we can do for them, Slowjaw. Not without revealing our garden to outsiders," Slee said, stroking his beak with all the sympathy she could muster. "We can only stay here in the garden, share our burdens, and wait for him to pass away. I'm sorry."

While Slowjaw could not understand her words, he could understand the images that came along with them. He groaned, standing up tall and extending his neck until he could see over the tops of the síanas.

Slee left him there, ushering the peaducks to follow her. She boiled solans and mashed them with herbs for her supper, drank hot mint tea, and chewed peppery hiralá leaves with her feet by the fire. All the while Slowjaw continued to peer over the hedge, sighing and humming, his poor heart aching with concern. Slee did her best to comfort him as the hours passed and the sun sank.

All life cares for all life.

The words surfaced every few minutes, itching her and disturbing her attempts to restore peace. Nothing could be done to close off the agony of the dying human entirely. No matter how carefully she mended the telethymic web between all the living things in the garden, an aura of pain and unease lingered in the air, grey and irritating as smoke.

She busied herself checking and double-checking the síanas for buds, flowers, and berries. There was little to find, for she had been cutting them three times a day since the elves nearly found her.

As her fingers combed the leaves in search of buds, her Mama's voice echoed in her ears.

Never become a farmer, who shuts himself in and nature out.

"I'm not like a farmer," Slee muttered.

All life cares for all life.

"I care for my garden and my animals," Slee said. "The day humans show any care for living things, I'll care for them, too."

In her circuit of the garden's border, she reached the hedges under Slowjaw's boulder-sized head. He turned his gleaming yellow eyes to her. It was a rare moment in which she wondered if he was not sharper and wiser than she had given him credit for. He almost looked as though he, too, could hear Mama's words.

Years ago, when she was a child, a trio of birds had pecked up a pile of tanberries she had picked. Shocked and upset, she had chased them all away, shouting, "Those were mine! *Mine!*"

Mama had sat her down and explained that she was only upset because she had indulged in the 'illusion of possession.' She was perhaps too young to grasp it the first time, but the lesson had repeated many times as she grew older.

Jealousy is a human emotion. Theft is a human crime. Elves have neither, and it is because they do not hold a thing and call it 'mine'. You are not upset at birds eating berries. They do that every day! You are upset because you thought the berries you picked were yours to keep. Nature knows better. That is the illusion of possession.

Those words echoed in her mind along with the others. She had been thinking of the garden as *her* garden. Slowjaw and the peaducks were *her* animals. They were hers to protect and care for, yes, but also hers to *possess*. Papa never minded that kind of thinking, but Mama would always loftily mention illusions and farmers, fences and walls.

Slee knew that the safety of *her* animals had to come before nature's laws and Mama's philosophy. Mama and Papa had died for that philosophy, more or less. They left the safety of the hidden garden and came back mortally wounded. Slee wouldn't leave Slowjaw and Felheim and all the rest alone the way she had been left alone.

If it weren't for Slowjaw's persistent vigil over the humans, and the warm aura of his concern, she might have been able to forget all about nature's laws.

The human's mortal wound still throbbed through the soil, the plants, and the animals. The dense web of telethymic threads eased the pain somewhat, but they could not dull the dread of the man who knew he would die, and the companion who knew he would soon be alone.

As Slee headed for the hut under glowing curtains of lichen, flanked by Felheim and the peaducks, she hoped that the human would die before dawn.

Chapter 7

*The order's coming down the chain,
We're battling at first light.
They'll send us marching right into
A hopeless sort of fight.*

'Fight the Enemy,' Second Stanza

The streets of Madea City were like an evening gown that's been through a field — shabby and muddy around the bottom, but progressively cleaner and prettier as one lifts one's eyes. Fentor's eyes were ever raised to the pinnacles: to the great soaring flags on flagpoles and ship's masts, to the steeples and belltowers, and everything else that rose above the common, filthy crowds below.

Proud black horses pulled carriages hither and yon, parting crowds of commoners. Two streets away, a parade boasted loudly with drums and pipes in honor of the Madean Land Corps. There was always a parade in Madea City. The street cleaners hardly had time to wash away mud and grime with all the discarded banners, streamers, and confetti.

The buildings themselves stood shoulder to shoulder, narrow, uniform, and three stories high. The streets cut them into perfect squares, like bizarre layer cakes of brick and stone, with bird droppings and gutter stains for icing. If you've seen one block of tenements in Madea City, you've seen them all.

The home of Her Excellency the Grand Toque Lady Elatea Talentus, which Fentor stood facing, broke this uniform pattern.

Where the streets chiefly ran east-west and north-south, her home and its extensive gardens were offset at forty-five degrees—a diamond in a grid of squares. A regiment of tall trees, each of them a towering monument to the topiarist, peering over her high fences at the surrounding streets. Fentor always rather thought that they seemed disappointed by what they saw.

The Lady's main house, sprawling in the centre of her otherworldly gardens, possessed a majesty that was second to none. While all agreed that the king's palace was larger, none said that it was grander.

Every one of Her Excellency's windows had a balcony, and each balcony had a stairway up to a floating mezzanine, some of which had yet other balconies. Every colossal marble column that lined her walls was carved

and painted, depicting Grand Toques of the past. The
house itself was an edifice, a monolith of pale grey stone,
with a tiered, sloping roof of copper-colored tiles.

Fentor, tricorne tucked under his arm, entered through
the front gate. The guards greeted him as they let him in,
but his mouth lacked the moisture for a reply. He only
smiled and nodded.

As he proceeded along the long, long path of crushed
white stone, his neck began to prickle. Some judgemental
eye lurked nearby, watching his progress, he was sure of
it. His own wealth was decent enough, but here he was so
thoroughly dwarfed by opulence that he felt like a beggar.
Even the haughty statues that lined the path looked down
at him with suspicion, as though he had stuffed the
silverware in his jacket.

At the door the head butler, who wore a powdered wig
crisp as snow, accepted his hat and his coat, then let him
in. Fentor's new silver-buckled shoes clacked loudly on
the polished marble. A more timid man might have
softened his steps, but Fentor stepped vigorously, letting
the echoes herald his arrival.

The butler's footmen at the end of the room opened
another door for him. He found himself in a long hallway,
also of polished marble, lined with massive windows that
looked out on a garden of red and white roses. At the end
he met yet another footman, who ushered him along yet
another hallway. This footman handed him off to a valet,
and together they climbed a wide spiral staircase.

At long last, they came to an especially ornate door,
wide enough for a parade to march through, tall enough
that it stretched all the way to the high ceilings. It took

three footmen, red-faced and sweating, to open the massive thing. Fentor, checking the alignment of his moustache with his fingers, drew a breath and entered.

Lady Talentus sat in uniform on a high-backed, golden chair. Her hair glowed in the light streaming through the high arched window behind her, like Providence itself had crowned her as a Saint. Frescoes covered the walls from floor to ceiling, depicting scenes of battle and the handsome Grand Toques that oversaw them. Fentor could not help but imagine his own face painted in such a scene. Grand Toque Fentor Lonochy, the scourge of the Elarím, Hero of Madea. It had a pleasant ring to it.

"Sit," the Lady said. She regarded him coolly as he came to the table and took the smaller, simpler chair across from her.

As he sank into it, he kept sinking into its plump cushion, until he was hardly able to look over the table to meet the Lady's eyes. Her elbows rested on the table; he could have barely rested his chin upon it.

"You cannot be rewarded," she said.

"No, my Lady. Of course not," Fentor said, dipping his head.

"The shot fired from my cannon killed elves, and our forces won a slight advance into their territory. That much is not denied," she said.

"Of course."

"But now, because of you, Junior Lancer Thorassa is gone," she said. She looked down upon him steadily over intertwined fingers, seeming to emanate a frosty breeze. She did not blink once. Fentor suppressed a shiver.

"Precisely what happened the last time you saw Thorassa?"

"When the battle broke out, we were separated. I handed command of the cohort to my trusted officers, and departed in his place to make the request."

"The request for my Great Bombard."

"Indeed, my Lady."

"How were you separated?"

The image of Thorassa cowering under a bathtub flashed before Fentor's eyes. "The fiery light of battle blazed in his eyes. He was hardly making sense, my Lady. Saying such things as, 'I'll feed these elves their own teeth, and when they come out the other end, watch them bite their own …' "

The Lady held up a slender pale hand, and Fentor broke off.

A lesser woman may have berated him, or scoffed at his story. Instead, the Lady gave him no reaction whatsoever, except for her raised hand. She continued to watch him. He'd had more lively staring contests with statues.

"How were you and Junior Lancer Thorassa separated?"

Daringly, perhaps, Fentor chose to tell the truth. He tried to raise himself on the seat, but the cushion had as much substance as a puff of air. He settled for leaning forward and half crouching by the table's edge.

"The Thorassa family … will they hear of this, my Lady?"

"They will hear whatever I judge to be fit for them to hear."

Fentor dragged his chair forward along the polished floor, producing an ear-splitting shriek. Then, with his fingers on the table's edge, lifted his chin above it. The Lady said nothing, but stared at his fingers with a needle-sharp gaze. Fentor withdrew his hands reflexively, as though he had narrowly avoided being pricked.

"The Junior Lancer … was not ready for battle. He hid when the arrows began to fall. I handed him an arrow, told him to stab himself in the leg and get himself a carriage home. I thought 'courageously wounded in battle' might sound better than 'hanged for cowardice' in the Thorassa family records."

"I appreciate that."

"Thank you, my Lady. To be honest, my best ideas are forged in the heat of crisis—"

"I appreciate your *honesty* in telling me that. The actions you took are still under scrutiny."

Fentor wilted back into his chair, feeling as deflated as the cushion beneath his rear.

"Are you feeling judged, Fentor?"

He swallowed. Her eyes were the color—and temperature—of an iceberg's underside.

"In truth, my Lady, just a tad," Fentor said, flashing an uncertain smile.

"Good."

Her Excellency drummed her fingers on the table. She did not tap with much force, but the sharp click of her fingernails filled the room with echoes.

"You said that you wished to follow my example. That you admired me. Was there even a drop of truth in that self-serving drivel?"

"Every word was the Saint's honest truth, my Lady," Fentor said. He even laid a hand over his heart. His mouth was so dry, it felt as though he'd bitten the end of a chimneysweep's broom.

"What part do you admire? My wealth? My home? My title and rank? Perhaps you aspire to have them write songs about you in every dank and dreary drinking hall in the city?" Lady Talentus said lightly. "Which part, precisely, do you want?"

"All of it," Fentor breathed. Sincere, honest, truth had escaped him with that breath. He could only hope it was the answer she was looking for.

As the Lady's eyes met his, a nigh-imperceptible twitch crossed her cheek.

"All of it?" She leaned back, eyes half-closed, looking almost bored.

An urge to convince her, no matter the cost, swelled inside him until it was unstoppable. A thousand words crowded about his tongue, breaking the seal of his lips like an army with a battering ram. Before he knew it, he was talking, and he could not stop.

"I swear that it's true. I would do anything — *anything* — to be seen the way you are. To stand so high above everyone else that I can hardly see the ground for clouds. No other Capilet has the same strength of will as I. None of them are as determined to see victory for Madea, with nothing left for the elves but charred leaves and broken arrows. Some days it's like the sun rose just for me, and it set all the world ablaze in my honor. I can almost taste the victories I'm due."

He almost went on, but he caught a glint in the Lady's eye, and his mouth suddenly regained the ability to close. He snapped it shut, and touched the ends of his moustache self-consciously.

"Quite the soliloquy," Lady Talentus said. "Though, a little strange to have been rehearsed for this occasion. 'It's like the sun rose just for me' … is that from a poem? A song, perhaps?"

"To my knowledge, they are my own words," Fentor said.

She stood and drifted away from the table, gazing up at the frescoes as she passed them. Fentor fell into step beside her, arms folded behind his back.

"I called you here because I need to know something," Lady Talentus said.

"What is it, my Lady?"

"Whether you are a fool that got lucky with the Bombard, or a … what's the word?" She tapped her chin with a finger. "I fear 'visionary' paints an overly flattering picture…"

"Perhaps, 'intrepid, bold, risk-taking, heroic—"

"I was rather thinking 'Grand Toque in the making'," the Lady said. She paused by a fresco depicting the Vichón the Great, a Grand Toque with a mane of fiery red hair.

"My Lady, you are too kind," Fentor breathed, chest fluttering.

"Hmm. I am still not sure which you are: a fool, or something more useful. The difference is determined easily enough. A lucky fool cannot repeat his successes. But how can your talent for success be tested, I wonder?"

"I beg you, my Lady, don't let me languish in Madea City. I'm *wasted* here," he said. "Send me back to the front. I'll prove that I'm good enough. I will do anything — things nobody else is willing to do."

"That last part is valuable information," Lady Talentus said. "However, you will not be leaving the city."

His heart, which had been soaring a moment ago, crashed to the ground like a kite made of rags and rat's tails.

"If you go back to the front, it will be as though I approved of your negligence. You'll have to remain by my side, under my watch," the Lady said.

"Will you instruct me in the ways of advanced military tactics?"

"Hardly. You'll take dictation, schedule meetings, and serve me in any other manner I wish. If you happen to pick up lessons along the way, then you can consider them side-benefits to being in my presence," the Lady said.

She turned from the fresco and looked squarely at Fentor.

"I'll grant you one free lesson now: it would have been better that Thorassa had died. Some of the idle rumors bandied about by the rank-and-file regarding the Common Power are true," the Lady said.

"You mean human prisoners are …?"

"According to what little I can gather from Dídac, yes. Utterly enthralled. No Madean that is taken prisoner by the elves ever returns … because once they are enchanted, they don't want to."

"The Common Power is that potent?"

"The Elarím never lack the power to bewitch a new supporter. You see, the very source of the telethymic craft is numbers. Each recruit adds more to the whole than they take. If they aren't stopped, the entire world will be yoked to the Common Power, thinking as one, puppets on a single string called *Crann Arborím*. Imagine glassy-eyed pawns, lurching about overgrown forests, unthinking, forevermore—all the gifts of Providence snuffed out. A dead soldier is a casualty. A dead officer of good birth is a tragedy. But a Madean taken prisoner is a gift to the Elarím."

"I understand. I shall never let it happen again."

"I should hope not. You are dismissed, Capilet. I expect you here tomorrow morning to commence your duties."

"Yes, my Lady." Fentor slid his heels together and saluted. "As always, your grace and mercy are greatly appreciated."

"Just remember: you would be in civilian's clothes if your little wager had not paid off," the Lady said.

Still holding his salute, Fentor said, "My Lady, that is why we call them 'wagers.' "

The corners of her eyes contracted and her lips twitched, only by one twentieth of a degree, but it seemed to be the beginnings of a mirthful grin. Perhaps, with enough effort, he would one day succeed in making her laugh aloud. "Indeed. The highest stakes yield the sweetest prize. You know, I gambled my name and my reputation on an elf once, and it gave me Dídac. If Providence continues to smile on me, I might just add you to the heap of my winnings."

"It would be an honor, my Lady," Fentor said with a smile, though his stomach turned at the comparison to Dídac.

He saluted and bowed, and she nodded toward the door. Thus dismissed, he followed valet after footman after butler through her labyrinthine halls. Step by step, his smile slipped, and his mood chilled. By the time he reached the street outside, he was scowling so frostily he half-expected his nose to sprout icicles.

A *clerk*. She was going to have him take her dictations and plan her days, and Providence knew what else. He was going to be *seen* taking her notes. Angsley and the others would be off fighting the elves while he trotted along in the Lady's wake, dipping his pen in ink like some snot-nosed pupil.

He was plunged at once beneath the ice of despair, into winter's deepest and darkest pit. There was no hell, no torment, no mutilation of the flesh or agony of the mind that could compare to the depravity of subjecting a man to *clerical duties*. His heart shrivelled up, dried out like an old, dead rose, and blew away on the wind.

Later, as he absently tossed a bronzer to a beggar with a gangrene-blackened foot, he thought that no individual in the whole of Madea could possibly say they had it worse than Lord Fentor did.

Chapter 8

A man with an arrow in his belly might survive as little as a few minutes or as long as a day or two. It depends entirely on luck — on which parts of his insides are pierced. The morning revealed that the wounded human still clung to life, but just barely. Slee considered the man's luck to be poor indeed. The doomed fare best when they don't linger.

She dressed and left her hut, kneading the soil a little as she yawned outside her door. The web shivered and throbbed with aches and cold despair. The human was barely able to stay awake, hardly aware of the extent of his pain. Soon, he would slip away, and Slee's garden would return to normal.

That morning, almost every leaf, branch, and bloom was covered in pale blue butterflies. Their wings winked in the young sunlight, opening and closing with the slow luxury a stretching cat. It looked as though all her plants had grown tired of being green and sprouted dainty sky-blue leaves instead. Slee breathed deeply and enjoyed the ethereal calm of the butterflies' presence. Some of the bolder creatures left their perches and lit upon Slee's head, shoulders, and chest.

The dying human was not forgotten. He served as a reminder, to savor all fleeting things before they pass. The blue butterflies had only stopped by to rest before floating away to their next destination. Life was the same: a brief visit, a moment of joy, and then a departure.

Slowjaw, still peering over the síanas, was evidently too distracted to appreciate the garden's gentle visitors. He stood at the centre of a dense, distorting aura, like fog lifted from a long, disturbing dream. His cavernous lungs heaved slow sighs, and two little streams of tears coursed down from his eyes and down his weathered neck.

Slee crept gently between her crops, disturbing as few butterflies as she could. As she reached the thick aura hanging around Slowjaw, she instantly felt heavy, tired, and heartbroken. The poor tortoise had kept his vigil the whole night through, pouring his heart out for humans that could not see him, let alone sense his presence.

She climbed onto Slowjaw's enormous shell, sat on its front arch, and hugged his neck tightly, her fingers just barely meeting at the front of his throat. He hummed gently in response to her touch, but with her ear pressed to his skin it sounded like a long rumble of thunder.

"I'm sorry, my love. It will be over soon," she said.

They're very hurt, he thought. *Poor humans, very hurt.*

Slowjaw turned to look at her, then back toward the hut. The oppressive cloud of sorrow that hung in the air seemed to clear a little. Slee followed his gaze and saw the peaducks sleeping in a huddle by her door. Slowjaw turned back to look over the hedge, and stood taller so quickly that Slee's stomach swooped. He raised one knotted, tree trunk-sized leg until it was almost above the hedge.

"Slowjaw, don't you dare!" she gasped, gripping his neck tightly.

Too late she realized that he hadn't calmed down because her hug had soothed him. No, he felt better because he'd decided to charge down the hill to the human's aid. With Felheim sleeping and Slee on his back, there was nothing to stop him but the hedge.

His foot hovered over the garden's border.

"Put your foot down and get back in the garden, right now!" Slee hissed.

He put his foot down — outside the garden. With this first act of defiance done, he lurched forward, and hurried out of the garden with all the haste he could muster. The hedge was flattened and crushed by the underside of his shell, and the hill began to rumble as his gargantuan feet pounded the earth in a bulky, lumbering canter.

Slee clung on as tightly as she could as his shell bucked under her.

Slowjaw could charge like a bull elephant when he was motivated. He could move his great bulk with his powerful legs, but once he got going, stopping was fairly difficult. He stopped running, but his momentum continued to carry him forward. As a result, he skidded down the hill, gouging a deep groove in the earth, knocking over saplings, casting up clods of dirt, leaves, twigs, and several indignant birds. He came to a stop with a great lurch, shook his head, and made a brief, gurgling sound in his throat.

Slee, bruised and sore, peeled herself from Slowjaw's neck and dismounted. It felt more like she had fallen down the hillside than ridden down it.

They faced the ivy-covered basin in the hillside. She didn't hear any human voices yet. Perhaps Slowjaw's thunderous arrival had scared them out of their wits. Perhaps they were waiting, guns loaded, to shoot her between the eyes.

Slowjaw, his enormous heart glowing, ignored any potential danger and thrust his head through the curtain of ivy.

"Good Providence above! Kill that beast!" a gruff human's voice shouted.

Slowjaw, not understanding, crooned at them and bent down to have a closer look.

Slee, half-paralyzed from fear, forced her trembling legs to march through the vines. She stood between the humans and Slowjaw with both arms outstretched. Each breath felt as though it congealed in her lungs, her vision went grey and her head swam, but she stood upright regardless.

"Don't hurt him!" she said in Madean.

Her vision cleared a little and she found herself nose-to-nose with the bayonet end of a rifle. The man holding it, an olive-skinned man with a thin black moustache, glared at her in warning. He was half-crouched over his injured companion, a pale, round-faced man with a shaggy blond beard and a crude bandage around his waist. The shaft and fletching of the arrow stuck out through the bloody cloth. He aimed a pistol at Slee, though his arm shook violently with the effort of holding it up.

Slee looked from one man to the other. The injured one looked wild with either rage or pain, blinking sluggishly, his teeth bared and his breathing jagged. The other looked protective, stern, resigned. His aura was drowned out by the sharp gusts of pain flowing from the arrow wound.

She chose to address the calmed black-haired man. "I am not one of them. I have no weapons."

"Cartín, what are you waiting … for?" the blond one said between gasps of pain. "Sh-shoot them!"

"She is unarmed," the one called Cartín said softly. To Slee, he said, "Send your beast away."

"He won't harm you. He's only … curious," Slee said, hesitating in her search for the proper Madean word.

"Make it leave!" Cartín barked, waving his rifle in warning.

Slowjaw made a trumpeting call that shook the leaves. He snaked his head left and right, trying to look past Slee at the humans. Cartín followed the tortoise's movements with the point of his rifle.

Slee waved her hands between them. "Alright! I'll make him move."

"Just … shoot them!" the blond one choked, though his eyes were glassy, and he was aiming at a tree to the left of Slowjaw.

"Don't! If you shoot me, he'll trample you both. Your guns won't save you from that. Just let me calm him, please," Slee said.

"I will give you until the count of ten," Cartín said. His tongue flashed across his lips, and a bead of sweat rolled down his nose. "Make him move, or we shoot."

Slee nodded, still holding both hands up, then turned toward Slowjaw.

"Slowjaw, my darling, you must slowly move away," Slee said. As she spoke, she hurriedly wove some telethymic threads together, drawing from her own feelings and the panicked aura of the humans. With both hands still raised, she had to weave them with sheer concentration, stitching a new web that human eyes could not see. It formed a crude image that she presented to Slowjaw, showing humans overcome with fear, shooting bolts of thunder that struck her in the chest. Slowjaw growled in consternation. Slee quickly knitted a new scene, depicting Slowjaw going back up the hill, calming the humans and saving Slee's life.

His plate-sized eyes closed, and he expelled a defeated sigh into Slee's face in a gale that almost knocked her backward. The colossal tortoise was stung to be sent away, but he understood that he had to go. He dragged his enormous bulk backward a few paces, then turned and slowly lumbered back up the hill toward the garden.

She turned to the humans. "There, he's gone. Lower your guns."

"You might be unarmed, but if we let you leave, you'll bring others who are," Cartín said.

"Others? What others? I live alone," Slee said.

"None of the Elarím live alone."

"I'm *not* one of them," Slee said.

"Spare me. I'm afraid your pointed ears give you away very clearly," Cartín said.

The trio faced one another, trapped together in the hidden basin like flies in spilled honey. The wounded man's eyes fluttered, and his lips were the color of ash, but he still gripped his gun. Cartín held Slee at the end of his gun, his face taut.

"Well, if you truly wanted to shoot me, you would have done it already."

"I try not to make a habit of shooting unarmed women. Elf or otherwise," Cartín said.

"So let me leave," Slee said.

The blond man, who had been sucking in each breath loudly through his teeth, suddenly went quiet. An aura like icy fog billowed over Slee's feet, and as she shivered, her mouth went dry and her eyes grew heavy. Blood loss was sending the man to a sleep he would never wake from. Deep, sinking despair weighed upon the aura, the particular despair that is a resignation to the end.

"Horvald?" Cartín said urgently, keeping his eye on Slee. "Horvald?"

"I'm … here," the blond man murmured.

"He doesn't have long," she said softly.

"We've been through worse," Cartín said. A glimmer of tears came to his eyes, and he blinked them away. "Haven't we, Horvald?"

Slee realized that at least some of the despair she had sensed came from Cartín.

"This is just—" Horvald coughed feebly. "A little splinter."

Slee stared at the humans. Something sparkled in the air between them, so faintly that it must have been imagined. It reminded Slee of Mama and Papa — a sparkling aura had always hung in the air between them, like golden dust caught in a sunbeam.

"You care for each other, don't you?" Slee said. "More than is usual for humans?"

Cartín went very still. "He is … a dear, dear friend," he said, his voice cracking.

"He doesn't need to die today. I can help him," Slee said. Despite herself, despite all her best instincts and the bayonet hovering near her nose, she had begun to care about the men.

All life cares for all life.

She shook off the thought as a horse shakes a fly, but the truth behind it remained. Simply being there, experiencing their pain, knowing how deeply the two men cared about each other, she could not help but care as well. She was drawn into the strange feeling, as though she had drifted to an unfamiliar place by a river current.

Telethymia opens up the heart, Sílandra, and lets the world in. The trouble is, you can't always choose what comes in.

Cartín had not moved, but behind him, Horvald steadily wilted. His eyes were almost closed.

"I can help him," Slee said again. "It's not too late."

She let tender threads of concern waft through the air towards the humans, but they found no purchase. It was as though the feelings she projected were in a language they could not understand.

Cartín stared at her, his face hovering between hostility and despair. The rifle did not move.

Horvald collapsed at last, as limp as a heap of clothes. Slee sensed a feeble heartbeat and shallow breathing from him, but nothing more. The air that had been thick with his pain was now chokingly thin.

Cartín trembled. "Horvald?" He stole a brief glance at his companion, then glared at Slee with suspicion.

When she made no move other than raising her open hands a little, Cartín turned and shook Horvald's leg.

"Horvald?" Cartín said, louder than before.

"He is still alive. We can help him," Slee said. She took a tentative step forward.

"Don't touch him, elf!" Cartín said, waving the bayonet in her face.

"Half-elf," she corrected, without thinking. "Look at me. Look at what I'm wearing. Look around us, at the empty woods! Have you ever seen an Elarím that looks like me, unarmed, all alone? I'm not one of them."

"Even if that's true, it's no reason for me to trust you."

"You care very much for Horvald, don't you?"

Cartín licked trembling lips. "What does it matter to you?"

"If you care for Horvald, that is reason enough to trust me." Slow, lethargic fog rolled from Horvald's aura across the ground, sleepy as a winter hillside. Slee shivered, then said, "He is fading away. You don't have time to deliberate."

Cartín's expression softened and his shoulders sagged. "I don't know what customs of honesty elves live by, but if you can look me in the eye and tell me this is not some trick …"

"I swear, this is no trick. We can take him to my home, it's hidden away up the hill. The Elarím won't find us there."

Cartín lowered his rifle. He placed a hand on Horvald's leg. The tension in the air eased slightly. Perhaps the calm Slee projected had affected him after all, or perhaps her words had. Whatever the case, he nodded to her. They lifted Horvald and carried him.

"Why would you even offer to help us?" Cartín asked, as they pushed through the curtain of ivy.

All life cares for all life.

Slee pursed her lips as she searched for the right Madean phrase. "I am only … obeying the law."

****

Opening the door to meet the dim, foggy, dawn in Madea City after an extended evening of carousal was a strange, introspective, hazy, dream-like experience. Indefinable magic hung in the air. Lamp-posts glowed through veils of fog, mysterious and alluring, promising adventure and intrigue like Will-o-the-Wisps. The usually overflowing streets were nigh deserted. The few souls one did pass first appeared as ill-defined, darkish blobs, then resolved to be nightwatchmen, beggars, or fellow drunks.

Fentor had walked the streets in that way more than a few times. The morning he rose to report to Lady Talentus, he had a rather different experience.

Sobriety extinguished all the magic he so fondly recalled. The fog was cold and clammy. Passing early morning revellers stank of the ale they'd spent the night soaking in. At least *they* were having fun. He, Fentor, was a miserable wretch who could only think of his cold fingers, and the sleep he was missing out on.

He reached her door, half-catatonic, and was ushered inside.

Her Excellency was already in uniform, looking well-rested and impatient.

Almost before he could catch his breath, the Lady whisked him out to her stables, where a four-horse carriage waited. There, he wrote a rapid barrage of her thoughts, though he wasn't completely sure where the pen and ledger in his hands had come from. One of the valets must have thrust them into his grasp. She dictated ideas for memoirs, quotations from Saints, and the names of the people she wanted to meet with. As the carriage lurched along the cobbled streets, Fentor's hands scribbled wildly in his attempts to keep up with the Lady's deluge of thoughts. It was like trying to contain a waterfall with a leaky bucket.

When she asked him to repeat back to her a particularly pithy thought she'd had, he scanned the illegible squiggles on the page, and was forced to improvise something that she plausibly *could* have said. She did not look pleased.

The day passed in this manner, too fast for him to get his bearings, yet somehow also too slow. Every hour felt like a dozen.

At long, long last, the day was over. He trudged stiffly to bed, woke up just as tired, and the torture continued.

Every day was a descent into a deeper, more forsaken corner of the Sinner's Abyss. He kept neatly ruled ledgers that tracked the movements of the Lady's many investments. He delivered her personal messages to various Lords and Ladies about the City. He attended her meetings, speeches, fittings, recitals (she played the harp with ethereal precision), and her meals. Every hour, every minute, every second, he felt as though an invisible vice had been clamped over his ears. As it gradually tightened, his brain liquified and dripped out his nose. The work was crushing his soul, in a very real, life-threatening way.

Boredom like that was a slow-acting poison, and he was approaching a fatal dose.

Despite his best efforts, though, he became quite competent at his duties. His handwriting developed into a form of short-hand, his memory for her dozens of appointments and meetings sharpened, and he even stopped yawning in full view of her noble hosts.

Every evening, he soaked himself in brandy and a hot bath. In the rose- and lavender-scented steam, he would behold grand visions of himself wearing so many medals on his chest it looked like chainmail. In the ecstasy of those fantasies, it was he who gave dictations, he who gave the orders, he who gave the world a shining example worth following.

As the hours of the day inched past him like a parade of snails, Lady Talentus would sometimes say some wise, pithy thing, then ask his thoughts. At first, hardly able to follow, he merely agreed with her. Later, as his boredom grew increasingly desperate, he clung to those philosophical moments like floating planks after a shipwreck.

"I think Saint Temlin meant that there *is* no society, not really," the Lady said, as they waited for the rain to pass inside the carriage. "There are providers and takers. The takers cannot help but depend on the innovations, leadership, and charity of the providers. Wouldn't you agree?"

"Of course, my Lady. Why, society's ills surely come from takers who *think* themselves providers," Fentor said. He spoke in a lofty, academic tone, but his neck grew warm out of fear that he had somehow exposed his ignorance.

"And vice versa, I should think. Madea would do well to ensure people are in their proper place. The climb to the top is too shallow, and the summit is too … comfortable," she said. She looked out the carriage window at the city, shaking her head slightly. "There are many *takers* at the top. I fear they are the reason the war has never been won."

Fentor said nothing. He dared not agree, or even ask who she referred to.

Her Excellency continued to survey the street outside, tapping her chin with a slender finger. She looked at the city as though it was her drawing room, and she was deciding which color and style the curtains should be.

"We ought to have won this war so very long ago," Lady Talentus said with a small sigh. "The Elarím are a nation of takers. The only thing keeping them safe is Crann Arborím. The Tree of Rubies, which sustains the Common Power. Without it, without their whistlers and their aegis, they would crumble in an afternoon."

"Perhaps, one day, we will advance far enough and take Crann Arborím for ourselves," Fentor said.

"I admire your optimism. But after a century of smoldering, this war has proved it shall not burn itself out. Conventional tactics have been exhausted. It's not enough to advance our lines, or to perfect our gunpowder, or anything else we've been doing. We need something new."

"A new tactic? A new weapon?" Fentor said.

"Ah! The rain has stopped," Lady Talentus said. She rapped on the roof of the carriage. A moment later, the driver opened the door and they stepped out into the street. The freshly unveiled sun glared up them, reflected in puddles underfoot.

"What could possibly be tried that hasn't been tried before?" Fentor asked.

"A new war altogether," she said. "One that's *meant* to be won."

Chapter 9

After a particularly gruelling day of taking dictation, the Lady told Fentor that he would be attending a particularly crucial meeting the next morning. It was a monthly event held at Grand Toque Walbough's home, where various military leaders and the king met to discuss 'The War Effort.'

"You'll be sitting next to me, not behind my chair," she said, eyeing his clothes and muddy boots. "Do try to dress like you deserve a place at the table."

There was no need for Fentor to peel himself out of bed the next morning. He shot out from between the sheets like a startled cat, and had Methúsel fetch him his best dress uniform, best oils, best combs, and, if possible, his best behavior.

"With regard to sir's best behavior," Methúsel droned, his puffy, white eyebrows raised. "How am I to fetch that?"

The ancient butler held up a silver platter with all Fentor's finest grooming accessories.

"You'll just have to think of something," Fentor said, snatching up a faux-pearl comb and pulling it through his hair.

"Of course, my Lord. I will search for your manners in the dustiest, most neglected corners of the house. It must be many years since last they were used."

"Oh, just get out," Fentor said, tiring of the game of wits. Too late, when Methúsel had left, he realized he should have retorted that high-quality butlers didn't misplace things or let the house gather dust.

He combed his hair back neatly with scented oil, shaved twice, then shaped his moustache with tiny scissors and a jeweller's loupe jammed in his eye. He trimmed his magnified moustache with the care of a surgeon, shaping it into thin needlepoints. Then, making a bold but hopefully fashionable choice, he greased the tips and curled them *upward*. Brush moustaches like Angsley's were standard, and most other styles in Madea City were straight or curled down. It took a man like Fentor to risk turning such a fashion on its head.

Later, arriving in Grand Toque Walbough's foyer, a trio of young footmen looked at him with pinched expressions, as though he was a dog squatting on their lawn.

They led him through to a dining hall that could have fit five tenement apartments within it. The polished floor of checked marble stretched so far in all directions that the long table at the center looked like a toy doll's furniture on a chess board. Twenty grey-haired, bushy-moustached Grand Toques had been seated already. Fentor took his seat beside Lady Talentus.

Grand Toque Walbough, a pink-faced gentleman of thin grey hair and bushy grey moustache, sat at the seat closest to the head of the table.

Over the following minutes, the rest of the empty places at the table were filled, except for the seat at the head of the table. Nobody spoke and nobody moved. As the minutes passed in silence, Fentor was forced to wonder if time had passed at all. The room had become a tableau, an elaborate living sculpture on display at a museum dedicated to boredom.

At long last, the house's head butler crossed the vast expanse of marble and whispered in Walbough's ear. The Grand Toque nodded, then stood.

"It seems that His Majesty will not be able to attend, as he is engaged in tasks of a most surpassingly urgent nature," Walbough said, in a clear, silky tenor.

A collective shuffling and muttering rippled along the length of the table. Many of the Toques relaxed their posture. One thick-necked man even undid the top button of his collar. Walbough raised a hand with a small smile as the chatter began to swell.

"Now, now! Order, please. We still have business we can address in His Majesty's absence," Walbough said. "Malthus, I believe you had something to present?"

Grand Toque Malthus, a gaunt man with a high forehead, stood and cleared his throat. His watery, sunken eyes looked like potholes filled with rain.

"Yes, thank you, Walbough. Today I am pleased to announce that I can present a new and innovative elixir. I call it the Malthusian Elixir of Power. The preparation imparts strength to the drinker proportionate to the animus input as it is distilled."

"The preparation does what to who with respect to what? Speak plain Madean, man!" said a small man with prominent ears farther down the table. Gruff chuckles met the interruption.

"Settle down, now, Quindly," Walbough said, half-rising out of his chair. "The floor is yours, Malthus."

Malthus, his thin cheeks reddening, glared around the table. "In simple terms then. If you put the strength of ten soldiers in, the elixir gives you the strength of ten men. If that is still too convoluted for you chuckle-brains to understand, then I shall demonstrate."

He held up a small glass vial for the table to see. It contained a mouthful of cobalt-blue liquid. Malthus drank it, then looked up and down the table, as though provoking challengers.

"Grand Toque Quindly," Malthus said. "Would you be so kind as to lend me your sabre?"

Quindly's neighbors nudged him and chuckled. Still, he stood and offered the sword to Malthus as requested, smirking.

"Thank you very much," Malthus said with slow deliberation. "Now watch."

Malthus took the naked blade of the sabre in both hands, and began to bend it. His face grew red as he strained. The blade began to kink in the middle, and then with a forceful crack it broke in half. Malthus, breathing hard, held up both ends of the sabre for all to see.

Mild applause broke out, as though a juggler had performed a simple routine for them.

"I hope you plan on paying for that!" Quindly said.

"Trust me, dear Quindly, with all the money I'll make from this mixture, I'll be able to buy you an entire armory," Malthus said. He handed the broken sword to Quindly with a gracious smile, then turned to the rest of his audience. "I propose that we produce the Malthusian Elixir of Power as standard issue for Land Corps officers."

"Speaking of money, what does this little potion cost to produce?" Quindly huffed, returning forcefully to his seat.

In answer, Malthus distributed some papers to his neighbors. They circulated from hand to hand, filling the vast, echoing room with ghostly flutters. When those who cared enough to look over the document had done so, Quindly stood, page in hand.

"I move that we ban all production of Malthus' Elixir of Strength," Quindly said.

"Elixir of Power," Malthus intoned.

"Whatever you called it. As I suspected, it is far too expensive for what it does. A snapped sword may seem impressive, but I fail to see how the elves will be perturbed by mere feats of strength," Quindly said. "Why, if the elves are close enough to see you break a stone or lift a horse, the battle has already been lost."

"The motion is noted, Quindly, but it shall have to wait until last. Malthus, thank you, you may sit."

Malthus, who was still standing, gaped at the other Grand Toques. When nobody met his eye or raised a comment, he sunk into his chair. His deep-set eyes were wide with disbelief.

After that, the table moved on to topics such as supply lines and incentives to encourage recruitment.

Fentor narrowed his eyes as he looked up and down the table. Nobody, save for Malthus, showed any interest at all in the demonstration that had just taken place.

On the notes he had been keeping for the Lady, he quickly scribbled, "Can't they see what the elixir could do?"

He showed her the page. She glanced down, then nodded, but held a finger to her lips.

Fentor slumped back into his seat. The meeting, with grey-haired Toques squabbling and joking about things that hardly mattered, was not what he had expected. He was reminded of what Lady Talentus had said about there being too many 'takers' at the top.

The primary concern of the table seemed to be how much it cost to advance into Elarím territory, to train and arm Bluefingers, and how much it hurt their pockets when ground was lost. Dozens of common-sense solutions were offered for problems, but they were all dismissed on the basis of cost alone.

Fentor, of course, could see some importance in those matters. Without funds, there would be no war. Cost had to be considered. But he began to get the uneasy impression that nobody seated at the table had even *considered* actually winning the war. It almost seemed as though their real motive was finding ways to keep it going, forever and ever.

Two columns of footmen entered, bearing trays of tea, brandy, cigars, and pork sandwiches. The head butler announced that luncheon was served, and it was the sweetest combination of words Fentor had ever heard.

Minutes later, every chair was emptied, and the Grand Toques stood apart from the table in little gossiping, guffawing, conspiratorial groups. The footmen offered refreshments to the guests with flourishes and twirls, as though they were in a choreographed dance. Fentor, all but tethered to Lady Talentus' elbow, took something from every platter, except tea.

She stood apart from the other Grand Toques, conspicuously so, and observed them each in turn with a cool eye. Nobody glanced at Fentor, even in passing. He was invisible. Her Excellency Lady Ironhands, on the other hand, drew the eye of most other Grand Toques at least once. Fentor watched as each of them—Walbough, Quindly, Malthus and the rest—reacted to her unabashed observations. Some met her eye, then quickly looked away. Some pretended to scratch their eyebrows to cover their face from her. Other, bolder souls, raised their glass to her, as though they were old friends. Fentor suspected that was not the case.

"I have decided how you're going to be useful to me," she said to Fentor in a low voice, as clear as the clinking of crystal.

"You have, my Lady?"

"I want that elixir," she said.

"You want me to speak to Malthus?"

"I can handle Malthus. I don't want them banning the elixir, nor do I want them producing it for the Madean Land Corps. I want it for myself. Your task is to ensure they vote the right way."

Fentor swallowed. A crumb of ash fell from the end of his cigar.

"You want them to vote against banning it, without voting to actually use it? My Lady I … I hardly know these men," Fentor said.

"And none of them know you. Use the advantage. I was ready for your … unique rhetoric, and yet you still twisted my arm into using the Great Bombard. This should be easy," she said. She looked at him, or rather, she looked *through* his skin and facial muscles to judge the underlying bone of his skull. He felt like a vivisected specimen pinned to a table.

His heart beat faster and faster with a stuttering rhythm, like a novice drummer practicing a drumroll. She had, at last, handed him a chance to prove himself. It was not a battle, true, but it tasted like destiny all the same. A faint hum enlivened the air, and his skin tingled. The sweet, sparkling aura of victory kissed his tongue, like the last drop from a champagne glass.

Now was his time.

He drained his glass, stuffed his half-eaten sandwich in it, and placed it on the tray of a passing footman.

"My Lady," he said, twirling the cigar slowly between his fingers. "The elixir is as good as yours."

The trace of a glint flashed across the Lady's eye. "Good."

Luncheon ended, and they resumed their seats.

Fentor felt revived. The past days of drudgery were erased, and he was his old self again. The gentle glow of destiny still hung about him, and he knew it was the shining light of Providence. Victory was inevitable.

"Beg pardon, Walbough," Quindly said, rising from his chair. "Can we speed through the agenda to ensure my motion is properly heard?"

Malthus shot him a filthy look.

"Well, there are a few matters we were going to discuss, but they were chiefly of concern to His Majesty …" Walbough said, tracing his finger down the page. "A request to change the Land Corps uniforms from navy blue to admiral blue … a summary of the changes to Bluefinger rations … a request to change the Madean *Navy's* uniform from admiral blue to cerulean …"

"His Majesty's wardrobe ideas can wait, can't they?" Quindly said with a smirk.

The table was split between groans and chuckles. Lady Talentus, of course, refused the indignity of either.

"Watch your words, there, Quindly … we're all patriots here," Walbough said, though he, too, was fighting a grin.

"With all respect to the good King Philliby, perhaps it would be best to set aside those matters until a meeting that he has actually attended?" Quindly said in a wheedling tone. Then, he muttered into his collar, "That is to say, never…"

"Well, I suppose—"

Fentor, seeing his chance, pounded the table with his fist and stood. "For shame, gentlemen! I can hardly believe my ears!"

"Who let this hayseed in?" Quindly asked.

"He is with me, Quindly," Lady Talentus said. Her voice had the delicate musicality of a harp, but Quindly flinched like a scolded boy.

"This is the good King Philliby est Wellendorf you are speaking of! I should think that a table attended by the Madean Land Corps' top officers would show the respect he is due!" Fentor said. He was, of course, not incensed or even mildly displeased. It was just better that the vote be put off as long as possible. "Providence above has gifted us with a wise, just, and vigorously intelligent ruler. I, for one, insist that we discuss the matters dear to him with as much consideration and detail as they deserve."

Despite the humble Capilet patches on his shoulders, the others cleared their throats and lowered their eyes. Even a scowling Quindly sat down. Fentor had to struggle not to grin.

"Very well ... thank you, young Capilet, for speaking your piece. I suppose you all agree to go through the agenda as planned?" Walbough said.

There was a grumble of non-committal assent. Quindly, lips pursed, gave a small nod.

"You have my humblest thanks, Grand Toque Walbough. Your spirit is as grand as your home," Fentor said with a bow.

"Yes, quite," Walbough said. Then he rifled through his papers, drew one out, and read from it. "*Ahem.* His Majesty wonders if navy blue is, perhaps, a color that causes the Madean Land Corps to appear ... *lackadaisical* ..."

Walbough continued to read the king's long-winded tirade against the color navy blue, and in favor of the more noble and fitting color *admiral* blue.

Even if he had slipped Vernan's Sleeping Tonic into the Toque's brandy glasses, he could not have done a better job sending them to sleep. Some rested their chins on their hands. Some folded their arms, leaned back, and struggled to keep their half-closed eyes from fully closing. Every so often, a hand was raised to conceal a yawn. Fentor, though, was rejuvenated by the droning list of reasons the uniforms ought to change. Every minute passed was another inch of ground gained against Quindly. Perhaps it was like a battle, after all.

Alas, Walbough reached the end of the statement, and the table voted swiftly to keep the uniforms navy. Principally, they cited the cost of changing dyes.

Then, Walbough dutifully read out a list of changes in the Bluefinger rations. As they moved onto the matter of changing the color of the Grand Madean Navy's uniforms, Quindly sat straighter in his seat. There was still time to hold the vote for the elixir, but Fentor's tactics were not yet exhausted.

"His Majesty feels that *admiral* blue does not suit our navy, as we do not actually have a rank that is called 'admiral'. We call our most senior officers Grand Toques, whether on the land or upon the sea …" Walbough droned. "Moreover, as a shade of blue, it is better suited to the Madean Land Corps."

Walbough continued for some time. Fentor felt like his body was tightening like an over-wound watch-spring. Looking across at Quindly, it looked as though he was feeling the same. Both were tense, ready to leap from their seats the moment Walbough finished. If they both stood at the same time, though, there was no question who Walbough would select to speak first. Quindly outranked him.

He had to think of something.

The table voted on the matter of the Grand Madean Navy's uniform. They kept it the same.

"Now, regarding the matter of Malthus' elixir—"

Fentor, Quindly, and Malthus all stood at once. Their chairs squealed as they slid across the polished marble. Walbough recoiled at the sound, then glanced between the three men.

"You all have comments, do you?" he asked wearily.

"Yes!" they said in forceful unison.

"Well, you can't all speak at once ..."

"Here, Quindly," Fentor said, whistling sharply. "Catch."

Fentor took his sabre, still in its scabbard, and tossed it across the table to Quindly. He caught it by pure reflex, blinking and open-mouthed.

"You lost your sword. Have mine," Fentor said.

Quindly stammered, unable to find a suitable a reply. Malthus, too, was speechless, though he was motionless.

"It seems the esteemed gentlemen may need a moment to gather their thoughts. My comments, however, are well-formed and ready to deliver. If you will permit me," Fentor said rapidly.

Walbough, apparently overwhelmed by Fentor's behavior, raised both hands as if in surrender. "Proceed, young Capilet," he said. "Be quick. There are precious few minutes left, and I've an appointment to keep."

The other men sat down, seeming unable to believe or process the turn of events. Quindly cradled Fentor's sheathed sabre awkwardly in his arms.

Fentor's chest glowed with inner fire, and swelled like a hot-air balloon. If he inflated any more, he might float away. Instead, since he was full of hot air, he parted his lips and made use of it.

"Firstly, I entreat the table to indulge in an exercise of imagination. *Think* of the applications Malthus' elixir might have!" he said. He paced around the table's perimeter with both hands clasped behind his back. "Imagine the strength of ten, twenty, thirty soldiers pumping through your veins! Imagine forty! Fifty!"

"Precious few minutes," Walbough repeated pointedly.

"I have a point, I promise you. Sixty, seventy, eighty men? Can you see yourself performing feats alone that would take an entire crowd working together? What about an entire cohort of Bluefingers?" Fentor said. "Grand Toque Malthus, does the elixir have a limit?"

"None that we have found in our testing," Malthus said slowly. He followed Fentor's pacing out of the corner of his eye, and tapped his fingers as though he was bored. Still, Fentor could tell he had Malthus' full attention. "Though, without funding, we only had access to a small pool of volunteers."

"What do your alchemists say?"

"They say that power *should* scale indefinitely with animus input," Malthus said. "They believe there is no limit except cost."

"Intriguing. What if one were to drink the Malthusian Elixir, as well as, say, Malcolm's Hardskin?"

"There is no need," Malthus said. "Those who drink my elixir can tolerate injury in proportion to the strength they gain."

"Remarkable," Fentor breathed, and he meant it. A growing part of him coveted the formula to the elixir for himself. "Picture it, gentlemen: a lone officer, swatting aside volley after volley of whistlers, cutting down elves like bunches of summer barley. A terror to his enemies, a …"

More than a few expressions around the table had shifted. Eyelids that had sagged under the heavy burden of boredom perked up. Moustaches bristled, chairs creaked, and spines straightened. Quindly was hunched over Fentor's sabre, lips in a tight scowl. He had their attention. Now for the difficult part.

"Next, I shall highlight an uncomfortable question. Who should have access to such an elixir?" Fentor said. "Authorized access … or otherwise?"

The Grand Toques looked askance at their neighbors.

"We keep vials of Malcolm's Hardskin locked away in secure chests in the Capilet tent. They are for officers' use only, for good reason. Yet every month, there are stories of Bluefingers picking locks, taking a swig, and disappearing into the trees, never to be seen again. We currently only deal with defectors. What would we be dealing with if a Bluefinger could snap his commanding officer in half like Malthus snapped that sword?"

Fentor continued to pace, waiting while his words soaked into the Grand Toque's minds. Some fidgeted in their seats. The room was not filled with the hazy silence of a bored group, but with the tense quiet of a breathless audience.

"We could supply ever more confounding, more costly locks, the kind that cannot be picked. They might keep the potions safe—at a steep price. We could limit the number of officers allowed possession of this brew. But which ones? It might take hours and hours, motion after motion to settle a matter as delicate as that. Special meetings, hearings, proceedings. As for the potion itself: Quindly said it best," Fentor said. He paused in his slow circle of the table, placing a hand on Quindly's shoulder. "It's far too expensive for what it does."

"Look here, whose side are you on?" Malthus squawked.

"The Capilet has the floor," Walbough drawled. Then, he turned a stern eye to Fentor. "For the moment."

"Thank you, my Lord," Fentor said. He gave the still-scowling Quindly's shoulder a little squeeze, then continued in his circuit. He felt like a hawk circling his prey. Now was the time to dive, and flash his talons.

"I have a third proposal for the table. As sensible, keen-minded men well-versed in these matters, you will naturally vote against Quindly *and* Malthus. You will then vote in my favor," Fentor said.

"Lord Walbough, he's a *Capilet!*" Quindly spat, shooting to his feet. Seeming to suddenly notice the sabre in his hands, he threw it on the table, where it spun on the polished surface like a compass needle. "Shall we invite the butlers and the chamber maids in? They can add their proposals, too!"

"Quindly, sit down at once!" Walbough said. He turned to Fentor and said, "He's right. You don't have the authority to add a proposal to the proceedings, young Capilet."

Lady Talentus rose from her chair with silent grace. Every eye in the room turned toward her. "You may consider Lord Fentor's proposal as my contribution. He has my full support."

She sat back down and neatly folded her hands on her lap. Her feather-soft voice produced a new stretch of shocked silence. Fentor caught her eye, and she nodded at him to continue.

"Thank you, my Lady. I propose that we keep the elixir where it belongs: in the private hands of those with the means to produce and safeguard such a potent formula. If we ban it, we discard a gift. If we provide it to officers, as Malthus wishes, it will be a matter of time before low-born, peasant hands find their way to the stoppers of the vials. If we give it to the private sector, the high cost alone will ensure that only worthy hands will ever handle it. Vote wisely, gentlemen."

Fentor resumed his seat with a flourish. There was no applause at the table. The Lady turned briefly to him, and gave him a small nod. In the privacy of Fentor's heart, that nod meant he had just received a standing ovation.

"Any comments Malthus?" Walbough said. He checked a pocket watch. "We have … three minutes left."

Malthus made as if to stand, then slumped back into his seat. He looked utterly drained of willpower. Fentor kept his face straight, fighting a shiver of glee that brushed his spine.

One down, one to go.

"Quindly?" Walbough said.

As Quindly stood, he flashed a sneer at Fentor. He held up the pages that Malthus had distributed, and recited the costs of the elixir in a slow, droning voice. In between each line he read, he paused to raised long-winded, repetitive complaints about the elixir. He called it a 'parlor trick' no fewer than a dozen times.

Fentor could feel all his hot air leaking out through a small puncture hole. The longer Quindly waffled about nonsense, the clearer it became that he had no intention of letting any votes take place. Fentor had to pin down one hand with the other. He worried that otherwise, he might take back the sabre he'd given Quindly and sheathe it in the scoundrel's belly.

Walbough stood, pocket watch in hand, and announced that time was up.

All at once, like racehorses shooting from starting gates, the Grand Toques shifted their chairs and hurried away from the table. They all muttered and grumbled about urgent appointments with tailors, barbers, and spouses. Quindly disappeared into the flurry, having left Fentor's sword on the table.

Fentor, still seated beside Lady Talentus, turned to find her staring intensely at him.

All his certainty melted away as her glacier-blue eyes peeled away his flesh, cut him into pieces, and labelled the parts to hang in a butcher shop window. His soul, bared to her scrutiny, shrivelled.

Only three minutes ago, he had been certain she approved of him. Now, she might have been thinking anything. He felt like the whole meeting had been a failure.

Worst of all, nobody had even noticed his curled moustache.

Chapter 10

War does not refute my theory of universal
love, but it makes it a damn lot harder to
write a book about it.

Love for My Enemy, Sage Aínan

With his rifle in hand, Cartín stood over Horvald and watched Slee's every move. No matter what she did, he scrutinized the way she did it. The dead metal eye of his gun had to watch her, too, it seemed. A cloud of fear and suspicion rose from him, until it filled the room like a swarm of stinging gnats. She neither understood nor cared why Cartín felt the need to be so hostile. Her attention was on Horvald, on his wound.

The arrow had pierced through his torso, so they had laid him on his side. She had applied a mash of cleansing herbs to the wound, bound his abdomen with clean cloths, and now fresh bandages were boiling. Steam thickened the already tense air.

As best she could while she worked, she knitted telethymic strands together. The mesh, seen only by her, billowed about her hut like a silk sheet, but found no purchase with Horvald's body or mind. Still, she kept weaving, if only to keep herself well-connected.

Horvald was pale, clammy to the touch, and deeply unconscious. Still, his heart and lungs were working, if only barely. The fight had only just begun.

Slee's hut was small and cluttered, but it usually served her well. Dried herbs hung from the ceiling here and there, within reach. Her fire pit and the black pot hanging over it dominated the center of the room. The walls were barely visible, being so covered with shelves overcrowded with books, jars, and crockery. The intrusive presence of Cartín and Horvald made her once cozy home seem as claustrophobic as a coffin.

Her efforts did little to improve Horvald's condition. His downward slide into oblivion seemed to have halted, at least. His color, pulse, and breathing neither worsened nor improved. She had to do something.

As she made for the door, Cartín barked, "Where are you going?"

"I need to get some things," she said. "Stay there."

Felheim, who had been standing guard by her door, quacked softly and waddled in her wake.

"Stay close, old friend," she said. "Help me watch the humans."

Felheim quacked a decisive affirmative. His gaudy plume stood tall.

"I heard that humans *eat* ducks for supper," she whispered, projecting the image of a grisly dinner scene. "Be vigilant!"

The peadrake quivered, then leapt up to the windowsill. He glared at the humans through the glass. If Cartín could hear Felheim's vicious thoughts, as Slee could, he would have fled in terror.

Slee gathered a few handfuls of the vines that snaked around her hut, taking care not to uproot any of them. As she pulled them free, she twisted them into a kind of crude rope. Once she judged that she had enough, she looped the vines over her shoulder and carried them inside.

"What in blazes have you got there?" Cartín demanded.

Slee leveled him with a glare that would hopefully quell foolish questions. "Beans."

"Providence above," Cartín breathed. He held his rifle close to his body. The paranoid miasma in the room thickened further, as though Cartín had some deathly fear of *beans*.

Slee took the bundled vines to Horvald's bed, then began to gently unwind them.

"What are you going to do with them?" Cartín said, agape, his expression at the boundary between consternation and disgust.

"I can't explain it to you," Slee said, focusing on the slender vines between her fingers. As she unwound them, she placed them gently over Horvald's legs.

"Now, look here! I trusted you! I let you take Horvald into this ... place!" Cartín said. "You owe me an explanation!"

As it often does in humans, his anger had sprouted in the fertile ground of fear. Red sparks even shot out from his temples, like he was a burning log.

Felheim rapped the window with his beak and fixed Cartín with a withering glare.

"It's not about what you are owed. It's that I can't explain it to *you* — a human," Slee said. She had begun to wrap the climbing bean vines around Horvald's legs. At the same time, she was weaving the plants' humble animus into the existing telethymic mesh.

"That's not for you to decide," Cartín said. He aimed his rifle directly at Slee's head. "Horvald is badly hurt, so I can accept many things if they might help him. I can stand in an elf's home and accept her help. I can accept that the Common Power may be the only way. What I cannot accept is you brushing aside my questions!"

"Lower your gun and I'll answer," Slee said calmly.

Cartín considered for a moment, then pointed his rifle away from her. "Why are you wrapping him in vines?"

"Telethymia," Slee said. When Cartín's expression went blank, she continued, "Not the Common Power. That refers to a type of telethymia that the Elarím use. My craft is broader, deeper. I connect living things with threads, share the energies needed for growth and healing. Humans can join the web, but they cannot make use of it. I have been having trouble stitching Horvald into the fabric of the garden. These living vines, I hope, will act like tethers for his life energy. From his legs and arms, through the vines to their roots, then through the soil and to everything that lives and grows in the garden, and then back again, his pain will leak out and healing energies will trickle in."

"You … you've done this sort of thing before?" Cartín said.

"Every day of my life," she said, unspooling a length of curly green vine and winding it around Horvald's forearm. "Not with a human, though."

"What about the herbs you have strung up everywhere?" Cartín said. "Why not use them? What good can wrapping him in *beans* do?"

"It's not the beans, it's the living vines. There are four principles that guide telethymia, four pillars — *telethían, aínan, crantarín, muanan*. Madean has no words for these, but …the more life, the closer it is, the stronger the bonds," she said. As she worked, she softly intoned, *"All life cares for all life … oe telethí aínar oen telethían."*

She finished wrapping vines around Horvald. He looked like a fallen log overgrown with climbers. With her eyes closed, she placed her hands on his chest and studied the feeble flicker of animus within. Horvald wheezed, his heartbeat feeling as weak as that of a mouse. The wound in his belly lay dormant, ignored by his hibernating body. Even with the whole animus of her garden wrapped around him, from Slowjaw's enormous heart to the tiniest ants in the soil, Horvald showed only a minor improvement. He wasn't connecting to anything.

Some of his pain had eased, and his heart gradually found a stronger rhythm.

Slee offered some of her own life energy, but it was like throwing a bucket of water into fierce wind. It simply couldn't reach the human. All it did was drain her.

"Did it work?" Cartín said.

"Not very well," Slee said. "He will not die. He could grow to be an old man, still wrapped in those vines. But he would never rise from the bed. He might never even wake up."

Cartín looked down at Horvald, eyes glistening. "He was minutes away from dying when you brought him here. Your magic kept him hanging on. There must be something … anything …"

"I'm not sure," she said.

"You can't have tried everything," Cartín said. "Use me, use my life!"

"That would take skill with telethymia no human could ever possess," Slee said, though it was only half-true. It took her Papa many years, and great effort to learn the craft from her Mama. "But there is something I can try."

"Whatever it is, you must try it," Cartín said.

Slee faced him. "It carries great risk. To him, to my garden. Maybe even to us."

"We have little choice," Cartín said, stroking Horvald's hair. The rifle now leaned in the crook of his arm, half-forgotten.

"No. Hardly any choice at all." Slee, whose ears rang with Mama's mantra, was referring to a different sort of choice. Though, the tender way Cartín looked at Horvald echoed with that phrase: *All life cares for all life.*

"I have something that I keep hidden. It may look like a trinket, but you must never tell a soul about it," Slee said. "I may lose everything I have."

Cartín laughed. Perhaps her word choices in the human's language had been poor. Cartín's laughter continued, with the trembling energy of one who breaks into mirth after enduring great tension. Slee frowned.

"What is it?" Slee said. "Some human joke I am unaware of?"

"No, no," Cartín said, wiping his eyes as the laughter subsided. "It isn't that. I just rather think I have more to lose than you. If my Capilet was to hear that I'd sheltered with an elf without shooting them, it would be *me* living out in the woods, eating the moss off rocks and doing Providence knows what else."

"You'd just tell them that I am not Elarím, wouldn't you?" Slee said.

"An elf is an elf."

"How tautological," Slee said. "Do all humans speak like that?"

"The way we speak … is the way we speak," Cartín said, with a glint in his dark brown eyes. Then, the smile slid from his face. "If it can help Horvald, then I swear to keep the secret of your trinket."

"Good."

Slee shuffled about the dirt floor of her hut, feeling for the hiding place with her toes. The mineral was buried deep, but its magnifying effect was easy to detect. She came upon the spot, which hummed under her feet like a tuning fork.

As she scratched dirt aside, the hum tickled her fingers. Healthy soil will support a whole world of unseen creatures. There under her floor, crowded around the geode Mama once used, a whole galaxy of motelings thrived. A rich, earthen scent rose as she parted the dirt, like the smell of the sun drying a forest after rain. Her fingers soon found the hard, rough edges of the mineral. When she pulled it free, every nerve in her body shivered.

It was more or less round, small enough to fit on her palm, and mostly a drab, mousey grey. A small wedge-shaped opening revealed an interior of tiny hexagonal crystal columns. Depending on the light, or perhaps the time of day, their color ranged from that of deep red wine, to the iron-blue of a stormy sea, to the inky indigo of the sky at dusk. At that moment they were the iridescent black of a beetle's wing.

She carried it with cupped hands to Horvald's bed.

Cartín peered into her hands. "What is *that*?"

"It's Horvald's last chance," she said.

"What do you do with it?"

"*I* do very little. The real work is done by the garden. This stone is just an enhancer or a … what is the Madean word?"

"A catalyst?"

"Yes, a catalyst, but also a magnifier. Like a seeing-glass that focuses light into a small, hot point."

Mama had explained so little about it before she died. She only said it was a tool for *anín oenan*, a phrase with so many translations it clarified nothing. It could be called an amplifier, a resonator, a bridge, a stitcher, a weaver, or any number of things.

"What is it made from?" Cartín asked.

"I don't know," Slee said.

Cartín rubbed his forehead firmly and sighed. "You're *sure* this is our only option?"

"Yes." Slee knelt beside Horvald, still holding the geode gently, as though it was a duckling.

"Let me see it," Cartín said, and reached a hand forward.

"Don't touch it!" Slee said, holding the precious stone away from him. "Do you know why humans cannot use telethymia? It's because the instinct of your kind is to take and consume and destroy. If you so much as *touch* the geode, you might drain the life out of Horvald, and me as well."

"Fine. I won't touch it. What *can* I do?"

"You'll be pulling the arrow out," Slee said, then she nodded at his rifle. "You'll need both hands to do it."

Cartín held the gun closer. The way he held it in front of him, like a shield or talisman, Slee wondered if he would ever relent the weapon. To him, the gun was just as much a balm to his fears as it was an instrument of war. She could see it in the dark, smoky aura that hung about him.

There are so many things to be afraid of in the world. A loaded rifle addresses only the fear of being attacked. If someone comes to shoot you, you can shoot them back. All the other things one might fear — losing a loved one, dying of disease, hunger, or the cold — with those things, a gun was no help. Yet Cartín clutched the rifle for comfort, as a child keeps nightmares at bay with a beloved toy.

"I will do it without you then," Slee said.

Before Slee could begin, Cartín set his rifle down and knelt beside her. His hands hovered near the arrow's fletching. Slee noticed that the tips of his fingers were stained, as though he had been picking blueberries.

She eased apart the vines that encircled Horvald's body, giving them more space to work.

"I'm ready," he said.

"Pull it, but don't tug it. Elven arrows may not be barbed, but you must still take care. I will focus on stitching his flesh and veins back together. He has little blood to spare, so we have only one chance."

"Understood," Cartín said.

"And you must *not* touch this stone."

"I won't."

From the moment Cartín had set his gun down, the dark smoke of fear had begun to dissipate. Now, he was calm and determined.

She held the stone a handspan away from Horvald's wound.

"Now," she said.

Cartín took hold of the arrow, and began to pull it.

At once, the glimmering mesh of animus roiled, until a vortex formed overhead. Like water draining through a sinkhole, it poured through the geode and then into Horvald's stomach. The curling vines took on a subtle violet glow, which spread out into the garden, touching every leaf, twig, and petal. As Cartín continued to draw the arrow out, Slee could feel Horvald's skin, flesh, and veins knitting back together as though they were her own. It was working.

The stone vibrated with such intensity that Slee's fingers were soon numb. More and more animus coiled through the conduit, irresistibly, until Slee's arms quaked. The arrow was halfway through when Slee realized, with a terrible jolt, that she was locked in place.

She couldn't move at all. Cartín pulled the arrow free, and still Slee was paralyzed. She clenched her teeth and strained every muscle, but the geode would not free her.

153

Horvald's stomach glowed violet, brighter and brighter every second.

Each thread of animus that the geode pulled from the garden was a peaduck, a síana, a beetle, a worm. Slee could feel them all, see through their eyes. They were weakening. Leaves were wilting, eyelids were drooping.

Horvald, still unconscious, was taking all of their life energy for himself.

The last veins stitched together, and his skin became whole. Still, the geode immobilized Slee, and its powerful hum resonated in her bones. Pins and needles erupted in her teeth, across her scalp, and in all her joints. Her own life force was diminishing.

Her vision turned grey, and she suddenly felt sleepy. They had saved Horvald. All it had cost was her garden and her life. *All life cares for all life*. The words came dimly to Slee, abstract and disassociated, no more than a curious sequence of syllables.

Warm hands closed around hers, and pulled her free.

She fell on her back, gasping like someone rescued from drowning, her senses slowly returned.

Two men crouched over her, one of whom was still holding her hands tightly. They were speaking, but their words were muffled like those spoken through a thick pillow.

"What?" she said.

"Are you alright?"

Slee shook her head, hard, and returned abruptly to reality. "Yes. I'm fine," she said. "What happened?"

Blinking hard, she saw Horvald and Cartín's faces, both close to hers.

"You were shaking like a fish on a line," Cartín said. "I had to take that thing out of your hands. I'm afraid I touched it."

"Well … thank you," Slee said. "I hadn't expected it to do that to me. It hasn't been used on humans before … as far as I know."

Slowjaw bugled urgently — a warning call.

Slee, despite her trembling legs, heaved herself upright and hurried outside. The humans followed shortly after.

The colossal tortoise stood by the perimeter of the garden, where the síana bushes were brown and wilted. With his enormous head raised above the hedge, he continued to call out harsh, trumpeting bleats.

Slee sprang onto his shell, and climbed to the top.

Down the hill, a dark-haired elf woman was looking right at her.

Chapter 11

The trouble with having an especially large bath was the volume of water that needed to be heated. The trouble with having especially *long* baths in a bath like that was that the house staff had to be constantly engaged in heating and carrying the water to it. The trouble with *that* was that in Fentor's house, the staff were overseen by Methúsel, a man whose unyielding competence was matched only by the sharpness of his tongue.

Fentor luxuriated in his lake of porcelain, watching the rose-scented steam rise to the ceiling. His troubles and failures evaporated too, curling and floating away until they condensed on the curved mosaic ceiling, ran down in rivulets, where they trickled into drains that led out into the garden.

Madeans, for all their virtues, failed to grasp the philosophy of bathing. For them, bathing was joyless. They scrubbed their skin raw with stiff brushes and harsh bricks of soap, with water so scalding that they reddened like crabs. Naturally, they endured the torture only briefly, and could not comprehend the joys of a long soak.

The fine porcelain of the bath, the artisan who had built it, and Fentor's luxuriant attitude toward bathing had all come from Norimand. It was his only remaining connection to the land Father had called home. Even their family name had changed, from 'de Lon-a-qis' to 'Lonochy.' The average Madean tongue could scarcely handle the musicality of Fentor's birth name, *Fédillion Charlemontaigne Besoinaux de Lon-a-qis*. All that had been scrubbed away by his simpler, adopted Madean name. By way of heritage, he was left only with a Norimandian taste for the ablutionary arts.

Fentor sighed in appreciation of the water's tender embrace, and the playful tannins of his aged brandy. A friendly tingle sparked in his stomach and spread to his fingertips. Soon a cheerful glow infused the steam, like a cloud caught in the sunset. He topped up his glass, and thereby topped up his optimistic mood. Some might have said his brandy bottle was now half-empty—Fentor preferred to say that his belly was now half-full.

Then, familiar, stern footsteps approached.

Fentor sought only to relax his weary body and over-wrung mind. Methúsel sought only to stick his ancient beak into Fentor's sore spots, like a crow pecking at a dying man's liver.

The steam stopped glowing.

The spindly-legged butler entered, wheeling in a large tub of steaming water with a tap in its front. Between his build and the tufty crown of white hair encircling a bald spot, he looked something like a half-depleted dandelion seed stalk. He brought the tub to the edge of the bath, and turned the lever on the tap. As the stream of boiled water flowed into the bath, Methúsel began the long circuit around the bath toward Fentor.

"Will sir require his towel and robe in the foreseeable future?" Methúsel said. "Whilst I am still young enough to fetch them, perhaps?"

"Don't start that with me, you old goat. I've hardly got wrinkled fingers," Fentor said.

The fresh, hotter water reached Fentor's toes with a delightful surge of heat. The bath's veil of steam thickened into a curtain.

"Is there anything else sir requires?" Methúsel droned. "Besides a copy of *The Manual of Better Manners*."

"Decant another bottle. I want it ready by the time I finish this one."

"A second bottle for sir drink—alone, in a bath, at this late hour? Is sir troubled?"

Fentor waved his brandy glass at Methúsel, spilling a little. "No! There are no troubles, not in here. I want all talk of troubles left at the door. This is my sanctuary."

"Of course. I shall decant your second bottle," Methúsel said, bowing deeply with smooth grace that belied his age.

"Thank you."

"I am forced to offer sir a tiny speck of advice. A little atom of wisdom, as it were," Methúsel said.

"I decline."

"It comes from the good Saint Chandon, patron of butlers, gardeners, and oyster divers," Methúsel continued, despite Fentor's glower. "He said, 'Wine pairs best not with cheese, but with a companion.' Perhaps sir ought to obliterate his brain, one lobe at a time, in the company of others."

"You left out the second part: 'Brandy pairs best with peace and quiet.' " Fentor spoke a little too loudly, the echoes of his voice somewhat undercutting the point of his made-up quotation. Still, he pointed to the door, and Methúsel bowed once more and headed for the door.

The tub had finished draining. As the ancient butler began to wheel it away, he turned, and said, "Your father kept his cup dry and his mind sharp, you know. He achieved a great deal because of it."

"Get out! You miserable … old goat!" Fentor barked, after straining to find something more quick-witted.

Methúsel closed the door behind him. The phrase 'your father' somehow still lingered on the air in the butler's absence.

Every knot of tension that the bath had eased now returned. He looked at his deeply wrinkled fingers, then plunged them back under the cover of the rose petals. The bath suddenly seemed conspicuously large to cater to the comfort of a solitary man.

No, not solitary. Certainly not *lonely*. He was going to make a name for himself first, then find a well-connected wife, then have children and do all the rest. One required a legacy worth passing on before producing heirs. Otherwise, he'd fall into living in comfort with a happy family — a fiendish snare that had claimed so many promising lives. Happy and fulfilled people do not aspire to greatness, scheme ruthlessly, or persevere in the hunt for glory. Fentor had to stay hungry.

"Your father kept his cup dry and his mind sharp!" Fentor grumbled, mocking Methúsel's raspy voice. "Your father never wasted energy on smiling! Your father slept on a carved rock instead of a pillow!"

Father's letter swam in the steam before him, a floating paper mirage. The actual brandy-stained copy was still folded in Jontain's bust in the study. Fentor had no need of the original to see every line burned in the air before him. A few choice insults stood out, as always.

Your mind is a blunt instrument and you have scarcely any talent, but you shall have to make do. After all, Providence gave me but one son — you — and I had to make do.

He glowered. He would 'make do', by Temlin, whatever the cost. Nobody could 'make do' like he could. All those happy boys brought up to be contented men lacked the one advantage Fentor had always relied on: nothing could fuel an eternal quest like the need to prove a dead parent wrong.

Rapid footsteps approached once more. It was too soon for another tub of hot water.

"What in blazes is it?" Fentor demanded as Methúsel opened the door.

"A carriage is approaching, sir," Methúsel said, wheezing slightly.

"A carriage? At this hour? What *is* the hour?" Fentor said, peering unsteadily at the dark windows above. His head felt too loosely screwed on for him to be receiving visitors. Begrudgingly, he tipped the rest of his brandy into the bath water.

"It is eleven thirty-four, sir," Methúsel said. He dabbed his liver-spotted brow gently with a small handkerchief, shattering his usual façade of perfect composure. He might as well have flapped his arms and crowed like an alarmed rooster.

It did not bode well.

"Providence above! Visitors at midnight! Who is it?"

"The coat of arms is difficult to see by the carriage's lanterns, sir," Methúsel said. "But I believe it is the crest of Talentus."

The house swarmed with maids, footmen, and chimney-boys like a beehive that had been kicked open. Cobwebs snarled with dust seemed to have materialized in every corner. Methúsel ordered the staff to clean only the entrance, foyer, and the front sitting room. Every other room and passage in the house were off-limits. If Her Excellency wished for a tour, they were to invent an excuse and politely deny her entry.

With the floors swept and the cobwebs cleared, the house staff dispersed into nearby rooms, ready to burst forth and clean at a moment's notice. A pair of footmen waited outside the front door. Fentor waited in the sitting room, fully dressed, a randomly chosen book open in his lap. He would greet her with polite nonchalance, as though he often received guests in the dead of night.

The sound of hoofs and carriage wheels approached, then stopped. Shortly after, the front doors opened. Lady Talentus' gently assertive voice floated through the halls, remarking on the subtlety and restraint of Fentor's humble home.

Fentor arranged his body, down to his fingers and toes, in a pose of perfect calm. He traced the words in the book with an index finger. Somehow, the words shifted and slid around the page, until they became a transcript of the failed meeting at Walbough's home. He read and re-read his failure to secure a favorable vote as Lady Talentus' soft footsteps drew near.

Methúsel entered and cleared his throat. "Lord Fentor, Her Excellency, the Grand Toque Lady Talentus is here."

The Lady entered, taking in the close-packed, spindly furniture, bookshelves, and the merry fire in the fireplace opposite. She wore pearl earrings, a short ponytail, polished riding boots, white trousers with gold trim, a sapphire-blue silk blouse edged with lace, and a thin necklace of gold.

"Do forgive me for coming in my shabby house-clothes," she said. "But this is an urgent matter."

Dídac entered the room and lingered in the Lady's shadow. His lips were so tightly sealed, he looked like a petulant child refusing his vegetables.

"Lady Talentus! Dídac! What an unexpected and genuine pleasure," Fentor rose from his chair, book in hand.

Methúsel, Dídac, and the Lady all raised an eyebrow at the book. Fentor looked down for the first time and saw the title: *Sultry Tales of Bridget the Misbehaving Maid.* Without missing a beat, he flung the book across the room and into the grate, where it quickly caught fire.

"I like to buy sordid books just for the pleasure of watching them burn," he explained—plausibly, he hoped.

Dídac tutted loudly, with a roll of his silver eyes. The elven facial structure, angled and cool, was already disposed to look smug. An elf in the deepest slumber might seem to be scoffing at their own dreams. Dídac's little smirk, therefore, was an especially aggravating thing to behold. Fentor almost slapped the prig.

"Please, have a seat," Fentor said, indicating the floral sofa chairs opposite to his own seat. "Methúsel, fetch tea and something to eat."

"I will have water," the Lady said.

Methúsel bowed and left.

"There is a problem, and I have the solution," Lady Talentus said. As she took her seat, the cushion expelled a puff of musty-smelling dust.

Dídac pinched his nose and waved it away.

"I love solved problems. I think they're the best kind," Fentor said.

"That depends on the solution," the Lady said.

"I am anxious to hear about this one, but please start with the problem. I prefer the suspense," Fentor said.

"Walbough has decided that you may not attend further meetings. In addition, Quindly has secured enough votes among his friends to have the Elixir of Power banned. By next month, it will be a crime to even discuss producing it," she said.

"He won't let me attend?" Fentor said, aghast. "Whyever not?"

"The given reason is that only Grand Toques will be permitted in future. The true reason is that Walbough probably grew tired of Quindly pestering him to change the rules."

"My Lady, I truly regret that I failed you. Because of me, we will never see what the Elixir of Power can really do," Fentor said.

"You failed, but not completely. You bought us an entire month. Therein lies my solution."

Fentor leaned forward in his seat, unconsciously pinching the end of his moustache. "What do you mean, my Lady?"

Methúsel entered with a tray of tea, cups, triangle sandwiches, and a tall glass of water. They watched silently as the ancient butler dispensed the refreshments, and then left the room.

"That group of gentlemen would never have voted to produce anything with the slightest chance of actually winning the war," the Lady said. "Malthus was a fool to bring it to them."

"With deepest respect, my Lady, they're Grand Toques. It's their *duty* to win the war, is it not?" Fentor said. Privately, he felt vindicated that his hunch about them had been correct.

"What was the name of the gunsmith your Father left you?"

Fentor blinked, caught somewhat off-guard. "Silvestron's, my Lady."

"How is business? Does it wax and wane?"

"Why, yes, it goes with the tides of the war. Right now, it's …" Fentor paused, and the Lady gave him a slow, meaningful nod.

"The Grand Toques *all* have gunsmiths, and krysite mines, and gunpowder manufactories, and all manner of related investments. Like all wars, this one is a racket. Ending it is the last thing they want," the Lady said.

"I can hardly believe my ears, my Lady. The whispered rumors of certain—dare I say—credulous Bluefingers would appear to be true."

"Well, a broken compass will sometimes swing north," Lady Talentus said. "And don't forget, some things on the ground are most clearly seen by those who live on the ground. We who raise ourselves ever higher can see farther outward, at the expense of perceiving the ground beneath our feet."

"I will remember that," Fentor said.

"I trust you also remember that I have been evaluating you," the Lady said.

"Little else has been on my mind," he said.

"I have judged that you are … useful," she said.

Fentor kept a straight face as fireworks erupted in his chest and bounced around his ribs. He took a hasty sip of tea, scalding his tongue, then set down his cup with a grateful smile. He became light-headed, and was submerged in the dream-like glow of destiny. Little winking lights frothed all around the sitting room, making Fentor feel as though he was bathing in a tub filled with Norimandian champagne. That, or he was about to pass out.

"You are too kind, my Lady."

"You bought us a month, and I intend to use it," Lady Talentus said.

"Simply tell me what you require, and it shall be done," Fentor said, fighting to keep his voice from trembling.

"I bought the patent for the Elixir of Power from Malthus for a pittance. A secret team of alchemists have gone northwest, to the Madean Highlands, to construct a high-volume distillery for me. Payment has been arranged for all the materials and personnel … but not the crucial ingredient."

"Krysite?"

"A substantial volume of it. The other costs have rather … compromised my liquidity."

Dídac leaned forward. "Make no mistake, Her Excellency's wealth exceeds her needs. It is simply tied up in investments, land, treasury bonds—"

"Thank you, Dídac," she said, raising a pale hand with a gesture like an orchestra conductor's command for silence.

"Whatever you need my Lady, you have only to ask," Fentor said.

At a nod from the Lady, Dídac drew a folded page from inside his uniform jacket and handed it to Fentor.

"This is what we need," Dídac said.

Fentor opened the paper, read it quickly, blinked, read it once more, and then temporarily forgot how to read. He continued to look at the individual letters and numerals—especially the long rows of zeros—and puzzled over their meaning. His vision blurred, his mouth dried, and then finally his brain detached itself, hopped across the room with little squelches, and threw itself into the fire.

The Lady Talentus said something, but it sounded to him like short toots of a foghorn.

"I beg your pardon, could you please repeat that my Lady?" Fentor said in a—perhaps excessively—bright tone.

"I asked you whether you would be able to invest that level of capital," she said, slowly, with the rhythmic enunciation and cadence of a fortepiano.

Fentor looked down at the page again, and at last understood the writing. They needed every last crown Fentor possessed, and then a few more. If he called every loan, sold every bond, and emptied every account down to the last bits and bronzers, he might just barely be able to scrape the required amount of money together.

Then he saw the line marked '*Expected 12-month return on investment,*' the impossibly, unfathomably high number written next to it, and almost fainted in his chair.

Either his investment would make him the richest man in Madea, or it would leave him destitute.

"Of course," Fentor said. "Of course, of course."

"You *are* able to get that together? We have precious little time," the Lady said.

"I shall have to make arrangements … see the bank people, loot the family crypt for jewelry," Fentor said with a weak laugh.

They gave him blank, unimpressed stares.

"Only joking. I can have it ready within two or three days," Fentor said.

"Make it tomorrow."

"Certainly," Fentor said, torturing his lips into a smile that hopefully appeared confident and not deranged.

"Good," the Lady said.

"If I may ask, how much will you be selling the vials of elixir for?" Fentor asked.

"Oh, no. We won't be selling the elixir. We'll be using it."

"Using it, my Lady?"

"Indeed. You and I, armed with the Elixir of Power, will destroy Crann Arborím and put an end to this farce they call 'war.' "

Chapter 12

The dark-haired elf woman had come alone. She climbed the hill with purpose, directly toward Slee's garden.

The síana hedge, brown and wilted, had failed.

Slee leapt down from Slowjaw's shell, half-choking on the fog of dread that had spread all around the garden. The colossal tortoise stamped his feet and whimpered. Felheim rallied the peaducks, leading them to and fro along the garden's perimeter with commanding quacks. He stretched his wings and raked the air with his webbed feet, which were tipped with vicious talons.

"What's all the hullabaloo about?" Cartín said, holding up a pale Horvald.

"An elf is coming. Get in the hut and don't come out," Slee said.

"I'll ready my rifle."

"No! Hide and do nothing else!"

The humans hurried back into the hut.

Slee hoisted herself up onto Slowjaw's shell once more, and peered over the top of the síanas. The stranger was drawing close to the garden, and would be there in moments.

"Hello up there!" The dark-haired elf called in the elven tongue, waving. "I come in friendship!"

Slee flattened herself, spitting curses onto the hard plates of Slowjaw's shell.

The intrusion of a hundred human soldiers might have been better. *Anything* would have been better than an elf. Humans might shoot her without bothering to know a single thing about her, and the ordeal would be over. Elves, though, would not rest until they knew every last thing about her and her parents. She'd be cajoled and seduced into becoming a part of their Common Power, a pawn in their war, another worker ant in their vast nest.

She hugged Slowjaw's shell, and hastily connected her fears with the panic of the animals in an effort to ease both. There was no chance that she could heal the síanas in time. Even if she could, the elf had spotted them. There was no option left to her but getting the intruder to leave, by whatever means necessary. Even if it meant an extreme and repugnant act — violence. *Uthuín.*

A private, shameful corner of her heart considered the ultimate betrayal of her parent's teachings. If the dark-haired elf happened to die in a struggle with Slee, then perhaps the other elves would assume she had been killed by humans. Slee's garden would be safe, at the cost of her deepest morals.

Slee checked the various pouches and pockets that covered her smock. As always, they were filled with enough seeds to start again somewhere new. She hoped it would not come to that.

"Hello? Can we talk?" The stranger called out from somewhere nearby. In moments she would be on the other side of the hedge.

Slee cursed a final time, then stood tall and glowered down at the intruder. "You are not welcome here."

The stranger halted in her approach. She was tall and willowy like most of her kind, yet her hair was black and lustrous as onyx. Her bright, curious eyes examined Slee and Slowjaw, with the rapt expression of someone utterly lost in a book. In contrast, her other features seemed somber, weighed down by some long-held burden. Despite trying to close off her telethymic senses, Slee received a waft of the stranger's inner despair, clean and cold, a scent like falling snow.

"I don't want you to be afraid. I just want to speak with you," the stranger said.

"We have nothing to speak about. Leave at once, before I am forced to make you leave," Slee said.

"It just seems as though you might need some assistance," the dark-haired elf said.

Slee narrowed her eyes. Mama and Papa had always warned her against accepting help from the Elarím.

"I don't need help. Especially not from you. I won't warn you again—go away!"

"My name is Sidarí. We have heard much about strange happenings in this place in my home clade, Rivumaí. A síana garden that appears and disappears. A pair of humans that vanished without a trace. A mysterious elven woman, neither Elarím nor Madean, but a witch! Many who live in my clade wished to investigate this place, with bow and spear. I convinced them to let me speak to the 'witch' alone first. If I fail, I fear they will come here, armed and suspicious."

Slee scowled. When Cartín had threatened to shoot her, he'd at least had the decency to be straightforward.

"So that's it, is it? Either I speak to you, or an armed posse comes to take me away?" Slee said.

"If you are no threat, there will be no abduction of any sort."

"I am no threat to the Elarím or to anyone else. There, we have spoken. You can return and tell them that."

"Actually, I have other questions I hope you can help me with," Sidarí said. "May I enter your garden? Calling across this distance is tiring — for both of us, I'm sure."

"You stay there," Slee said.

She slid down Slowjaw's shell, and was immediately confronted with a swarm of peaducks around her ankles. Some of them nipped at her toes, puffing their feathers and quacking rapidly. Agitation and anxiety had spread through the garden, until the air was swarming with little red sparks. Slowjaw, radiating flushes of hot anger and clammy fear, lowered his wide golden eyes to level with hers.

"Don't worry. I'll make sure she goes away, and everything will go back to normal," Slee said, stroking Slowjaw's cheek. "Just wait by the hut, but be ready."

She tried to calm their confusion and alarm, but she couldn't even keep her own emotions in check. All the living beings in the garden, from the animals, to the plants, to the motelings under the earth, had been weakened too

172

greatly. They could not resist the thickening atmosphere of panic, but fortunately, they did not seem willing or able to attack the stranger either.

Slee couldn't outright order them to wait for her. She could only project her desires and suggestions to the animals telethymically. Thankfully, the animals understood the urgency of her request, and they left her side to crouch in the shelter of the hut.

Trembling in the midst of her own anxious, slate-grey aura, she pushed through the dry síana hedge and faced the intruder.

The dark-haired elf wore a tepid smile. It warmed neither her face, nor her melancholic presence. Slee could not picture her ever wearing a genuine smile.

"Thank you, my friend. This is much more suitable," Sidarí said. "You know my name. May I know what you are called?"

"Slee."

"A pleasure to meet you. Do you know the greeting of our kind?" Sidarí held out her hand and gently closed it into a fist.

"We are not the same. We share no 'kind.' "

"My apologies. It is just that you use the elven art, telethymia, in your garden. Did the one who taught you the art also teach you the greeting?" Sidarí asked, still offering her fist.

"I know it," Slee said, but she made no move to reciprocate the gesture.

"It is the best way for you to know that my intentions are true. After all, Sage Nyendi once said, 'Words can deceive, but *telethí* never lies.' "

Slee frowned. *Telethí* was the elven word for a telethymic bond. Mama had taught her that saying, along with the proverbs of many other Sages. To hear Sidarí repeat them felt like a trespass, as though she had trodden on the soil above Mama's grave.

Still, the words were true.

Slee raised her hand slowly, made a fist, and touched her thumb to Sidarí's.

A spark of animus jumped between them at the contact. All in one moment, a trace of Sidarí's memories and intentions flashed across Slee's mind. Everything the elf had said was true, though it reassured Slee little. Intermixed with those thoughts came images of dead brothers, sisters, cousins killed by war, all compressed into a single moment of overwhelming grief. Suddenly, unpleasantly, Slee understood part of the reason for the wintry aura of sorrow that followed Sidarí around.

She wondered how much Sidarí saw of her life, her garden.

"Thank you for sharing telethí with me, if only for a moment," Sidarí said. "You know that I am no threat, and I know the same about you. 'With common ground, find common purpose.' "

"That's another Sage's proverb. Do you have any of your own words?"

"Some. Enough to fill a few books."

"So why did a writer like you insist on coming all the way out here to speak with me?" Slee said.

"Because I am in desperate need of your help," Sidarí said, with a passionless smile.

Slee could not even think of a reply.

Slowjaw chose that moment to blurt out a stream of worried, guttural calls. Slee raised her voice and told him to be patient, and wait in silence. When she turned back to Sidarí, she almost shivered.

The elf appeared to be wreathed in a flurry of glinting ice crystals, as though she had been carried to Slee's garden by a deep winter wind. The ice was not real, not in the physical sense, but the aura chilled Slee's arms all the same. Along with the deep cold came a deep, sinking sense of despair. Sidarí's need was indeed desperate.

Words can deceive, but telethí never lies.

"You need my help?" Slee said.

"A request for help may not be quite what you expected, I know," Sidarí said.

"It is, actually. I always knew your kind would come to recruit me. I just thought the coercion would be less transparent," Slee said.

"I promise you, there is no coercion."

"But there is!" Slee threw her hands up, soaking up the frustration and anxiety clouding her garden like a cloth in a puddle of ink. "Your emotions may be honest, but your actions are not. You mean for me to feel badly for you. You are so pitiful, you elves and the foolish war you're losing! You want me to weep for you, join your ranks, then fight and die for your borders. I tell you now, compassion will not overcome my better judgement. I won't help you, no matter how desperately you need it."

Sidarí nodded slowly, as her shoulders and arms sagged a little, like a marionette held slack on its strings. She was much taller than Slee, but her diminished posture seemed to rob her of her height. Her frosty aura was unchanged.

Only her bright eyes moved, darting here and there as though searching for some tiny thing she had dropped.

"I understand you," Sidarí said, squaring her shoulders. "I won't try to recruit you. But I would still like to ask for your help—if you would let me complete my question first?"

"Promise you will leave immediately after," Slee said.

"I promise. May I ask it?"

Slee searched for dark spots or shadows in Sidarí's aura, and found none. It either indicated honesty, or an expertly told lie. She nodded.

"Long ago, almost out of recorded memory, the Elarím were a hidden folk. They say that we observed the outside world, but did not participate in it. We were happy to be left alone. Somehow, the art of hiding through the Common Power was lost. Even the wisest Sages do not know why. All we know is that war came to us soon after. We had always lived in the forests north-east of Madea, but our arrival was looked upon as invasion. Now they claim that our land has always been part of Madea.

"No lasting peace has ever been made between the Elarím and Madea. I believe no peace can ever be made. We cannot win through force, either. The only way for us is to recede from the world like a wave from the shore, to hide once more under the shelter of our trees. Your garden—a miracle of our past blooming in the present day—could be the salvation of the Elarím. Will you teach me the art of hiding?"

"You speak as though you are innocent victims, and maybe you believe it," Slee said. "Tell me, how often have the elves been the ones to fan the embers and reignite the violence?"

"You speak as though you understand the realities of war," Sidarí said.

"I understand well enough," Slee said. "Until *you* understand, the art will always be out of reach."

"What do you mean?"

"I mean that I could give you the very tools you need, and they would wilt in your hand. The Common Power may be a form of telethymia, but it is one that ignores nature's law."

" 'All life cares for all life,' " Sidarí said, raising her eyebrows. "We do not ignore it."

"Knowing the words is not enough. You must live it."

"Tell me how, and I will," Sidarí said.

Slee was lost for words. She could only shake her head in disbelief. How could she possibly make it clearer? High above, from the vantage of a crooked branch, a raven watched her and cawed drily. It almost sounded like a warning.

Sidarí waited patiently for Slee's answer. Motes of ice eddied and swirled around her shoulders and arms, a telethymic aura of frosty despair that she could not — or would not — keep to herself. The longer they stood there, speaking to one another, the deeper the chill in Slee's bones. All the burdens and sorrows that weighed on Sidarí's shoulders had slowly begun to infect Slee. Something had to be done to save the Elarím. Nobody deserved to feel so wretched and hopeless. Perhaps Slee could be the one to help them …

No, Slee would not let herself be drawn in.

She took hold of the fearful energy pervading the garden, and wrapped it around herself like a cloak. She had to worry about her own home first. With her palms sweating and her heart racing, there was no room left for a stranger's concern. Fear could be very insulating.

"There is nothing else I can tell you," Slee said. "Go back to your people. Tell them I am no use to you, that I have nothing worth taking, and that I am no threat. Leave me be."

Slee turned away, scowling deeply, and headed for the síana hedge.

"Wait! Please!" Sidarí rushed forward and caught her arm.

At the moment of contact, a scalding cloud of anger overwhelmed her. All the animals felt it too, and fed into it with their own fury. The ground rumbled under Slowjaw's feet, and the air rang with Felheim's commanding calls.

Slee wrenched herself from Sidarí's grip, and spat, "Don't touch me!"

Sidarí released her at once, and backed away.

The immense heat and volatility of Slee's sudden rage surprised her, but she welcomed it nonetheless.

"Slee, I'm sorry," Sidarí said, in a soothing voice that only deepened Slee's anger. "Please, just listen to—"

"I did what you asked! Now get out of here at once!" Slee shouted.

The síana hedge parted, and Slowjaw's enormous head loomed over Sidarí. His golden eyes flashed in the sunlight. The next moment, Felheim landed in front of

Slee, along with his cohort of peaducks. The dark-haired elf backed away further, both hands raised in placation.

"Please, I am unarmed," Sidarí said.

"Slowjaw!" Slee barked.

The colossal tortoise let loose a hill-shaking roar, then charged at the elf with speed that belied his bulk. Sidarí cringed and covered her head with her arms, but she did not cry out. Slowjaw lunged at her with his beak opened wide, then snapped it shut a handspan away from Sidarí's head.

For a moment, everything was still.

Sidarí did not flee, nor did Slowjaw continue his attack.

A moment later, the reason became clear. Telethí never lies, and Slowjaw had stopped the moment he'd felt what Sidarí was feeling. Slee felt it, too. Sidarí had not feared for her life, even as Slowjaw had threatened to crush her head like a chestnut. She had only worried that she had failed those who depended on her.

Slowjaw, whose heart was too big for his own good, had given into his sympathy for her. He crooned softly, nudging her with the end of his nose.

"Hello," Sidarí said, her voice cracking a little.

She reached out a hand tentatively and stroked Slowjaw's beak. He closed his eyes and rumbled with contentment.

"Slowjaw might not hurt you, but I will," Slee said. Her rage had not diminished even slightly.

The tortoise turned slowly, blinking his wide, yellow eyes at her. Sidarí sidestepped him and slowly approached Slee.

"Your tortoise knows nature's law better than either of us, I think," Sidarí said. "I think he can see that I am sincere."

"His heart is large and soft. It can be fooled," Slee said.

"Perhaps. I see that I have done all I can. I will take my leave," Sidarí said.

"Not a moment too soon," Slee said. Felheim quacked fiercely, as though he agreed.

"I feel bound to warn you that your days living like this, in peace, are almost over," Sidarí said.

"Is that another threat?"

"Not at all. It is the humans who are a threat. Every season, they clear more land for their mines and farms. One day soon, there will be no corner of this world that is not fenced up and sold off. I hope that when that day comes, you will join us."

"If the war was reversed, and it was the Elarím conquering all the land, my days of living free would likewise be over," Slee said.

"Well," Sidarí said, with a long sigh. "There are different ways of being free."

"So there are. And I choose my way."

"I'm sorry that you feel you must be alone to be free. You know, I do not even wish solitude on my worst enemies. Exile is a punishment we reserve for the most vile acts of *Uthuín*," Sidarí said. "It is strange for me, to see your pointed ears, then to hear you choose exile willingly."

"These ears don't define me like they do you," Slee said.

"I can see that now. Farewell, Slee. You will always be welcome in my clade," Sidarí said, then held out her fist in offer. At Slee's scathing look, she let her hand drop, then turned and started down the hill.

Slee, Slowjaw, and the peaducks watched Sidarí climb down the hill.

All life cares for all life.

Slee snorted. Sidarí was everything Mama had warned her about. The elves, shooting the humans full of arrows and thinking they uphold nature's law. Only the Elarím could tie their minds in such knots.

Once the elf was out of sight, Slee led the animals back through the hedge.

The garden was in a dire condition. Between healing Horvald and the shock of Sidarí's intrusion, the great store of animus was nearly depleted.

The humans emerged from the hut, each with a rifle slung over their shoulder. Horvald, looking pale, leaned heavily on Cartín's shoulder.

"Is she gone?" Cartín asked.

"For now," Slee said. Without breaking her stride, she pushed past them into the hut, and began gathering essential things.

"What's going on?"

Slee barely heard the question. She ran her hands over the shelves, which were stuffed with all manner of preserved food and books, unable to decide which was more precious. The books she had read many times, but they had belonged to her parents. Food could be foraged, but that was never guaranteed. Slowjaw's back, broad as it was, could only hold so much.

Packing up to leave was never easy.

"What are you doing?" Cartín said, watching her make a harried circuit of the hut's shelves.

She turned to him briefly, holding a large jar of pickled onions under one arm and three volumes of an encyclopedia on amphibians under the other.

"Leaving," she said. Then, nodding at her shelves, she said, "Help me take these."

"Leaving? Are we in danger?" Cartín said.

"I'm in a little danger. You're in more."

"I thought the elf woman left?"

"They know where I am now. It's only a matter of time before they come to drag me away and burn my garden down. It could be later today, it could be in a month. I can't risk waiting to find out."

"Horvald can hardly walk. What if they catch us?" Cartín said.

"I have a way of escaping. Set him down and help me load these things onto Slowjaw's back," Slee said.

She carried her things outside with breathless haste, then lashed them to Slowjaw's shell with lengths of vine. In her hurry, she ended up grabbing things at random, then securing them to any free spot on the tortoise's back. With all the vines and lumps of luggage, he began to resemble a boulder overgrown with moss.

Felheim trotted about her ankles, nipping at the ends of vines, or carrying spoons and loose leaves in his bill. The other peaducks watched nervously from a distance. Horvald watched Slee and Cartín in silence from the cot, his arms crossed over his belly.

Before long, Slee declared that nothing more would fit. She wiped a bead of sweat from her flushed face, and looked around her half-empty home. In the end she had chosen to take most of her books, because they could not be replaced.

Cartín hooked Horvald's arm around his shoulder, and together the three of them went outside.

"Slee, you almost forgot this," Cartín said. He held out the geode.

Slee snatched it from him and plunged it into her deepest pocket. She barely wanted to look at it. Part of her had wanted to leave it behind, but in the end it was more important to keep it out of Elarím hands.

"Climb up and secure yourself. You won't want to fall off," Slee said.

"I used to break young, impetuous colts who'd buck all day long if you let them," Cartín said. "I think I can manage the slow, lumbering gait of a tortoise."

"Trust me, our method of escape will make those colts seem like sleepy old nags," Slee said. "Tie up Horvald first, as securely as you can. He won't be able to hold on."

For all their other shortcomings, the humans at least knew how to tie decent knots. Cartín explained that it had been part of his training with the Madean Land Corps. Horvald still said very little, only giving Cartín hushed, one-word answers to his questions.

Slee watched as Cartín secured Horvald's arms and legs, with great tenderness and care. The strength of the bond between them was undeniable. Even if Slee had not possessed the art of telethymia, there would still have been an aura, a warmth in the air between the humans. Most humans were not capable of such a bond. Perhaps these two were rare ones, sensitive to telethymic energies, like Papa had been. Cartín brushed aside Horvald's blond hair and kissed his forehead.

The wilted garden and ransacked hut looked more like the site of a battle than the home Slee had nurtured into existence. The dry síana leaves chattered in the wind, and the door moaned as it swung, sounding like an abandoned calf. Slee could still remember the feel of the loose, barren soil when she had planted the first few crops. Now it was rich with motelings that she was forced to abandon. It takes uncounted hours of toil to build such a densely connected galaxy of life in a place, and that toil in turn deepens love for the place. Now, in the blink of an eye, all that toil and love had come undone.

Slee turned away from the others. She allowed herself a small lump in her throat, and a few stinging tears, as she knelt to brush her fingers across the soil one last time. With that inadequate farewell, she got heavily to her feet. She blinked hard, and coughed to clear her throat.

A few minutes later, all three of them were enmeshed in the vines near the top of Slowjaw's shell. Felheim and the peaducks swarmed around Slee's legs and waist, jostling for a better position.

"Let's go, Slowjaw," Slee said. "To our next home, wherever it might be."

Slowjaw rumbled his assent, and started forward. His heavy, lurching footfalls were at first quite jarring, but Slee soon found the rhythm of leaning into the motion.

They pushed through the síana hedges at the rear of the hut, then continued up the hill. Cartín laughed in short, nervous bursts. Every so often, he said, "This is absurd! Riding a tortoise with an elf!"

Horvald was either too unwell to laugh along, or his taste in humor followed a different sensibility.

Slowjaw reached the top of the hill, where they overlooked a slope so steep it was almost vertical. Aside from a few stunted trees and tufts of grass, the incline was bare. Way below, where the ground leveled out, there was a dense carpet of forest. Just beyond was a glittering, serpentine river.

"Good Providence above!" Cartín said.

"I hope you tied yourselves well," Slee said.

"You can't seriously mean to throw us over the edge!" Cartín said.

"Don't worry, Slowjaw is more than capable of getting us down safely. The worst that might happen is a pickle jar or two breaking."

"I rather think there are worse possibilities than that! Being flattened! Being launched like a cannonball!"

"It's the only way to put enough distance between us and the elves. They'll have to go all the way around on foot," Slee said. "Ready, Slowjaw?"

The colossal tortoise raised his head and trumpeted with confidence.

"I can't watch …" Cartín moaned.

"Best to close your eyes, then."

She gripped the vines with both hands, so tightly that it felt like her knuckles might burst from her skin.

"Now!"

Slowjaw tucked in his neck partway, shuffled his feet, then pitched forward, and he plunged down in a mad descent, an avalanche of one.

Chapter 13

*Some say the clouds must be sad, to drift
so high above us, without the chance to feel
the warm earth. To them I ask: What do you
think rain is?*

Sage Nyendi

As Slowjaw groaned and blinked at the end of a trench of his own making, Slee and the humans clumsily disentangled themselves from their leafy moorings. The chaotic descent had seemed to take forever while they were falling. Now, after an abrupt halt, it seemed to have taken only an instant.

At last, they broke free of the vines, and Slowjaw heaved himself upright. A few books had lost bindings or pages, and some jars of preserves had cracked, but otherwise damage was minimal.

Felheim and the rest of the peaducks, who had flown down, landed in their midst. At once they began nosing through the leaf litter in search of grubs and beetles.

"Well done, Slowjaw," Slee said as she leaned heavily on Slowjaw's cheek, half in embrace, half to keep herself upright.

"What now?" Cartín said.

"You need to go upriver to your own lands. I need to go wherever the elves won't find me," Slee said.

Cartín gaped at the dense trees surrounding them. "Which way to the river?"

"That way," Slee said, pointing.

"Well …" Cartín said, glancing at Horvald, who was resting against Slowjaw's shell.

"What?" Slee said.

"These lands are often patrolled by the Elarím. We'll be safer together. Shall we at least go to the river together and then part?"

Slee searched for a reason to disagree, but found none. "I suppose."

"You look pale. Can you walk?" Cartín asked Horvald, feeling his forehead with the back of his hand.

"Course I can. I could carry you on my back, if you'd like," Horvald said with a weak smile, half-slurring his words.

"Ride on Slowjaw. Save your strength for the long journey home," Slee said.

"No, no," Horvald said. "I can manage."

He stood shakily, then collapsed forward into Cartín's arms. Despite his protests, Horvald was at last deposited on a secure seat on the ridge above Slowjaw's neck.

They set off as a group, like the world's most bizarre merchant caravan: a half-elf, two humans, a flock of peaducks, and a colossal tortoise loaded with pickled tubers and books. The trees there grew in clumps, from which crooked, slanted trunks and boughs branched out high overhead in a dense canopy. There were squat, thin-leafed peelbarks, and pale pepperspecks, and sprawling, orange-leafed cornbirches with raised roots that snaked everywhere underfoot. The forest was pleasant and tranquil to the eye, but something about it was off.

Cartín walked with his rifle slung over his shoulder. Slee eyed it, remembering too well how recently it had been aimed at her.

"Was it really necessary for our escape to be so … dramatic?" Cartín said.

"Absolutely. Slowjaw can only walk so fast, especially loaded with all my things. I needed a good head start," Slee said.

"What did the elf say?"

"Typical Elarím nonsense. She tried to recruit me, then begged me to teach her what I know," Slee said.

"What did you say?"

"I let her spin her little tale of woe, then told her to be on her way."

"Then Slowjaw charged and showed her what-for, didn't he?"

Slee grunted neutrally, unwilling to admit that he had gone soft at the last moment.

They continued on their way, wherever Slowjaw could fit between the trees. When he could not, he flattened them and forged his own way. They would make a clear trail regardless, so a few fallen trees would make little difference.

The air was fresh and clean, though curiously thinner than Slee was used to. They encountered few birds, and spotted no signs of larger animals either. Despite all the trees, and the nearby source of water, the stretch of forest felt bereft of animus. The forest's aura should have been nigh incandescent with motelings and insects. Without a telethymic web to anchor herself in, she felt as though she had been robbed of a sense as vital as sight.

She kept probing the sparse threads and auras they passed through, hoping to find some rich reserve of life.

She could hardly concentrate on her surroundings, because Cartín and Horvald insisted on asking a barrage of questions. Every word she said, for whatever reason, seemed to inspire more of their endless curiosity.

Why did she live alone? She wanted to. Where was her family, her parents? Gone.

Do many elves live alone, the way she does? She didn't know. What does she have against the Elarím? Too many things to count. Why not join the Madeans, then? In many ways, they're worse.

Where did Slowjaw and the peaducks come from? She hatched them from eggs.

Despite Slee's best efforts at dull, blunt answers, they still went on and on. At last, her thinning patience snapped.

"Do humans never run out of questions?" she asked.

"Sorry. I suppose we're curious," Horvald said. "You aren't what I expected."

"What did you expect? An Elarím zealot?"

"Something like that," Horvald said.

"You seem to be one of a kind. I'm not sure exactly *what* kind you are one of, but it's certainly not the Elarím kind," Cartín said.

"I'm flattered … I think," Slee said.

Slee felt a prickling agitation that she could not trace. The forest, so sparsely populated, somehow seemed to be watching them pass by. She paused as Slowjaw noisily toppled another tree.

"Something rather strange happened when I came to," Horvald said.

"What do you mean?" Slee asked.

"Before I passed out, I was terrified. I thought gentle Slowjaw was a monstrous beast, and you an Elarím soldier. But when I woke up, all that terror was gone. Even before I properly knew where I was I just … knew I was safe."

"Knew that you only meant to help us," Cartín said, nodding.

"Exactly."

"That makes no sense," Slee said.

"Perhaps it is different for elves and humans," Cartín said. "The strongest bonds of trust are forged when a life is saved."

"You risked a lot to help me. It says a lot about your character," Horvald said.

"I didn't do it because of my 'character,' " Slee said.

"Whatever your reason, we thank you for it," Cartín
said.

Slee grunted. She didn't *want* thanks. She wanted her
garden back. She wanted to be left alone, now and forever.

The chance of explaining nature's fundamental law —
her real reason for helping them — seemed far too slim.
How could a bird explain its instinct to build a nest?
Nature's laws were all the same, for all creatures. The
problem was that humans and elves had insulated
themselves with culture and industry. They cut fields into
pieces with fences and cut the land into pieces with
borders. Those things gave them the arrogance to ignore
the basic things that even a wren knows.

Rather than try to explain it all, she simply said, "You're
welcome."

"That's the river now, if my ears don't deceive me!"
Cartín said brightly.

"Cartín, would you be a Saint and find me a walking
stick?" Horvald said.

"At once," Cartín said, raising a merry salute. He
hurried ahead, scattering fallen leaves and inspecting
potential branches.

The rush of water could indeed be heard close by.
Slowjaw continued to trudge in the gaps between the
trees. His enormous feet left long drag marks, as lethargy
increasingly weighed him down. Horvald sat upright in
his makeshift saddle, the color in his cheeks much
improved. He watched Cartín with half-lidded, fond eyes.

"You and Cartín are not what I expected, either," Slee
said. "I can hardly believe you are humans."

"What do you mean? That we're more like elves?" Horvald asked gruffly.

"I wouldn't insult you like that," Slee said, letting slip a small smile. "I just cannot see how a nation like Madea could be made up of Madeans like you two."

"Well … people like Cartín and I are not exactly darling sons of Madea," Horvald said. A small aura like a cloud of steam rose from his head as he frowned and tugged at his beard.

"What do you mean?"

He waved his hand, as though instinctively clearing the cloudy aura which he could not see. "Never mind. Most Madeans are decent folk who do the best they can. It's the kings and nobles that make Madea what it is."

"Why do you let them?" Slee said.

At this, Horvald only laughed. Once again Slee was faced with the riddle of which questions were funny to humans and which were not. When he was finished laughing, though, he frowned, lost for words.

Cartín returned, with a long, leafy branch in hand. "This ought to do. Do you have something I can cut it with amongst your … luggage?"

"You can ask Slowjaw to help," Slee said.

They brought the massive tortoise to a halt. Cartín gingerly offered Slowjaw one end of the branch, which he bit clean through. Then, after stripping it of twigs and leaves, he offered the rough, makeshift cane to Horvald. Horvald accepted it, as well as a kiss, then slid down gently from his perch.

"Thank you. This'll work fine," Horvald said as he tested his weight on the stick.

They continued on, and soon came to the banks of the river. The water was crisp and glittering, tumbling over and around stones smoothed by erosion, lapping on shores of gravel and sand. Great sprawling trees with pendulous branches leaned over the water, dropping leaves like tears. Here and there, tufts of reeds bowed languidly to the wind. The scene was beautiful, but in some unseen way, profoundly wrong.

"Just in time! I'm parched," Cartín said, and he knelt by the riverbank and lowered his cupped hands into the water.

"Don't drink it!" Slee cried.

The two humans stared at her.

Slowjaw approached the river's edge too, and she rushed over to block his way.

"We cannot drink this," Slee said. "Something is wrong here."

Slowjaw gave a deep chirp of concern. Felheim and his flock, perched on Slowjaw's shell, peered down at the water with suspicion. The colossal tortoise sniffed deeply at the river, then sneezed with a blast like a cannon, and lurched backward, away from the water.

"Good Providence above," Cartín said.

"There's something horrible in the water," Slee said. "Look around. Where are the dragonflies? The birds? There's hardly a thing living in the water, or in the soil around it."

"If I'm not mistaken, this river is fed by Bianlock," Horvald said. A shadow passed over his brow as he looked meaningfully at Cartín, then Slee.

"What is that?"

"A lake in the Madean Highlands."

"Do you think they would …?" Cartín asked in a hushed tone.

"I wouldn't be surprised," Horvald said.

"In Bianlock? Surely not."

"What are you two talking about?" Slee asked.

"Whenever lush woods or fertile waters go barren, it means some alchemist has dumped the waste of his experiment there," Horvald said darkly. "Everyone knows it, but we can't do a thing."

"This river has been deliberately poisoned?" Slee breathed.

"Now, for all we know it was not deliberate," Cartín said. He pulled on the ends of his moustache, lost in thought for a moment. "A wagon of reagents might have fallen in the river. Or they might have thought their waste was harmless."

"Or there were too many crowns on offer for them to care about consequences," Horvald said.

"It might be nothing at all! We are far downstream from Bianlock. Perhaps this is the way the river has always been," Cartín said.

"None of nature's rivers are this way," Slee said quietly. Her feet on the damp ground had either been numbed by the foul waters, or there was not a single moteling living under the sand. If it weren't for the robust animus of Slowjaw, and the many threads between the peaducks, Slee might have become unanchored from the world and floated away. She held to the telethymic strands as though they were lifelines.

*Life is like air, Sílandra. When it is all around, you take no
notice, but a sudden absence cannot be ignored.*

"It doesn't matter," Horvald said. "There's nothing we
can do. We should just move on."

"What are we going to drink? I doubt we'll find any
other waterways that don't go back to Bianlock," Cartín
said.

"There are ways to get clean water," Slee said. "First, we
must get away from the river."

"Back toward the Elarím?" Cartín said.

"We ought to head upstream first, then cut deeper into
the woods," Horvald said.

"Are we sure a little drink from the river will kill us?"
Cartín asked.

"Kill us? Perhaps not," Slee said. "But anything that can
make a river barren is not worth risking."

"I suppose we'd better get moving, eh? If my tongue
dries out any more, we might as well pluck it out and keep
it as sandpaper," Cartín said.

As they went on, Slee saw the woods with fresh eyes.
The trees, sprouting in clumps, suddenly looked like they
were huddling together for safety. The air, so anemic and
scentless, carried too little of the signs of growth and
decay. It would not be long before the whole area was a
brown, dusty welt on the face of the land.

After making some progress upstream, they turned and
headed back into the woods. Slee probed around the soil,
finding more and more moteling life the farther they got
from the river. At last she declared a spot to be suitable.

At her request, Slowjaw gouged a large hole with his
beak, then spat out the dirt at his side. The creation of the

hole had harmed a great host of motelings, and severed many roots large and small. Slee knelt beside the hole and silently paid them respect before summoning the water.

Damaging nature to sustain yourself was no sin. After all, nature made the lamb as well as the wolf. The only sin was damage that goes beyond one's needs—anything done to quench a thirst that is never satisfied.

The process of obtaining the water was not taxing. Slee only did what trees routinely did, through moteling messengers around their roots. She asked.

With her hands half-buried in the soil, she let the surrounding woods know of her thirst, and the thirst of her companions. At once the hole, as large as a bathtub, began to fill with water.

Slee withdrew her hands and smiled slightly. Cartín and Horvald gaped at her. The men shared a curious, clouded aura that was difficult to read. She thought they would be pleased, but the subtle tendrils of black smoke that snaked around their necks were what Mama used to call 'the collar of horror.'

"Don't you want water?" Slee said.

"How did you *do* that?" Cartín asked.

"Can all elves conjure water?" Horvald breathed.

Slee folded her arms. "First of all, I am a half-elf. Secondly, I conjured nothing. Water is everywhere in the woods. You just need to know how to ask for it."

Their auras lightened a little, and their collars dissipated, but they said nothing.

When neither of the humans moved, Slee drank her fill. The peaducks crowded around the makeshift pond's edge and dipped their bills into the water. Slee sternly told them not to swim in the water, and to hold their droppings until they were far away from it. At last the ducks were finished, and Slowjaw opened his cavernous mouth to take a drink.

"I'm sorry, my darling, but you must go last," Slee said, stroking the tortoise's nose. She relayed an image of the humans drinking first. He groaned, and shuffled away from the water.

"I thought you were thirsty?" she asked Cartín, who was eyeing the water with open distaste.

"I am! It just looks a little brown," Cartín said.

"So it is," Slee said.

"I just wonder if the river water isn't ... cleaner," he said

"This water is cleaner than rainfall," Slee said. "Close your eyes if you must."

Slowjaw nudged Cartín with his nose and let out an impatient bugle. Cartín almost fell into the water, but Horvald caught his arm.

"Gently, now, Slowjaw," Cartín said. "I'll drink, I suppose. I *am* rather thirsty."

Cartín and Horvald knelt by the hole and drank the water in tentative sips. It was indeed clouded with a few drifting specks of grit, but otherwise was clear enough that Slee could easily see the bottom. Humans were a finicky lot. How could poisoned water that merely *looks* clean be more enticing than pure water from the earth?

Cartín soon began taking long gulps, and continued drinking long after Horvald withdrew with a dripping beard. Slowjaw inched closer and closer with his beak half-open, until his shadow fell across the entire pool of water. A drop of thick saliva stretched down like a glob of molten glass, descending ever closer to Cartín's head. Horvald, noticing the drool, pulled Cartín out of the way just in time. The tortoise's viscous spittle splashed heavily in the water.

Cartín, wrinkling his nose, said, "I suppose it's all yours, now, Slowjaw."

With one beakful, Slowjaw took all of the water, and some of the hole it was in. His long, leathery neck ballooned as he swallowed. The look of gratification and proud achievement on Slowjaw's face made Cartín chortle.

An echoing report of gunfire in the distance cut him short.

It was hard to tell where the shot had come from. All of them were frozen, straining their ears under hushed trees that also seemed to be listening.

Another volley of hissing shots rang out. Slee, pointed ears twitching, pointed west.

"That way. They're getting closer," Slee said.

"Are you sure?" Horvald said.

"I can tell the age and type of a tree by the sound of its falling leaves. I think I can tell the source of a gunshot," Slee said, tapping the end of one ear.

"That will mean that whoever they are shooting at is coming this way," Cartín said.

Horvald swung his rifle off his shoulder, flipping open its hatches and flicking its levers. His walking stick lay on the ground, forgotten.

"I believe this is where we must part, Slee," Cartín said. He extended his open hand to her.

She frowned for a moment, then remembered reading about a 'handshake.' As she grasped his hand and then Horvald's, she felt flashes of fondness and gratitude leaking both ways through the contact. They *liked* her, and she was surprised to learn that she felt the same about them.

Felheim had already led his flock to perch at the top of Slowjaw's shell. A low, continuous moan of unease bubbled in the depths of the tortoise's chest.

"What are you going to do?" Slee said.

"What must be done. Sorry, Slee, it's war," Horvald said, then ripped a package of gunpowder open with his teeth.

"With any luck we'll be able to draw the elves away while you go downriver," Cartín said.

"Downriver? But I need to find out how the river was poisoned," Slee said.

Cartín took her by the arm and spoke with low urgency. "It's not worth your life. You saved Horvald; let us save you."

"You don't understand," Slee said. Strangely, she felt no urge to wrench herself free of his grip. In fact, through the point of contact, she felt the flicker of a strangely familiar telethymic sensation, like a butterfly's wings brushing against her skin.

"I know you have your convictions, and they are admirable. But this is war. Convictions get you killed. Whatever is happening in this river, it is not worth your life," Cartín said.

His dark brown eyes, open wide, searched hers for an agreement that she could not give him. She gently shook her head, and his shoulders sagged, and his hold on her arm eased slightly. At last, she recognized the flickering feeling passing between them: nature's deepest law. Some buried instinct had sprouted in him, like a seedling chasing the sun. In a way—a flawed, narrow, human way—he was thinking: *All life cares for all life.*

"I hear you, but I am able to make my own choice."

"Cartín—movement," Horvald said. He was leaning into the crook between two thick boughs, rifle in hand.

They followed Horvald's gaze to see a distant shower of gleaming red sparks.

"I'm going upriver," Slee said.

She turned to climb up on Slowjaw's back, when a hard object knocked against her leg. The ink-black geode glittered when she pulled it out. While it had saved Horvald's life, the cost had almost been everything she held dear. She threw it into the makeshift waterhole, and had Slowjaw cover it up with his rough feet. Cartín watched it leave her hand, but said nothing.

There was a loud burst of gunfire not far off. Though she could not see those who had fired, she could smell the sour, metallic gun-smoke.

"Well, if you cannot be convinced, then we only have one choice, don't we?" Cartín said, his tone droll.

"And what is that?" Horvald said, still watching for the enemy's approach.

"Draw them all away from the river," Cartín said.

"Of course. Easy as hagapple pie." The tense, clotted aura congealing around Horvald's head belied his cheerful tone.

"Stay safe, Slee. I hope we meet again," Cartín said.

"Farewell!" Horvald called over his shoulder. He was now leaning his rifle across a nearby branch, aiming down its sights.

Slee nodded to them, unsure of what to say. At last, she simply said, "Goodbye."

As she mounted Slowjaw and guided him toward the right direction, an errant shot from the nearby skirmish hit an overhead branch and showered her with splinters.

"Don't linger, Slee. And remember: most humans will kill you on sight. If anyone gets curious about your allegiance at all, it will be after you are cold." Cartín nestled himself behind a fallen log not far from Horvald as he spoke.

"I will remember it."

Slowjaw trundled between the trees, scraping bark from them and crushing small plants underfoot.

The crackle of gunfire drew nearer, as well as the hideous shriek of elven arrows. Just before she was out of earshot, she distinctly heard Cartín say, "Don't you dare get shot again and leave me all alone."

"Don't be absurd. Nothing can happen to me: I'm with you," Horvald said.

Chapter 14

All the pastoral landscapes hanging in the Madean Academy of Arts had lied: the Madean countryside was a dreary, desolate, loathsome place. Countless oil paintings depicted a sun-drenched paradise of rolling green hills, with rose-cheeked women tossing grain for the chickens like wedding confetti. As Fentor rolled past grey, fallow wastes and their gaunt, gap-toothed denizens, he saw not quaint farms, but hovels. The only reprieve was when rain or fog drew a curtain over the unsightly vista.

His creaky carriage limped along in the wake of Lady Talentus' four-horse rolling throne room. The towns they lodged in were simply horrendous. The common folk reacted in one of two ways upon their arrival. They either crowded around the coaches, hands outstretched, begging for alms, or jeered, spat, and threw stones. In either case, the mobs were dispersed by a few judicious cracks of the drivers' whips. Lady Talentus seemed to have an endless supply of coin purses, which she gave to the mayor of each town. Inspired by her generosity, the noble guests were always given the town's finest beds—often the mayor's own.

The farther they got from Madea City, the greater the displays of ingratitude. Fentor spied a gangly old man at a lonely fork in the road, holding up a crudely-written sign. It read, "I grew the wheat, you got the bread, I got a crumb back." Fentor shook his head and tutted at the indecency.

The crowds in the outer towns gave louder jeers, and threw larger rocks. It now took a dozen cracks of the whip to fend them off. Fentor quickly gave up on reasoning with the crowds. He wasn't *their* landlord, he told them. He wasn't taking *their* wheat. Perhaps if they spent less time sowing discontent and more time sowing grain, he said, their plight would not be so dire. Even the most unassailable logic fell on ears sealed shut by ignorance.

After investing his entire fortune in Lady Talentus' enterprise, he was just as penniless as they were. He wisely judged that mentioning this fact would not draw the sympathy it deserved.

The Lady withstood the fist-shaking populace with stoic grace. In fact, she refused to acknowledge them so resolutely that they seemed robbed of any power over her. At one misshapen cluster of shacks and pigpens, however, a particularly belligerent mob formed. An errant rock thrown by them caught Lady Talentus on the chin. It left a small red mark, no larger than a fingernail.

In response, the carriage drivers, Dídac, and the mayor's constables all rushed at the crowd with whips, cudgels and sabres drawn. The Lady halted them all with a word, and instead proposed she make a deal with the town. She disappeared with the mayor into his home and emerged shortly after. He announced an increase in pay for all workers in the town, then mumbled that some conditions were attached. The mob cheered, then knelt and kissed the Lady's hands.

As they made for their carriages, Fentor asked her what the conditions were.

"Some believe that obedience requires either the carrot *or* the stick. I believe in using both," she replied. She did not elaborate further.

Fentor had lost count of the days when at last they approached the site of the secret distillery. Nature, here, put on a show more in line with the city's painted fantasies. The thin, cool air carried a bracing shroud of mist. On high ridges all around, pines pricked the sky like orderly rows of bayonets. The shy morning sun hid her face behind the trees and cast golden beams all across the surrounding hills. Fentor found it quite charming.

They came up over a pale gravel ridge onto a rough path carved beside the lake. At the end of the long path lay their destination.

The distillery itself was an odd building of steel beams, turning gears, and hammered brass panels. At such a distance, it resembled a little clockwork toy. A steady ribbon of blue steam rose from its riveted chimney, and a stream of blue liquid drained through a pipe into the lake.

WAR WITH ELVES: FOR PROFIT AND AMUSEMENT

Their carriages came to a stop in the shadow of the distillery. Thick dust raised from the chalky gravel enveloped them, then passed, revealing the structure like the drawing of a curtain.

What had earlier seemed like a toy now towered over Fentor. It was as large as a barn, but strangely, it gave him the same breathless feeling as the Saint's Cathedral in Madea City. The feeling, he noted, was that of being in the presence of a higher power.

Lady Talentus gazed up at the distillery with a gleam in her eye. Otherwise, her bearing was the same as always. She stood with square shoulders, arms folded in the small of her back, chin high, and an expression of controlled neutrality. With nothing more than a little glint in her eye, she seemed to charge the very air around her with a crackling vitality, like the build-up before the crash of thunder.

Fentor recalled a passage from his copy of *Illustrated Writings of Saint Temlin the Exiled: Exclusive Limited Anniversary Edition:* "One day, Providence will grace us with a Saint unlike any other. By their hand alone, the war between man and elf will end, and it will end forever."

It would have been a ludicrous thing to say aloud, so he kept quiet. Still, Fentor could not help but wonder if he was witnessing the prophecy coming true. As if on cue, a cloud shifted, and the distillery was caught in shafts of intense, golden light. One beam, reflected from a hammered panel, fell gently upon the Lady in a dappled golden square, like a spotlight cast down from Providence itself.

"It is a remarkable structure, my Lady," Dídac said, hovering just behind her.

"Wait until you have seen what is inside," she said.

She led them to the front door, a large panel of riveted steel set on rails. It slid open smoothly as they approached, as though of its own accord. Then, stepping inside, Fentor saw that it had actually been opened by two Bluefingers using a pulley mechanism.

The distillery was a warehouse, an alchemy laboratory, and a military barracks all in one. Two dozen Alchemist-Lancers hunched over their work on long tables of polished steel. They boiled, titrated, measured, mixed, distilled, scooped, dripped, and swirled reagents of all colors and kinds. Between whistling spouts of colorful steam and clouds of acrid-smelling powder, Fentor could hardly make sense of the chaotic procedures.

Beyond the alchemists were great stacks of wooden crates, of which some reached as high as the ceiling. Indeed, most of the space in the distillery was taken up by the crates.

Bluefingers patrolled the space, though they did not wear the admiral blue uniform of the Madean Land Corps. Instead, they wore coats of ash-grey, bearing the Talentus coat of arms.

Lady Talentus introduced them to the head alchemist, Capilet Galton. He had the stocky build of a boxer, a bald spot on his crown, and mutton chops which almost joined his moustache. His hands and forearms were stained with splotches of every hue.

At the Lady's request, Galton gave them a tour of the facility. He pointed out the various reagents, and how the refining processes worked for each. Fentor nodded at appropriate times, and murmured, "How interesting!" Soon, though, the highly technical alchemy was beyond his ability to understand.

There were simpler things, like the transmutation of ferric oxide and wood ash into caustic red-ash. Then there was the process for oil of telium, which was derived from 'saponific matrices' and other things Fentor could not pronounce. Then came ethyl vitriol, which Fentor dimly understood to be an alchemical cousin of plain, everyday alcohol. Last of all was the enriched kryside, a product Fentor knew well for its role in making blue gunpowder. However, the complicated methods of reducing, combining, oxidizing and compounding the many ingredients with raw krysite soon had him utterly lost.

The truly enlightening thing about the distillery was not what they made, but *how* they made it.

Rather than have one alchemist make a single potion from start to finish, the highly specialized tasks were divided among them. One particular alchemist would stand at the bench for hours on end, producing vial after vial of a single reagent, and then pass it on. Each reagent passed from hand to hand, to be mixed or refined in some way at each spot. At last, the mixtures were combined into their final form, the Elixir of Power.

Working this way, Galton explained, increased production eightfold.

"Eventually," he said brightly. "We'll have no *need* of fully-trained alchemists. With each process simplified and separated, even the simplest dock worker could be taught to do it. *Boil this until it changes color, then pour it in that flask.* A thrilling thought, isn't it?"

The Lady agreed.

For the entire tour, Dídac had hung in the Lady's shadow. He appraised the spindly glass instruments and crates of reagents with an expression of detached, casual interest. Every so often, though, when the elf thought no one was looking, Fentor caught a spark of greed in his pale eyes. In those moments, pulling his lips back in an unconscious grimace, he almost looked like a cat licking its lips by a butcher's window.

Galton then led them to a large trapdoor, which he opened by pulling on a heavy lever. A steep spiral staircase of wrought iron bars was revealed, and they descended into a cold underground chamber of stone, easily twice the size of the distillery above. Each of their steps on the iron stairs sounded like the peal of an off-key bell.

"My Lady, how were you able to build such an enormous place so quickly?" Fentor breathed.

"Masons and builders have a saying: 'You can get decent work or fast work, but for both you need a miracle.' To that, I replied: 'With sufficient funding, I shall have all three.' "

As Fentor gawked through the bars at the vast chamber below, he understood how the Lady had, in her words, 'Compromised her liquidity.' He began to estimate how much it would have cost in materials alone, and soon gave up. An unwelcome question occurred to him, like the twinge of a cramping muscle: Why had she needed *his* investment, which was so meagre in comparison?

The vast underground space, which Galton called the 'Extraction Chamber,' was filled from wall to wall with scores of soldiers on low canvas cots. There was a diffuse twilight glow, which seemed to have no particular source, and washed everything sapphire-blue. Between that and the cool, damp air, Fentor felt as though they were submerged in a sea-cave.

As they reached the bottom of the stairs, Galton continued in a hushed voice. Fentor peered at the nearest row of soldiers. They seemed to be deeply asleep. A nest of wires and glass tubes surrounded their heads, terminating in a row of needles across their foreheads. It looked as though they were in the embrace of long-legged metallic spiders. As Galton explained, raw animus was extracted from the unconscious Bluefingers, collected in large barrels, then sent upstairs to the alchemists via 'winch-lift'. They watched as one such platform carried full barrels up toward the ceiling by a system of chains, gears, pulleys, and counterweights.

"We are in luck, the shift is over! I'm sure they will all be thrilled by your presence, Your Excellency," Galton said.

"Indeed."

Gradually, the soldiers began to stir. Some sat up, drawn and haggard, slouching on the edges of their beds. Others lethargically plucked the needles from their forehead. Most, still lying down, seemed unable to do more than blink and flex their fingers.

Before, Fentor had only been able to see the bizarre extraction equipment. Now, seeing the soldiers properly for the first time, he noted that many were older, or amputees, or bearing deep burns and shrapnel scars on their faces.

"Clear the cobwebs from your eyes and look smart! We have a guest!" Galton called. His booming voice was joined by a chorus of echoes.

The Bluefingers, looking like ghosts of themselves in the curious blue light, stiffly rose to their feet. Then, realizing who their 'guest' was, they broke into cheers and applause.

"My Lady!"

"Lady Talentus is here!"

"Thank you, Your Excellency! Thank you!"

She raised a slender hand in acknowledgement, straight-faced as always.

Fentor spotted a hazily familiar rosy-cheeked woman halfway across the chamber, but could not match a name to the face. She waved at him with an eager smile, and he waved back as though he remembered her.

The Lady dropped her hand and cleared her throat. The room fell silence at once.

"I appreciate your kind welcome. If you will indulge me, I wish to say a few words," she said. She spoke in an icy yet invigorating tone, like a swift wind skittering over snow drifts. The silence in the room was so complete, that she hardly needed to raise her voice at all. "Most people are destined to merely witness history as the world changes around them. Together, in this distillery, we are *making* history. We shall achieve a victory against the elves that has long been called impossible, and that is only the first step of many. Once Madea knows peace, we shall see transformation. Alchemy is the art of transformation.

210

Transmutation. The mundane remade into the remarkable. In the same way, I shall take the plain clay of Madea and sculpt wonders that have never before been seen. A land free of want, a leader of world affairs, a people free of the humiliations they have long been forced to bear.

"I heard some of you thank me, but I am afraid I cannot accept. Thanks are for favors or acts of charity. Transactions of mutual benefit — the true foundation of any society — require no thanks. You all have pledged to work, and I have pledged to pay you all enough to purchase land to call your own. Direct your gratitude to Providence, for permitting us this chance to reach out and grasp glory that has so long eluded us.

"Remember, I came from modest beginnings. If one like me can rise from nothing to such great heights, then the same can be true for all of you. With my guidance, Madea will no longer be a land where the wounded and unfortunate must suffer the indignity of begging for subsistence. Instead, I shall build a new nation, founded on the principle that all may be employed in meaningful work. A nation of unlimited freedoms. A nation that will manifest Providence on earth, where we can all have the chance to live as Saints."

The soldiers broke out into a cacophonous roar of stamping, cheers, and applause. Many eyes shone with joyous tears. Even Fentor found a lump in his throat.

The Lady was a Saint, through and through. Fentor would willingly bet that every single soldier in the room would agree. The only thing left was a formal confirmation from the Church of Providence.

Despite all that, Lady Talentus somehow managed to look bored.

"Shall we carry on? I'm afraid the last stops of the tour are the least engaging—dormitories and such," Galton said. The stocky man swept his arm toward a nearby corridor, offering to lead the way.

"No. I am sure they are built to specification. Dídac will no doubt wish to inspect the facility fully once it is his to oversee," the Lady said.

"Of - of course," Galton said, blinking. The parts of his cheeks not covered by mutton chops reddened. "My Lord Dídac, it will be a pleasure to work under you."

Dídac's hand was briefly engulfed by Galton's, and they shook hands. Judging by the elf's obviously limp grip, it must have felt something like shaking the fin of a dead fish.

It occurred to Fentor that Galton had expected to be the one running the distillery.

"I'm sure the pleasure is mine," replied Dídac, in a drawling voice that was the very antithesis of 'pleasure.'

"For the moment, I would rather inspect the troops, as it were," the Lady said.

Lady Talentus paced between the rows of cots, stopping to speak with the soldiers she passed. A loose crowd formed as many lingered nearby, hoping the Lady would grace them with a visit. Dídac, Galton, and Fentor followed dutifully in her wake.

Someone caught Fentor's arm, and he turned to find the familiar rose-cheeked woman, supported by her crutches. She beamed blearily at him, forcing her eyes to stay open with apparent effort. It looked like she had gone days without sleep. Fentor, still rummaging through his mind for her name, opted to greet her with total, enthusiastic ambiguity.

"Of all the places in Madea, it's here that I find you! How *have* you been?" Fentor said.

"Why, it's a surprise for us both, my Lord. To think, that not one but *two* of my saviors would visit. I'm either blessed or dreaming!" she said.

"Well, it's time to thank the Saints, because this is no dream," Fentor said, gracing her with a warm, genial smile that he had rehearsed many times.

"It's quite overwhelming, truth be told!"

"I'm sure it is. Tell me, how did you come to be here?" Fentor listened closely, hoping for some clue as to her identity.

"By the grace of Providence itself, my Lord, I'm sure of it," she said. "I so sorely needed this chance, and it came right as hope had left me."

" 'The worthy need never despair, for the riches of Providence are theirs,' " Fentor said, nodding slowly so he could appear sagely. "Divine favor has a way of coming just in time, does it not?"

"Don't misunderstand, my Lord—freeing me from the burden of rent has been a miracle of its own," she said.

All in a flash, Fentor remembered—Charlotte! Charlotte Wicksling or something, *that* was her name. He almost blurted out her name in reflex.

Charlotte continued in a rush, "I was able to free an aunt of legal troubles—penury laws, you see, enormous debts—and *she* was able to help watch my children, and it freed me to accept the blessing of this work."

"Charlotte, you have no idea how it warms my heart to hear of your triumph. You deserve every blessing. All the poor and destitute of Madea ought to look to your example," Fentor said, adopting the august tones of a benevolent king.

"My Lord Fentor, you do me too much kindness," Charlotte said, bowing her head and flushing a deeper shade of rose.

Far above, there was a grating metallic noise. The trapdoor at the top of the stairwell opened, and a piercing column of light dispelled the ethereal gloom.

A soldier rushed down the first few steps, then bellowed, "Intruder! There's an intruder approaching!"

Chapter 15

I sneak into my Capilet's tent
And draw my shiny knife.
I'll have to kill my enemy
To save my stinkin' life.

'Fight the Enemy,' Third Stanza

Few places could match the ability of a lake to nurture vast communities of living things. So much depended on a single lake. From the tiniest motelings, to the fish in the depths, to birds on the surface, and the beasts on the shores, a lake was the sum of all the life within it. Truly, it could have a life all its own.

Bianlock Lake, however, was dead.

Slee, riding on Slowjaw's shell, looked out across the lake with a numb heart. The absence of bird calls and

215

humming insects left the whisper of wind as the only sound. No living thing could be seen, except the stern regiments of pine trees around the lake. Nor could she sense a single telethí thread, not even among the nearby trees. It was as though the entire web had been torn away. The lost connections numbed the lake, and in turn numbed Slee's heart.

Some anger goes beyond heat. Some injustice defies words.

Slee could only gape in her shock, unable to comprehend.

Across the lake stood the culprit: an ugly lump of metal, spewing fumes and liquid waste. The longer she looked, the more her heart thawed. Soon, hot flashes of anger roused her from her stupor. The air around her crackled with forked lightning, a blood-red tempest of rage. She would see the building crushed, and its inhabitants strewn across the shore like rag-dolls. Their blood would be the only thing she would allow to drain into the lake.

Slowjaw, concerned at the searing heat of Slee's aura, turned and crooned. *Please don't hurt people,* he thought. *Not even bad people.*

As always, his heart was too large, too kind. Slee ignored him, and urged him to hurry forward.

She wanted to reach the building with her righteous anger intact.

****

Out across the shores of Bianlock, Fentor beheld the most bizarre 'intruder' he had ever seen.

A tortoise, easily as big as an elephant, lumbered around the lake's perimeter. Atop his massive shell sat an elf woman with light brown complexion, and a flock of what appeared to be ducks. They were all wreathed in a great, billowing cloud of white dust which rose up from the chalky gravel.

At the Lady's direction, Dídac raised a spyglass and studied the new arrival.

In the flurry that the elf's approach had inspired, Fentor had been handed a rifle and a pistol, which he held close to his chest. The weapons provided some measure of comfort.

Lady Talentus had restored order swiftly to the alarmed soldiers and alchemists. She and her Capilets would handle the intruder, she had told them. The soldiers and alchemists were to stand by, inside the distillery, and do nothing unless ordered otherwise. They were, however, permitted to watch. As a result, it seemed as though the entire population of the facility was crammed into the threshold, jostling each other for a better view.

"What do you make of her?" the Lady said, as casually as one might ask a guest how they were enjoying their tea.

"She is unarmed," Dídac said. "Dirty, like a farmer. It looks like she made her own dress from scraps."

"An unlikely choice for a scout," the Lady mused.

"She is brown of skin and hair, and not slim like a true elf."

"A half-breed?" Lady Talentus asked.

Dídac flinched slightly, then lowered the spyglass, as though it had stung him. His cheeks flushed pink. "A …

half-elf, yes. If her ears were not pointed, I might have thought her a Norimandian vagrant."

"An unarmed half-elf and a flock of ducks riding on a tame colossal tortoise. Thoughts, Fentor?"

"Either she has come to ask for a 'crumb from the table,' or this is the most peculiar ruse the Elarím have ever deployed," Fentor said.

"If it is a crumb she wants, she will be sorely disappointed," Lady Talentus said. "But why a tortoise? Why ducks? Do they have some significance in Elarím culture?"

"No, my Lady. The Common Power does not extend to animals." Dídac frowned deeply, squinting through the spyglass.

"With your permission my Lady, shall I fire a warning shot?" Fentor said.

Lady Talentus did not answer for a moment, seeming transfixed by the strange trespasser. She unconsciously raised a hand to cradle her chin. It was an unremarkable gesture for others to make, but to see the Lady's usually severe composure broken suggested a profound disquiet. A marble statue might as easily have come to life to scratch its nose.

"Yes, a warning shot. Ready and load, Fentor. Fire on my command," Lady Talentus said.

"Aye, my Lady."

Fentor lay the pistol at his feet, then set about loading the rifle. The comforting ritual busied his hands and dispelled some of the tension. The sequence was so familiar that his old instructor's barked commands echoed

in his ears. *Powder! Cast about! Load! Ram it home! Hold
ready!*

The half-elf and her mount rounded the final curve of
the lake's edge, and headed directly toward them. Fentor
drummed his fingers on the barrel of the rifle. Perhaps
shooting the stranger would be simpler.

As they watched and waited, Fentor hastily loaded the
pistol, too. One could never be sure that one shot would
be enough.

With the pistol on his belt and the rifle in hand, he
awaited the Lady's order. When the tortoise was within
two hundred paces, the Lady said, "Aim."

Fentor sighted a spot just in front of the beast, in the
hopes that gravel might spray up and give it a scare.

"Fire."

The shot went off with a sharp fizz-crack, and a large
plume of dust and crushed stone burst under the tortoise's
nose.

Rather than retreat, it paused, then sneezed.

The massive, lurching ejection rocked the creature's
shell so hard that it almost unseated its passenger. Then,
ignoring the warning, or not comprehending it, they
continued to approach the distillery.

"Load your weapon once more," the Lady said.

Dídac, glowering through the spyglass, said, "The half-
elf looks rather wrathful. Warning shots are no deterrent."

"Surely a wretch seeking a crumb from the table would
have fled, or cowered. She has come here with a purpose,
and it is one she would risk her life for," the Lady mused.
Her voice rose and fell melodically, like the opening
phrases of a symphony. Not only did her hand still caress

her chin, but her eyes narrowed. Then, she whispered, "Why have you come?"

"Shall I dispatch her, my Lady?" Fentor asked.

"No. In fact, hold your fire altogether. I must know who sent her," Lady Talentus said.

"With respect, Your Excellency, it is doubtful that the Elarím would send anyone alone, even as a ruse or distraction," Dídac said.

"I agree. I find myself rather overcome with curiosity. If the Elarím did not send her, then who did?" the Lady said. "I cannot accept that mere chance has brought a half-elf to a distillery built under the strictest secrecy."

"What are we to do with her, my Lady?" Fentor said.

"Speak." The Lady advanced a few paces, waved at the stranger in greeting, then folded her arms behind her back.

"Are you going to shoot an unarmed woman?" the half-elf called out in Madean, with a slight Rodessian accent.

"Of course not. Come closer and we can talk," the Lady called in reply.

The half-elf dismounted, and walked—on bare, dirty feet—across the rough gravel. Fentor wrinkled his nose. The tortoise followed gamely in her wake, turning his enormous yellow eyes from Fentor, to Dídac, to the Lady in turn. Something in its manner reminded Fentor of a curious dog, eager to meet strangers. A low, constant rumbling sound emanated from the tortoise's large throat.

The largest, most colorful duck, in contrast, somehow managed to look down on them from his perch with naked contempt. Fentor had never seen such expressive animals in his life.

The half-elf drew close enough for conversation, but no closer. Her hair was unbrushed, but not matted. Her hands were dirty, but not her face. Together with these things, her proud, defiant bearing belied the notion that she was simply a beggar-woman. She was a strange specimen, neither Elarím nor Madean. Most peculiar of all was the pure rage that curled her lips and puckered her brow. One might have been able to start a fire by holding kindling to her nose.

Fentor waited with his rifle ready.

"I am Grand Toque Elatea Talentus, Duchess of Astralan, Countess of Shorovia, and the chief designing engineer of Talentus Heavy Ordnance," the Lady said. "Who are you?"

"Slee," the half-elf said curtly.

"I beg your pardon?"

"My name. It's Slee."

"I see. Well, Slee, what brings you here?" the Lady said, with the air of a hostess greeting a new arrival to luncheon.

"This." The half-elf Slee pointed past the Lady at the distillery.

"I am afraid I don't follow. You have come because you are curious about the building?"

"No. I've come to stop it. All that stuff leaking out — it's poison," Slee said.

"Poison? Good Providence. How can you be sure? Are you an alchemist?" the Lady asked politely.

"I don't need to be an alchemist to see what is killing the lake."

"Whyever should the lake's well-being be your concern? Do you own it?"

"No," Slee said. "No one does. People can't *own* a lake."

"You are incorrect there, I am afraid. You see, it *is* my lake. As Countess of Shorovia, Bianlock Lake is under my stewardship. Beyond that, the private deed for this land — including all bodies of water therein — is in my name. This is my distillery and my lake, and I may dispose of effluent as I see fit."

"You can't just poison water!" Slee marched forward, raising her fists.

Fentor blocked her way, and aimed his rifle between her eyes. The half-elf stared down the sights at Fentor with such naked, twisted hostility that he almost pulled the trigger just to wipe the expression away.

"Stand down, Capilet," Lady Talentus said softly, but with staccato precision.

Fentor backed away, still locked in a mutual scowl with Slee.

"Let's all agree to comport ourselves with a touch more civility," the Lady said. "Shall we?"

"Good. It's about time you acted *civil*," Slee spat, imbuing the last word with venom.

Dídac scoffed. Slee shot him a withering sneer, and Fentor could not fault her for it. After all, it *was* Dídac.

Slee then said something to Dídac in the elvish language which flushed his cheeks pink with anger.

"Are you aware of the Madean law against trespassing?" Lady Talentus asked.

"I know a great deal about trespassing. People where they don't belong. As for Madean law, I cannot imagine a worse thing to waste my time learning," Slee said.

"You are new to these lands, so your ignorance can be forgiven. Under the law, I have the right to remove trespassers from my land by any means I deem necessary. I regret to inform you that you are not welcome here, and I must ask you to return to your place of origin," the Lady said.

"My place of origin? You mean my home? I no longer have one," Slee said. She stood tall with both fists curled, making no sign that she intended to move.

"That is not my concern. You have been warned. If you continue to refuse to leave my land, I shall have no choice but to authorize deadly force," the Lady said.

Fentor took half a step forward, holding the rifle ready.

"No laws or deeds could give you the right to poison this lake," Slee said. "I'm not moving until it stops."

Lady Talentus and the half-elf faced one another, a juxtaposition of such extreme opposites that any poet would call it trite. The Lady stood with the noble bearing suited to her birth and station, cool, rod-straight, and poised. Slee all hunched and tense, was overcome by the heat of her irrational passions. She wore a silent snarl that would have looked more fitting on an enraged badger.

"Fentor." The Lady inclined her head slightly in Slee's direction.

Fentor came forward once more, and aimed the rifle at Slee. The bayonet grazed her nose. She neither flinched nor stepped back, even when drops of blood wetted the blade.

A great rumbling shook the earth beneath Fentor's feet, and his first thought was that there had been an explosion in the distillery. In the next moment, though, he saw that the massive tortoise had sprung forward and was now towering over him. Two massive, golden eyes glared down at him, and Fentor was almost overcome by the instinct to avert his eyes. It would have been easier to stare at the sun.

"Hold your fire, Capilet," the Lady drawled.

The tortoise snorted with enough force to blow the hat off Fentor's head.

Biting his tongue and tensing his legs to conceal their trembling, he turned his focus to the half-elf at the end of his rifle.

How on earth could she stand at the end of a loaded rifle without so much as blinking?

Either she sincerely believed a lake was worth dying for, or she had lived alone so long in the woods that it had warped her mind. It now seemed entirely out of the question that the Elarím might have send her. They sent showers of arrows, not envoys dressed in rags.

"Do it," Slee hissed, eyes wide and teeth bared. She pressed her nose harder against the bayonet, shaking as though a storm was trapped in her body. "Shoot me. See how Slowjaw here responds."

Fentor's finger wandered close to the trigger.

"Stand down, Fentor," the Lady said quietly.

He stepped back once more and held his rifle to his chest, point upward. The Lady's understated, melodic command produced silence and stillness at once.

"You are more than a simple hermit with concerns, are you not?" the Lady said. Her eyes flashed as she looked up at the colossal tortoise, and then back down to Slee.

"What are you talking about?" Slee spat.

"Your arrival here was not by chance. And these animals are something more than simple pets or livestock. They are something … stranger," the Lady said.

"For the first time, you're right. But what does it matter?"

"Magic led you here. Elven magic."

Slee shrugged, and said, "That is no secret."

"It is all too clear why you have come here. You are spy sent by the Elarím," the Lady said.

Fentor, despite all his better instincts, shared a glance with Dídac behind the Lady's back. Both raised their eyebrows slightly, then resumed neutral expressions. It seemed they had shared the same thought: *Surely the Lady knows that's not true?*

Fentor shuddered at the idea of agreeing with Dídac. He needed a bath.

The half-elf scoffed. "I am no more Elarím than you are!"

"Perhaps not, but you *were* sent by them. Nothing else can account for such bizarre events," the Lady said. She tilted her head slightly, hands behind her back. To Fentor, it looked as though she was assessing the flaws of a mildly engaging work of art.

"No one sent me," Slee said. "I came because I had to."

"Enough time has been wasted on this. Dídac, apprehend her," the Lady said.

As Dídac started forward, Slee jabbed a finger in his face and said, "Don't lay a hand on me!"

Dídac grabbed her wrist, then twisted it. Slee cried out. One instant later, her tortoise opened its enormous mouth and let out a roar so loud that the lake's surface rippled, and the gravel underfoot shivered. Fentor was so overwhelmingly deafened that he went half-blind, as well.

There was a great flurry of colorful feathers, as a quacking object flew through the air. Fentor, dazed and disoriented, raised his rifle and fired.

A stunned silence followed, as the tortoise ceased its roar, and all eyes watched the plumed peaduck flop onto the gravel.

"Felheim!" Slee screamed. She reached out for the duck, which fell a few paces away from her.

Dídac wrestled with her, twisting her arm behind her back and forcing her to the ground. The half-elf all but ignored him, calling the duck's name over and over until her voice cracked, reaching pitifully toward the motionless creature.

At that moment, Fentor was struck in the chest by a battering ram.

He landed on his back with a jolt that drove the breath from his lungs. With his hands wrapped around his belly, he rolled over in time to see his rifle snapped into splinters by the tortoise's massive jaws. The 'battering ram,' it seemed, had been the beasts' massive head colliding with him as it snatched the gun from his hands.

The monstrous reptile advanced on Fentor, who still could not draw a breath, let alone escape. He could only watch as a scaly foot the size of a tree stump rose above his head, blotting out the light of the sun, then came down with great force.

A slender, pale hand halted the foot's progress with grace and ease. Fentor gaped at the Lady Talentus, who held the tortoise's limb aloft as though it weighed no more than a silver platter. The beast strained against her hold, but the Lady was unaffected.

She took the tree-trunk sized leg in both hands, and threw it upward so hard that the tortoise fell onto its back with a thunderous crash. The flock of tawny ducks took flight just before the impact, and scattered in all directions. Some books which had been lashed to the great green shell came fell to the gravel.

"How?" Fentor gasped.

In answer, the Lady Talentus pulled a small, empty vial from her pocket. A cool smile crossed her face, and a strangely crystalline glint came to her eye.

Slee, now gagged and bound, strained against her bonds and tried to scream through the cloth stuffed in her mouth. Dídac stood, pink-faced and panting, with his foot on her back.

"Well done, Dídac," Lady Talentus said, brushing dust from her clothes with small, delicate motions.

The tortoise flailed its legs and cried out pitifully. It arched its neck and rocked its massive bulk side to side in futile attempts to get back on its feet. The feeble noises that gurgled in its throat sounded partway between sobs and the toneless notes of a rusted trumpet.

Fentor regained his breath and his feet at last, and looked down at the brutish creature without a shred of pity.

Then, as though by sheer will, the tortoise began to rock in greater and greater arcs, until it was on the cusp of turning back onto its feet.

"I rather think this is an opportunity to properly test the potency of the Elixir," the Lady said.

Rubbing her hands like a gymnast, she approached the edge of the enormous, wobbling shell. She took hold of it, and the rocking stopped. Then, with one mighty heave, she lifted the entire tortoise above her head. It looked as easy as lifting a bag of flour. She crouched, then sprang up and launched the tortoise high into the air. Hundreds of pages torn from the books on the creature's back fluttered away on the wind.

The sight of watching such an immense creature sail so far left Fentor breathless.

The tortoise turned over and over in the air, seeming almost weightless. Then it landed with a crash that threw up great sheets of gravel and shook the earth.

Deaf to the desperate, muffled cries of the half-elf, Lady Talentus studied her own hands with wide eyes, spellbound by them, as though she had never seen them before.

Chapter 16

Not far from the distillery, there was a small, hidden place in the shadow of a crooked tree. Its weathered trunk was bent like an old man's spine, as though it was tired of holding its heavy boughs up for so long. The tree's leaves were still healthy and dense. Moss and pine needles softened the ground. It was sheltered, not only from the wind, but also the eyes of humans. It was a good place.

Felheim couldn't care for the flock. That meant it fell to his mate, Gretka. Once she had found the spot under the crooked tree, she had gathered all the other peaducks and brought them there. Then, with two of her daughters, she went to retrieve Felheim's body.

Quacking softly to one another in the shadow of the pines by the lake, they first made sure that no humans were lurking nearby. Felheim's body was unwatched, discarded, a ruffled lump of feathers and flesh on the pale gravel. Slowjaw, though, was nowhere to be seen.

The peaducks waddled up to the disturbed gravel where the tortoise had fallen, sniffing carefully around the area. They found no scent they could follow, so they hurried to Felheim.

As Gretka drew close to her mate, he lifted his head feebly and met her eye.

She could hardly contain her quacks. She rushed to his side, flapping to speed her along. The other peaducks soon caught up, and together they fell upon him with a flurry of affectionate nibbles. Felheim's breathing was labored, his feathers were matted with blood, and when he opened his bill to quack, he made no noise. He could only manage to blink.

They took hold of him with great care, took flight, and carried him back to the hidden place under the crooked tree.

A great chatter of excited quacks greeted their arrival, and Felheim was swarmed as every peaduck jostled to nuzzle him or preen his feathers. Gretka spread her wings and ordered them to leave him be with a series of stern quacks.

The peadrake's wound gave him great pain. The hurt filtered through the threads of their shared bond, but without Slee or Slowjaw, the bond was too weak to bring relief.

Gretka was heartbroken. Her mate, so strong and fearless, had faced the enemy without a second thought. But the fight was cut short before it had a chance to begin. His wound, dealt at a distance, was not a fair reward for his courage.

She nestled in close beside him. The bullet had pierced his wing close to the shoulder, passed through and then grazed his back. The wound smelled like many human things did — metallic, artificial, *wrong*.

On a bed of pine needles and moss, the peaducks huddled together and tucked their bills under their wings. Gretka took on as much of Felheim's pain as she could, and the rest of the flock did their best as well. Soon, they settled into a sort of shared hibernation, their only refuge against the strange, uncaring world.

They did not have Slee, or Slowjaw, or the garden, but they had each other.

****

In the stone corridor which led to the detainment cell, with everything washed blue by the strange light, attended by a host of echoed footsteps, Fentor could not suppress a little shiver. It seemed more like the lair of some fairy-tale wizard than a state-of-the-art alchemy facility.

The half-elf had already been escorted into her cell. Lady Talentus stopped Fentor and Dídac halfway along the passage. Between her flawless posture, refined features, and the diffuse phosphorescence illuminating her, she looked more like a statue of herself than ever. A perfect likeness, but artificial.

"We have precious little time to spend on questioning this … anomaly," she said, wafting a hand in the direction of the cell. "Do not forget, our Good King Philliby will soon outlaw our enterprise."

As she led them to the dungeon, Dídac elbowed Fentor out of the way for the privilege of being one step closer to the Lady. Fentor bit his tongue to halt a gasp of pain. His ribs were still bruised from his encounter with the giant terrapin.

The detainment cell was an early feudal dungeon in all but name. It was a large space, dark and cold, lit only by a small, barred window near the ceiling. There was no ghostly blue glow to banish the shadows in the far corners. Long chains with shackles hung at intervals along the wall. Fentor counted twenty-four pairs. The intruder had not been expected, but clearly, the need for a dungeon had been anticipated. Who had the Lady been intending to shackle in there?

The half-elf, iron cuffs on her wrists, sat hugging her knees, with her face hidden.

"What did the Elarím offer you?" the Lady asked.

Slee made no response.

"How long have you been their spy?"

Silence.

"Perhaps the Elarím did not send you, but *someone* did. Who?"

She gave no answer.

The Lady continued to ask similar questions, and the half-elf remained motionless and silent.

"My Lady, if I may have a brief word?" Fentor asked, struck by an idea.

Lady Talentus looked him up and down for a moment, then nodded. In the far end of the shadowy dungeon, Fentor grimaced and pulled at the end of his moustache, as though he was weighing his words.

"Out with it, Fentor," she said.

"It's just, I wonder if she refuses to speak because certain parties are present," Fentor whispered—a deliberately loud, carrying whisper. He nodded meaningfully toward Dídac.

The Lady, half-covered in shadow, said nothing. Despite the risks of speaking out of turn, he chose to push his luck.

"Who knows what she might think of an elf like Dídac? A traitor to the cause, perhaps, in her eyes," Fentor said.

A full minute passed as the Lady deliberated, during which time Fentor enjoyed the puckered, bitter look on Dídac's face.

"Very well," she said.

The Lady dismissed Dídac. He graciously accepted the order to her face, then shot a caustic scowl at Fentor behind her back. The heavy dungeon door closed behind him.

Slee slowly raised her head. Fentor could have punched the air in jubilation. Dried blood stained her chin, and dried tear trails coated her cheeks. Her eyes, which had recently held such volatile and frenetic rage, were now flat, almost lifeless.

"Are you ready to tell us who sent you?" the Lady said.

The half-elf nodded, sagging her shoulders and dropping her gaze, as though ashamed.

Fentor held his breath. The Lady would have her answer, all thanks to Fentor's suggestion. Dídac would never forget how he had been outmanoeuvred. Fentor would make sure of it.

Slee's lips moved, but she only produced a thin rasping sound. She beckoned the Lady closer. When she did not move, the half-elf gestured more urgently, saying something in a voice too raw to rise above a whisper.

Her Excellency Lady Talentus had probably never crouched to let someone whisper in her ear in all her life. Indeed, she stood so straight and tall, Fentor wondered if her spine and joints were even capable of crouching. After a moment of hesitation, the Lady sank to one knee, and offered her ear to the captive.

Slee lunged at the Lady with clawed hands. Lady Talentus smoothly stepped out of reach, but the half-elf continued to rake the air where her throat had been.

The Lady tutted, and straightened her jacket. "I ought to have expected such behavior."

Slee sagged back against the wall, her face gnarled with loathing.

"We have wasted enough time," the Lady said gently.

With a crisp nod to Fentor, she made for the door. He followed closely behind, then paused by the door to look back at the half-elf.

Her glaring eyes and bared teeth produced a strange effect in Fentor. In the way a yawn is echoed by those nearby, or a laugh spreads like contagion, he began to feel somehow infected by her festering rage. It radiated from her like heat from a furnace. He could almost see a dull, reddish glow spreading through the dungeon, could hear blood pounding in his ears. His lip began to curl, his shoulders began to tense.

He stepped out into the clammy corridor, and the feeling was gone.

Around the corner from the detainment cell was a guarded room that Lady Talentus referred to as 'the pantry.' It turned out to be half-armory, half-storeroom, filled with racks of guns, shelves of cheese and other sundries, sacks of oats, and crates labelled: 'Caution! Explosive Bluepowder Within. Handle Gently.'

Dídac paced among the shelves with a discerning frown, prodding things, smelling them, and weighing them in his hands. He looked like a merchant inspecting his wares.

"Take what you need, Fentor. We shall be setting off shortly," Lady Talentus said.

Fentor was drawn at once to the guns. Many were standard-issue, but a few had a sleek, alluring look Fentor had never seen before. The barrels shone like silver, and the stocks were tapered and curved, like shapely legs peeking from under a skirt. Instead of iron sights, each had a ring of curved glass fixed to the top, something like a monocle. As Fentor reached out to caress one of the weapons, he felt somewhat scandalous.

Lady Talentus drew up beside him, took one of the guns, and inspected it from every angle. "These were custom-made for our use. The alloy in an invention of mine called 'Aurinium', which can withstand the ignition of triple-enriched bluepowder."

"They are marvellous," Fentor said.

"Here," she said, handing him the rifle, then she took one for herself. "A word of caution — do not attempt to fire it unless you have taken a dose of the elixir. The recoil, I'm told, is capable of slicing one's arm clean off the shoulder."

It was heavier than it had appeared. Looking through the glass sights, he found that they magnified the target considerably.

As Fentor explored the gun, clicking the hammer and opening the frizzen, Lady Talentus addressed Dídac.

"The half-elf is unlikely to volunteer the information we need," the Lady said.

"Precisely my thinking, my Lady."

"Do what you must. Those who sent her may come looking when she doesn't return. Whoever it is — elf or otherwise — you are authorized to use any necessary force. This facility *must* remain secret," Lady Talentus said.

"Understood, my Lady."

"Good."

A few minutes later, Lady Talentus and Fentor were armed and provisioned. Fentor dressed himself in an available grey overcoat, packed his own rucksack with rations, and stocked his own ammunition and weapons. Dídac did all these things for the Lady, fussing over her like an overly eager butler.

They made their way back to the cavernous Extraction Chamber, where Galton was waiting with a tray of thin glass bottles of elixir. Lady Talentus opened her overcoat and stowed twelve of them in special loops that had been sewn into the lining. Fentor, concealing his disappointment, took the remaining six.

"That will be all, Galton. We must depart at once," Lady Talentus said.

Galton barked an order, and every Bluefinger in the room stood at attention. Then, at another bark, they lifted hands stained by bluepowder in a salute. Many eyes glistened with the tears of those overcome by patriotism or religious fervor.

Lady Talentus headed for the spiral stairs, walking so smoothly that she might have been floating. Her eyes fell upon the Bluefingers with a sapphire glint, accepting their salutes as a monarch might accept rose petals. Fentor followed her, basking in the reflected glow of adoration and awe directed at the Lady. One day the spotlight would shine on him. He would make sure of it.

The hard vials of elixir pressed into his chest, clinking gently as he walked. He could not help but be aware of their presence. Nor could he keep himself from imagining what it might feel like to drink them. How had Lady Talentus felt, tossing that enormous tortoise through the air as though it weighed no more than a kitten?

When Fentor had first fired a rifle as a lad, and seen the bullet-hole in the target, he had felt such a rush of pleasure. Father had explained that it was the feeling of power, which all men crave. Now he knew that a lifetime of firing muskets had been a mere appetizer.

As he looked around, all the tearful, saluting soldiers appeared to be wreathed in a diffuse golden light. The taste of glory teased his tongue—a single drop spilled from the cup of the gods.

Soon, the apparition was complete. As he followed Lady Talentus out of the distillery, onto the pale gravel and along the shores of the lake, a phantom crowd blew trumpets, threw confetti, and cheered Fentor's name.

The gilded path to glory stretched out before him, beckoning, promising to lead him at last to the victory he had so long been entitled to.

Chapter 17

Slowjaw blinked and looked around. He tried to remember where he was, but he couldn't. It was a dark place with lots of trees. It wasn't Slee's garden.

Something really hurt. His belly-shell had been cracked, and all his insides felt bruised. Breathing hurt. It hurt a great deal, but he had to keep breathing anyway. So he kept breathing, kept looking, and kept trying to remember. It was all very hard.

Then he remembered. Two bad humans and a bad elf. They shot a gun and hit Felheim. Slee was thrown to the ground. Where were they?

Then he had dragged himself into the forest so he could hide. He must have fallen asleep.

The dark trees crowded all around him like strangers. Scary things might have been hiding in all the shadows. But if Slowjaw stayed put, he would never find Slee or the peaducks.

He raised his heavy head and bugled in the tongue of tortoises, *Slee? Felheim? Where are you?*

No answer came. He called again, even though it hurt his belly. Still no answer.

He stood up. His legs were shaky and sore, and they couldn't hold him up. He fell back to the ground heavily, making a lot of pine needles jump up.

It was getting close to sun-down time. Would he be stuck there all night?

Slee? Slee! Where are you? Please help me! I'm hurt! He called again and again, as loud as his sore throat would allow.

Slee was in trouble. That was why she hadn't come. She needed him more than he needed her. How could he lie there and expect her to do everything for him?

He tried to stand again. His belly felt like a cracked egg, ready to split open and spill out his inside on the ground. Something smelled like blood. Everything quickly went dark, even though the sun wasn't gone.

Slee? Where are you?

He dragged himself along the ground, half-blind and weak and sore. He was also getting sleepy, but he was afraid of closing his eyes. He didn't want to be alone. He wanted the garden. He wanted Slee.

As big and strong as his legs usually were, they failed. He couldn't move them at all. Big tears fell from his eyes as he pulled his head back into his shell. It was hopeless. It was the end.

Sorry, Slee. Sorry, he mumbled into a heap of pine needles.

It was his job to protect her and he did it badly. He cried and cried until his eyes were too heavy to hold up. It made him so sleepy that he forgot about his sore belly. Maybe it wouldn't be too bad to rest his eyes.

He closed his eyes, and everything went dark.

****

Slee hammered one manacle against the other until her hands and wrists throbbed. She continued until they stung with pins and needles, and then until they went numb altogether. The shackles did not dent or show any sign of damage. Soon the mindless, clashing rhythm served more as a ritual to channel her rage than a true escape attempt. After all, she was keenly aware of the bars on the window, the locks on the door, and the humans guarding her. The moment she stopped trying, though, would be an admission that she had abandoned her animals.

Slowjaw's distinctive, trumpeting call came as though from a great distance. Slee had barely heard it over the clanking chains. She held still, straining her ears. The longer she waited without hearing a second call, the surer she was that she had imagined it.

As the silence wore on, the lack of telethí became impossible to ignore. After years of cultivating connections to living things, immersing herself in the ebb and flow of animus, she felt airless, desolate, forsaken. She was as dead as the stone she sat on, cold as the iron on her wrists. The depths of her isolation eventually confused her senses. Her vision went numb, her hearing itched, and her body could not see.

241

She bashed her shackles together, as hard as she could, over and over. The sharp pain in her wrists was a welcome relief.

The heavy lock on the dungeon door clicked, and it opened. The pale elf called Dídac, who wore human clothes and a human look of contempt, came in. He stood by the threshold, looking her over with pale, grey eyes.

A human wearing a grey coat came in, bearing a tray with scraps of bread, hard cheese, and a clay cup. The soldier set the tray down by Slee's feet, then turned and left. The door was locked, and she was alone with the elf.

"Who sent you?" he asked in a thin, nasal voice.

Slee did not say a word.

"You know, we might have avoided all this unpleasantness if you'd only answered the first time you were asked. Tell me now, and we can settle this affair. Who sent you?" he said.

"No one sent me," she said.

He sucked in his thin, anemic cheeks, briefly giving him the look of a skull in a wig. "I see," he said with exaggerated cadence. "*No one* sent you."

The elf paced back and forth, as though lost in thought.

"I wonder — did the Elarím promise to reverse your exile?" he said.

"There's nothing to reverse. I never lived among them," she said.

"*Liar*," he breathed, grey eyes flashing. He paused in his pacing, perhaps to accentuate his accusation, then continued. "What did you do that was worth the sentence of exile?"

"I was *never* exiled."

"Oh, and I suppose you freely chose to grub in the dirt, dressed in rags, eating nothing but weeds and duck's eggs?" Dídac said. "Is that what you're telling me?"

Slee said nothing.

"Nobody chooses to live like that. You were exiled. You can't have lived with the humans. I know what happens to those with pointed ears. You must have lived with the Elarím, and been expelled," Dídac said. He crouched close to her, eyes wide. "Tell the truth."

"Why were *you* exiled?" Slee said.

Dídac stared at her.

"That's why you work for the humans, isn't it?" Slee said.

The elf raised an open hand and braced himself, as though preparing to strike her. She blinked and tensed up reflexively, but did not cower.

Dídac let his hand fall, then resumed pacing. He pointed at the food tray.

"Aren't you going to eat? All the excitement must have made you hungry," Dídac said.

Slee, seized by a defiant impulse, kicked the tray. It shot across the stone floor, scattering the bread and cheese and breaking the cup.

"Temper, temper," Dídac tutted. "Go hungry, then."

"If I starve, you'll be rid of me," she said.

"That is a fair point. However, I'm prepared to force your dinner down your throat if that's what it takes to get an answer." He stooped, grabbed her face, and forced her to meet his eyes. "Who sent you?"

"Nature sent me," Slee spat, scowling deeply. "You broke her highest law."

Dídac released her and backed away, eyes wide. For a moment, something other than petty scorn flashed across his pale eyes. A bare, quiet look, almost like confusion. The next moment, the demeanor he had been taught by his human masters returned, and he slapped her.

She curled up as he kicked her again and again with his heavy boots. The blunt pain of his assault shocked her at first, and she cried out. As it continued, she focused on keeping silent and showing no reaction. Eventually the attack was over.

"You will tell me who sent you," he said between wheezing breaths. "Or that will be my daily gift to you."

The heavy lock clicked, Dídac left the room, and she was alone again.

Even the slightest motions provoked sharp aches in her ribs, so she kept still. She didn't even dare to breathe too deeply.

In the cold silence that followed, Slee instinctively reached out telethí threads so that she could share the pain with her animals and plants. Then she remembered — they were all gone. The agony was hers to bear alone. Just the thought that she couldn't be with them was worse than all the aches of her body.

Her longing was so overpowering that she kept imagining she could hear Slowjaw's long, mournful call in the distance.

Chapter 18

After a few hours of trudging through the pine forests, all thoughts of triumph and renown were gone. The glowing visions leaked out Fentor's ears and drifted away on the highland winds, like kites with severed strings. Instead of a cheering crowd, he'd acquired a fizzing swarm of midges. Lady Talentus, somehow, avoided their attention.

Elarím territory was still many days away on foot. Crann Arborím — whatever it was — would certainly be in the very heart of their lands. Fentor grew more and more certain that if elven arrows didn't finish him, trudging through clouds of midges day after day would. Something had to be done. Even a vague idea of where they were headed might make the ordeal bearable.

Crucially, he would have to approach the issue from a subtler angle than directly expressing impatience with insects.

"My Lady, I'm afraid a quandary of sorts has come to my attention," Fentor said. His vigorous swatting somewhat undercut his genteel tone.

"A quandary?" she said, as she avoided a low-hanging branch with a graceful bob like a ballerina's plié.

"A miniscule issue, really. It seems unlikely that we will reach our destination before the elixir is formally outlawed. How can we make it in time if we must proceed on foot?"

"This has just occurred to you?" the Lady asked.

They passed single-file under an arch formed between a half-fallen tree and the neighboring pine it leaned against. Fentor used the moment to grimace at his misstep. He had all but accused her of failing to consider something obvious.

"As - as I say, my Lady, the issue is surpassingly minor—"

"Do not address me in that way," she said. Then, she came to an abrupt stop, pulled out a spyglass covered in dials and switches, and surveyed the surrounding terrain. She clicked and turned the controls until, apparently satisfied, she nodded and stowed the gadget away.

"How shall I address you?" Fentor asked, baffled.

Without even a glance in his direction, Lady Talentus resumed a quick march at a sharp angle to the left of their previous bearing. Fentor hastened to catch up, slapping his midge-covered cheeks. If she intended to wrong-foot him, she was doing it well.

"Call me Elatea," she said.

"Very well … Elatea," Fentor said. He cringed, half-expecting a thunderbolt from Providence to strike him down. "May I ask why?"

"No. You may not."

They began ascending a steep hill, which took all of Fentor's spare breath. Lady Talentus — or rather, Elatea — climbed without breaking her usual stride. She reached the top as Fentor was still halfway up, negotiating with his burning legs, which were threatening to resign in protest.

Once again, she surveyed the surrounding lands through her curious spyglass. The moment Fentor crested the hill, Elatea started back down the way they'd come. Not wishing to groan or grumble, he channelled his despair into giving a midge on his arm an especially forceful smack.

"May I ask what you are using that rather unique spyglass for?" Fentor asked, after hurrying downhill to catch up with her.

"If it was necessary for you to know that, I'd already have told you."

"I understand. My apologies."

"A question is attempted theft, you know," she said sharply. "One party asks another for knowledge, and expects to receive it for free. That is theft. It's why we have patent laws."

"That is quite enlightening," he said, despite being thoroughly confused.

"If it were up to me, requesting a cup of sugar from a neighbor would carry the same sentence as pick-pocketing. The concept is little different." Elatea's jaw moved in a subtle, rhythmic way that looked as though she was gently chewing the inside of her cheek.

"Consider questions to be banished from my personal grammar," Fentor said. The instant the words left his mouth, he was suddenly bursting with questions.

"Good. Be grateful. The less you know, the less you'll be able to divulge if you are captured and tortured," Elatea said in a tone as gentle as the breeze.

Fentor wanted to ask: *Is that a likely outcome?*

Instead, he said, "I see."

They continued in silence for a time, crossing streams, vaulting over fallen logs, and marching under the branches of uniformly spaced pine trees. As charming as the landscape had first appeared when they arrived at the distillery, Fentor now found the woods to be unbearably dull. Between the prohibition of questions, the endless grey-brown carpet of pine needles crunching under his boots, and the incessant midges, Fentor seriously considered turning back.

Then, a brilliant idea came to his rescue.

He would use the old rhetorical trick of playing the fool. If he was careful, he could state things *just* obtuse enough to provoke Elatea into correcting him. The answers he craved would come without a single question asked.

"Crann Arborím must be well-guarded, as far from the Madean border as possible. I suggest we make for the cape on the north-eastern coast," Fentor said with great confidence.

"At the very edge of their domain? I think not. No creature keeps its beating heart in the tip of its tail," Elatea said.

They passed through a recess between steep, mossy rocks. Elatea halted and inspected their surroundings with her spyglass, then put it away and continued.

"We're fortunate indeed to have Dídac on our side. You must have been perceptive indeed to spare him from the firing squad, knowing how loyal he would become," Fentor said.

"Firing squad? Who told you that?" she said, shooting him a glance almost sharp enough to break the skin.

"I misspoke. I suppose I forgot the details of how you recruited him. With such wild rumours flying around about him, one can hardly be blamed," Fentor said.

"I never told you how I recruited him. I only said that he was a gamble that paid off."

"I do apologize, Your Excellency. Oh! I mean, Elatea," Fentor said. He made sure that she saw a self-conscious frown cross his face. She would, hopefully, think he was a foolish chatterbox, and not a sly fox pilfering answers from her.

They continued for a while without another word spoken. Fentor could only hope he had guessed right — that Elatea would not be able to resist correcting him.

At last, after consulting the spyglass once more, Elatea spoke. "Dídac was not a captive of war. I found him on the streets of Rodessia. He had blackened his hair with soot, and covered his ears with bandages, but there was no disguising his elven features. He held a sign which I remember to this day, which read, 'I will do *any* work for *any* pay.'

"As you might imagine, few accepted the offer of a poorly disguised elf. I spoke with him for a time, and confirmed my suspicion that he had been exiled. Banished from his home and his people for the crime of ambition. He had only wanted a better station in life. I offered it, and in return, I would receive his undying loyalty. No more and no less."

"Dídac is a true Madean at heart," Fentor said as sincerely as he could, though the words were as bitter as poison. He needed a stiff drink to wash out the aftertaste.

"He is indeed. I have shared this knowledge with you because it is instructive. I expect no less from you than the utter devotion Dídac affords me. Should I say the stars are spinning tops and the Earth rests upon a silver platter, you must accept that it is true. *That* is loyalty."

"You have my devotion, Elatea. Whole-heartedly." Fentor was a little relieved to say something true. Then, pressing his advantage, he risked it all, and said, "I see now why he shared the location of Crann Arborím with you."

She came to an abrupt stop, turned, and looked directly into his eyes. He felt something like a mouse transfixed by the gaze of a blue-eyed cat.

"I know what you are doing. Enough." Even though she spoke in an even, neutral tone, he felt his heart shrivel and freeze like an orchid in midwinter.

Then, leaving him to stew in his dismay, she performed a smart quarter-turn and once more peered at the surrounding forest with her spyglass. After a few minutes of turning the thimble-like dials and flicking the many switches, she nodded. With clockwork motions, she put away the spyglass, then pulled out a vial of the Elixir of Power.

"I have determined that we are not being observed," Elatea said. "Drink one of yours, and I shall share one of the elixir's many secrets."

Fentor seemed unable to direct his limbs to move. If they weren't being observed—if there were no enemies nearby—why would they drink elixir? A small lift of Elatea's eyebrows shocked him out of his daze.

He reflexively took out a potion and pulled the stopper off. Then, as Elatea raised hers to her lips, he followed suit. The Elixir of Power stung the gaps between his molars, burned his throat, and left a distinct aftertaste of polished silver.

At once, a vigorous shudder coursed through his core, and fiery heat spread to his extremities. Every muscle in his body simultaneously felt as hard and heavy as stone, while also feeling as light and flexible as a coiled spring. He saw the forest around him with truly new eyes. Not only did he have sharper vision, but he also saw each rock, leaf, twig, and tree as distinct, solitary objects, separate from their surroundings. It was like he could peer at every minute detail through a magnifying glass, while the rest of the world faded into a uniform grey void. For a few moments, he was thoroughly disoriented.

"Each bottle contains the distilled strength and endurance of five hundred soldiers. An entire cohort that fits in one's hand," Elatea said, flexing her hands slowly. "The dose remains potent until all that strength is spent."

"I feel as though I could topple the Rodessia lighthouse with a little push," Fentor said.

"The feeling is accurate. But I have other plans for this dose."

"Like what, precisely?" Fentor said.

The muscles at the corners of Elatea's mouth dimpled slightly as she tightened her lips. Fentor shook his head, trying to focus on more than the smallest details of her face. He had asked a question, and displeased her. Yet somehow, he did not care in the slightest.

"We are going to run," Elatea said, with delicate emphasis on each syllable. "We shall run farther and faster than anyone ever has before."

Chapter 19

*Hope does not end. If it ends, it was not
hope.*

Sage Nyendi

It was not true that the dungeon was entirely devoid of
life.

A rat lived there.

Slee first became aware of her cellmate when she heard
the quiet pitter-patter of small feet across the room. By the
slivers of moonlight coming in through the barred
window, she could sometimes see the outline of the little
creature. It moved furtively, in sudden spurts, nose
twitching. Through all her bruises and aches, Slee sensed
the rat's flickering life force. It only brought the smallest
measure of comfort, but it was better than being utterly
alone.

Hardly daring to breathe too loudly, Slee gently extended a thin strand of telethí to the rat, the way one might hold out a finger to a kitten. The pale thread snaked through the air toward the rat, as soft and ethereal as spider silk waving on a midnight breeze. The rat didn't respond. Even when the telethí passed right through it, there was no reaction. Living creatures could normally feel the touch of telethymia, the same way a daisy could feel the touch of the sun and know it was time to bloom.

The little rat must have closed itself off. Perhaps a lifetime of hardship had closed its mind, or perhaps it simply chose to live that way.

Whatever the case, Slee could only watch as the rat collected bits of bread and cheese that she had kicked across the room. What had been a paltry prisoner's supper was now a rat's midnight feast. At least the food was going to some good use. Slee had never been particularly sensitive to hunger, but watching the rat gnaw on scraps of bread made her stomach growl.

Dawn was hours away, and the cold grew more and more bitter. Slee kept her feet and hands tucked within the folds of her thin smock, but it could not keep properly warm. Her whole body throbbed in a constant aching tempo that was somehow hypnotic. The pain was sharpest where she could still feel the outline of Dídac's boot, and dullest where long contact with the hard floor made her numb. She could not tell which hurt worse.

Hours passed like an endless, hazy dream. The rat left as the sky began to brighten. Slee missed its company at once.

A distant shout drifted in through the window. More followed, some from elven throats and others from human ones.

Slee, realizing she was not dreaming, lifted her head and tried to listen. There was no way to discern what the faint voices were saying, but there was little need to. Humans and elves only met for one reason.

Her heavy heart almost convulsed, roused by a powerful, impossible, audacious surge of hope. Never in her life had she welcomed the arrival of elves, but in that moment, she could have cheered out loud.

Stiff and trembling, she eased herself upright, leaning heavily on the wall for support. The view through the barred window was limited, but she could see parts of the opposite shore of the lake. She leaned this way and that, as far as her chains would allow, but still could see nothing. The shouts continued, somewhere out of sight.

Then, with a sound like harpies wailing, a volley of bright red arrows flashed among the trees. In answer, guns barked and crackled, raising a cloud of blue-grey smoke. If any were killed in the exchange, Slee could not sense it.

The battle had begun. Slee stood with her shackled hands clasped to her chest, torn between her lifelong abhorrence of the war, and a sudden, ferocious desire to see the humans slaughtered.

****

Of all the intoxicating substances, Fentor was most familiar with alcohol. It whispered false praises, and

255

promised more than it could deliver. It was the friend who offered to pay for everything, only to vanish when the bill came. In one moment, it would convince you that you were charming, powerful, and graceful, only to betray you a moment later with charmless words and stumbling steps.

The Elixir of Power warmed him with a similar heady rush of certainty, strength, and prowess. The difference was, it kept every promise it made.

Elatea and Fentor hurtled between the trees, and sometimes broke right through them without breaking stride. Nothing compared with the savage pleasure of shooting through a fully-grown pine and shattering it into splinters. They had travelled in this way for hours and hours, all through the night and past the dawn. With the animus of an entire cohort condensed in his veins, Fentor needed no rest. Indeed, with his senses so sharpened, and the novelty of his immense strength, he hardly noticed time passing at all.

He was a bull charging through daisies; he was a flaming boulder shot from the belly of a volcano; he was a gale, a tempest, a force of nature.

Drunk on the savage pleasure of his stampede, he began to wonder why he had meekly agreed to stop asking questions. He was curious, and Elatea had the answers. If questions displeased her, then she was welcome to endure displeasure. What could she do to punish him, after all? Send him back? Kill him? No, if she had been able to complete her mission alone, she already would be alone.

The fact that she needed him proved he was safe. He was like collateral in some great loan she had taken on. Or, perhaps he *was* the loan? He shook his head. Thinking in terms of metaphor had become tricky. Either way, he was safe. Perhaps he *was* a safe, or he was locked *inside* a safe …

He cast off the strange thoughts and turned his attention to his surroundings. They had left the grey-brown, pine-dominated Madean Highlands and were now charging through a denser, wilder, more colorful woodland. His vision enlarged every detail as though seen through a spyglass. Fleeting images were caught in his mind as though encased in amber, or trapped in a spiderweb, or captured in a painting, or …

A dragonfly flew alongside him for a moment, its veiny wings beating sluggishly, the cells of its compound eyes reflecting Fentor's face. There was a tiny white flower filled with motes of yellow pollen, each unique and delicate. Fentor crushed it underfoot. There was a tree stump with a rusty brown ant climbing it. By coincidence, there was another ant right behind it, then another ant, then another. The moment before his foot crashed through the stump and reduced it to matchsticks and sawdust, he realized that the individual ants were actually part of a line, and had been climbing the stump together. After the splinters settled, he forgot all about it.

Kicking through the stump had taken some effort, and he felt a slight twinge in his toe. Soon after, his lungs began to burn, his legs began to ache, and his pace slowed to a trudge.

Elatea came to a stop, her face flushed pink, holding her ribs. Fentor drew up beside her, wheezing.

"Where are we?" Fentor asked.

She pointed at a nearby lump of vines and hanging lichen. "Close."

Fentor stared at the overgrown lump, and tried to make sense of her answer. Close to what, weeds?

Then he spied a cracked roof tile, a rotting windowsill, and a gaping black doorway. It was no lump, but an abandoned house, so overgrown that it had blended in with the surrounding greenery. The house was kidney-shaped, made with uneven timbers intact branches, and decorated with words in a foreign, curling script.

"An elf house," Fentor said.

"Astute as ever, Fentor," Elatea said. She had recovered her breath, and now the only sign of exertion were two small pink circles on her cheeks.

A moment later, Fentor turned and saw they were surrounded by a dozen half-rotten, ivy-strangled buildings. There was even a weedy gravel path winding between them, which should have been obvious. His eyes had seen only the individual rocks, not their function. As the Elixir of Power waned, his perceptions slowly returned to normal. Trees together made a forest; buildings together made a village. So strange that he had forgotten those things.

"Abandoned settlements like these litter the border. All that graffiti carved into the boards — they are the words of the great elven Sages, I'm told. Most common is the famous refrain, 'All life cares for all life.' " Elatea paced along the gravel path, looking down her nose at the nearest structures as though they were mildly engaging museum exhibits.

"A brilliant proverb if there ever was one," Fentor said sardonically. "Obviously, the wolf cares for the lamb, the leech for its host, and the vulture for its carrion."

"That it can be so easily disproven is the basis of its insidious power. Everything the Sages say follows this line of thought. Elves are expected to look at reality, reject it, and embrace the Common Power instead," Elatea said. " 'All life cares for all life' translates to 'All elves must obey.' "

"Obey *whom,* I wonder," Fentor said.

"They obey obedience itself. Leaderless rabbles cannot endure otherwise," Elatea said. "Do you see how imperative it is that we free them all from these bonds?"

"I had … never thought of it like that," Fentor said slowly. The question seemed to have sprung out of nowhere—a trap, surely. She had never before spoken of *freeing* the elves. What was she trying to snare him in?

Maddeningly, she fell silent. They strolled side by side through the dead village like sightseers. Each of the hollowed-out, crumbling buildings was stranger than the last. One resembled a stack of shelf mushrooms, made of linen, canvas, timber, and the trunk of a living tree. Another was a simple stone cottage that might have belonged to a Madean farmer. Another had no walls at all, consisting only of a circular, sunken pit with decaying furniture, and a canopy of thatch supported by timber beams sculpted to resemble coiled snakes.

At the end of the winding gravel path was a large clay dome, glazed and painted to resemble a tortoise shell. Inside there was a litter of discarded packets of Madean rations and tobacco, crumpled up paper, two thin bedrolls, and a heap of cold ashes.

"Patrols are sent through this place from time to time, but they needn't bother. The Elarím have not attempted to reclaim this territory in years," Elatea said.

The sight of a resting place, even one scattered with rubbish, was deeply tempting. Fentor wanted nothing more than to cast the pack of his aching shoulders and dive headlong into an eighteen-hour sleep. Elatea continued past the strange clay structure, and Fentor trudged onward. Between his aching feet, the straps cutting into his shoulders, and the increasing heaviness of his eyelids, he was rapidly approaching a mood that Methúsel called 'fussy.' In truth, fatigue and the fading elixir made him defiant.

As they left the overgrown ruins behind, he said, "I want to know about Crann Arborím. I think I've earned that knowledge."

Elatea fixed him a familiar stare, devoid of all expression and yet somehow able to congeal the air between them. Fentor met her eyes without flinching.

"In fairness, that was not a question," he said.

"I suppose it wasn't."

They came to a high ridge overlooking a heap of sharp rocks and tangled brambles, then turned to follow its length.

"Crann Arborím. The Secret Tree of Rubies. The nexus of the Common Power," Elatea said. "It is a loom that weaves the threads which bind the elves. It is a monument to the fallacy bred into every elven mind — the compulsion to stitch every free individual together into a single

subjugated, enthralled, uncontrolled, undifferentiated
mass."

"It's a real tree, then?" Fentor said.

"Perhaps, but most likely not. I anticipate that the name
is that most loathsome of devices — a metaphor."

"I take it you are not a great admirer of poetry?"

"Most verse is unbearable, but a select few poems are, at
least, engaging," Elatea said. "I can tolerate Saint Temlin's
Ode to the Alchemist, for instance."

The ground leveled out, and a large wall of brambles
came into view. The gnarled, weathered, branches curled
and coiled into an impenetrable barrier that stretched as
far as they could see. Thorns like iron spikes stuck out on
all directions. Fentor could almost feel their sharpness just
by looking at them.

"There it is," Elatea said. "Beyond is Elarím territory."

"And Crann Arborím, wherever it might be," Fentor
said, his voice soured by fatigue and a pervasive feeling
that everything in life was unfair. "I wish I knew."

"So do I," Elatea said, with a sapphire glint in her eye
that *might* have been amusement.

She took out a bottle of the Elixir of Power and held it
up to the light. She looked as though she was searching
the liquid for a speck of something elusive.

"The Common Power has ways of keeping its secrets,"
Elatea said. "Much is locked inside those borders — the
elves, the prisoners, and even certain kinds of knowledge.
Even exiles that have been cast out of the Common Power
find their memory to be patchy, their lips unable to shape
certain words. But as with all things kept behind a lock
without a key, one need only apply sufficient force."

"You mean Dídac…?"

"He was a willing volunteer. I took nothing from him that he did not ask me to take. Elves respond differently to pain than humans, you know — it was quite a riveting set of boundaries to test." Elatea drank the elixir, then closed her eyes and tilted her head back as a shiver moved through her.

Fentor averted his eyes, feeling as though he had witnessed something private. He hastened to take his own dose of the Elixir of Power. Instantly, he was alert, strong, and brimming with a restless and relentless energy that craved release. All of a sudden, the massive hedge of thorns looked less like a daunting wall of barbs, and more like a bouquet of fingers beckoning him forward. Destiny called, and he would answer.

"I may not know precisely where Crann Arborím is," Elatea said, with a hint of a smile lurking around the corners of her mouth. "But I know how to find it."

Chapter 20

The early morning battle on the shores of Bianlock, among shadows, shafts of slanting light, and silver clouds of discharged gunpowder, seemed more like a skirmish between ghosts than one between elves and men. Slee strained against her shackles and stood on her tiptoes, desperate to make sense of the whip-crack of gunfire and the shriek of blood-red arrows. The window was too small, and the bars sliced her view into pieces. There was no way to get a sense of the whole. She could hardly tell how many were fighting, let alone which side might have the advantage.

She caught a glimpse of a dozen soldiers in grey coats speeding around the edge of the lake, led by the silver-haired Dídac. She lost sight of them, and held her breath. A few minutes passed. Then, a series of deep blasts shook the trees. There was a short pause, and then came another thundering salvo.

Silence fell. Large clouds of gunpowder smoke drifted between the trees; a silvery gasp expelled from the lungs of dying ghosts. Slee realized then, with a deep pounding in her chest, why the battle had felt ethereal, imagined. She *knew* there had been death, but she had not *felt* it happen. Without telethymic connections to the world, the violent end of the battle had no substance. She willed herself to care for the dead strangers, but her heart remained hollow.

The stinging cold of the air pricked and prodded her skin, so she curled up on the floor once more. Just like Slowjaw would retreat into his massive shell, she pulled her hands and feet into the relative warmth of her clothes. Whatever hope had been flickering in her chest, it was now cold ashes. No one was coming to her rescue.

Numb hours passed with no life, no movement. The only interruption was when an unshaven soldier brought Slee food, water, and a thin blanket. His slow-blinking, red-rimmed eyes made it look as though he hadn't slept in days.

In spite of the hunger clawing her insides like an iron rake, she set aside a crust of bread and a corner of cheese from her daily meal. She tucked them inside her smock. Hunger hurt, but isolation was worse. With luck, the rat might visit again. That thought kept Slee from eating the scraps.

There were handfuls of seeds in her pockets, too. Some were edible. What kept her from eating them, she did not fully know. She simply couldn't bring herself to eat them.

She needed to plant them in the new garden. If she ate them, there was no garden.

As a result, she sat wrapped tightly in the blanket and her thoughts. She thought of the bread, the cheese, the seeds, the hunger, the rat, and the bread. Hours passed while she was stuck in the loop.

A passage of some half-remembered philosophy followed the trail of thoughts, like dried leaves caught in a vortex of wind. *The Self moves only in relation to the Other. Without the Other, there is no movement. The Self is defined only in relation to the Other. Without the Other, the Self remains undefined …*

The door opened, and Dídac entered. Her strange hunger-induced trance broke.

For a long while, he stood with his hands clasped behind his back and a hawkish glint in his eye. He looked at her as though he was about to pounce on her in a flash of talons.

"There were no survivors," Dídac whispered. "Such a shame. You would have appreciated a cellmate or two, I'm sure."

Slee remained silent and stone-faced.

"At least, in death, they spared me the tedious chore of questioning you," Dídac said. "I'm no logician, but I have a fair idea of why they came here so shortly after you did. Cause precedes effect."

Slee did not react. She could have insisted that she was not Elarím, that the elves had not come there for her. But Dídac, with his angular face set in a triumphant sneer, would never believe it.

"No tears for your fallen allies?" Dídac said, closing the distance between them with slow, deliberate steps. The hard click of polished boots on stone punctuated his words. "I can hardly blame you. It's cold outside the Common Power. Isolation is bleak, especially to those who cannot recognize the freedom it comes with. Few exiles last. They would do anything to be welcomed back into that warm embrace."

He dropped to one knee—beyond where she could reach—and studied her with narrowed eyes.

Now that he was closer, Slee could sense his presence, but not in the usual way. Whatever half-dormant telethymic perception she still had, it registered Dídac as a dark spot. He was unlike all other living things, which glowed with at least *some* telethí strands. Rather, he was a sinkhole, a place where light was drawn in and extinguished.

Looking in his pale grey eyes, she saw that same cold nothingness.

"The humans don't understand it. They *can't* understand it. I, at least, know what drove you," Dídac said. "*All life cares for all life,* after all."

"You haven't got the slightest idea of what drives me," Slee spat, her throat rough from disuse.

"Perhaps, perhaps not." Dídac placed his hands on his knee, then stood with a theatrical sigh. "In truth, I could hardly care less. Now that I have everything I need from you, I am *thrilled* to bid you farewell. Enjoy your new home."

He turned to leave.

"Kill me," Slee hissed.

Dídac stopped, turned sharply, his thin lips curling with the beginnings of derisive laughter. "Who are *you* to make demands of *me*?"

"You must kill me or let me go," Slee said. A savage heat had built up inside Slee, until her heart pounded and her ears burned. She would *not* be discarded so easily. If she could never be free, then she would rather use her remaining freedom to demand death than obediently waste away. "What will you do, feed me scraps until I perish? Save yourself the trouble of starving me and kill me now. Or, if you lack the stomach, admit as much and let me go."

Dídac looked as though his feet had been nailed to the floor. He leaned slightly, first one way and then the other, the bitter smirk frozen on his face. His pale, thin fingers twitched and flexed at his sides, as though preparing to strangle, break, and tear. At last, he faced the door, and expelled a long hiss between his teeth.

"A tempting thought. But it's not your decision to make," he said, still facing away from her.

"It's not yours either, is it? You need the Lady's say-so. Why, I'd wager you aren't allowed to use the chamber pot without her permission," Slee said.

Dídac stormed to the door, wrenched it open, and slammed it behind him.

Seeing him so affected gave her a few glowing minutes of vindictive pleasure. Then, as all the warmth and defiance slowly leeched out of her into the stones and iron chains, she curled up once more. She withdrew into herself, body and mind, until she was an unfeeling, unthinking lump.

The minutes dripped by like an hourglass filled with cold lard. *All life cares for all life.* The words had lost all meaning, but they echoed around the dungeon walls all the same. Sometimes, they came in Mama's voice, and sometimes in Dídac's.

At dusk, a small, flitting movement by the window caught her eye. For a minute, everything was still. Then, a little grey creature darted in through the window and down the wall, where it twitched in the dark corner. Two pinprick points of light stared out at Slee.

The sudden appearance of the rat struck her like lightning from a clear sky. She was paralyzed for a moment. Then, she slowly took out the crumbs of food she had saved. With controlled, gentle movements, she set the food down nearby, then waited. She stilled her breath, her body, and her mind as much as she was able.

The little rat took a few tentative steps forward, pink nose twitching. A small spark of animus trembled within the rat, weak as a guttering candle flame.

To Slee's telethymic sense, it was like seeing the sun after spending days in the dark.

****

The brambles grown by the elves were fruitless, leafless, gnarled tangles of knotted branches with spikes that could skewer a chicken. They had been bred to form a foreboding, impenetrable barrier around the Elarím lands. Breaking through them proved no obstacle for Fentor, however. He made it through to the other side without a scratch.

268

His clothes had not fared quite as well.

The sleeves of his coat were shredded to ribbons. His trousers were filled with holes, some large enough to put his hand through. His rucksack had picked up so many thorns, it looked like an overgrown hedgehog was riding on his back.

Elatea's clothes were similarly tattered. The tears in her clothes revealed patches of porcelain skin, from which Fentor averted his eyes. If she felt self-conscious about her torn clothes, she showed no sign of it.

They continued through the increasingly dense foliage at a gallop that rivalled King Philliby's prize racehorses. Tiny, isolated details still caught Fentor's eye. He did his best to remain unfocused, to look at nothing in particular. With his vision so discombobulated, the forest melted into a continuous blur, as though smeared by a painter's brush loaded with green. He followed in Elatea's wake, through clouds of fine splinters caused by her violent passage through the trees.

Without warning, Elatea dug in her heels and cried, "Stop!"

She swung out her arm, catching Fentor painfully in the chest like a steel girder, driving out his breath. There was a crunching sound, and the front of Fentor's clothes grew wet.

They both came to a stop mere inches from the edge of a cliff. One more step, and Fentor would have barrelled over the edge, plunging into the deep ravine below.

At the bottom, a narrow river studded with sharp rocks sparkled in the sunlight. Across the gap, at the cliff opposite, the dense forest continued. The river and the ravine happened to follow the exact same, curving shape. Fentor thought it an odd coincidence. What were the chances of a watery thing and a rocky thing following the same line? Rivers and canyons were different things. They couldn't communicate, let alone cooperate in the construction of a gorge.

It must have been like Saint Chandon said: Providence owns the secrets of nature, and mortals may only lease them.

Elatea cleared her throat and picked a few leaves from her hair. "We'd have survived the fall, of course, but it would have wasted valuable elixir."

Fentor peeled his soaking coat from his chest. Two of his remaining vials had been smashed to pieces, while another had cracked and was slowly leaking. Only one was left intact. Elatea sniffed at the blue liquid staining Fentor's front.

"You ought to be more careful," Elatea said icily.

Fentor gaped at the soggy mess. Gripped by an overwhelming urge to somehow undo the damage, he opened the cracked vial and downed it, then licked the excess from his palms. Then he wadded up his dripping clothes and sucked the liquid out of them. Elatea wrinkled her nose, but he didn't care. Was he supposed to let it all go to waste?

When he had extracted all the elixir he could, he cleared his throat and straightened his coat in an attempt to regain his composure. "See? No real harm done," he said.

"No real harm? Half of the priceless potions I entrusted to you have been broken. Do you have any idea how many crowns' worth of damage that is?" Elatea breathed.

"Perhaps there were blunders on both sides," Fentor said, shrugging with controlled affability. Hopefully, he could defuse both Elatea's rage and his own. Spiteful words began slowly worming their way up from the pit of his gut to his lip. If he accused her of carelessly breaking the vials and then blaming him for it, then he would most likely find himself flung over the edge.

"What blunder, precisely, was there on my side?" Elatea said.

"Never mind all that! After all, it was Saint Pembly who once said, 'All forgiveness, except forgiveness of debts, is divine.' I'm sure you will gladly share with me from your many remaining vials of elixir should need arise," Fentor said quickly.

Elatea's eyes bulged slightly. Between the splinters dusting her hair and the tears in her clothes, she looked wild as a cornered wolf.

"Share?" she hissed. "*Share?* Oh, no, Capilet. There will be no charity here. You shall have to make do with what you have left. That includes the elixir you slurped up."

"I've only got one *bloody* vial left," Fentor spat between his grinding teeth. "I'm only thinking of the success of our mission. One assumes that your infallible genius will lead you to conclude that it would be more effective if we both had elixir, rather than you having a full ten vials to yourself."

"On the contrary, for the success of the mission, I require every single one."

"Why?"

"That's a *patented* secret!" Elatea punctuated the word by jabbing his chest with a finger as hard and sharp as a chisel.

Fentor rumbled like a storm cloud, no longer able to contain the words he longed to say. "You broke the vials! It's your fault!"

Elatea's cheeks turned rose-red. She opened her mouth to respond, but nothing came out. Instead, she abruptly looked over Fentor's shoulder, and wore the sort of smile one might wear to greet a cherished, unexpected guest.

Fentor turned to find the forest bristling with bright red arrows, brass-colored chainmail, pointed ears, and wispy locks of silvery hair. He forgot every word he and Elatea had just said.

He flexed his fists, and gave the elves a welcoming smile of his own.

Chapter 21

An elf with a severely pointed chin stepped forward, sword in hand. He twisted the hilt, and a number of interlocking gears clicked smartly. The sword sprouted a long haft, its blade retracted partway, and became a spear.

Fentor, with his eyes so sensitive to details, realized that the contraption underwent the transformation by way of an intricate, spring-loaded telescoping mechanism. The haft was actually composed of a series of interlocking pieces that nested within one another. He frowned and nodded in appreciation of his own cleverness.

"Draw your weapons slowly, then lay them down," the elf said, pointing the spear at them.

"No," said Elatea, with a sweet and placid smile.

"Lay down your weapons at once. There need be no bloodshed," the elf said, louder.

All around them, two dozen or so elves still held their glowing arrows at full draw. Fentor wondered idly how the scrawny elves could find the strength to do so without so much as a wobble. Then he spied one of them turning a brass dial near the grip, which tightened a catch that was holding the arrow in place. The elves weren't holding their arrows by some feat of strength; the bows were doing the work for them.

There was something so delightful about things that click, twist, and ratchet. Perhaps it was the new clarity afforded by the elixir.

The elves spoke in their own language for a time. Each clipped, sibilant syllable was less intelligible than the last. By their heated gestures, it seemed some were losing their patience. The elf with the brass spear and the geometric chin cut the others off, then turned to Elatea.

"If you will not put your weapons down, then hold out your hands so I can bind them," he said. "If you do not, we will open fire."

"I did not hear you say 'please,' " Elatea said in a delicate sing-song.

The elf's feather-down eyebrows rose sharply. He gaped, incredulous, at the elves around him. Some of them shrugged, others looked at Elatea with doe-eyed pity.

"Do as she says," one of the elves said. "Look at their clothes all in tatters. They've clearly become lost and gone without sleep. They likely don't even know where they are."

With a rough sigh, the spear-holding elf said, "*Please* will you hold out your hands?"

Elatea graciously offered her hands, palms down, as though expecting a manicure. Fentor did the same.

Two of the elves set down their bows and came forward with ropes in hand. They bound Fentor and Elatea with tight, precise knots. It was quality rope. Fentor estimated that it likely had the tensile strength to lift a bull — provided it wore a suitable harness.

He pulled his wrists apart, and the rope burst in a cloud of small fibers. Then, he took the elf's hands and crushed them. That elicited a sharp, anguished scream. Next, Fentor tugged hard on the hands. The elf's arms came free at the shoulder with a pretty spray of crimson blood. That cut the scream short. Not knowing what else to do with the limbs he was left holding, Fentor tossed them over the edge of the cliff.

Ten or so arrows struck his chest with as much force as a swarm of fireflies. As Elatea dismembered the elf that had tied her hands, Fentor shrugged the Aurinium rifle from his shoulder and began loading it.

Despite all the blood and screams and projectiles crowding the air, the routine of loading the rifle was calming.

Once that was done, he took aim at the heart of the nearest elf, who was in the process of charging forward with his spear ready. When he pulled the trigger, the spear stayed in place, while the elf holding it was thrown back forty paces. On his way there, he collided with a few other elves, and several trees. The shockwave of the shot also knocked down a number of elves who'd been nearby. In the end, with one shot, Fentor had gouged a neat welt across the forest floor and dispatched a handful of enemies.

A moment later, Elatea fired her weapon with a brilliant flash and a resounding boom. Another half-dozen elves were flung backward — some of them still intact.

Fentor weighed the time it would take to re-load the weapon against the more immediate option of simply using his hands. Another volley of whistlers peppered his chest. He decided that it was best not to dither.

He barrelled toward the enemy, snatching up the fallen spear without breaking stride. Not wanting to break the flimsy thing, he delicately pierced a number of vital organs as one might lance a boil with a hot needle. Despite all his extra care, the wide-eyed elves tripped over themselves in their clumsy attempts to avoid him. One elf even shielded a companion, knowing they would not get away. Fentor skewered them both.

To his disappointment, he looked around and found that there were no enemies left. Elatea had continued to fire her rifle, though he could only dimly remember hearing it go off. He had been too focused on his own task. In any case, between them, they had dispatched all the Elarím before Fentor had been able to even work up a sweat. He frowned at the anti-climax.

"What were we talking about just before?" Elatea said.

Fentor tried to remember, but it evaded him. He squinted at the sky, as though the answer might be there.

"I think … we wanted to cross the ravine," he said with confidence.

"Yes. I suppose we could climb down and then back up. Or, we could leap across."

"Indeed we could. You know, in training I was the best long jumper in my cohort. Or, I would have been, if all the others weren't such cheats."

Elatea stepped over the limbless torso of an elf and approached the cliff's edge, tapping her chin thoughtfully. She looked down, then across the gap, then left and right.

"Ah! A bridge," she said, pointing. "A well-guarded bridge. See?"

Fentor peered in the indicated direction, but saw nothing except more trees and more ravine.

"Here," she said, and put her custom-made spyglass in his hands.

When he looked through it, he was reminded of a kaleidoscope. Tiny fragments of the world were separated in a fractal pattern that ran in concentric rings around a central focusing point. Unlike a kaleidoscope, which confuses the eye to create a beautiful illusion of scattered light, the spyglass took the world's beautiful illusions, dissected them, and then laid them out for careful inspection.

He saw a timber plank, then another, and another. He saw a series of ropes, the hair, eyes, nose, lips, and chins of several elves. He saw the individual fletching of individual arrows. Turning the dials at random, the splintered pattern of the bridge shifted and swirled, showing him a different set of details at different levels of magnification. The prismatic array ought to have been dizzying, but for Fentor, it made perfect sense.

"There it is," he said.

"It runs on the same basic principle as alchemy," Elatea said. "Atomization. Purification. Distillation.

Recombination. All the elements that make up the world carefully separated, then recombined into more useful forms."

"It is quite a remarkable instrument," Fentor said, handing it back to her.

As he did, he suddenly remembered his broken vials of elixir. She had broken them and then blamed him, and the elves had interrupted their disagreement. How could he have forgotten?

Just as he decided to say something, Elatea opened her coat and drank two vials at once. With his commanding officer a full two cohorts stronger than him, he decided that keeping silent was the more prudent choice. Perhaps it was best that he did *not* remind her of the things he had been interrupted in saying.

"Soon all Madea will follow that same principle. After all, you hear it in the words of the Saints. Why do we not live by them?" Elatea gazed into the distance, beholding some enrapturing scene that Fentor could not see. "We've let the elves poison our thinking, with sentimental notions that reek of the Common Power. It is time to return to true human nature. We must all stand *alone* so the greatest among us may stand *out*."

"Wiser words were never spoken," Fentor said.

Elatea blinked rapidly and looked around at Fentor. "What words?"

"The … ones you just said. About human nature," Fentor said.

She blinked again. "Ah. I did not realize I had been speaking aloud." She frowned. "What else did you hear me say?"

Fentor repeated back all that she had said.

"Good, good," Elatea said absently. "You understand, of course. Some things are not for your ears …"

Not quite understanding, Fentor said, "I understand."

"We *could* cross this little gap with a modest leap," Elatea said. "Or, we could pay the elves guarding the bridge a visit."

On one hand, the elixir was still sizzling in his veins, urging him to pull triggers and throw punches. On the other hand, he only had one vial left.

"Perhaps we ought to adopt a more cautious —"

"To the bridge," Elatea said, driving her fist into her palm. "Each elf left alive is a threat to fair Madea, to everyone we love. They must be stamped out."

Fentor narrowed his eyes. Were the elves to be stamped out, or freed from the yoke of the Common Power? He couldn't make sense of it. His mind had become scattered, kaleidoscopic, as though waking from dream after dream. Perhaps he *had* misremembered what she had said.

"Aye, Elatea. Understood."

She seized him by the arm, turned him to face her. Her blue eyes slid between his, unfocused, one pupil wide, the other a tiny pinhole. He felt like a rabbit in a hawk's talons.

"Don't ever rewrite history with me," Elatea said. "I told you to stop. I held out my arm. *You* ran into it. You have no one to blame for your lost elixir but yourself."

Fentor could only watch as she turned toward the distant bridge, drew her rifle, and disappeared into the trees. He had to follow her. He *knew* he had to follow her. His legs just would not move. It felt as though a colony of ants was crawling over his scalp.

Then, he shook them off, and raced after her.

****

The guards at the bridge were of indeterminate number.

Each of them was visible from the vantage point Fentor and Elatea had chosen. The number of elves was not necessarily hard to determine or calculate. It was just that every time Fentor tried to tally them, he lost count, then forgot what he was doing.

What he *could* see was one elf after another, one strand of silken silver hair after another, a bow, a spear, an arrow, an ear. He also saw targets. Prey. He saw hapless ducks sitting in the reeds, just waiting for the hunter's rifle to snatch the breath from their little lungs.

Beside him, Elatea took out every vial of elixir she had, and drank them one after another. When she was finished, Fentor could almost see every iota of tension in her body evaporating and floating away. Only she remained, serene and pure. All the world looked muddy, chaotic and accidental, in contrast to her deliberate, pristine, exquisite poise.

Squaring her shoulders at perfect right angles, holding her rifle at forty-five degrees, and her head aloft like the golden head of a lamppost, she marched toward the bridge. She was like a wind-up tin soldier made by a master craftsman. She was like a porcelain swan. She was perfection.

Fentor hurried to swallow his own bottle of elixir, then kicked through the ferns and vines in his haste to catch up to her.

Perhaps the extra dose unscrambled his eyes, or perhaps he had become more accustomed to the alternate view of the world. Either way, the fragmented, variegated objects arrayed before him came together into a cohesive scene.

The elves watched as Elatea and Fentor marched toward them along a swept path. On either side of them, the trunks and branches of the trees formed a continuous arch, like a corridor. Fentor imagined that all the forest was bowing in respect of their arrival. No — he *knew* it.

The elves, rudely, did not bow. Instead, they formed ranks on either side of the bridge. Four hundred and twelve elves, in total. They possessed approximately one thousand, eight hundred and forty-two arrows, assuming a standard quiver size. The count of silver strands of hair roughly totalled forty-one million, two hundred and eighty-nine thousand ...

"Halt, humans!" one elf called. She spoke loudly and clearly, but without alarm.

The rest, almost in unison, nocked their arrows, but did not yet draw them. Fentor could not help but smile. The elves should have opened fire immediately. Did they not know their own doom when they saw it?

"Surrender your weapons and prepare to —"

Elatea raised her rifle, and pulled the trigger. Fentor, standing a few paces behind her, first experienced the shot as a flash that turned the world sky-blue, then as a trembling roar that could have shaken his teeth out of his gums, and at last as a voluptuous fireball which left a smoldering crater where two dozen elves had been standing.

He fired his own rifle shortly after. The result was not nearly as impressive, and seemed like a timid cough next to the almighty roar of Elatea's weapon. Still, he managed to catch a decent number of targets in the blast.

The elf that had recently spoken now appeared to be gone, but Fentor knew better. The ground she had stood on was now blackened and empty, yes. The particles which had constituted her body, however, had not vanished. By means of a sudden exothermic reaction (combustion) she had merely been rapidly dispersed into a cloud of water vapor, ash, and various gasses. Nothing had *really* changed. There had just been a rearrangement of which particle was adhering to which.

Together, Elatea and Fentor reloaded their weapons, and prepared for another round of elf *dispersal*.

The Elarím raised an aegis of red so deep it was almost opaque. Even so, it would stop Fentor's bullets about as effectively as a faint breeze or a stern suggestion.

Whistlers whistled at him, and he whistled back. Whereas the swarm of glowing missiles whined tunelessly, Fentor puckered his lips and blew a rousing marching song. He merrily loaded the pan with concentrated bluepowder, tamped the bullet home, replaced his rammer, and peered through the glass sights in search of a suitable target.

A shower of arrows struck Fentor, everywhere from his forehead to his toes, but they might as well have been matchsticks. Frustratingly, some had struck his rifle. Most bounced harmlessly off, but one had cracked the magnifying glass.

He was livid. How dare they damage such a delicate instrument?

Tracing back the offending arrow to its source, Fentor pulled the trigger. The aegis vanished like a pricked soap bubble. The charred culprit was thrown over the cliff along with a few of their nearby fellows.

"Ha! Tit for tat," Fentor muttered, then resumed whistling.

Elatea fired at another knot of elves, who underwent a process of rapid oxidation (they were incinerated), and drifted away as a cloud of smoke.

The elves showered them with a near-continuous volley of glowing arrows. The ground around them was scarcely visible for all the arrows littered everywhere. The incessant shriek of whistlers tested both the capacity of Fentor's ears to endure noise, and his rapidly thinning patience.

As he tried to reload his rifle, arrows struck it, causing it to jolt left and right. He spilled powder, dropped bullets, and couldn't get the rammer to go in the barrel properly. He ground his teeth together with enough force to turn normal teeth to powder. An irrepressible wave of frustration came out of nowhere, and overwhelmed him. He stood, took the rifle in both hands, and snapped it over his knee like kindling.

The next few arrows that hit him *stung* slightly.

He started toward the nearest elves, who stood between deep ruts of smoking, blackened earth. The Elarím sent whistler after whistler at him, but nothing slowed his approach. Every elven eye was wide, every brow dusted with soot.

At the moment Fentor's fist collided with an elf's pale, delicate jaw, the battle had been going for precisely three minutes.

Fentor leapt and dodged, struck and kicked, twisted and pulled, and turned the elves' own weapons against them. By the fourth minute, the elves on their side of the ravine had all been dispatched, dismembered, or *dispersed*.

Some of the Elarím on the far side of the bridge were hacking at its moorings with axes. Just as Fentor rushed to cross it, ropes snapped, timber planks fell away, and the bridge detached from the opposite cliff face. It fell apart, loose and limp, with a great clattering of wood that resounded through the ravine until the pieces fell into the river far below.

Fentor froze with his foot jutting over the edge, holding a short piece of the remaining handrail. He blinked, looking from his foot to his hand. He had been so *sure* that he would be able to make it across before the elves finished cutting it. They must have cheated, must have sabotaged the bridge before his arrival just to spite him.

Another volley of whistlers rose high above the ravine, then converged on his chest. None of them broke the skin, but they left a vaguely tender feeling where they hit him. This reminded him of something he had forgotten: people can be killed by arrows.

The fear brought by that thought was brief and indistinct. It was scattered, kaleidoscopic, as though he had woken from an unsettling dream. He wondered briefly how much longer the elixir in his veins would last. Then, Elatea appeared beside him, and he forgot the fear.

"Well?" she said, in a sweet, wind-chime voice. "Aren't you going to jump over the gap?"

"Of course I am. How else will I get over there?"

Despite what he'd said, he still lingered at the edge of the ruined bridge. A new, bright red curtain of whistlers took flight, and as they arced gracefully toward him, he could not tear his eyes from them. He also couldn't help but shrink away from them — just slightly.

"Well?" Elatea asked sweetly.

"Yes, yes, of course. Just a little skip, really. A little hop over a puddle. That's all it will take," Fentor said quickly.

The arrows continued their rapid descent. Fentor's feet didn't move. He insisted that they budge, but they refused. An unrelated thought barged in: he had very little elixir left in his system.

"All I have to do is jump, and I'll be across ..." Fentor murmured, as the sky above him was blotted out by the wave of ruddy, screeching whistlers.

"Allow me to assist," Elatea said brightly.

She grabbed him about his middle, then lifted him above her head. Then, without any apparent effort, she tossed him high in to the air.

He felt the way a bullet must feel.

Cold air slapped his face, forced his eyes closed, and rushed past his ears. A cloud of sharp, little objects pricked his skin — the whistlers, he supposed. Then, he caught a glimpse of the ground rushing up to meet him.

His meeting with the ground, while not fatal, was certainly not pleasant.

He struck the dirt face-first, then rolled over and over as the world corkscrewed around him. He came to a stop, dazed and slightly nauseated. The elves and trees around him slid in and out of focus. His mind had become scattered, kaleidoscopic, as though waking from dream after dream. He kept forgetting his own thoughts, only to have them again moments later.

Kaleidoscopic. *Ka-lei-do-sco-pic.* The word went round and round inside his head, the individual letters splayed out in colorful, ringed patterns. He blinked hard and shook himself. It was like he was waking from dream after dream …

A moment later, a blonde, person-sized object landed with a meteoric crash in the midst of the elves. Before the veil of dust settled, the elves began to scream.

Fentor rushed to his feet and joined the fight.

He pummelled and punched and shoved and tore every part of every elf that came within his reach. Great sprays of blood filled the air, and corpses littered the ground, but Fentor knew better. After all, blood is just the colloidal suspension of red cells in plasma, along with a smattering of other cells and particles. And 'corpse' was merely an irrational term for a body whose respiratory processes have been discontinued. They were all made of the same stuff as before, weren't they?

At last, Fentor understood. Everything Elatea had said about separating and recombining, how she had wanted to liberate the elves from the Common Power … it all became clear. He *was* liberating them. As he freed arms from sockets and heads from necks, he also freed the elves. One limb at a time. One thread of the Common Power after another.

They were no longer pawns of the all-dominating influence that bound them all together. They were free.

One ungrateful elf drove a spear into his chest. Or, rather, she *tried* to. The spear point curled back on itself without drawing a single drop of blood. It did, however, inflict a moment of dull pain on Fentor.

"Ouch!" he spat, covering the sore spot with his hand.

The gaggle of elves facing him exchanged looks among themselves. Fentor cursed himself for his moment of weakness.

The Elarím renewed their assault on him. Arrow after arrow stung his shoulder blades, his thighs, his stomach, and his head. Each one stung a little more than the last. They prodded him with their spears and slashed at him with their swords. Before long, he was forced to shield his face with one arm, and continue killing with the other.

Then, the sabotage began.

Some elf must have secured weights to his feet. They dragged heavily across the ground, weakening his tired legs. Some others had sucked the air out of his lungs, so that he had to gasp for every breath. They had also, somehow, covered his brow with sweat and stolen the strength from his arms.

A previously comatose part of his mind stirred, stretched, and indulged in a long yawn. Then, catching a glimpse of the world through the window of his eyes, it leapt up and shouted: *They're not sabotaging you, you bloody fool! You're running out of strength. They're going to overwhelm you!*

Panic gripped his heart. He cowered from the tangle of spears aimed at him. All around him were elves—

hundreds of them in the branches of trees above, in a circle around him, and embroiled in a large melee around Elatea. Each wore the same brass chainmail, the same red cape, and the same expression of deep, passionate contempt.

There hadn't been this many elves before. Had he miscounted? Or had reinforcements come?

The elves closest to him all fell to their knees in perfect unison, though no order had been called. Whistlers flared bright red in a ring all around, then streaked through the air toward him. They struck his back, sides, and chest all at once with enough force to knock him down. He rasped out an airless moan and curled up into a ball.

Slender, rough hands seized him, pulled him upright, bound his arms, and tied a cloth about his mouth to gag him. He cringed, expecting them to beat him and spit on him. Despite the pink flush on every cheek and the naked hatred burning in every eye, they did not do so.

He looked over to where Elatea was still fighting, and his spirits rose. Their weapons could not so much as scratch her, and she flicked away elves like they were ants. She was strong, stronger than he had ever been. They could still win.

In a pause between the flurries of whistlers raining down on her, her eyes met Fentor's. For a moment, she paused, paying no heed to the spears and arrows still prodding fruitlessly at her. Though her clothes were torn and her hair caked with blood and dust, her poise in the face of the onslaught was untouched. Time itself seemed suspended for her benefit. Standing alone, framed by her enemies, brushed with colors from the palette of battle, she stood like a portrait of herself.

She smiled.

It was the tranquil, beatific smile who has seen the final outcome of all things, both of Providence above and earth below. A smile of religious culmination.

She slowly raised one pale, slender hand, open palm outward. As she lifted her hand, she rose an arm's length above the ground. A sphere of pale blue light engulfed her, alternating in shades of the deep sea and the gentle dawn. Her dark silhouette could still be seen, holding the same pose.

The elves gawped, transfixed by the display. A few stray arrows halted mid-air just outside her aura. For a moment, nothing moved. The cosmos held its breath.

Then, Elatea closed her hand into a fist, and the sphere collapsed with a brilliant flash. There was a loud thump, then silence.

Her Excellency, the Lady Elatea Talentus stood encased inside a heavy crystal. The many facets of sapphire-colored cocoon caught the light and scattered it into rainbows of indigo and teal. In the heart of the crystal, she still wore that same placid, knowing smile.

Chapter 22

Weeds grew in cracks. Rather, humans gave that name to any plant that could sprout from a gap, along an edge, or from barren soil. A name that means unwanted, out of place. Slee knew those sorts of plants for what they really were: survivors.

Now, like a stubborn dandelion poking through a crack in the stone, something had sprouted in her heart and begun to reach for the sun. It was no garden, but it was a start. She had a friend. It helped that Dídac had not visited, either.

Since the first evening visit of the little female rat, Slee had fed her many crumbs and enjoyed having her simple company. She'd even given her a name to match her squeaked greetings: Dit-Dit.

At first, Dit-Dit only came during the darkest, quietest hours. These visits were brief, little more than an exchange. Slee fed her crumbs, and Dit-Dit gave her a few minutes of companionship. It was enough to make Slee briefly forget the bruises, stiffness, and numbing cold that dominated her waking attention.

Slee persisted in offering a telethymic bond to her new friend. No matter how Slee tried, she could not get the rat to accept the silken strands she extended. Dit-Dit was startled by everything — shadows, sudden movements, faint sounds, and scents too faint for Slee to perceive. As Slee sent thicker and thicker cords of telethí snaking across the floor with no response from Dit-Dit, she became irritated. Even when she flooded the room with telethí and coiled around the rat's mind like a snake, the rat did not even flinch. No normal rat could close itself so completely to one like Slee.

Would a bird born in a cage know why it has wings? Would a fish born in a bucket yearn for the river?

Mama had once said that about the Madeans, but Slee could not help wondering if it was the same for Dit-Dit. Creatures of all kinds rely on telethymic bonds, from the simplest motelings to the leviathans that swam in the ocean deeps. Would a creature that lived its whole life without them even know what was missing? Was Dit-Dit deliberately ignoring Slee's onslaught, or was the rat simply unaware?

Whatever the case, Dit-Dit's visits grew longer as the days passed. She would scamper up Slee's arm to perch on her shoulder and sniff her cheek. Sometimes, she would even burrow into Slee's blankets to warm up before leaving. One night, when Dit-Dit started carrying the crumbs to Slee's lap to eat them, she knew she had truly made a friend.

Early one morning, as Slee blew warm air into her icy hands, an enormous crash resounded through the distillery. It sounded as though the entire roof had fallen in—a thought that gave Slee a stab of savage pleasure. A great confusion of yelling followed, and persisted for some time. As the sun rose, the general level of noise fell, though occasional shouts still funneled down the corridor to Slee's dungeon. There were too many voices for Slee to indulge any hopes that the humans had all been crushed by falling bits of distillery.

All that mattered was whether Dit-Dit had survived, and whether the cacophony had scared the rat away for good.

Then, a clamor of overlapping shouts drew closer, until their confused echoes filled the dungeon. They mixed with the sounds of heavy boots, scuffles, and faint thuds. The humans were headed her way.

The heavy dungeon door clicked and creaked, and a knot of struggling legs and arms squeezed inside. Most of the legs and arms belonged to several red-faced soldiers in grey coats, while one set of limbs belonged to the man they had dragged in. Slee caught a glimpse of a blond beard before the others blocked her view. There was a clinking of heavy chains, a string of curses, and grunts of effort as the guards kicked the new prisoner. Their victim, perhaps fortunately, was spared from more savage blows because all the guards crowded so closely around him that there was too little room to swing their heavy boots.

Not long ago, in quiet moments in her garden, Slee had been able to sense the wilting of a single flower. Now, though a man was enduring great pain across the room, her telethymic senses told her nothing.

Dídac sidled through the doorway, looking down his nose at the prisoner.

"I suppose that's enough," he said coolly. "Her Excellency made it clear that human deaths ought to be minimised, after all."

The grey-coated guards cinched their belts, straightened their tricornes, and filed out the room. One spat on the bloodied wretch. The last to leave was Dídac, who shook his head, and gave a short, humorless laugh before leaving. He hadn't so much as glanced at Slee.

When the heavy door closed and its rough locks slid into place, her new cellmate groaned softly. He hung limply forward, and might have fallen face-first on the stone if the chains weren't holding him up. Blood dripped steadily from his nose. Even though she could only see the top of his head, he was strangely familiar.

Gradually, so faintly Slee thought she imagined it, a clammy aura of pain spread around the room like a fog. It almost felt as though the stones themselves were throbbing softly. Slee thought she recognised the rhythm of the aches, and tried to place the vague feeling. It was like the words of a childhood song she had half-forgotten.

As she extended a wispy telethí strand toward the man, the vague sense of recognition grew stronger. The strand found nothing to hold on to, but it brushed against the boundary of his mind. She had not expected to make a bond easily with a human. Still, tortured for so long by her solitude, she had no choice but to try.

The man coughed, then raised his head. Fresh cuts and welts covered his face, and one eye was almost swollen shut. His blond beard was streaked with drying blood.

"I'd hoped we would meet again," he rasped. "Pity that it's in here."

"Horvald?" Slee breathed. "What happened? How did you get here?"

He opened his mouth to reply, but coughed weakly instead. After a series of restrained coughs and throat-clearings, he spat out a glob of bloody spittle. When he spoke, his voice was still rough as bark.

"Long story. Throat hurts," he rasped. "Cartín's here, too. They accused me of breaking that winch-lift contraption, threw me in here."

"*Did* you break it?" Slee asked.

Horvald shrugged, tilted his head with a roguish smile, then was overcome with another fit of coughing.

"I'm sorry. You should rest your voice," Slee said.

Horvald eased back against the wall, every breath bubbling and wheezing.

The human's aches, which lingered in the fringes of Slee's perception, ought to have been as overwhelming and urgent as a hurricane. No matter how she focused on connection, on Horvald's feeble telethí, she could not join him. Without a strong bond, his pain would remain as hazy as a forgotten dream. To help him heal, she would need to feel it all.

The art of telethymia had failed her, first with Dit-Dit, and now with Horvald.

Horvald slid into a deeper and deeper slouch.
Eventually, his breathing became regular and his eyes
closed.

Slee's legs had become stiff, numb, and ungainly from
long disuse. As she watched Horvald sleep, she feared that
her heart had become the same. She felt neither great relief
at his sudden appearance, nor horror at his injuries. The
pale ghosts of both emotions were there, lurking
somewhere out of sight, faintly coloring her mood.

The cruelty of fate made sense, in a way. After all, only
a sliver of sun and a breath of wind could reach her
through the high, barred window. It followed that only a
shadow of her former self remained—a hollow Slee,
uprooted from her garden, withering from the inside out.
She could no more nurture feelings than the dungeon
could nurture a garden. Her heart had gone numb from
disuse.

All she wanted was to climb onto Slowjaw's back and go
to some isolated corner of the world where she would
never be found again.

Without the freedom to do that, she did the only thing
she could—watched over Horvald while he slept.

****

Horvald woke many times over the following hours, but
only briefly. Sometimes he whispered Cartín's name upon
waking. Slee urged him to rest, assuring him each time
that Cartín was coming.

The day ended, and no guards had brought her daily
rations. With no crumbs to offer, and a new, loudly-

breathing cellmate, Slee worried that Dit-Dit might stop visiting.

Long hours trickled by. Slee's hunger grew so strong that she could taste it on her own breath. The little rat did not come. Disappointed, Slee wrapped herself more tightly with her blanket, and readied herself for sleep.

At that moment, the heavy lock of the dungeon door turned over with a grating click. A wedge of blue light spread across the floor as the door opened, and a man holding a strange lantern entered. Slee could only see his dark outline behind the glare. By instinct, she drew in her hands and feet,

The man turned a dial which dimmed the light, then set the lantern down and crouched beside Horvald. Slee immediately recognised the thin black moustache, the smell of pipe-smoke, and the tender way his hands held Horvald's face.

"Cartín?" Horvald said hoarsely. "You interrupted the most pleasant dream. I was all battered and bruised, shivering in a dark dungeon with our good friend Slee."

"They must have knocked the sense right out of your head," Cartín said.

Horvald gave a laugh peppered with coughs. "I was only joking."

"I know—that's the problem. Forget all that. I can't stay long," Cartín said. He reached into a large pocket on his grey coat, and pulled out a small cloth bundle. "Here. It's not much, just bread and cheese."

Horvald took the bundle then pulled Cartín close. The two rocked each other gently in a long embrace, with Cartín resting his chin on top of Horvald's head. When they parted, Cartín kissed his forehead, the tip of his nose, then his lips. It looked to Slee like an affectionate gesture they had shared many times.

"I really can't stay long," Cartín said.

"Not to worry. I have all the company I need," Horvald said with false brightness.

"I'll return as often as I can. But Dídac and the others are watching."

"Would it be a terrible bother if I asked you to bring a cup of hot tea next time? Perhaps something sweet for afters?"

Cartín smiled. "I'll do my best."

Cartín crossed the dungeon and knelt in front of Slee. "I never expected to see you again, my friend. Least of all in a place like this."

"How did you two come to be here?"

"After we last saw you, we were drawn into a days-long skirmish with the Elarím," Cartín said, handing Slee a similar bundle to the one he'd given Horvald. "We joined forces with the other Bluefingers, hiding from the elves, tracking them, trading shots with them. We ended up near Bianlock. Then, Dídac appeared and … a few seconds later, he was the only elf still standing."

"Those explosions were so loud, they made the chains rattle," Slee said.

"Yes. Relieved as we were that the battle ended, I could not help but shudder when I saw it. Scorch marks where there had been trees and elves … ash falling like snow," Cartín said. He smoothed his moustache.

"They call this place a distillery. What, exactly, is being distilled?" Slee said.

"The Elixir of Power. The next great innovation in warfare. Perhaps in many other things, too," Cartín said bitterly.

"Power? Such a thing cannot be distilled and brewed into a potion. Power is a *relation*," Slee said, echoing the words of the Sage Amenídes. The absurdity of it almost angered her more than the harm it had caused.

"We may need to save debates of metaphysics for when we have our freedom back, Slee," Horvald said. He had opened the bundle and was eating small pieces of bread.

"Breaking you two out will not be easy," Cartín said. "The Greycoats—Lady Talentus' own private mercenaries—are loyal to Dídac. They watch every corner of this place, night and day."

"You are wearing the same sort of coat," Slee said.

A shadow slid across Cartín's face. "Yes. Dídac made us choose—join the Greycoats, or put those *things* on our heads and have our animus sucked out. We aren't allowed to leave, not now that we've seen the secret distillery and the elixir in action. They are 'patented secrets,' it seems. Hopefully, I chose well. I can learn their ways as an insider."

"Wear the coat if you must. Just take care it doesn't wear you," Slee said.

Cartín looked quickly at her, then away.

"Good Providence, Slee! What did I just say about philosophizing?" Horvald said in a tone of mock exasperation. The simple meal seemed to have lifted his spirits.

"I have to go. But there is one last thing," Cartín said. He reached into the inside pocket of his coat, and pulled out a small, glittering object.

Slee recognized it the moment he placed it in her hands. It was the geode Mama had left her.

"How…?"

"Forgive me. It was too precious to leave buried. If it could save Horvald, then perhaps it can save us now," Cartín said.

Slee held the geode away from her body, as though it was a crab with splayed pincers. The crystals in its core were dark as ink, glittering faintly in the lantern's light. At length, Slee tucked the stone away in her blanket, conflicted. She pressed it hard against her chest, where its weight was hard to ignore.

"I will do everything in my power to come again soon," Cartín said.

"Thank you," Slee said softly.

Cartín and Horvald shared another long embrace, until Cartín insisted once again that he could not stay. He picked up the lantern, gave Slee and Horvald each a strained smile, then left.

The moment the lock clicked into place, Horvald sucked air between his teeth, then stifled a low groan. A ripple of aches and twinges spread across the dungeon floor and lapped over Slee's feet. She recoiled at the sudden clarity of Horvald's pain.

"What's wrong?"

"Ah, it's just Cartín held me a wee bit tightly for the liking of my bruised ribs," Horvald said between shallow gasps.

"Why didn't you tell him how badly it hurt?" Slee asked.

With the lantern gone, the only illumination was the pale square of moonlight on the far wall. Slee could only see Horvald's outline, hunched and huddled.

"He didn't have to know about it," he said.

Slee shook her head, perplexed. Papa had always hidden the extent of his injuries from Mama, and Slee had never seen the benefit or logic of it. He explained to her it was a human quirk that he was still trying to overcome. But what is pain *for* if it is not a signal those around you? Do humans think they can wish it away by keeping it hidden? Is it some treasure they must jealously guard?

All life cares for all life.

Horvald's pain beat on, an urgent drumming that kept time with Slee's own throbbing aches, adding a fresh, stinging layer to the matured rhythms of hurts. By instinct, she unspooled some threads of telethí and extended them toward Horvald.

Unseen by him, her silvery telethí snaked through the air, and his own frayed threads rose to meet them. She held her breath, hardly believing her good luck. As they twined together, Slee's pain sharpened, then eased. The connection not only brought Horvald's pain across to her, but by the sharing of the burden, began to mend their wounds.

Horvald groaned, though this time with sleepy relief. "This feels pleasantly familiar. Are you doing your magic, Slee?"

"Yes. My geode is finally working," Slee said.

She almost closed her eyes and let the soothing current carry her off to sleep. Then she caught sight of the wandering telethí filaments—they had all become concentrated on a single point. The geode in her hands bound the threads, coiling them, steadily pulling in new threads from Slee's heart. A black wave of sleep rose up, closing over her like a smothering pillow.

Startled, she shook herself awake. Then she shifted her blankets and dropped the stone an arm's length away.

At once, the silvery threads that filled the air faded, unwound, and retreated to their origins. They did not disappear entirely, and some of the pale telethí that remained drifted here and there like seaweed stirred by waves.

Horvald winced and held his sides. "Ah! Some warning would have been appreciated."

"I'm sorry," Slee said. "It was taking over. If we'd fallen asleep, we may might never have woken up."

"I *told* Cartín we should have left it in the woods," Horvald said.

"Maybe you should have. Mama and Papa could never tell me quite how it works. I think they didn't know, themselves," Slee said. "But it has such tremendous potential …"

"What are we going to do with it, then?" Horvald asked.

Slee considered the question for a moment. Her first instinct was to fling it through the window. Then she thought of Slowjaw, Felheim, and the other peaducks. If any of them were still alive, they would be hurt, afraid, and alone. Without Slee they would not survive for long. She stared at the geode and the glittering crystals within, which were now blood-red.

The little rock held great potential, but its power was unruly. It was like fire—destructive in careless hands, yet life-saving in times of great need.

"I will learn to use it as best I can," Slee said. "Then we will break out of this place. We will have to risk everything on it. Either the geode will free us, or it will kill us."

Chapter 23

*When we die, the Actuaries of Providence
tally up the worth of our earthly labor. Every
good deed in life is a penny in the bank of the
afterlife. Your eternal paradise will depend
on the dividends of this fund, so I say to you:
invest wisely.*

Saint Temlin.

Soft, rhythmic scratching woke Fentor. Reports of dire
aches, bruises, and sprains trickled in from the far corners
of his body. The order to open his eyes was intercepted on
the way, so they remained closed. He marshalled all the
intact faculties he still had, and puzzled over his present
location and how he had come to be there.

The chief sensory report was the sound of dry
scratching. It came sporadically and quite faintly, as
though distant.

The sound inspired a memory of dry leaves skating down the cobblestone streets of Madea City. Combined with his pounding head and unresponsive eyelids, a theory of his whereabouts formed.

He must have overindulged at The Crown Upon a Crown, and then taken a brief nap outdoors. A little breeze tickled his clammy skin, confirming his guess. It carried fresh, woodsy air, which suggested that he had staged his repose in one of the city's great parks.

At last, his eyes belatedly obeyed the order to open, and he wished they hadn't. Gentle sunlight filtered through a canopy of waving leaves high above, and pierced through his eyes to the back of his skull. Despite the pain, he kept them open, and solved the mystery of the scratching sound.

Brown leaves fell from the canopy like a steady, fluttering rain. Then, some way above Fentor's head, they brushed against an invisible barrier, then tumbled away to the side. It was as though some perfectly clear sheet of glass was floating above him.

He sat up and frowned at the colorful vegetation, and a small audience that had been watching him.

He was not in Madea City.

A dozen or so elves lounged on the grass or perched on low-hanging boughs, watching him with open-mouthed fascination. All of them were silver-haired save one — a female with long, dark hair, and a look on her face like she had received word of a dear friend's death.

The grass was peppered with little flowers of all colors. Squat berry bushes, waist-high mushrooms on thin stalks, and trees of all shapes with leaves of orange, green, and purple surrounded the area. Garlands of tinkling bells and colorful streamers hung high in the trees, adding a gentle undercurrent of music to the wind. Fentor glowered at each of the assaults on his senses.

None of his spectators spoke or moved, so Fentor took the initiative on both counts.

He stood—shakily, creakily, battling a rising tide of aches—and addressed a nearby male, "Might I trouble you to answer a question for me?"

"Ask it and see," he replied. He was tall, silver-haired, and fair-faced, which did little to distinguish him from the others. His only unique point was that he was the closest.

"Could you please tell me where we are, good sir?" Fentor said. Swaying a little, peering at the silver-haired onlookers, he began to suspect that something about the scenario was *off*.

"Rivumaí is the name of this place," he said. The elf stood, crossed his arms, and frowned slightly. He was wearing long robes of white cloth, decorated with flowers stitched with black thread.

"Pardon my additional query, but who might you be?" Fentor said. His head pounded so hard that small black circles bloomed in his eyes with each pulse.

"My name is Kinam," he said.

Borne along by the current of reflexive politeness that had been cudgeled into him at a young age, Fentor said, "And I am Lord Fentor Lonokai, Capilet of the Madean Land Corps."

"You're bleeding," Kinam said, pointing at Fentor's face.

Fentor touched his brow, found a wet spot, and inspected his now bloodied fingers. "Ah. I am, indeed. Thank you for pointing that out, er, Kaneem."

Feeling quite dazed, Fentor searched his pockets and belt for a handkerchief. His hands found that nearly every pocket was torn open, and he had no scabbard, gunpowder, or, in fact, any other possessions. A sudden recollection broke free in his mind, like a chick pecking its way out of an egg. All at once the events rushed at him in a blur: the elixir, the bridge, the battle, Elatea, the Aurinium rifles, the elves, the defeat.

For a moment, the only sound was the continued scratching of leaves on the invisible ceiling.

Another elf approached and offered Fentor a roll of gauze. "I can put on bandage … if you like," she said in halting Madean. She wore hard leather vambraces, silver armbands, a heavy apron of black cloth, and an odd sort of cape made of hundreds of colored ribbons.

Fentor stared at the strange garments for a moment before taking the gauze. "Thank you, but I can manage on my own."

"As you wish," the elf said, before turning and bounding away with a colorful flash of her cape.

A drop of blood reached his eyebrow, and threatened to fall into his eye. Rather than unwind the bandage, he simply pressed the whole roll on his forehead to stem the bleeding.

"Tell me, Kenwim—" Fentor began.

"Kinam."

"Of course. Tell me … am I a prisoner?" Fentor said.

"I should have thought that was obvious," Kinam said, gesturing at their surroundings.

Fentor, spying no bars, doors, chains, shackles, or guards, was privately inclined to disagree.

"Say I turned and ran for freedom. I daresay a barrage of arrows would hit my back before I made it two steps, would they not?" Fentor said.

"No," Kinam said, drawing the word out and narrowing his eyes. "Of course not."

"Are *you* a prisoner, too? Or are you a guard?"

"Neither."

"Are any of these elves prisoners or guards?"

"No," Kinam said, a little testily.

"Well then, in what sense is this a prison?"

"In the sense that you may not leave," Kinam said. "Now that I have explained things to you, it is time I get back to work."

"But you haven't explained a single thing!" Fentor said.

"Others will be able to answer further questions if you have them."

Kinam turned abruptly and began to leave.

"Now, listen here!" Fentor said, reaching out and taking hold of Kinam's shoulder. "I am a highly respected officer of the Madean Land Corps, and—"

As Fentor attempted to turn the elf around, it felt as though a dozen invisible threads wrapped around his wrist, and they wrenched his hand off Kinam's shoulder. Stunned, he halted and gaped at his own immobilized hand.

"I do not know how humans usually comport themselves. Here, however, a gesture like that could be interpreted as aggression," Kinam said over his shoulder, still facing away from Fentor.

"What are you, some sort of sorcerer?" Fentor said, eyeing the elf's curious robes.

"Not at all. I'm a philosopher," Kinam said, and continued the way he had been going as though there had been no interruption.

Fentor's hand was released, and he hugged the offended arm to his chest. The elves that had been watching him dispersed, speaking softly among themselves like audience members leaving the theatre. The dark-haired elf remained for a minute, and studied Fentor, still sitting in the elbow of a low-hanging bough. She stood, then sauntered away. Fentor was left alone.

Dead leaves continued to rattle across the invisible barrier above. Fentor watched as they fell on a downward slope, tracing the outline of a large, curved barrier. With Kinam gone, it seemed he would have to find answers for himself.

The bleeding on his forehead seemed to have stopped, so he placed the wad of gauze in one of the few still-intact pockets of his coat.

He followed the course of the tumbling leaves, dodging between densely-growing trees, flower-bushes, vines, and violet stalks of grass as tall as him. At last, he came to a place where a knee-high wall of leaves had been deposited. Among them were feathery seeds, twigs, acorns, and other detritus shed by the local flora. Fentor, wading through a patch of transparent flowers that looked like champagne flutes, approached the barrier with both arms outstretched. He inched closer, until his hands were an inch away from the skittering leaves.

Holding his breath, he made a fist and probed the air with a knuckle. He intended to knock on the barrier, as one might a door, but his hand passed right through to the other side. With a little laugh, he put both hands on the other side of the invisible wall and caught some of the falling leaves.

"Ha! A wall that keeps leaves out, but doesn't keep prisoners in," Fentor said. "I suppose I was expected to stay put out of some sense of fair play."

He made to step through the unseen curtain, but hesitated. Even though he had reached through to the other side, his eyes clearly saw leaves trailing across an invisible, yet defined surface. The proof of the growing wall of leaves at his feet made his body protest against taking a simple step forward. His *mind* knew there was nothing there, but his *brain* insisted that there was.

To overcome this impasse, he took a few steps back into the tinkling, clear flowers, then ran headlong at the barrier.

He did not smash into a solid wall, nor did he break through a pane of glass. He also did not pass cleanly through to the other side. Those were the outcomes he had been expecting.

The outcome he received was to be caught mid-air like a fly in a web. Indeed, he could feel scores of unseen strands pressing against his body. Some of his momentum stayed with him, and it carried him deeper and deeper into the invisible web at an excruciatingly slow pace. Leaves tickled his nose and cheeks as he continued to drift into the strange structure. There came a point where it seemed the barrier had stretched to its limit. As with all things that stretch and contract, he expected his momentum to shift, and for his body to be flung with great force back in the direction he had come.

That expectation was confirmed.

He was thrown back into the mercifully soft vegetation. Still, a new pain in his lower back joined all his existing injuries.

"The barrier won't let you through, no matter what you try," said someone with a thin, piping, curiously familiar voice.

"Valuable information — had I received it ten seconds ago," Fentor croaked.

"Most have to experience it for themselves. They end up taking a run at it sooner or later, no matter how clearly you warn them," they said.

Fentor hoisted himself upright by pulling on nearby tangles of branches. The man he'd been speaking to stood on the outside of the barrier. He wore loose linen clothes and boots, but he was no elf. He had a little, twitchy nose, watery eyes, and pronounced, but definitely round, ears.

"Thorassa?" Fentor breathed.

"Hullo, Fentor," Thorassa said, with a warm smile. Gone was his anxious tremor and shifting eyes. The Lancer now stood tall, and seemed altogether much less rabbit-like.

"You were presumed dead!" Fentor said.

"Many people here are. Presumed, that is — not actually dead."

"Well, that hardly matters now. Look, Lancer, I can't stay here. Tell me what you know about this barrier," Fentor said.

"The barrier is not a priority at the moment," Thorassa said.

"Of course it bloody is! I'm in the middle of a mission of surpassing importance! Critical! I need to get through it now while no elves are watching," Fentor said.

"Wouldn't you rather meet the others?"

"The others? What has gotten into you, Lancer?"

"I'm not a 'Lancer' any longer," Thorassa said.

"You're right about that! The moment we get back to Madea, I'll demote you so thoroughly you'll have to scrape your way back up to mucking out latrines!"

Thorassa raised his eyebrows and bared his teeth in a jovial grimace. "Oh my, that *does* sound unpleasant. If it will make you feel better, I shall answer. The barrier is impassable to all except the Elarím. Only they can get in or out."

"Well, that's a start."

"There's nothing we can do about the barrier just now. Why don't we go and meet the others?" Thorassa said.

"I'd prefer a bath, a change of clothes, and a generous glass of brandy. I need to be in peak mental condition to find a way to thwart the barrier," Fentor said.

"I'm not sure about the brandy, but we can get you cleaned in the main part of the village. The others are there, too—Hess, Crauford, Angsley, and even Lady Talentus," Thorassa said. "In fact, I came all this way to see if the rumors she'd been captured were true."

"Hess? Crauford?" Fentor said. His mouth felt as dry and rough as a sea sponge left in the sun. "For Temlin's sake, why didn't you mention that earlier?"

"I tried rather valiantly to, Fentor," Thorassa said, shrugging.

"Hang on. You spoke as though we were going to see them together. How do you expect to do that?"

Thorassa, still smiling with genuine warmth, strolled through the invisible barrier without impediment.

Fentor stood transfixed, too aghast to speak, too shocked to give so much as a suitably dramatic gasp.

Thorassa had joined the enemy.

Chapter 24

Slee hardly slept that night, but dread and discomfort played no role. Purpose stoked the fire within her, woke her leaden limbs, and propped up her drooping eyelids. The little rock sat on the floor, its jagged crystal mouth leering up at her. She studied it for hours, watching the pale moonlight winking on the points of the crystals. That yielded nothing.

Mama or Papa *must* have said something about it that she couldn't remember. If she could just force herself to remember, wring the memory out of her mind like drops from a damp washcloth, she'd be able to use it. All she could bring to mind, she already knew: the geode was a rare and special thing, it could weave threads of animus together, and it was best to leave it alone.

A familiar squeak broke through her ruminations. A rush of affection warmed her heart as she saw Dit-Dit appear at the window, who paused to sniff the air. The moon outlined her body and whiskers with a silver glow.

"It's safe to come down, my friend," Slee whispered.

With an unpleasant twinge, she remembered that she hadn't kept any crumbs. She hoped the warmth of her blanket would be enough to make the rat's visit worthwhile.

Dit-Dit stood on her hindlegs, with one paw on a bar and her nose twitching. Horvald gave a loud snore. Immediately, Dit-Dit made herself small and froze. Slee was nearly tempted to throw the geode at the noisy human, but restrained herself.

A little puff of dark smoke rose from Dit-Dit, a quivering shroud of fear. Slee hardly dared to believe what she was seeing—a telethymic aura. She opened her heart and let her telethí wander freely. It is not taxing to free the part of yourself that connects to others, but it can be a difficult part to find when it has been abused, neglected, and starved. Dit-Dit's aura, faint as it was, proved that the little rat had not lost the part entirely.

Just as Slee's telethí reached toward the window, Dit-Dit turned and fled.

Horvald sniffed loudly and stirred, causing his chains to clink. "Did you say something?"

"No. You should get back to sleep," Slee said.

"I would if I could. I had dreams somebody was pelting rocks at me," Horvald said. He yawned and stretched like an old, rheumy cat, gingerly uncurling one stiff limb at a time.

With Dit-Dit gone, Slee's telethí hung in the air like filaments left by hatchling spiders. Faint inklings of animus touched the threads, and they shivered. From little tufts of moss to tiny insects and worms searching blindly

for food underground, life of all kinds flickered nearby.
Every time a telethí crossed through the geode, it hummed
with resonance like a tightening harp string.

She watched and waited, ready to withdraw. There was
no telling what might trigger the geode to drain her
completely.

"Cartín hasn't come back yet, has he?" Horvald said. "I
thought I might have dreamed ..."

"No, he hasn't."

"He'll come soon, Providence willing. Then we can
really work on breaking out."

"Will he be able to do it alone?"

"Unless the other Greycoats have a miraculous change
of heart, he'll have to," Horvald said. "We can only rely on
ourselves in this wretched place."

Horvald then explained the workings of the distillery,
and how he had decided to sabotage it. After only a few
days of being forced to work for Dídac, he had seen
enough to know that he could not allow production to
continue. The elf forced the Bluefingers to work longer
and longer shifts. The soldiers, drained of animus and
lacking sleep, feebly protested. As Greycoats, Horvald
and Cartín were ordered to intimidate and beat any
complainers into silence.

Cartín spoke with Dídac, implored him to see reason. If
he kept demanding so much of the Bluefingers' life force,
some were sure to die. Dídac was unmoved. Horvald told
the elf that well-rested soldiers would give more long-
term, and any deaths would cut into the profits. He was
ignored.

The other Greycoats were even less concerned than Dídac. Some only wished to follow orders. Others were eager to give out beatings.

Despite Cartín's insistence on caution, Horvald decided to take matters into his own hands.

The winch-lift carried animus from the lower level to the alchemists above. Without it, production would grind to a halt, and the Bluefingers would get a brief reprieve.

Inspecting all its pulleys and ropes and gears and counterweights, Horvald noticed a steel belt of interlocking teeth which connected crucial pieces together. With an old hammer and a 'deft bit of bashing' while no one was looking, he managed to render it too mangled to function.

Unfortunately, rather than grind the winch-lift to a halt, it collapsed entirely. The noise drew Dídac and the Greycoats to the room, and Horvald was caught.

"In the end, it was hardly worth it," Horvald said. "Dídac just ordered the poor blighters to carry their own animus upstairs, bottle by bottle. The winch-lift has probably been repaired by now."

"You should have seen that there's nothing one person can do to stop this place," Slee said.

"Oh? And what was it that got you thrown in here?"

"That was different." Slee hugged her knees tighter. "I had Slowjaw."

"Well, we don't have him now. What we do have is Cartín," Horvald said.

"And the geode."

"What have you learned about it?" Horvald asked.

"Very little."

"Here, pass it to me," he said.

The mere thought of handing a human the geode filled Slee with apprehension. At once, the wandering telethí threads contracted. Her small links to nearby life-forms wavered, then broke off entirely.

"It is not safe in your hands," Slee said. "It must stay with me."

"I won't *do* anything with it, I just want to look," Horvald said. "Here—"

"Humans cannot use telethymia. In the unlikely event that this thing *does* respond to your touch, it would only be to drain your life away. A process which, without telethymia, you would not sense happening until it was too late," Slee said.

Horvald raised his hands slightly, as if in surrender, which rattled his chains. "I yield. I was only offering to help."

"Sorry for being abrupt," Slee said. She glared at the geode, seized by a vague notion that the strange little rock was responsible for the anxiety needling her ribs.

"Don't worry. Even the Saints of Providence themselves couldn't sit shackled for so long without getting a little irritable," Horvald said.

"A comforting thought." Slee was sure the comparison was meant as a compliment, but it felt oddly like an insult.

Horvald stood up, with much groaning and the clinking of chains. Once he was on his feet, he twisted his body and stretched his limbs as far as they would go. The motions drew sharp gasps, but he persisted with them.

"Aren't you a little too hurt for calisthenics?" Slee asked.

"On the contrary," Horvald wheezed. "These bruises prove how crucial it is to keep the body limber."

"I saw them kick you with those heavy boots. You shouldn't be standing, let alone doing whatever you call this," Slee said.

Horvald, with his legs and arms crossed in what looked like a hopeless tangle, laughed drily. "They are Saint Tagustine's 'Scout's Confinement Drills.' They look strange, but they keep the body strong. I had an especially restful sleep after the little stone worked its magic on me. Moving like this might smart, but at least I *can* move." Suppressing pained grunts, he eased himself back onto the floor. "You should move around too. You don't want to turn to stone."

"I will consider it," Slee said.

"Good. Now, if you won't share your little pebble with me, could you at least share your thoughts on it?" Horvald asked.

Slee explained everything she knew about the strange rock, and everything she didn't know.

"Any number of things could be causing it to draining too much life from us. It could be that it cannot work for humans, or perhaps just severely injured ones. Or it could be something else entirely, I suppose," Slee said.

Horvald nodded pensively. "A mystery worth pondering."

Slee glowered at the little geode, rubbing her hands together under her nose. "I feel like the answer must be right in front of —"

A chorus of shouts in the corridor cut her off.

Slee hid the geode between her back and the wall.

Moments later, a tangle of shouting men spilling into the room. Greycoats wrestled with Bluefingers, yelling and grunting in a confused mass. With a shock like a blow to the stomach, Slee saw Cartín among the Greycoats. He helped the Greycoats pin one of the Bluefingers to the wall and shackle him. Slee could hardly believe what she was seeing.

A moment later, as the Greycoats backed away from their new prisoners, Cartín looked over his shoulder at Slee and Horvald, and gave them a subtle wink.

"Your grandchildren be paying off that spoiled animus long after your dead," a bald Greycoat with a neat grey moustache said. His cheeks burned red from the recent exertion.

In response, one of the three new prisoners spat at his feet. The Greycoats crowded in and began kicking at once.

Slee closed her eyes and turned away at the harsh sound of boots meeting bodies. Small fountains of pain bloomed with each kick, falling like rain on Slee's senses.

"What are *you* looking at? Do you want some?" Cartín's familiar voice rang out, filled with an unfamiliar tone of hatred.

Slee opened her eyes, and her heart turned cold. Cartín loomed over a cowering Horvald. Before Slee could cry out, Cartín pulled him to his feet by his collar, rammed him against the wall, then punched him hard in the gut. Horvald wheezed and collapsed, holding his arms protectively across his middle. Cartín glared at him with narrowed eyes, then scoffed and turned away.

"Come on, you lot. I need a stiff drink," Cartín said, flicking his fingers lazily at the others.

"Hold on. Dídac *did* say we ought to feed them," the bald Greycoat said. His face was flushed deep red, and a little vein in his temple stood out like a fat worm.

"Right you are," Cartín said.

With sudden ferocity, he took a lump of bread from one of his deep coat pockets, and stuffed it into Horvald's mouth.

"Didn't your mother ever teach you table manners? Take *smaller* bites or you'll choke," Cartín said, tutting.

The other Greycoats laughed heartily.

Such rage built inside Slee that she felt as though the heat of it could burn the very shackles off her wrists. She pushed herself upright, despite the sharp pains in her joints.

"Slee, don't," Horvald groaned, the wadded bread in his hands.

"How dare you! You – you—" Slee began, but Cartín reached her before she could get another word out.

He grabbed a handful of her hair with one hand and covered her mouth with the other. With wide eyes and soft, high eyebrows, he whispered, "Pretend this hurts."

Slee was so shocked at being grabbed that she hadn't realized that he wasn't pulling on her hair all that hard.

She made the best sounds of pain she could, and pulled at Cartín's hands as though desperate to get them off.

"Good, now I'll hit you. Ready?" he whispered.

He drew his fist back, then brought it to her belly with a quick, savage motion. However, Slee only felt a light tap.

Cartín released her, and she fell to the floor, unhurt. She gasped for air as though the wind had been knocked from her, and looked up at Cartín with an expression of anguish. Cartín gave her a barely perceptible wink, then turned away.

"Come on lads, we'll be in here all day if we carry on," Cartín said. "Pennald lost the last hand, it's his turn to fetch the ale. Kleuger, you deal us in."

The Greycoats filed out, red-faced and panting, mopping their brows of the sweat raised by the beating. Cartín was last to leave. As he passed Horvald, the two shared a look that, to Slee, looked full of sparks.

Their eyes must only have met for an instant, but Slee somehow felt it contained an entire conversation. She saw — or imagined she saw — little lights winking between them, like starlight on water. The harder she stared, the fainter the lights became, until they disappeared entirely. Her own weary eyes must have conjured them. The moment passed, Cartín left, and the door closed with a heavy clang.

Horvald, who had been curled up and groaning loudly, quietly sat upright and then started tearing the bread into pieces.

Slee, too, abandoned her act of being in terrible pain. She rubbed her eyes.

The new arrivals, who had been chained up at the far end of the dungeon, stared at them. The first was a thin man with dark skin and finely chiselled features. The second was young, his pale skin mottled by acne, especially on his round chin. The third seemed to be the oldest, with streaks of grey in his long whiskers, and one milk-white eye.

"What's going on?" the young one asked. "Were you two pretending to be hurt?"

"Hullo," Horvald said brightly, and held up a piece of bread. "Are any of you hungry? This piece didn't touch my lips."

"No, thank you. Not hungry," the thin man said.

"What are you doing with that bread, Horvald?" Slee asked.

Horvald, now sitting amid the snow of torn pieces of bread, held up a small silver object and cried, "A-ha!"

"What is it?" Slee asked.

"A key."

Slee leaned forward as her heart struck up an eager tempo. "Does this mean …?"

"Well, it's a kind of key," Horvald said, squinting at the thing in his hand. "More of a sturdy little pin that can be used as a key."

"You'll never break out of here. Not even with a proper key," the pimply youth said.

"How did we get caught? I was so sure no one saw us," the thin, dark-skinned man said. "Dídac sees everything, somehow."

"Wretched bloody piss-stain, that elf is," the older man said.

"Saw you do what?" Horvald asked.

"We put charcoal into a day's worth of animus. Renders it useless, apparently," the young man said. "We put it in one little handful at a time while no one was looking. Or so we thought."

"Piss-stain. Absolute, ruddy piss-stain, he is," the older man grumbled.

"Alright, Tybalt, we heard you the first dozen times," the youth said.

"In truth, we were inspired by your little act of mischief, Horvald," the dark-skinned man said.

"I am thoroughly flattered. But where are my manners? Have you met my dear cellmate, Slee?" Horvald said, pointing at her.

The three men glanced at her briefly.

"The half-elf?"

"Yes, Slee is her name. What are you gentlemen called?"

"This fellow is old Tybalt," the youngest man said, pointing to the oldest. "And I'm Batha."

"My name is Aizman," the thin, dark-skinned man said.

"Pleased to meet you all," Horvald said.

"Why did you all take such a risk?" Slee asked.

"Sorry, I doubt an elf would understand," young Batha said.

"Try her. She understands a great deal more than you do," Horvald said.

"Well, the situation out there is desperate. People are about to crack from the strain," Aizman said.

"I'd rather be in here than out there, getting the goo sucked out of my brain, and that's the truth," Tybalt said.

"But if things are that bad, why doesn't everyone just stop? If you all refused Dídac's bidding together, there would be nothing he could do," Slee said.

Batha scoffed softly, looked between his feet and shook his head.

In the ensuing silence, the sound of gentle clicks came regularly from Horvald, who had stuck the pin into the lock of his shackles.

Aizman frowned thoughtfully, then said, "Most depend on this pay to provide for their families. They obey because they have no choice."

"I told you an elf wouldn't understand," Batha muttered.

"I may not comprehend the depths of human folly, but I understand the situation. It's *you* and the other Bluefingers that need to understand. If you just looked around you, this place would fall in an instant," Slee said.

"A-ha! Got it!" Horvald said brightly. His shackles fell from his wrist, and he raised his freed arms in triumph, pin still in hand.

"Excellent!" Slee said.

"What are you celebrating? There are locked doors, an exposed staircase, and all Dídac's Greycoats standing between you and freedom," Batha said.

"Suit yourself, young man. I, for one, shall enjoy the freedom to walk about," Horvald said.

He came to Slee's side and began the process of unlocking her shackles.

"Don't trouble yourself. We'll only have to put them back on if the guards come," Slee said.

"We'll worry about that when those ears of yours hear their boots approaching," Horvald said. "Besides, it's important you keep your body moving. Our chance might come at any time, and you'll slow us down if you're limping on pins and needles."

"I suppose," Slee said.

Her shackles opened with a click, and Horvald gently helped her stand.

She winced as her joints creaked, her tendons strained, and her weakened muscles shivered at the task of holding her body upright. The blanket fell from her shoulders, covering the geode.

"There we are. Let's walk it off." Horvald smiled through his thick blond beard, and offered the crook of his arm to her.

Slee took hold of him, and together they walked in a slow circuit around the dungeon. The more they worked, the more Slee's numb, tingling pains became muted, dull aches. She was not entirely sure the trade was worth it. Still, movement became easier.

The other three prisoners watched in silence as Horvald led her back to her place, then resumed his own spot across from her.

"Horvald, how'd you come to get so chummy with an elf like *her*?" Batha asked, pointing at Slee with his round chin.

"She saved my life," he said simply.

"Did she desert the other side, then?" Aizman said.

"I was never on any side except my own," Slee said.

A brief silence followed, in which the three new prisoners looked blankly at Slee.

"You know, gentlemen, since she clearly speaks Madean, there's no need to pose your questions through me," Horvald said.

Batha looked at both of them, then cowed his head slightly and said, "Sorry, I suppose."

"Good. We'll all have to be on good terms if we're going to escape together," Horvald said.

"How do you propose we do that?" Aizman said.

Slee felt the hard geode against her back, and flinched. She had almost forgotten it was there. As she reached back to adjust it, she was struck by the answer that had so long eluded her.

"We're not going to escape," Slee said. "We're going to grind this place down to rubble."

From the back of her memory, the yellowed pages of an old Elarím tome opened before her. Breathless, eyes wide, she silently recited the principles of telethymia. *Aínan, Muanan, Crantarín, Telethían.* Four things strengthen the bonds between living creatures: love, urgency, common purpose, and allies.

"What is she yammering about?" Batha said.

Slee ignored him, and instead addressed Horvald, "I know why things went wrong before. I connected telethí to you, but *not* to Cartín. I excluded him."

"Why would that change things?" Horvald said.

"*Aínan, Muanan, Crantarín, Telethían,*" Slee said in a rush. "The four strengths of the art. Love, urgency, purpose, allies. Don't you see?"

"I'm afraid I understand less than before," Horvald said with a bemused smile.

"It means that if I'm right, Dídac won't stand a chance," Slee said.

With a broad smile that lifted his grey whiskers and revealed a gold tooth, old Tybalt said, "You know, I don't much care for elves. But if Slee here wants to help us get rid of that dung-smear Dídac, I might just make an exception."

Chapter 25

My hands are red, my enemy's dead
I killed the Capilet in his bed.
He'd have sent me off to die;
I'd rather hang instead.

'Fight the Enemy,' Stanza 4

Thorassa had joined the Elarím.

Fentor was paralyzed for a fraction of a second. He could not think of a sensible response to the situation. He *could*, however, think of many non-sensible responses. After all, Thorassa, a junior officer under his erstwhile command, had joined the bloody enemy.

And the bastard was *smiling* about it.

"Why, you treacherous little worm! You cur! You – you custard-brained, needle-necked, tallow-catching, swine-fondling … hoddy-doddy!" Fentor rounded off the barrage by launching his fist at Thorassa's jaw.

In the instant before he struck, his arm was halted as though caught in an invisible web. The sensation was becoming unpleasantly familiar. The next moment, his fist was thrown back over his own shoulder. As his body twisted, one foot crossed awkwardly over the other, and he lost his balance. Just before he fell into the patch of crystal-glass flowers for the second time, Thorassa caught him by the arm.

"Woah there, Fentor. I've got you," the young man said. Still holding Fentor, his face shone with nauseatingly sincere concern.

"Unhand me, traitor!"

Thorassa released him. "You aren't hurt, are you? The Common Power doesn't allow aggression, I'm afraid. It can be quite strict on that point. You will have to find other ways to express yourself."

Fentor felt like an overheating boiler straining to contain the pressure of his rage. He could almost feel rivets popping off his forehead and spouts of steam gushing out the gaps. His impotent, balled fists trembled at his sides, but otherwise he did not move.

"Let's get you to your friends. Seeing them might calm you down," Thorassa said in a soft, warm voice that only deepened Fentor's fury.

"They've joined the enemy as well, haven't they? That's why you're so eager to take me to them," Fentor growled.

Thorassa laughed gently. "Oh, no. They are as loyal to Madea as ever. But then, so was I when I first came here."

Fentor glowered at the implication. Thorassa, still smiling, beckoned him to follow. Rather than allow himself to be led about by a turncoat, Fentor pushed past him and headed in a direction of his own choosing.

Thorassa, perhaps sensing the dynamic, followed a few paces behind and whispered directions to Fentor.

"Left along this path … right at this tree …" Thorassa would murmur.

Each time, Fentor pretended not to have heard him, and barked, "This way! Quickly, now."

Admittedly, Fentor *did* take the route that Thorassa suggested. Part of him was content to simply appear as though he was leading the way. The other part couldn't stand the sight of Thorassa's rabbit-like face.

Each patch of dense vegetation was indistinguishable from the last. Thorassa, however, seemed to navigate as though each tree held a signpost, and each clover-choked dirt path was a cobblestone avenue. They pushed through curtains of vines and low-hanging branches. They tramped across mossy, weedy, marshy, grassy ground. They swerved between crooked trunks, steep hills, and trickling streams. Everything was bursting with so much color that Fentor's tired eyes soon longed for the sedate grey-brown of Madea's muddy streets.

All the way, dead leaves continued to scrape against the invisible dome overhead.

They reached the main village. Rather, they reached a place where buildings stood out among the still-dense vegetation. There, pale, silver-haired, sharp-eared, willowy elves were everywhere.

Each of them seemed to be engaged in work that ebbed and flowed with strange rhythms. Many carried baskets, buckets, and trolleys filled with goods from one place to another. Once the loads were delivered, some other elf would take the empty vessel and carry something else somewhere else. Food, cloth, tools, books, nails, timber, water, and weapons changed hands so fluidly that Fentor could not see where one process ended and another began. He might have had better luck guessing at the workings of an anthill.

"We'll probably find Hess, Angsley, and Crauford in that building there," Thorassa said, pointing to a crude building at the opposite end of the village.

The structure stood out among the others not only in its shoddy construction, but also by its style. Most of the village had been constructed the elven way, with timber, glass, metal, and stone crafted into curved, irregular shapes. The building Thorassa had indicated had straight timber walls, a rectangular door, and a sloped roof. Except for the many gaps, crooked nails, and misaligned joints, it looked thoroughly Madean.

Many elves stared at Fentor as he passed. He held his head high and refused to meet their gawking eyes.

When they reached the wonky building, Thorassa rapped on the door with a crookedly affixed iron knocker.

"Hess, Angsley, Crauford, you have a visitor," he called.

There was a sound of scraping chairs and hurried steps. The door was thrown open — almost off its flimsy hinges. Fentor felt rather unprepared to meet his friends.

Hess, Crauford, and Angsley all crowded into the doorway, wearing the same stunned expression. Crauford

and Angsley had grown beards, though the tips of their
moustaches stubbornly stuck out. They all wore elven
clothes of soft linen, including navy blue jackets that
vaguely resembled the Bluefinger uniform.

"Fenny?" Hess said at last.

"Hullo, you three," Fentor said. "How have you —"

Hess and Angsley pulled him into an embrace so tight,
it cut off his air supply. With his face pressed hard into
someone's collarbone, someone else's hand patted his
back with great force and three overlapping voices
chattered in his ear. At last, the constriction eased. He held
his friends at arm's length and gulped the free air.

"Good to see you, Fentor," Crauford said. He flashed a
controlled smile while adjusting his spectacles.

"When we heard Lady Talentus had been captured, we
hoped and hoped you survived," Hess said. She pulled on
the many frayed edges of Fentor's shredded clothing.
"What's *happened* to you? Were you mauled by a thousand
bears at once?"

"Don't say a thing, Fentor. Here, have some sapwine. I
wouldn't say it's good, exactly, but in time you'll find the
taste extremely tolerable," Angsley said, as he steered
Fentor toward a long table that looked vaguely familiar.

He looked around while Hess and Angsley continued to
talk over each other. The walls were lined with stacked
casks, and shelves holding strange glassware. Overhead,
crude paintings had been daubed on the wall, perhaps by
children. One broad timber hanging above the back door
read: The Crown Away From Home.

"Have you lot recreated The Crown Upon a Crown?"
Fentor said.

"Well, as best we could. The elves wouldn't help us unless we joined them. Of course, we told them we never would," Hess said.

"It might not look quite like the one back home, but it serves us well enough," Crauford said in his mild, even voice.

"It may look rough, but it certainly smells better," Fentor said. "I suppose there hasn't been enough time for liquor and vomit to really soak into the floorboards."

The others laughed with almost manic eagerness. The swift, joyful, forceful welcome had left Fentor somewhat dazed. He felt as though his brain had been squeezed out by the embrace at the threshold. Now, as a vague sense of unease settled over him like a fog, he began to gather his thoughts.

"Hold on a minute," Fentor said heatedly as they reached the table. "Something isn't right here."

"Well, I did my best with it. I had to do it from memory, and with foreign tools too, you know!" Angsley said, stroking the table as though calming a distressed horse.

"No, not the table. This situation. We're *prisoners* here," Fentor said.

"Keenly observed," Hess said drily.

"Why are you all so happy? Why did they let you build this place? Shouldn't we all be chained up somewhere, under lock and key?" Fentor said.

"This is where I must take my leave," Thorassa said softly.

Fentor turned, startled. He had forgotten Thorassa was still there.

"Get going, then," Angsley said flatly.

"Don't hurry back," Hess said.

"I understand why you're all cross with me. Hopefully, you will see things the way I do soon," Thorassa said in an infuriatingly placid tone.

"Where, exactly, are you going?" Fentor asked.

"I have to return to my work."

"Work? What work?"

"Oh, this and that," Thorassa said with a smile. He gave a soft wave, then left.

"Little prick," Angsley muttered. Then, with a broad grin, he said, "Now that he's gone, what's say we fill Fentor in over a glass of the worst drink he'll ever have, eh?"

"If it's so bad, why drink it?" Fentor said, wrinkling his nose as Angsley poured honey-colored liquid into a quartet of odd-looking glasses.

"It's the only thing around here that can get you drunk," Hess said. "And there is *nothing* else to do."

Fentor shrugged. "That logic is sound enough for me."

He took a place at the table next to Hess and across from Angsley. They each took a full glass and raised them in a toast.

"To Fentor, to reunion, and to the first few glasses of sapwine. May we drink them so swiftly that our tongues grow numb to the taste," Angsley said.

They touched their glasses together, then drank.

The cup, Fentor realised, was fashioned to resemble the strange cup-like flowers he had fallen into earlier. Up close he could see tiny veins running through the glass, and the little folds where one petal joined the next.

A careful sip of the sapwine revealed a bouquet of flavors that clashed horribly. It tasted like some old widow had spilled her perfume into a bottle of Madea's cheapest wine, then diluted it with ditch-water to disguise her mistake. He took a bigger mouthful, hoping that the first impression would quickly pass. Instead, it introduced a lingering aftertaste, which tasted strongly like the bottom layer of straw in a neglected stable.

He set his half-drunk glass down, keeping his mouth tightly closed. Parting his lips might have given the wine an escape route.

"Yes, we all felt that way about sapwine at first," Angsley said. "The trick is to sort of throw it *past* your tongue and swallow as quickly as possible."

"Now, Fenny. Let us explain how things work around here," Hess said, placing her warm hand over his. As he turned, he found her freckled nose and green eyes rather close to his. A feather brushed against his heart.

At that moment, the door opened, and a dark-haired elf woman came in. A sabre-spear hung from her belt, and a brass bow was slung across her chest. She was carrying a small bundle under one arm. Without waiting for invitation, she approached their table.

"Pardon my interruption," she said. "I thought that this one might want new clothes."

"Who is that?" Fentor hissed to the others.

"The enemy," Angsley said softly. "A recruiter. They say she only had to say one word to turn that weasel Thorassa."

"Don't give her anything. She'll twist your words into knots," Hess said.

"I hardly think anyone, elf or otherwise, could ever turn me against Madea," Fentor said.

"That smug attitude is precisely what she'll use against you," Crauford whispered. "Be vigilant. Anyone can be turned at any time. You won't even be aware it's happening."

The dark-haired elf reached them, and placed the bundle on the table. It looked to be a cream-colored linen shirt and trousers tied together with a tea-colored scarf. She looked directly at Fentor, but he said nothing.

Her expression was neutral, but her face was not. The downward curve of her mouth and the furrow in her brow gave the impression that some tragedy had long ago weighed them down. Her blue eyes, however, were bright and active. They roamed across Fentor's face, restless and curious, as though questioning everything they saw.

"My name is Sidarí," she said.

"I can't pay for these. I seem to have misplaced my coin purse—among other things," Fentor said.

"There's no need to pay," Sidarí said. "In these lands, there never is."

"Then what do you expect in return? A favor? Loyalty, perhaps?" Fentor barked.

No elf would catch Capilet Fentor falling for such an obvious trap. *One moment, you accept a simple gift of clothes. The next, you find yourself helplessly ensnared. That's how they get you.*

At least, that was his working theory.

"I expect nothing. They are simply yours, if you want them," Sidarí said, narrowing her eyes.

"Oh, really? And I suppose you expect me to blindly—"

"Fenny, the clothes aren't a trick," Hess hissed in his ear. "They *do* just give us things."

"Ah," Fentor said. Suddenly, he could feel the breeze tickling his skin through the many holes in his tattered clothing. "Very well. I shall change into them momentarily."

"I am glad. After you have put them on, you may come with me to see Lady Talentus, if you like," Sidarí said, her inquisitive eyes searching his face.

Hess tugged on his sleeve. "That's the trick!" she hissed.

"Yes, thank you, Hess," Fentor said drily. He turned to Sidarí, and said, "I shall see her later. If you could just point the way ...."

"Unfortunately, that is not permitted," Sidarí said. "She is under rather strict protection. You will need my help to see her."

"Very well. All four of us will accompany you to see her," Fentor said.

"No. Only you," Sidarí said.

"In that case, I must decline," Fentor said. "Good day, and thank you for the clothes."

"I understand completely. After all, you are no longer bound to follow her orders any longer, are you, Fentor?" Sidarí said with a gently taunting cadence that sent a delightful, yet confusing, thrill of loathing up Fentor's spine.

Despite himself, Fentor pushed his seat back from the table. Angsley and Hess each took one of Fentor's hands and pulled him back in.

"Don't listen," Angsley said. "Ignore her."

"Stay here with us, Fenny. Drink some sapwine and forget all about it," Hess said.

"Her … orders?" Fentor said, pulling his hands away from the others.

"Sit down!" Hess hissed.

"Block your ears and hum loudly," Angsley whispered urgently. "Don't let her bait you, there's a good chap."

"What orders?" Fentor asked, ignoring them.

"Oh, for Temlin's sake," Hess spat.

"Well, we tried. He's as good as gone," Angsley said.

"Try have a little faith in me, won't you?" Fentor said heatedly to his friends. Then, turning to Sidarí, he said, "What do you know about her orders?"

Sidarí cocked her head one way and then the other. "In truth, I don't know much. I only heard things second-hand from those guarding her. *Strange* things."

"What in Providence are you talking about, elf?" Fentor said.

"Rubbish, that's what she's talking. Utter baldershite," Angsley murmured around the edge of his cup.

"I heard that she relayed an order to those guarding her, that Fentor should report to her 'on the double,' " Sidarí said, stroking her chin slowly as though deep in thought. "But that's not the strange part. The strange part is *how* she relayed it."

"How?" Fentor said.

"Well, she spoke directly in their minds. She is encased in a kind of crystal skin, so it seems her lips are sealed shut. I hoped you might be able to shed some light on such a curious phenomenon," Sidarí said.

"She ordered me to report to her?" Fentor said.

"She did."

Fentor looked from one face to another. His friends all shook their heads, hissing at him to ignore the elf. They didn't know, however, that Elatea had drunk several vials of the Elixir of Power. Disobeying someone so powerful was never wise. If the Lady could truly speak inside the minds of her captors, what other strange new powers might she possess?

A golden aura seemed to creep in through the cracks in the timbers of the makeshift tavern. He was afire with anticipation. Could it be, that they were still on the verge of glorious victory?

"Very well, Sidarí. Just give me a moment to change," Fentor said.

Hess groaned, buried her face in her hands, and slumped on the table.

"Watch yourself, Fentor," Angsley said darkly. "They say this elf weaves black magic into her words. She could convince a fox to befriend a hen."

"Oh, no," Sidarí said with a somewhat lighter expression. "I don't use magic of any kind. I am a philosopher."

Fentor's new clothes were soft and warm, but their loose design gave certain parts of him undesirable freedom of movement. He felt like he was floating naked in a bath. To compensate, he tied the scarf rather tightly and cinched the ties on his trousers as far as they would go. The strange shoes, at least, were soft inside and sturdy on the outside. They were made of overlapping cloth strips that had been coated in some strange glue that repelled liquid like a duck's wing. He learned that particular fact when Angsley spilled sapwine on them.

They left the Crown, and Sidarí led him through the village. In response to the stares of the elves, he threw his chest out and strode proudly.

The scene had changed. No longer were there flurries of goods changing hands. Now, the elves had coalesced into groups, and were absorbed in strange and varied crafts.

One knot of elves toiled away in a half-complete building. Fentor was not sure whether they were constructing it, or tearing it down. There was no mortar, no bricks, no frame, scaffold, or foundation. Instead, the elves seemed engrossed in a wall of colored, stacked rocks that formed a sort of mosaic. While some held the wall steady with ropes and poles, others took pieces out and tried to cram them back in elsewhere.

Other elves were toiling over large tubs filled with liquid. Fentor's first thought was of a tanner's curing vats. The elves probed the thick liquid contents with long stirring paddles. One elf reached into a tub and pulled out a lumpy clay object. Thick, viscous drops of purple and yellow liquids slobbered from it. They set the lump down, cracked it with a hammer, and pulled out shining brass tubes.

When they passed a large group that was crushing fruits and boiling them into jam, Fentor at last understood something. At least, he *did* understand until he saw how many of them ate the fruits as they worked, without a single cry of, "Thief!" How did they expect to have anything left for jam if they ate all the fruit?

Without overseers and foremen, it seemed, the elven style of work was a breeding ground for petty theft, inefficiency, and poor discipline. Why, judging by all the smiles and laughter Fentor saw among the Elarím laborers, not a single one of them was working to their fullest.

Good, productive, obedient workers never smile. Not in Madea, at least. Back-breaking work teaches human workers discipline, and judiciously meagre wages teaches them gratitude.

No wonder the elves were destined to lose the war.

As that thought spread a smile across Fentor's face, Sidarí led him to the base of a steep hill at the village's outskirts. A winding path snaked across its face, cut with irregular steps of timber and stone.

"Lady Talentus is being held at the top of this hill," Sidarí said. "The barrier we placed around her is unlike the one that surrounds Rivumaí. I would advise you to treat it with more caution."

"Your sage advice is noted," Fentor said.

"Ah, but I am no Sage. My advice was of the normal kind," Sidarí said.

"I wasn't being literal."

"Nor was I. Perhaps my wit was too subtle for you," Sidarí said.

Fentor was sorely tempted to give a scathing retort, but bit his tongue when she looked at him. It was little more than a sidelong glance, but he sensed that she was testing his response.

Instead he said in his smoothest tone, "Actually, I prefer it subtler."

They climbed the long, winding path side by side. Fentor kept his eyes to the treacherous, uneven ground and the crumbling steps. Sidarí, however, looked outward at the sights of the village and the forest around it.

"Lady Talentus is quite well-known, you know. Even here. I have never heard of you, though," Sidarí said.

Fentor almost snapped at her again, but crushed the words between his jaws. How was it that every word out of her mouth was designed to sting his pride?

He cleared his throat, laughed, and said, "Ah, well. I am a lesser noble. Almost a nobody, really. Most haven't heard of me."

"Strange that she should choose *you* as her companion, don't you think?" Sidarí said. "Out of all the renowned and decorated officers of Madea, she chose you."

"Well, she was impressed by my great potential," Fentor said, fighting to keep his voice even. "She saw greatness in me."

"And now, all your potential is wasted," Sidarí said, shaking her head sombrely. "Pity, pity, pity."

Eager to win, trembling with the need to put the elf in her place, he almost, *almost,* bragged about the Lady's remaining power. He had even drawn in a breath to say it with. No, his potential wasn't wasted. Greatness was still on the horizon. He simply had to refrain from spilling all the secrets of the Elixir of Power to the enemy.

"Yes, it's a pity to be in this prison. But at least some of my cellmates are dear friends," Fentor said.

"A wise perspective," Sidarí said. "The pursuit of greatness oft ends in bitter disappointment. Friendship and community are pursuits that never fail."

"Now *that* is the kind of subtle wit that I appreciate!" Fentor laughed with deliberate unkindness. "Friendship and community, indeed!"

Sidarí seemed unaffected. She only kept looking out across the village, her eyes tracing rooftops and following the dancing leaves.

Fentor briefly indulged a vision of putting Rivumaí to the torch.

"There are different kinds of greatness," Sidarí said softly, hardly seeming to address Fentor. Then she spoke a string of elven words, which sounded to Fentor like the recitation of a list.

There was a brief silence. Fentor simultaneously enjoyed the reprieve, and also strangely hoped the contest would continue. Finding a worthy opponent in a contest of wits was rare, after all.

Despite taking care on the uneven steps, he stepped on a slick of moss and fell to his knees. His shins met the sharp edge of a stone step. Despite the breathtaking pain in his bones, he ignored the hand Sidarí offered and staggered onward unassisted.

"Tell me, is Lady Talentus in any danger?" Sidarí asked.

"Only from your kind," Fentor said.

"Actually, we cannot harm captives."

"I doubt that—I've had your wine. I might never recover."

"What I mean is that the Lady does not appear to be breathing," Sidarí said.

"You think she's dead?"

"Not quite. Rather, she seems to be *unalive*."

Fentor narrowed his eyes. "What in blazes does that mean?"

Sidarí sighed and muttered a word that may have been an elven curse. "Ah! Forgive my poor phraseology, my Madean can sometimes be … maladroit. Put simply, the Common Power detects all things that live in our domain. Me, you, the grass underfoot, but not Elatea. She does not move, she does not breathe, she does not eat or sleep. She may not be dead, but we cannot tell whether she is truly *alive* inside her crystal cocoon."

"She's alive. The dead don't give orders. If you told the truth about her requesting my presence, then she is alive."

"Sound logic. You would make a fine philosopher," Sidarí said.

"A philosopher? How dare you," Fentor said drily.

"I cannot help but wonder, though. We elves define life by its cycles, processes, and connections. Cut off from all that, can we truly call the Lady 'alive?' "

"Arguing semantics might suit philosophers fine, but the rest of us prefer to get on with things," Fentor said.

"That is a valuable insight. We cannot dwell on things that we cannot know. Alive or not, the Lady's condition cannot be guessed. Let us therefore 'get on with things,' " Sidarí said. She turned and raised her eyebrows. "I only hope she is not slowly dying inside her shell …"

Fentor's retort evaporated off his tongue as they reached the top of the hill. If it were not for the Lady and her strange prison, the wildflowers and soft grass would have made the hilltop the perfect setting for a picnic.

Her Excellency stood like some priceless gemstone that had fallen from the stars and taken human form. She still wore the same knowing smile as when she had first been captured. Her lustrous sapphire cage threw shards of light across the faces of the fifty or so Elarím guards.

The chainmail-clad guards held sabre-spears ready, tense as mousetraps about to spring. One, in stark contrast to the others, was completely bald. His face was square, stern, and strangely commanding. Had it not been for his pointed ears, Fentor might have thought him human.

"Take my hand. There is an invisible barrier here that only Elarím may pass," Sidarí said. She held out her hand to Fentor.

He gave her pale, slender hand the same look he might have given a snake.

"It is best not to keep your superior officer waiting," Sidarí said, once again lifting her eyebrows.

With a wrinkled brow to show his misgivings, he took her hand. They stepped carefully forward once, twice, and a third time with nothing happening. Fentor began to doubt that there had been any kind of barrier at all. What could she have to gain from tricking him to take her hand?

Then, as they took the next step, Fentor walked into an unseen net of strong fibers. They pressed on his nose, tugged at his ears, pulled on his arms and legs. Sidarí paused, still holding his hand. She gently took another step, and dragged him along with her. A new, stronger set of ghostly threads hot as summer sunlight coiled around his hand and hers, binding them together. The resistance of the barrier began to give way. In the next moment, the pressure was gone, and Fentor stepped forward freely. The instant they were through, he wrenched his hand away from hers.

WAR WITH ELVES: FOR PROFIT AND
AMUSEMENT

The Elarím guarding Elatea kept their eyes forward, except the bald one. He turned and glared at Fentor with a curled lip, then glanced at Sidarí before turning away. Fentor could only wonder why it had taken so long for someone to look at him with naked hostility.

As she led him through the guards, Fentor reflexively rubbed his hand. The memory of the invisible threads' touch lingered on his skin, unpleasantly warm.

Fentor soon stood in the glistering shadow of Elatea's unearthly crystalline form. Up close, the sheer splendor of her jeweled cocoon dazzled him half out of his senses. He could only stare. The Lady, scattered and reflected in glittering pieces all along the facets of her shell, appeared to have hundreds of ethereal eyes, dozens of phantom limbs, and several gently curving smiles. Fentor looked from one fragment to the next, unable to tell which was real and which was merely a reflected image.

"Has the Lady ... said anything?" Sidarí said softly. "Perhaps you should say something first."

"Well ..." Fentor said, still distracted by the way the light struck the crystal.

Then, coming to himself, he raised a salute and said, "Capilet Fentor Lonokai reporting as requested, Your Excellency."

Nothing happened.

The Lady continued to glisten, prism-like, splitting the sunlight into bands of indigo and blue. Fentor held the salute as Elatea's fractured eyes stared, unseeing, right through him. Doubt bubbled up from his belly like tar. Hess and Angsley were right. Sidarí must have hoodwinked him with the tale of the Lady speaking in the minds of the guards. She could only have brought him there as part of some unfathomable elven joke.

He let his hand fall, then turned to glare at the dark-haired elf.

"I suppose you find this terribly amusing. Well, I won't be made the subject of fun. I may be your prisoner, but my dignity remains int—"

A thousand cannon blasts went off just behind his eyes, cutting his words short. He clapped both hands over his ears and fell to his knees, deafened, stunned, sure he was about to die. Then, as the echoes of the blasts faded, a discordant tinkling noise splintered inside his head, as though someone was pouring broken glass through his ears. Out of the piercing cacophony, a voice like the hiss of steam spoke to him.

Listen closely, Fentor. This costs me tremendous effort.

Fentor could only clutch his head and pray for the agony to pass.

All of this is as I planned. You must gain the enemy's trust. Learn the location of Crann Arborím, by whatever means necessary. When you find out where it is, free me. My guards are few, but they are holding me down with the whole weight of the Common Power. Tell no one of this task. Fail me, and I will screech in your mind until it breaks. I will not repeat myself.

The ear-splitting noise subsided, and Fentor realized that he was curled up on the ground. His throat was raw, and tracks of tears and saliva criss-crossed his face.

A pair of elves pulled him upright and brushed him off, despite his croaked protests.

"Fentor. Are you alright?" Sidarí asked. She came in close to his face. "You were screaming. That looked like quite the ordeal."

"Nothing a stiff glass of wine can't fix," Fentor said, though his words were betrayed by his weak, raspy voice and his tear-stained cheeks. He wiped his face vigorously with his scarf. All fifty guards, he noticed, were staring at him. The bald one wore a crooked, amused smile. The rest had the audacity to looked concerned.

"Well, hopefully her message was worth hearing," Sidarí said lightly.

Fentor did not reply.

Sidarí pulled him back through the barrier, then asked if he could find his way back alone. He assured her that he could.

As he descended the steep hillside, then pushed through the busy elves of Rivumaí, his mind turned around and around like a gear. Elatea's blaring words still rang in his head. He felt like the clapper in a church bell that has just finished ringing. He would not have been surprised to discover his ears were vibrating.

How she expected him to follow her orders, he could not fathom. The Common Power wouldn't even let him hit Thorassa's weaselly face. Defeating fifty armed Elarím was outside the realm of possibility.

As he continued to evade the elves and the loads they carried every which way, he kindled a tentative hope that he might get used to Elatea's psychic screaming. Perhaps, if it came to it, he could simply puncture his eardrums.

In the shadow of the ramshackle tribute to The Crown Upon a Crown, he was shoved aside by several elves who carried a barrel full of some liquid that smelled strongly of fish offal. They wore thick cloth wraps around their faces, apparently to lessen the stench.

"Watch out there! Make way!" one of them grunted.

Fentor tutted at them, loudly enough for them to hear, and watched them as they disappeared into the crowd.

When he turned back to The Crown, he found an elf blocking his way. Their long, silver hair was tied back neatly, and their eyes narrowed over the white strip of cloth that covered their nose and mouth.

"Look here, that was their own fault. They should have been looking where they were going," Fentor said sharply.

The elf rushed forward, and Fentor dazedly observed the thin, talon-like dagger in their hand. Forgetting his surroundings, Fentor could only throw up his hands, eyes locked on the blade's rapid advance.

All at once, nearby elves gave shouts of alarm, the dagger whipped forward, and a tangle of bodies converged around them.

The blade sliced Fentor's forearm, then his cheek and nose, tracing a searing line in his skin. At the same time, what felt like a dozen arms enfolded him and pulled him away. A second crowd of elves wrenched the dagger from his attacker's grasp. Once the weapon was out of their hand, they squirmed free and dove into the crowd, out of sight.

Amid the distraction and shouting that he could not understand, Fentor wrestled himself free from the elves holding him. In doing so, he smeared his blood all over them. Seeing how much blood had painted their clothes made him feel faint. He barked at them to get away from him. He needed space. He needed air. Above all, he needed to work out what in blazes had just happened.

As they backed away from him, he turned in every direction, disoriented by the abrupt end of the ordeal. It felt as though his heart, in a desperate bid for escape, had climbed into his throat and got stuck there.

His would-be assassin was nowhere to be seen.

Chapter 26

A trio of elves wearing leaf-green aprons stuffed with bandages and spindly brass tools promptly appeared at the door of The Crown. Only one of them spoke Madean. They had come, apparently, to 'tend the human's lacerations.'

While Hess and Angsley blocked the door and refused them entry, Crauford cleaned Fentor's face and arm over a washtub filled with rapidly reddening water.

"I must insist," the elf healer said. "Human healing arts are notoriously poor."

"We will be fine!" Hess snapped. "If you want to help, you should catch the little shag-bag who attacked him!"

"Get thee gone, pointy ears!" Angsley bellowed. "No elf will lay so much as a finger on Fentor while I still live!"

"What happened?" Crauford said, inspecting Fentor's wounds with his glasses balanced on the end of his nose. "Did they say anything before they attacked you?"

"No. Some elves carrying a stinking barrel rammed into me. They all had cloths tied around their noses. The one that did this had their face covered too, but now that I think of it, I don't think he was one of them," Fentor said. "Or she."

"We can arrange for warriors to watch over you and your friend," the elf said. "Such terrible violence is not tolerated here. The Common Power stands united against such acts."

"For the last and most *emphatic* time, no!" Hess shouted, then closed the door with great force. The gesture might have had more weight if the door had not continued to swing lazily back and forth on its uneven hinges. As a result, each swing gave them a view of the departing healers.

"By the grace of Providence, these cuts aren't deep enough to need stitching. I doubt they'd let us have needles to stitch with. We're not even allowed to eat with anything sharper than a spoon," Crauford said.

Angsley stomped over, followed quickly by Hess.

"How is he?" Angsley said, tugging on the ends of his beard.

"They missed his eye and didn't sever any major blood vessels," Crauford said. He steadily wound a length of gauze around Fentor's arm. At first, it blushed bright red, until successive layers managed to contain the bleeding. "If you ask me, some Saint of Providence is smiling on our Fentor."

"Well, if they'd been smiling a bit harder, Fentor wouldn't have been all sliced up in the first place," Hess said. Her auburn hair had come partially loose, framing her heated expression like a cloud of cinders.

"I appreciate, but reject, your concern," Fentor said. "Talk about something else, would you?"

"First things first. I'll get the wine," Angsley said, and went over to the table and began pouring.

"Curiously, it's not all that easy pulling conversation out of thin air when your friend has just been slashed to ribbons," Hess said.

"Tell me how you all got here, then," Fentor said. "Did the elves take the Gutter Trench?"

"Hold still while I plaster your face," Crauford said softly, leaning so close that Fentor could see every pore on his nose and the individual hairs of his beard.

As Crauford brushed thick white paste on his wound, Angsley set down a pair of overfilled glasses beside them. The sapwine looked like urine to Fentor, and was equally inviting.

"May the Saints forever curse the bull-toad that got us stuck here," Angsley said darkly. Raising a glass in a toast to no one in particular, he drained it in one, then headed back to the table for more.

"The tale of our capture is one of surpassing hubris, shocking cowardice, and peerless maladministration," Hess said.

"Such a vivid and eloquent introduction," Fentor said, wincing a little as Crauford continued to gently apply the paste.

Angsley returned, full glass in hand, and paced to and fro with a stern air of gravitas. If he only had a white barrister's wig, the image of a dramatic trial would have been complete.

"Grand Toque Quindly," he said, enunciating the name through a slight growl. "He took command of the Gutter Trench cohorts in the Lady's absence."

"Ah, Quindly. He and I have crossed paths," Fentor said.

Crauford began smoothing see-through strips of gauze across his cheek. Once they contacted the paste, they began to harden.

"Years ago, some unrepentant scoundrel must have seduced a dimwitted oaf in the alley behind the original Crown Upon a Crown. Only a union like that could have produced a villain like Quindly," Angsley said.

"He drank in his tent. Loafed about. Gave unreasonable orders without ever doing a thing himself," Hess said.

"Which, in controlled doses, are the rewards of achieving high command," Angsley said soberly, with a finger raised. "However, with excessive indulgence, men like Quindly erode morale and grind loyalty down until only dust is left."

"He did exert great effort on one thing: pompous speeches. Destiny and greatness and Providence and victory and all other nonsense," Hess said.

"That ought to hold," Crauford said softly, prodding the plaster.

"Many thanks, Lancer," Fentor said.

The plaster on his cheek pulled tightly on his skin as it dried, dragging his eyelid down and making the exposed eye water. He therefore was forced to dab away tears in between pungent sips of sapwine as the others continued the tale of their capture.

"Oh yes. The man could bloviate. In his first speech about 'working towards glory,' it was abundantly clear who would get all the work, and who would get all the glory," Angsley said.

"He paid no heed at all to the recommendations of subordinates," Crauford said with a little sniff.

"One day he called the other Capilets and I to his tent, and asked us why we hadn't gained any ground since he'd arrived," Angsley said.

"Don't tell me you told him to his face," Fentor said.

"No, but he should have," Hess said.

"Regrettably, I gave excuses. I told him the Gutter Trench was famously hard-won, and advancing further would depend upon successes in other areas of the front," Angsley said. "My advice was to keep the ground we had and wait for an opportunity to ripen."

"What did he say?"

"He said that if he had wanted excuses, he would have asked his son to explain why he keeps failing out of the M.L.C. Academy," Angsley said.

"He gave the order for a full advance," Hess said. She took a long swig of sapwine with a puckered, sour look that could have been from Quindly or the wine's taste.

"Just like that?" Fentor said. "Full advance?"

"All his cohorts were to advance. No support. No artillery. According to him, we hadn't been shooting straight. Having the targets closer would therefore help our aim," Angsley said.

"We might have mutinied, but half the other blockheaded Capilets supported Quindly," Hess said.

"The worst part was early in the advance. We marched under the trees without seeing any sign of the enemy," Crauford said. "Until, all at once …"

"A thousand whistlers lit up on every branch," Angsley said. "I don't know how many died in that first volley."

"We're alive because of Angsley," Hess said. "He didn't fire a single shot. The moment those arrows appeared, he dragged me and Crauford into cover."

"Well …" Angsley murmured, a shadow falling over his face as he scuffed his feet. "I always thought I'd die fighting if it came to it. One last blaze of glory. A feat of ultimate defiance. Instead, I shrank away like a coward …"

"The greatness of your act cannot be measured. Quindly's only thoughts of glory were for himself. He would've had us die for nothing," Crauford said, laying a hand on Angsley's broad back.

"There you have it, Fenny. Here we are in an elven prison, trying to find out how many cups of sapwine it takes to forget we aren't at home," Hess said.

They returned to the long table and each took a stool. Fentor braved another sip of wine, shivering as it befouled his tongue.

"What *is* this stuff made from?" Fentor asked.

"Sap," Hess said.

"Ah. Of course it is," Fentor said.

"They ferment the sap of a particular tree, the *crúcwain*. A small portion is kept for drinking, while the vast bulk is used in the processes that make their weapons and tools."

Crauford adjusted his glasses and fanned out his fingers on the table. "Their manner of industry could not be more different than ours, and yet there are—"

Angsley reached into his pocket, then dropped a handful of dice noisily on the table. They were crudely carved from some course-grained wood, their edges frayed from use. "Enough of that, now, Crauford. The less we talk about the elves, the better." He shook the dice then cast them on the table, jabbing them as he counted his score. Then he said, "I almost forgot—what happened with Lady Talentus?"

Angsley passed Fentor the dice.

"Oh, nothing. I shouldn't have gone after all. They only wanted to laugh at my reaction." The little wooden dice kept skipping excitedly from his fingers as he reached for them. At last, he snatched them all, shook them like a fox shakes a hen, then cast them with so much force that half of them fell off the table.

Elatea's cold, crystal-fractured, blue eyes flashed before him for a single, airless instant. Fentor's fingers vibrated like tuning forks.

All the others gawped at him.

"He's gone pale," Crauford said softly.

"Get some color back in your cheeks, there's a good lad." Angsley slid Fentor's glass closer to his trembling fingers.

Fentor drank the jaundiced liquid in one, sloppy gulp. Mercifully, he could not really taste it.

"There. Pour me another won't you? Crauford, it's your roll," Fentor said in a rush, drumming his fists on the table.

Tell no one of this task.

Fail me, and I will screech in your mind until it breaks.

Elatea's voice, or the memory of it, drowned out
Crauford's gentle reply.

"It's no wonder he's all out of sorts, he's just been
attacked by a maniac!" Hess shot a venomous look at the
door.

"I'm not out of sorts, I'm 'in of sorts' … I am suitably
within my usual sorts. I simply need to lie face-down in a
dark corner after we finish playing dice," Fentor said,
struggling to shepherd his lazy tongue through the
sentence without slurring. His dry mouth called out for
more wine. His hand obeyed the call, if a little clumsily,
tipping half the liquid in his mouth and the rest down his
front.

The others continued to fuss and cluck over him. What
they failed to understand was how little the knife attack
bothered him. He couldn't correct them, however, without
risking Elatea's wrath.

No conceivable plan could possibly fulfil the Lady's
wishes. She wanted not only escape and the location of
Crann Arborím, but she also wanted him to achieve those
ends alone.

He swallowed down a pork-knuckle-sized lump that
had settled in his throat. He looked at Hess' nose for a little
while. It had gone pink, from the wine or perhaps from
indignation. Either way, the new coloration partially
obscured some of her freckles. The color was like the rosy
aura of a slow dawn, when the sun must first surmount a
bank of sea-foam clouds before it can show. All that just
on a nose. Remarkable.

"Fenny? Fenny! Fentor!" Hess flapped her hands vigorously in front of her eyes.

"Eh? What?" He blinked and reached for the dice, guessing that it was his turn. No dice were on the table.

"What are you staring at?"

"I'm afraid I was lost in thought. Whose turn is it?"

"We stopped playing after you dropped all the dice," Angsley said.

"It's time you had a lie-down, my friend," Hess said as she got up.

Tell no one of this task.

Tell no one.

Angsley and Hess lifted him from his seat and led him around the back of the shelves stacked with glassware. There were four unfurled bedrolls in a nook that, in the original Crown Upon a Crown, would have been the barman's counter. Fentor's protests were met with gentle dismissals.

"Temlin's tears! Can't a fellow let his thoughts drift without being manhandled?" he rumbled as they forced him down onto a nest of blankets.

"You're battle-stunned," Crauford said. "You didn't only 'drift off.' You were catatonic for long stretches. I've seen countless Bluefingers go through it in the wake of gruelling combat."

"Get some rest, now, Fenny. We'll keep watch. They won't set foot in here while I'm watching."

Fentor, finding himself swaddled in blankets, closed his eyes. He just needed a moment to straighten his tangled, knotted thoughts.

With a long sigh, he said, "I'm fine, really. I admit that I may have had a little fright—"

"Who are you talking to?" asked Hess.

He opened his eyes.

Night had—somehow—instantly fallen. Hess stood nearby, holding a strange lantern. It had no visible flame, yet it cast a pool of ruby-red light around her. The rest of the room was dark.

"Ah," he said, half as reply, half as a yawn. His cocoon of blankets came loose as he stretched out his stiff limbs. "I suppose I fell asleep."

"How are you feeling?" She dropped to one knee next to him, placing the lantern behind her.

"Not excessively wretched," he said.

The makeshift beds around him were all empty. The sound of clattering dice and clinking glasses came softly from the main table.

"Crauford and Angsley?" he asked, tilting his head toward the noise.

"We've all been keeping watch, taking turns to sleep."

"Have you had your turn sleeping, then?"

"Actually, I was about to settle in." She leaned close. He could see every spot, every fiber in her moss-green irises. "But now, I'm wide awake."

"I, er …" Fentor's mouth and mind dried up. He fished for something to say, feeling rather like he was casting out a herring-net into sand dunes.

As Hess' face—especially her lips—drifted closer to his, his heart pumped loudly enough to drown out his thoughts. He could only watch.

Then, an instant before disaster, he pulled himself away. She leaned back on her heels, eyes wide. As her cheeks turned pink, he stammered, hoping to craft some phrase that would make her understand everything.

If they were, in fact, doomed to rot in elven prison for the rest of their days, then all the obstructions of polite society would be cleared away. The circumstances of her birth and his would count for nothing. If there truly was no escape, then he'd have gladly let the moment proceed.

But Elatea had thrust a secret burden upon his shoulders. Success in his mission mattered more than anything else. And once he succeeded, they'd return to Madea. He didn't dare give Hess any part of him that Madean convention would tear away.

He wanted to express all that, somehow.

Instead, what he said was, "Could you be a Saint and fetch Crauford for me?"

She sucked her teeth. "Crauford? Why?"

Unknown to him, an idea had brewed deep in his mind while he slept. Now, it bubbled to the surface. He was forbidden to *tell* anyone of Elatea's mission. But, so long as he kept them ignorant of his intentions, he could certainly *use* their help. It would take all Fentor's mastery of subtlety, but it just might work.

Fentor couldn't suppress a grin at his own genius. "I'd like to try brewing a potion or two."

Chapter 27

Slee woke to choking terror.

As it wrenched her from sleep, she only knew only the color and outline of the terror. Somewhere, the specter of a pale, screeching monster lurked out of sight. Slee sensed it with the incoherent certainty of a nightmare. The beast flashed its acid-yellow eyes, folded its vast wings as it dove, reaching toward her with talons longer than her arms …

The dungeon was silent and cold. Slee squinted into the gloom and saw the rumpled forms of Horvald and the other prisoners. None of them stirred.

She wrapped her thin blanket tighter around her legs. The vision had been so vague and yet so vivid. It felt like it belonged to another dreamer, but had been thrust inside her mind. The memory of the screeching persisted as a high-pitched whine in her ears.

Just as she calmed herself enough to try returning to sleep, the monster rose before her again like a phantom spun from moonlight.

Blind terror froze her, and she could only watch as grasping talons closed in. Then, the outline of the beast clarified in the moonlight, and a stern, round face with glaring black eyes loomed before her. All at once, Slee realized that it was no dream—it was a real owl.

The owl was hunting Dit-Dit.

Using telethí to guide her, she reached out to her little friend in the dark. Dit-Dit was shivering, unable to move, beneath the trees that ringed the lake. Slee touched her mind. Urgency erased the distance between them, and in the space of a single heartbeat, the telethí bound them as one united mind. The black fog of fear that had overwhelmed Dit-Dit filled Slee's heart. As their bond solidified, the fog thinned and then dispersed, and the little rat shone like a beacon of courage.

"Run!" Slee breathed.

Dit-Dit shot out from under the owl's shadow. She evaded the grasp of the claws, but one talon grazed her back. Dread and alarm postponed the pain—Slee had no idea how serious the cut might have been.

The little rat continued to dart over arched roots and through soft piles of pine needles. The owl, screeching somewhere in the darkness behind, took flight once more and wheeled overhead. Ahead, the mountain-sized distillery gleamed in the moonlight. The little window that led to the dungeon filled Dit-Dit's little mind, leaving no room for other thoughts.

Slee urged her friend on, hardly aware of the dungeon around her, or even of her own body. She saw through Dit-Dit's eyes, felt the rush of wind against her whiskers, heard the skittering gravel under her paws. The dungeon window was still far off, and there was no telling where the owl might be. Slee squeezed her eyes shut, bracing for the moment she would have to feel Dit-Dit enclosed in the predator's grasp.

Anxiety turned to dread as Dit-Dit began to slow. Her little legs had carried her so far already, and now her strength was almost spent.

"Horvald!" Slee hissed. "Horvald!"

With a sharp sniff, Horvald sat up. "What is it?"

"My friend is in danger. Help me!"

"What? Help you how?" He cleared his throat.

"Telethymia," Slee said softly. "Lend your strength to me."

"But I'm human! You said —"

"There is no other way. I will have to lead you." Slee began to open herself up to the world, and let all her animus unfurl. "Imagine that we are in a small boat on stormy waters. I will steer. You must avoid capsizing us — don't push or pull or do anything. Does that make any sense?"

"Not really."

"It will have to do. Hold yourself loosely. Don't resist."

Slee took hold of Horvald's faint, frayed telethí. She twined them together with hers, and let their combined animus flow toward Dit-Dit.

The little rat risked an upward glance. The owl wheeled around, a shadow against the moon, then folded in its wings as it dove.

The strength Horvald and Slee sent to Dit-Dit gave her a new burst of speed. She scrambled over gravel as large as boulders, flitted past weeds as tall as trees. She ran the fastest a rat could run, but no faster.

The dungeon window was just ahead. The owl's wings whispered just behind, not even a hand-span away. Slee held on with every bit of strength she had, urged Dit-Dit onward. There was nothing in the world but the promised refuge of the window.

Dit-Dit's body jerked suddenly to one side.

Slee slapped a hand over her mouth, strangling an involuntary cry. She waited for the pain, for Dit-Dit's body to be torn apart by talon and beak.

But death never came.

Dit-Dit kept running, and hurtled in through the dungeon window. The owl flapped noisily against the bars, then turned and flew away.

Dit-Dit sped along a crack in the wall, and came down into Slee's lap. The little rat shivered and panted, sharing Slee's surprise that she had lived.

"What happened?" Slee breathed. "How did she…?"

"I think I might have … rocked the boat," Horvald said, with a woolly, sheepish aura rising faintly from his ears.

Slee stared at him. "What do you mean?"

"Well, I did as you asked. I tried not to do anything, and just let you pull me along. But when the owl was almost upon your friend, I kept thinking, 'Move aside!' " Chains clinked as he rubbed his face and smoothed his beard anxiously.

"You made her move?"

"I think she *chose* to jump to the side. Maybe. I don't really know what happened. I'm sorry," he said.

Slee stroked Dit-Dit between the ears. The choking smog of the recent terror began to fade, and in its place the dungeon shone with the remaining telethí. The threads were thicker, brighter, and more numerous than Slee expected. Most tethered Slee, Dit-Dit, and Horvald together, but some wandered elsewhere. After a moment exploring the bonds, Slee realized that Cartín had become entangled with them, despite being in his bunk on the far side of the distillery.

"Don't be sorry. You were right," Slee whispered. "I was urging her to go forward. She would have died if you hadn't intervened."

"Well, I'm glad your friend made it through. Though, you *did* fail to mention that she is a rat."

"What did you think I meant by 'friend?' "

"I suppose, in hindsight, that's exactly what I should have expected."

"How are you feeling?"

"Fine. A little drained." Horvald slouched back against the wall. "Do you suppose the other three are awake? This would have been quite the thing to eavesdrop on."

"No, mate, we're fast asleep," old Tybalt said in a voice gruff from recent sleep.

"We didn't wake up from the sound of you two muttering and rattling about," whispered Batha sardonically. "No, we're peacefully dreaming, clearly."

"You know nothing of—" Slee began.

"Terribly sorry, dear friends. We didn't realize we were making such noise," Horvald said.

"Just keep it down after dark, will you? Hard enough getting to sleep with these chains digging into my bones," Tybalt grumbled.

"As you wish. Sleep well, gentlemen," Horvald said.

The prisoners all fell silent, but the air in the dungeon held no peace. Slee guessed that none of them would find the sleep they needed.

Dit-Dit's little mind had calmed enough that Slee was able to glimpse some of her simple thoughts. A vision of the steep hills surrounding the distillery leaked across the bond. The pine trees, from Dit-Dit's perspective, towered so high above it seemed they went on forever. The little rat remembered the arduous journey between them, following a faint but intriguing scent. She paused often in whatever nooks of shelter she could find, her little nose twitching.

The memory had a vague air of importance that Slee could not place. It didn't seem like an idle train of thought. It felt more like Dit-Dit was thrusting the vision into Slee's mind, showing her something crucial.

Dit-Dit remembered the scent rising to its strongest as she approached a curiously tangled thicket. Slee knew the smell too, but could not place that, either. The little rat approached with great caution, despite a nearby rumbling sound that shook her whiskers. She poked her little head in between the dense leaves, and spied an enormous tortoise surrounded by a flock of peaducks.

Slee choked back a sob, half of relief and half of despair. She let her tears fall in silence, let her mingled aura spread. Horvald and Cartín soaked up part of her hope and grief, perhaps unaware of the comfort they gave her.

Slowjaw, Felheim, and her peaducks were alive, and together. But they all were clinging to life by the slenderest of threads. The great crack across Slowjaw's belly and the bullet-wound in Felheim's wing were not healing well. The group was nestled in a kind of hibernation, their weak telethymic bonds the only thing sustaining them.

They were dying.

****

The sound of heavy boots approaching frightened Dit-Dit—she darted into the deepest folds of Slee's blanket. The prisoners exchanged wary, meaningful looks.

Slee met Horvald's eyes last. They silently acknowledged what they both sensed—Cartín was approaching, but he was not alone.

Distant clanging and shouting could be heard also, but Slee could not tell the cause of the commotion.

The door swung open, groaning heavily. Cartín entered first, his lips thin and his eyes flashing with warning. He brought a tray of food over to Slee and knelt down.

"Give it to me. Quickly," he breathed.

Along with his sparking, agitated aura, he projected an image of the geode.

Slee dug the stone out and handed it to Cartín, who tucked it away at once. He glanced at the other Greycoats, who carried identical trays to the other prisoners.

"Dídac's coming," Cartín hissed.

Then, with his lips curling in disdain, he tossed a wedge of cheese and a burnt corner of bread on the floor beside her.

"Pick it up," he said, loudly enough that the others would hear.

Slee snatched up the meagre meal and ate it quickly.

The other Greycoats treated Horvald and the other prisoners with contempt that was not staged. A stout man with a wiry, red moustache stamped on Horvald's fingers. Cartín watched intently, but did not intervene. He pulled his hat low over his eyes, but Slee could almost feel the heat radiating from his glare.

Horvald's nostrils flared and his cheeks reddened, but otherwise he gave his tormentor no reaction. When he steadily reached for his food with his other hand, the Greycoat kicked it away.

Dídac's arrival halted the petty torments. All the Greycoats stood stiffly at attention, limbs drawn in and eyes forward.

The elf regarded each of the prisoners briefly, with open disgust, as though they were puddles of vomit, and looking at them any longer would make his own stomach evacuate.

"Why, you all look miserable," Dídac said. "Just as miserable as every other gang of arrogant malcontents."

Batha drew in a breath to say something, but Tybalt kicked him and shook his head.

"Your kind are always the same. You think you'll make yourselves rich by destroying that which better people have built." Dídac paced along the length of the dungeon,

seeming to punctuate his words with the click of his heavy
boots. "You never create anything for yourselves. You
simply consume the fruits of civilization, gnaw on society
until the bones show. Nought but *rats,* all hunger and no
thought. It never even occurs to you to thank the betters
who furnished you with all your comforts."

Batha shouted, "The only rat here is you!"

Dídac paused in front of the young man who glared at
him in defiance. All the air seemed sucked out of the room
as Dídac stood there, rigid and composed. Tybalt and
Aizman both averted their eyes.

Slee ground her teeth together, cringing in anticipation.
She half expected the elf to draw a sword and impale the
young prisoner, but she couldn't sense a thing about his
intentions. Dídac lacked even the faintest hint of an aura.
He carried with him only empty, ionized space.

Batha's eyelids flickered, then he dropped his gaze to
the floor.

Dídac continued pacing as though there had been no
interruption.

"A few weeks ago I had an obedient cohort. They were
happy. Happy with their task and their pay." The elf
paused in front of Slee. "I wonder why all that changed."

Slee replied in elvish, "A few weeks here with you, and
only *now* they're unhappy? They lasted longer than I
would have."

Dídac gave her a lofty, unaffected look, but his cheeks
turned pink. "Stand up."

"Don't you hurt her!" Horvald shouted.

Cartín raised a hand as if to strike him, and when Horvald flinched, he let it fall with a chuckle. "Keep your mouth shut."

Slee, looking straight into Dídac's eyes, was sorely tempted to refuse. Dit-Dit still shivered in the blanket, though, vulnerable and small. Swallowing her defiant remark, Slee slowly stood. With the same motion, she bunched up her blanket around Dit-Dit and let it fall in a heap. The elf looked from Slee to the blanket with narrowed eyes, but said nothing.

Though it hurt to stand, the exercise she'd done at Horvald's insistence made it bearable.

"Unlock her," Dídac said.

The stout Greycoat plodded over to Slee and removed her shackles. The scent of ale clung to his long, red whiskers.

"We're going to have an exchange of ideas, you and I," Dídac said with a bow, waving Slee toward the door with a flourish, as though he was ushering a monarch. "Come along, now."

The Greycoats, including Cartín, chuckled.

"We can speak here." As she spoke, she shifted her focus to Dit-Dit, reassuring her and imploring her to stay hidden. The little rat was torn between the safety of her shelter and her instinct to flee. Only the bond with Slee kept her in the blanket.

"Hm. I asked nicely. They say honey catches more flies than vinegar, but that only leaves me wondering what to do with something much nastier than a fly?" Dídac looked around at the Greycoats. "Any ideas, gentlemen?"

The nearest Greycoat, leering and laughing quietly, pulled her arm, then shoved her toward the door. She staggered, then drew herself upright and walked of her own accord. As she passed Dídac, he raised a finger to stop her.

"Check her blanket," Dídac said.

"No!" Slee lunged toward it, but Dídac caught her by the arm.

Despite his crushing, immobilising grip, he expended no apparent effort. His hand did not even move when she struggled, as though he was made of stone.

The red-whiskered guard nudged the blanket with his boot, and lifted the corners.

"It stinks," he said.

"Your poor nostrils. What is she hiding?"

Slee poured all her strength and courage into her bond with Dit-Dit. She was frozen with fear in a fold of the blanket, clinging to it with her claws as the Greycoat pawed clumsily through it. At any moment she would be exposed, and the little rat would need all the strength she could get to run away.

"There's nothing," the red-whiskered Greycoat said.

"Idiot! Get out of the way," Cartín said as he stomped forward and snatched up the blanket.

Holding it bunched in both hands, he raised it off the ground and gave it a violent shake. Nothing fell out. Then, as he made to throw it back down, a corner of bread bounced at his feet.

Through the shining telethí between them, Slee had seen what Dídac could not—Cartín had held Dit-Dit carefully in his hands while he shook the blanket out. Now, placing the blanket and Dit-Dit safely back on the floor, Cartín held up the chunk of bread.

"Saving it for a special occasion, were you?" Cartín jeered.

It was a curious feeling, sending Cartín a burst of gratitude along their invisible tether, while also scowling as deeply as she could. The cold and hot emotions mixed, like a bucket of steaming water added to a freezing bath, raising gooseflesh on her arms. Cartín, likewise, acknowledged her thanks with his lip curled.

Dídac sighed and waved his hand at Slee. "Such emotions over a lump of stale bread. Take her."

Two Greycoats flanked Slee and pulled her toward the door.

"To those of you still in chains, I have a proposition," Dídac said. "As the great Saint Temlin the Exiled once remarked, 'By striking a deal, any two men are made equal.' Fair exchange is the very bedrock of civilization. Therefore, I come to you with an offer that will mend your woes *and* mine."

The Greycoats took Slee from the room, closed the door, and she heard no more. The curious glow of the corridor dyed everything blue, as though in deep water.

"Saint Temlin the Exiled," Slee muttered. "Such blithering nonsense. I'd exile him, too."

"Shut it, wench!" one Greycoat barked.

"You may be godless, but you'll speak of the Saints with respect! Especially the great Temlin, the only Madean who ever returned from Elarím captivity," the other said.

Both men tightened their hold on her arms, and pushed her along jerkily to make her stumble.

"You're godless too, you know," Slee said. "The Church
of Providence isn't theistic."

"What?" one Greycoat said.

"You have Saints, not gods."

"What difference does it make?"

"No, well, she's not *wrong*." The Greycoat unlocked a
door near the end of the corridor, and they led her inside.
"She's just splitting hairs, is what it is. The Saints function
as a traditional pantheon, but there *is* ongoing debate as to
the nature of their divinity in the afterlife. See, in this life
they are flesh-and-blood people, but what about after? Are
they gods or demi-gods, or are they just notable
individuals who are posthumously honored by the
Church?"

The tiny room had barely enough room to hold the table
and the stool they deposited Slee on. Regardless, the
Greycoats squeezed in, standing chest to chest.

"What in the – what are you *talking* about? Where did
this come from?" the Greycoat said.

"I studied theology. I was going to join the Church."

"How'd you end up here, then?"

"This pays better."

Dídac appeared in the corridor outside. The two
Greycoats made a hasty exit, and cleared the way for the
elf.

"Shall we stand guard, sir?" the theological Greycoat
asked.

"No. Keep an eye on the Blues, see they don't sabotage
anything else," Dídac said.

"Sir." The Greycoat nodded, and left.

The elf watched Slee with the rigidity of a cat watching a bird. The little smile he wore did not belong on his face. It was like his lips were drawn in a different style than the rest of his sharp, straight features. After a moment, he padded into the room and closed the door behind him.

We can't let him hurt her.

We won't. Hold on, Slee.

Cartín and Horvald spoke in her ear, as clearly as if they were right beside her. She flinched.

Dídac caught her recoiling, and seemed to think she was reacting to his presence. The little smile widened.

Cartín? Horvald? She sent her thoughts along the telethí. No replies came.

Dídac seemed to fill the room from the ceiling to the floor. Bathed in the blue light, he seemed almost translucent, and the irises of his eyes appeared white.

"This morning's little *outburst* has already been quelled. The Bluefingers are back at work in the Extraction Chamber. All you achieved was a tightening of rations for the perpetrators. Of course, you don't care about their fate, do you?"

"What outburst?"

Dídac shot air through his thin nose. "Don't try. I'm warning you now—very nicely, I might add. This is the honey. You don't want the vinegar. Don't deny your role in the sabotage. We aren't here to talk about that."

Slee, deeply perplexed, truly had no response. Sabotage? If there had been sabotage, it certainly had nothing to do with her.

Cartín? What is this sabotage? Slee reached out across
their bond, though the telethí felt strained, like a hair on
the verge of being plucked out.

Slee? Cartín's voice came to her, faint as an old memory.

"No. I understand what you did and why you did it.
What I must know is how," Dídac said, leaning over the
table, enunciating each word.

"You want to know how," Slee repeated.

"If you would be so kind," Dídac said, the words hissing
against his teeth.

"How I did … what, precisely?"

Dídac brought his hand down on the table, as though
swatting a fly. The gesture, made with little visible force,
was still enough that it broke the table into three jagged
pieces. Slee jumped at the noise. Dídac, too, pulled back
his hand quickly. It seemed he had not expected the table
to break, either.

Slee! Is he hurting you? thought Cartín, or perhaps
Horvald. The telethí connecting them seemed thin and
stretched.

Quickly resuming a posture approved by the Madean
Land Corps, Dídac brushed his hands together and said,
"Even my vast and much-tested patience can wear thin.
The next thing to splinter will be your bones. Do *not* deny
what you did."

Slee said nothing.

A manic, colorless light shone from his eyes. "By all
means, explain your methods! You and I both know that
humans can't use the Common Power—at least, not
outside Elarím territory. Without Crann Arborím, under
constant supervision, they can't so much as glimpse a

single thread of telethí. They can't even *think* the way elves do. I doubt they're even aware of the way you got them bobbing about on your strings, the poor puppets. How did you do it?"

Slee did not answer, thoroughly confused. What could she say that he would even accept as an answer? She could not confess to a crime she knew nothing of, nor could she deny it.

She could only sit there in silence.

One of Dídac's eyelids fluttered like a bee's wing.

Then he slammed his fist into the wall with a sound like a cannon blast. The stone he had punched was now recessed a hand's width deeper than its neighbors.

Slee!

Are you hurt?

What's going on?

Cartín and Horvald's voices overlapped in her ear, stronger than before. Even Dit-Dit's thoughts of concern joined them.

Slee could not still her trembling legs, nor could she swallow properly. She couldn't have spoken a word, even if she knew what to say. All she could do was watch the elf flex his fist, and cling to the telethí that linked her heart to her friends'.

Help me, she thought.

If they heard her plea, she did not know. All fell silent in her heart.

She had to have courage. Papa had always said there were different kinds of courage.

Whatever you stand up to, it's the standing up that's courage.

Then came Mama and Papa's other words—their mantra, their greeting and farewell.

All life cares for all life.

"First, one of them breaks the winch-lift. That's easily repaired," Dídac said, with poorly forced calm. "Then *three* of them are caught stuffing charcoal into barrels of animus. That ruins them, but we can make more. Now a dozen of them have staged a *coordinated* fit of vandalism, of bedlam and property destruction, all without any possible means of organizing it. I took away their little whispered meetings, I gave them separate break times, I kept them at work longer, I gave them no time at all to talk. And yet, talk they did, and out of their mouths came the words of elves. I have lived among humans long enough to know they didn't come up with those ideas alone. Someone put them there."

The elf crushed the remains of the table underfoot, stamping it into smaller and smaller splinters as he closed the distance between himself and Slee. He leaned closer and closer, bringing the humming, sterile aura of nothingness to Slee's face.

" 'The rich draw wealth from the poor, as a tick draws blood.' So said the Sage Nyendí," Dídac said in a soft and silken tone. Then, he scoffed, and straightened. "The Elarím honor no Sage above her. And yet, just the other day I heard the humans whispering. Comparing Lady Talentus and I to leeches. Blood-suckers. I saw through it immediately. No human says such a preposterous thing unless an elf has coached them to say it."

"Perhaps you haven't met the right sort of humans," Slee said. Despite her dry throat and trembling legs, she managed to say it all in a steady tone.

A brief laugh burst from Dídac's unsmiling lips. His aura, so close, became more and more unpleasant by the moment. It was like the sound of buzzing flies translated into a color; it was like the smell of distant lights being extinguished. It defied and disconnected the senses.

"How did you do it? Did you whisper to the guards?" Dídac asked.

"No."

"Did you smuggle all those Elarím books in here?"

"No!"

"Did you write messages on beetle's wings? Have elven writings flown in by pigeon? Answer me!"

"Alright! Yes, I trained pigeons to fly in pages from Nyendí's *Questions for Questions*. I had ants cut the paper into squares, and parade past in a sequence so all the humans could read it. Is that what you want to hear?"

Dídac seized her hand and slowly, inexorably tightened his grip. Slee gasped at the overwhelming pain. Her bones felt as though they were grinding together, on the verge of snapping like kindling.

"Tell me what you did, at once! Humans can't use the Common Power. Tell me why they're acting like they can!"

Help me, please!

Dit-Dit, Cartín, and Horvald wordlessly gave what strength they could. Though the straggling telethí were limp and thin, the little surge of animus they carried blunted the pain slightly.

"I'll tell you the truth, Dídac," Slee said, unable to help herself.

"Go on." He did not release the pressure on her hand.

"You *are* a parasite. I didn't need to show the humans a single thing. They can see for themselves that you're sucking the life out of them."

Dídac bared all his thin, straight teeth and squeezed her hand, all the tendons and veins on the back of his hand bulging.

At the same time, a tide of animus swelled across the telethí and warmed her hand. Dídac's grip hurt a great deal, but the bond with her friends blunted the pain. He squeezed tighter and tighter, until it felt as though her knuckles would shoot off like corks and her fingers would crumble like dry leaves. The skin on her hand began to turn purple.

The door burst open. Cartín, breathless and flushed, stood in the doorway.

"There's a fire upstairs! Quick!"

Dídac narrowed his eyes, glanced over his shoulder, then studied Slee. "A fire?"

"It's out of control! If it gets to the krysite …"

"Get out of the way," Dídac said. He released Slee's hand and pushed past Cartín.

A moment later, a dozen Greycoats stormed past, the sound of their heavy boots loud in the corridor. Cartín, however, waited for them to pass, then ducked into the small room with Slee.

"Is there really a fire?" she asked.

"Yes. A small one." Cartín flashed her a sidelong grin, a twinkle in his eye.

"How careless of them to let a fire break out at just this moment."

"Indeed. They really should pay more attention. There are so many flammable things lying about, so many out-of-sight places where a fire can start."

Cartín stood with his shoulder pressed against the door, perhaps bracing it, perhaps listening to the receding footsteps.

Slee massaged her aching hand, which was still discolored from Dídac's grip.

"How quickly can you move?" Cartín asked.

"Not very."

"Not to worry, I'll help you along."

"Cartín, are you thinking of doing something foolish?"

"It was Horvald's idea." He gave her a quick smile. "He's the brash one, after all."

"What's the idea?"

Cartín paused, pressing his ear to the door. "They're gone. Let's go!"

"Wait," Slee said, standing up. "We're not going anywhere."

He stared at her open-mouthed, as though she had spoken elvish. Sweat dotted his forehead like dew, and he was still breathing heavily. "Slee, this is the only chance we may get," he said. "We have to get you and Horvald out of here while we can!"

"I'm not leaving." Slee folded her arms, tucking in the injured one tightly. "I'm going to stop Dídac or die in the attempt."

"What about Horvald? I can't break him out and leave you here!"

"You can go. I'm staying."

A heavy shadow fell across Cartín's face. "Saint's tears, I can't just lock you back in there. You've got to see reason! We've wasted too much time already. We'll never get another chance to escape, never mind a chance to destroy the whole place!"

"This won't be our only chance. We'll make our own chances, if we have to."

Cartín's shoulders fell. He pulled on the ends of his straight, black moustache, slowly shaking his head.

"What about your animals? If Dit-Dit is right, they don't have much time left."

"It's no use saving them if we let this poison keep running into the lake. Where would we live? How would I ignore the dead lake with all its rivers dying?" As she said it, she could not help but see the peaducks huddled and shivering in Slowjaw's enormous shadow. It made her eyes sting. How would she explain to them that she had left them alone longer than she needed to? How would she live with herself if she was too late to save them? "I need to do what's right. The evil of this place spreads farther than you, me, Horvald, and the animals."

Cartín let go of the door. All was quiet outside in the corridor. He moved closer to her and held her arms. "Sometimes, the fight cannot be won. This elixir is not something we can overcome. I do not know how it is for elves — or half-elves — but I was raised to care for my own. You do not need to carry the fate of all living things on your shoulders. In dire times, with little hope, sometimes all you can do is hold on to the ones you can."

Slee looked into his brown eyes, saw his sincerity, felt his concern pulling on the telethí strings. The warmth in his voice and his aura was brotherly, earnest. In the end, though, his feelings were not the only ones that mattered.

"Give me the stone," she said.

Cartín reached into a deep pocket, then handed it to her. He looked at her warily.

"There are many unhappy people in this place," she said, looking down at the glittering stone. "It's time we start sharing our displeasure."

"You're staying, then?"

"Yes. Will you help me?"

Cartín turned to the door as distant footsteps approached. Little black clouds of anxiety rose from his head as though he was smouldering.

"Of course. Whatever you need."

"Find the ones who hate this place. Talk to them."

"It can't be done. Dídac is watching everything. Any word uttered to the Bluefingers will reach him."

Slee turned the geode over in her hand, feeling its weight. Loose, wandering threads of telethí began to gather to it like iron filings to a magnet. She maintained control, so the focusing power of the stone would not overwhelm her.

"Well, we won't speak out loud, then," she said.

WAR WITH ELVES: FOR PROFIT AND AMUSEMENT

Chapter 28

Blessed are the rich, for they are righteous.
Blessed are the righteous, for they are rich.

Saint Pembly.

When Fentor saw the deplorable state of his facial hair, he knew the day had started on a sour note.

Long, painstaking hours of perfecting the shape, volume, length, and lustre of his moustache was undone by the black carpet encroaching on his chin and cheeks. Worse still, his hairline seemed to have receded another half-inch. He was starting to look like a man who'd been lost in the desert, or worse, like someone that had actually *chosen* to grow a full beard. The elves didn't permit prisoners to have sharp objects. To his great shame, therefore, his unkempt face went unshorn.

Thankfully, Crauford and Angsley were likewise almost unrecognisable. Angsley could still be discerned by his booming voice, and Crauford by his quiet manner and tiny, glinting spectacles. In Fentor's mind, the three of them were beginning to resemble the sweepings on a barber's floor. At least he was not alone in his suffering.

Fentor had a mission to get on with, so he got on with it, despite his sour mood.

First, he needed the unwitting cooperation of the other three.

Crauford had already agreed to help him brew a potion, thinking Fentor wanted protection from assassins. The Thambrian did not know, however, that it would be the Elixir of Power, and it would help Fentor break Elatea out.

Next, he needed Angsley and Hess to find the other prisoners still loyal to Madea. As far as they were aware, they would simply be coming to the Crown Away From Home to share a drink with their countrymen.

In truth, it was because the animus for the Elixir had to come from *somewhere.*

Fentor convinced them easily enough over their breakfast of sapwine.

The final, and perhaps most daunting task, was learning the location of Crann Arborím. For that, he needed to leave the Crown and speak with an elf alone. While the knife attack had been a brief inconvenience to Fentor, it had somehow become lodged in the imagination of the others as a surpassingly significant event. As such, they were unwilling to let him out of their sight.

"You see, if I stay holed up in here, *they've won*," Fentor said over the rim of a rapidly emptying glass of sapwine.

"I'd counter that by saying that they've *actually* won if they stick you in the guts," Hess said. "Which, if you leave this building, is bound to happen."

"This fortress?" Fentor pointed around the room at the many loose, ill-fitted timbers of the ramshackle building. "This place can't keep a light breeze out, much less an armed assassin. If the elves really wanted me dead, they'd have done it already."

"That's because we're here, watching you," Angsley said.

"I'm telling you, it was an isolated knife-wielding madman. Every village has one. I need to stretch my legs in the fresh air or I'll risk becoming one myself. Is that what you want?"

"What are you not telling us?" Hess asked, slapping the table. "You only get this way when you're after something. Tell us or we'll never let you out of here."

"Whatever do you mean, 'get this way'?" Fentor said with mock indignation. He gulped the last of his sapwine, and held out the glass for Angsley to refill it. "I'm always this charming, whether I want something or not."

Angsley scoffed.

"Lady Talentus gave you orders, didn't she?" Crauford said softly over tented fingers. His dark brown eyes, enlarged by the lenses of the spectacles on the end of his nose, darted across Fentor's face.

Fentor knew that the wrong answer, or even the wrong tone, would damn him. As he searched for a cunning reply that would remove all suspicion, he became aware that he had left too long a pause. So he said, "No she didn't."

Then he hid his face with a long drink of wine.

"So that's it," Hess said. She shook her head, half-weary, half-pitying. "Fenny, why didn't you just tell us?"

"I haven't told you a thing. She didn't give me orders." Fentor felt itchy heat climbing his neck until it burned his ears and cheeks. All the excess hair aggravated it, until he was sweltering. Providence damn that beard!

The others glanced at each other. Angsley muttered something to Hess.

"No, no, stop that at once! The Lady didn't give me orders, do you understand? If she thinks I've told you, she'll — argh!"

A terrible, piercing, world-consuming whine filled Fentor's head. It sounded like a poem written on a pane of glass by a thousand metal shards. It blocked out every other sense, until he was alone in a shapeless abyss with no light, no time, only an unbroken, deafening scream.

A moment later, the sound ceased. He found himself on the floor, ears pounding, tongue dry, and trousers also — he checked them quickly — thankfully dry.

"Fenny! Fenny, what happened?" Hess, who had been across the table from him, was the first to reach him and help him up.

Brushing himself off, Fentor looked at them all meaningfully. He gave each word as much clarity and weight as he could. "I cannot say a word. Now, I'm going to go for a stroll. A very important stroll. Alone."

Hess, Angsley, and Crauford all stared, open-mouthed. As a group, they awkwardly brushed off his clothes and clapped him on the shoulder with a series of gruff, supportive comments.

"Be careful out there, friend," Crauford said.

"We'll do everything we can," Hess said. "You don't have to say a word. We understand."

"If another elf comes for you, we'll make sure he regrets it!" Angsley said.

"Thank you all. Enjoy the rest of your breakfast."

Fentor walked to the door through air thickened by silence. He could feel the others watching him, their eyes poking and prodding his spine.

Opening the door, he was greeted by a semi-circular crowd of about a hundred elves. He froze mid-step, hand still on the wobbly door handle.

Reassuringly, none of the elves were armed. Less reassuringly, every one of their pale grey eyes tracked his every motion.

They wore clothing of all kinds, in every hue, and ranged in age from youths to elders. It seemed as though they had been waiting for Fentor's appearance. He could not tell from their blank expressions whether they saw him with fear or fascination. Either way, he thought it best to greet them.

"Hullo," he said. He waved.

No response.

"I don't suppose any of you know the way to the barber?"

The crowd remained silent.

Then, wondering if he could disperse the crowd by startling them, he closed the door quite loudly and sprang out onto the road.

"Boo!" he cried, lurching toward them with clawed hands.

None of the elves so much as flinched.

Exhausted of ideas, he decided it was best to ignore
them.

As he struck out in a random direction, the elves kept
pace with him, while also keeping a few arms' lengths
away. The dark-haired Sidarí was nowhere to be seen. He
had decided late the previous night that she would be the
best victim for his subterfuge. She seemed to possess the
same neurotic, academic detachment from the world that
made Crauford soft-spoken and half-present. If he could
appeal to her intellectual side, she might not see the blunt
reality that someone like Angsley would smell from a mile
off.

More importantly, he did not want to learn the names of
any more elves.

So he strolled through Rivumaí with his flock of
spectators, feeling like a chicken farmer with a bucket that
was leaking grain. The main road curved and branched off
in all directions. Buildings of all sorts clung to the main
vein like strange beasts drinking from a stream. Tall,
stilted buildings leaned over squat, half-buried huts. Wide
open-air halls housed dozens of elves, and slender larders
stuffed with food sprouted everywhere in between.

The air carried the smell of every activity of the village
all at once. Between the roasting, curing, tanning, sawing,
soaking, drenching, and fermenting of various substances,
Fentor could not tell where one scent ended and another
began. A trio of elves in brass-colored chainmail climbed
the hill where Elatea was kept. Somewhere in the distance,
a choir sang an overlapping set of melodies that they wove
together in strange harmonies. A mason split a perfectly
square granite block into ugly, uneven chunks.

Fentor walked through it all, trying his best not to take any of it in.

There was no sign of the dark-haired elf anywhere.

"I don't suppose any of you know where I might find Sidarí?" Fentor asked his followers.

He stopped, as did the crowd. Nobody answered him.

"Sidarí? Dark-haired elf? Looks a little like a bad mood was permanently chiseled into her features?"

"She's coming," a nearby elf wearing an enormous rose-colored scarf said.

"She's coming here now?" Fentor asked.

"Yes. We called for her when you mentioned her name."

"I didn't hear anything."

"Why would you?"

Fentor looked around at the crowd. They looked back at him. A few of them blinked — perfectly in time.

Of course, the Common Power connected them at every moment. When they said they 'called' for Sidarí, they really meant that they had summoned her with a thought. No wonder his crowd of followers had followed him in silence. They could gossip about him all they wanted without saying a word.

A few minutes later, Sidarí appeared. She wore a belted smock embroidered with little birds, green leggings, and a somber expression. Her fingers were covered in ink stains.

"Fentor? I hope you are mending well. You've been through quite the ordeal."

"Ordeal?"

"The attack." She pointed at the gauze plastered to his face.

Raising his fingers to touch the half-forgotten bandage, he said, "Ah, yes. Mending well, indeed."

"I suppose our healers were not up to the … standard you are used to," she said, eyeing his frayed bandages critically.

"It's an issue of trust, really."

"I see. Well, you haven't been attacked again, at least. The increased security appears to have worked."

"Security?"

"Yes." Sidarí nodded at the crowd of elves standing all around them. "Your security."

"Is that what they are? I thought I was something like a new animal on exhibit at the Madea City Faunatorium. Something exotic to gawk at."

"There is an element of that. Why else would so many have agreed to watch over you?"

"You could pay them."

Sidarí gave a brief, ironic smile. "And yet, we don't."

"Is there some secret Elarím phrase that will get them to stop following me?" Fentor glanced around. Dozens of unsmiling elves stared back at him.

"Have you tried asking them to leave?" Sidarí asked.

"He shouldn't be left alone. It's not safe," a nearby elf said.

"He is free to choose. Unfortunately." Sidarí folded her arms.

The look she gave him somehow reminded him of the maid who, at his vehement insistence, had let him touch a hot stove. He'd only been a child, for Temlin's sake. When he inevitably burned his hand, she clucked her tongue and said, "See, young master? It's hot like I said it'd be. You won't be doing that again, will you?"

Fentor blinked, looked around at the nearby elves, and cleared his throat. "You are all dismissed. You may go now."

Half of his spectators shrugged and wandered off in various directions. The rest, wrinkling their brows and clucking amongst themselves, did not move.

"Begone! Shoo! I don't want you here!" Fentor said, flapping his hands as though they were, indeed, a flock of chickens.

The rest of the crowd dissolved and dispersed, leaving Sidarí and Fentor alone on the main road.

"You seem to have a—what's the word? A *cavalier* attitude toward your own safety." Sidarí closed the distance between them, giving him the same look that Crauford gave a rack of test tubes filled with dangerous reagents: fascinated, yet cautious.

"Oh, please. They weren't even armed. What could they even do?" Fentor said.

"Same as they did last time."

"And what if more attackers came, with bigger weapons?"

"The Common Power responds in proportion to the danger."

By some unconscious decision, the two of them began to walk along the main road. Dry leaves skittered along the barrier high above, birds swooped and sang among the rooftops and upper branches, and working elves sang and called and grunted as they toiled.

WAR WITH ELVES: FOR PROFIT AND AMUSEMENT

Every time Fentor looked at Sidarí's face, a little glowing spot flared to life deep in his stomach. It had a giddy, nauseating, exhilarating effect that he found unacceptable. As a result, he kept his eyes forward, and not on the graceful arch of her eyebrows, the depths of her curious eyes, or the fleeting smiles that touched her lips.

He decided — forcefully — that he was only feeling nervous about Elatea's mission.

"Did you find the one who did this to me?" Fentor pointed to the plastered gash on his cheek.

"Yes. She was found. Unfortunately, we have more questions than answers."

"It seems simple enough. She hates humans, and took it upon herself to try and kill one."

"Overcoming the Common Power to harm a prisoner is not so easy, I'm afraid."

"Then it's a mystery." Fentor now kept his eyes on the ground, placing his steps to crush the little white clover flowers that dotted the path.

"You don't want to know about the attack at all, do you?" Sidarí asked, narrowing her eyes and leaning closer, as though his thoughts might be printed on his forehead in tiny script.

"All my questions have been answered. We humans take that as a cue to stop asking new ones," Fentor said.

"You might benefit from reading Nyendí's work, then," Sidarí said with a small laugh. Fentor carefully did not look at the way her cheeks formed little dimples.

"Perhaps I would. Truthfully, Sidarí, I asked to speak with you because there are things I must say. Things that cannot be said around your friends … or mine." As he spoke, he affected the nervous twitching of a man confessing his deepest guilt. He let his gaze dart about his surroundings, and even checked over his shoulder. Then he stroked his beard — a deranged gesture that Father had always said only suited raving vagrants. The only reason a man should touch his facial hair in public, Father had said, was to re-position a moustache made askew by battle.

"Is that so?" Sidarí slowed down, looking at him sidelong.

"Yes. I have questions … questions about Madea. Grave doubts. All my life, I feel I have been lied to."

They left the main path, and began a gentle ascent under the boughs of trees with waxy, star-shaped leaves. A few elves flitted here and there among the trees, carrying little bundles of firewood or climbing up to gather pale, cherry-sized nuts.

"How have you been lied to?" Sidarí said, in a low voice that rasped like the dry leaves overhead.

Fentor paused, scratching his beard as though he was beset by fleas. He let the silence go on, both for dramatic effect, and to come up with something plausible. What *did* discontented Madeans say?

"I grew the wheat, you got the bread, I got a crumb back," he said, pulling the memory of the old man at the crossroads from the murky depths of his mind.

"I don't follow. I thought your wealth came from property and gunsmiths, not wheat farms. Is the wheat metaphorical, perhaps?"

"In a way, yes," Fentor said slowly. The point he wished to make was still forming in the back of his head. To buy himself time, he fell silent and shot paranoid looks at the trees around them.

They came to the end of the path at the crest of a small hill. A small stream cut them off from the next, higher hill, where Elatea glittered at the top like a hailstone dropped from heaven. Looking up at her, Fentor suddenly knew what to say.

"The rich in Madea claim all the fruits of the labor done by the lower folk. They demand ever higher rents from their tenants. The poor are ground to mince on the front lines, while their superiors count their money in the rear. The tables in all the manors groan under the weight of food they could never eat, while urchins that steal a loaf of bread are shot."

Where he had picked up such lies, he did not know. Everyone knew that reality was the opposite — that the poor would starve in their hopeless ineptitude without the guidance of the wealthy classes.

All that mattered was the effect his false diatribe had on Sidarí. She folded her arms and drew in her chin, withdrawing into herself as though in the onslaught of an icy wind. All that moved was her eyes, which leapt to and fro as though she was solving some complex, invisible equation written in the clover at her feet.

A subtle, high-pitched whine came to Fentor's ears. It was not piercingly loud as the scream he heard before, but was more like someone had struck a tuning fork next to his ear. Elatea in her crystal skin seemed to flash in the sun above him, as though in warning. He could almost hear her words underneath the ringing in his ears: *Tread carefully, Fentor.*

Trust me, my Lady. All is going to plan, he thought. The ringing continued. There was no way of knowing whether she had heard him.

"Forgive me, Fentor — you speak of the rich mistreating the poor of Madea. But aren't *you* rich?" Sidarí looked at him with a pinched, confused look. Fentor, despite trying not to, noticed that it looked like she was about to sneeze.

"Not out here. You've yet to invent money."

Sidarí blinked at him.

"Which is something I admire greatly," Fentor added hastily. "The Madean lust for coin causes more problems than it solves. I'm glad that I'm destitute. Thrilled, really."

"I see ..." Sidarí nodded slowly, turning slightly to the side. She looked down at the stream as though with great interest, interlocking her ink-stained fingers behind her back.

"You don't believe me," Fentor said. "Well, this will prove it. There was a woman, Charlotte Wembley, back in Madea City. A tenant of mine. She was struggling terribly to make ends meet, so *I* made them meet, so to speak. She seemed like a good sort, so I forgave the rent she owed me *and* I gave her a generous gift of crowns."

"That *is* generous. Few in your position would have done something like that."

"Now can you see the doubts that plague my heart?" His pressed a palm to his ear, which was still ringing like a crystal glass.

"I can see that you're very troubled." Sidarí studied Fentor, looking him up and down with her active, curious eyes.

He tried to arrange his face to look anxiously sincere, the way Thorassa would. The elf tilted her head this way and that, as though seeing him from different angles would reveal something.

The ringing in his ear swelled to a buzzing, loud enough to drown out the ambient pitter-patter of leaves and the rustling of the tree-nut pickers.

"You don't sound like the other prisoners who express their doubts," she said at length. "Your words reveal a mind that is still very … Madean."

"Madea is all I've ever known. The stench of it clings to me. I loathe the hypocrisy of the Grand Toques, the inaction of the King, the greed and ambition and hollowness of it all. I need you to teach me a new way to think … a better way."

"It would be my pleasure to teach you how to think," she said, with a twitch in the corner of her mouth.

"Please! I am your humble student."

"I'm not entirely sure you're ready."

"I promise you, I am."

The buzzing in his ears continued, vibrating his teeth and obscuring Sidarí's words. The sound rose and fell, following the same cadence of Lady Talentus' voice, only harsher. It felt as though Elatea was leaning over his shoulder, inspecting his progress.

"Very well. Tell me more about Charlotte," Sidarí said.

"Who?"

"Charlotte Wembley?" Sidarí said. "Your tenant?"

"Ah! Yes, of course. *That* Charlotte. What about her?"

"Is she typical, as your tenants go?"

Fentor frowned, vaguely sensing a trap. "Typical? I suppose. I see no reason why they'd be atypical."

"Haven't you met them?"

"Why would I?"

"I suppose I'm not clear on the duties of your profession. They pay you in return for a place to live, correct?"

"That's right." In addition to the buzzing in his ears, cold sweat began to dampen his armpits. Sidarí's questions seemed innocent enough, but he felt strangely like a fish being herded into a net.

"So somebody else collects the payment on your behalf?"

"Precisely. A junior clerk from the bank makes the rounds, I believe."

"But why is the money yours to collect? Did you build the house?"

"Well, no. My father built the houses, I inherited them," Fentor said.

"I see. So your father built them — he sawed the timber and laid the bricks?"

"Well, no. He hired the builders."

"Neither you nor your father built the homes of your tenants? I confess that I am more confused than before. Perhaps the ways of humans will always carry an element of mystery. Let me return to Charlotte. In a way, you rescued her from poverty."

"I did. It was my proudest moment," Fentor said, with a rising feeling in his chest. The words were not entirely untrue.

"I'm sure it was. For that reason, I won't relish asking this next question: this money you generously gave to Charlotte, where did it come from?"

"Why, my own personal wealth. It was as though I gave her the clothes off my own back."

"Your personal wealth … the wealth that is built upon the rent Charlotte and others like her paid to you?"

"I own a gunsmith as well. There's also my salary from the Madean Land Corps."

"Of course. But the vast bulk of your money?"

"It comes from rent." Then Fentor, sensing skepticism in Sidarí's wrinkled brow, hastily added, "A fact which brings me great shame."

"Why is that?"

Fentor froze. Wringing out his brain like a wet cloth, he tried to extract a reason she would believe. What was it the ruder tenants wrote in their letters of complaint every time he increased the rent?

"Because I'm trapped. I dislike collecting rent as much as tenants dislike paying it. If there was a way out of it, we'd have found it. But *someone* has to own the dwellings, and that someone needs a way to support themselves. Hard working folk can always make rent, and in return I always treat them well. Better than a lot of landlords do, I can tell you that! Having said that, it wouldn't be right to give handouts to *every* one of them. The more you give to the poor, the less they're able to fend for themselves, you know. I'm sure Rivumaí has its share of slackers and layabouts. It's an unfortunate truth of life, but there it is."

Fentor, incandescent with pride, knew that Saint Temlin himself couldn't have put it better. His compassion for the poor was beyond question, now.

Sidarí smiled at him, but it was a fixed, cold smile. The glow in Fentor's chest guttered, then went out completely. As the silence stretched between them, Elatea's buzzing presence in Fentor's skull grew even more piercing.

"Well, this has been a productive conversation. Unfortunately, I must be getting—" Sidarí began, but Fentor cut her off.

"Wait! You haven't heard the thing I've been driving at this whole time. I want to join the Elarím," Fentor said, widening his eyes to a degree he hoped was more earnest than manic.

Still wearing the same fixed smile, Sidarí said, "No, you don't."

Her response struck him like a pail of icy water. Before he could determine why she doubted him after everything he said, she gave him a small wave and began to turn away.

"I must be getting back to my writing, now. I cannot escort you to your safe haven, but I can call some trusted friends who will if you like?" she said.

"Don't go just yet! I truly want to join the Elarím. I do!" Fentor had to speak louder and louder over the increasingly teeth-rattling buzz that filled his skull. If Elatea hadn't distracted him the whole time with incessant noise, he'd have succeeded.

"Do you want an escort or not?"

Fentor deflated, rubbing his pounding brow. "No, no, I'll go back alone."

"As you wish. In truth, there is a chance the danger has passed. Your attacker was exiled, though we are still not sure how she thwarted the Common Power law against violence."

"A mystery for the Great Sages to ponder, I'm sure," Fentor said between gritted teeth. The gentle light of Rivumaí had somehow become bright enough to sting his eyes.

"Are you unwell? Do you need medicine?"

"No, thank you. I merely overindulged in sapwine."

"If you're sure." Sidarí turned and swiftly went back the way they'd come.

Once she was out of sight, Fentor doubled over and pressed both hands hard over his eyes. Fireworks burst across his eyelids, as the buzz inside his head built to a screech.

Fool! Your efforts were utterly transparent! Do not fail again!

Elatea's voice pierced his eardrums like splinters of ice. A moment later, her presence withdrew, and the shrill whine left his ears.

The relief of the sudden quiet was so deep that he remained doubled over, hands over his eyes, to better enjoy the absence of light and sound.

A few minutes later, he got to his feet and made his way downhill under the nut trees. Elves were still overhead, shuffling along the branches, and he paid them no mind.

He knew the problem. He was so thoroughly Madean, so exceptionally well-bred, that it was impossible for him to forsake his heritage in a convincing way. This was not a mark against him. In fact, it would be the sort of thing they would one day write about. *The Life of Grand Toque*

Fentor Lonokai rang pleasantly in his ears. Or perhaps, *The Wisdom of Saint Fentor the Cunning*. The potential titles were countless—he'd think of more later on.

All he needed to do was find someone to put the right words in his mouth. He could then say them to Elatea, and she would believe him. A certain rabbit-toothed, watery-eyed candidate came to mind.

Some careless elf showered him with nuts, twigs and leaves. He called up in displeasure at the half-visible nut-picker. They didn't give him so much as an apology. They just looked down at him.

Muttering about incompetence, he continued on. The sounds of elves rattling continued all the way down the hill, always seeming to be right above him. Doubtless, the fools had no idea how much of their produce was falling right onto the main thoroughfare. Couldn't they have picked nuts from more out-of-the-way trees? Fentor had to think. The constant rain of nuts and leaves impeded that.

As he neared the bottom of the hill, a length of rope fell from above, whipping him on the shoulder.

"Watch what you're doing, for Temlin's sake!" Fentor shouted.

Another rope fell, and then another, dangling from low branches and draping around his shoulders like scarves.

"Now, really, this is just deliberate!"

As Fentor pulled the tangled ropes from his shoulders, the branches overhead rustled loudly, and voices clamored harshly in elvish.

The ropes tightened.

One arm was trapped against his side, the other was pulled away from his body. One loop encircled his neck, and as it lifted him from the ground, it constricted. Struggling and kicking with all his strength, unable to draw breath, his vision quickly turned grey.

He had always expected his last thoughts would be significant. That he would utter some phrase of surpassing wisdom on his deathbed, an insight worth engraving on the plaque beneath his statue.

Instead, all he thought at that moment was, *I've been done in by a pack of bloody nut-pickers!*

Chapter 29

With each second that passed, the world grew dimmer, and Fentor's head filled with more and more pressure. The sharp pain of the ropes cutting into his skin faded as he slipped away from consciousness. He couldn't think of anyone who had been Sainted after being garrotted like that, but then, he couldn't think any thoughts at all.

Lightheaded and unable to struggle further, he was drawn by a powerful current to the edge of an abyss, a final, deep sleep.

Through that darkness, a piercing whine stabbed his ears.

This is more than you deserve.

All at once, with a small snapping sound, the pressure was released, and his arms and neck were freed. After a brief rush of cool air on his face, he collapsed onto the clover. The impact seemed to cudgel some alertness back into him. He would have groaned as he turned over, but his crushed throat reduced his voice to a hoarse whisper. Blinking through the sudden burst of green light, he became aware of other bodies that had fallen to the ground nearby.

Pushing himself upright proved too much for his enfeebled arms. The blurry elves, all dressed in black, were slowly getting to their feet. Feeling about as sturdy as a feather duster, Fentor pushed the ground away with every one of his muscles, and came queasily up to a standing position.

Two short paces away, a fallen sabre glinted in the clover. With the ground pitching under him like a skiff in a storm, he navigated the short distance, using all his concentration. Picking up the thin, whippy sword, he found himself facing four elves, three of whom held sabres of their own. Their faces were covered with black cloth, and their eyes glinted like shards of glass. They fanned out and advanced, including the unarmed one.

A lungful of air inflated his chest as though someone had blown it in his mouth with force. Shortly after, his muscles surged with new vitality, and his balance returned. At first, he attributed the sudden strength to his superior constitution. A familiar, ringing presence in his ears, however, indicated outside assistance.

Fentor squared his feet, holding out the sabre at an angle and tucking his free hand behind his back. He lunged experimentally at the nearest elves, swiping at their shoulders in quick succession. Both deflected the attacks easily, though with flat feet. Fentor, on the other hand, caught his foot on a stone and nearly fell over as he made his retreat. The elves made no counter, and only continued to steadily encircle him.

His opponents had poor stance, and one of them even lacked a weapon. His sword arm was still a little weak, but the sabre was light enough. His throat still burned, but his head was fairly clear. All things considered, the only advantage the elves had was numbers.

The empty-handed elf hung back a pace farther than the others. Fentor made sudden advances toward the vulnerable enemy, cutting the air haphazardly with his blade. Each time, the others closed in to protect their ally, parrying Fentor, who then swiftly retreated. He had no intent of doing real harm, only of forcing a reaction. They could not be allowed to surround him.

Sweat coated his palms and ran down his nose, and his legs quivered from holding the Madean-Land-Corps-approved half-crouch position. Time would run out for him before it would for them. They were patient, defensive. Even when he had slipped or overextended, they made no efforts to exploit their advantage. Therefore, he would boldly press the attack.

The decision did not come with the ringing of distant trumpets or the subtle golden glow of destiny, as it usually did. Instead, he felt like an unlit stove in an empty kitchen.

Regardless, he lunged. Targeting the elf on his right side, he drove at them, whipping and jabbing his blade from all sides. The elf—Elf One in Fentor's mind—backpedalled as they parried Fentor's onslaught. The other elves hurried to keep him penned in.

As Fentor continued to prod Elf One's defences, Elves Two and Three charged from the rear. He crossed blades with Elf One, then rushed forward until they were nose to nose. They pressed harder and harder into each other, blades locked. With a twist and deft sidestep, Fentor knocked aside the elf's sabre, traded places with Elf One and sent them stumbling into Elves Two and Three. Fentor slashed the elf's back as they passed. A long red line appeared between their shoulders. The unarmed Elf Four rushed forward to help.

Such a wound seemed impossible. Apparently, the Common Power wasn't watching.

Good.

Elves Two and Three advanced on Fentor, chopping at him with wide, undisciplined swings. He met their sabres with his, turning their own momentum against them with gliding parries. As he slid his blade down theirs from tip to hilt, he turned his wrist, gained leverage, and threw the blade and its wielder off-balance. Parry after parry, it went the same way. They could not touch him.

Elf Four, now holding the weapon of their injured companion, charged into the fray. With a clever twist of the hilt, the sword sprang into its spear form.

Now fending off two swords and a spear, Fentor soon ran out of all the techniques in his repertoire. Besides, there was no time to execute Temlin's Offhand Thrust or the Shy Capilet's Feint or even the Drunk's Stumbling Yield. He could only knock the weapons aside and retreat.

Then, he had an idea.

A moment later, the brass-colored spear flashed toward him. He batted it aside, but it wasn't knocked clear. The spear tip stung the top of his left shoulder before withdrawing.

Fentor cried out in annoyance and surprise. The other two elves seized their chance, each thrusting a sabre at his sides, like a pair of pincers. Fentor spun, crouched, and twisted the hilt of his weapon.

There was a scraping, metallic sound like the sharpening of knives. Fentor, now holding a spear, had diverted both sabres. At the same time, the tip of the spear had sprung out, and was now lodged in the chest of Elf Three. They all froze, human and elf alike, and stared at the wound.

Then, Elf Two kicked Fentor, dislodging his spear and knocking him on his back. The breath was driven from him. He held his remaining attackers at bay with wild jabs of his spear. With a great effort, he pulled himself upright.

Despite his bleeding shoulder and his bruised body, he wore an irrepressible grin. Only moments ago, he had been certain of his own doom. He had doubted the glorious future of fame and Sainthood awaiting him.

We all make mistakes, I suppose, he thought. *It's best to acknowledge them with a smile.*

Just as he had formed a plan to dispatch his remaining enemies, the grove came alive with armed, black-clad elves. Every face was covered, every sabrespear flashing. They converged on Fentor like ants to a beetle on its back.

His confidence deserted him as quickly as it had come.

My Lady, if you can hear me, I am in need of assistance, he thought.

There was no response.

My Lady? I beg you, help me!

No whine or buzz came to his ears, nor could he hear Elatea's crystal-chime voice.

Fentor held the spear as tightly as a drowning sailor clings to flotsam. Two dozen blades formed a circle around him, their gleaming points cutting off any chance of escape. Grey eyes burned like white ash in the heart of a fire, fixing him in place, wilting his resolve.

Elatea, please! They'll kill me!

A sharp whine split his skull. He almost fell to his knees from the pain.

I have done all I can already. Your fate is in your hands alone.

As quickly as Elatea's piercing presence had come, it was gone.

The ring of foes faced him in silence.

"Whatever our differences may be, I'm certain we can resolve them peacefully," Fentor said, his voice still a rasping mess from the rope.

No one replied. Their blazing eyes continued to spark and smolder with menace. Fentor could almost imagine a red glow suffusing the air, like the aura around a blacksmith's forge.

Help me, please, anyone! Saints, Sages, Hess, Angsley, Crauford — blast it, I need someone!

As one, the circle of elves began to contract. Sabres and spears drifted closer as their wielders crept toward him with small, coordinated steps. Soon, the weapons were within his reach. He grazed the tip of his spear against the nearest ones, pushing them aside one by one. The circle continued to close, and the aura around them seethed, deep red with anger.

Sweet Temlin, I pledge the first million crowns of my fortune to the Church if you rescue me from this …

Shouts came from the other end of the orchard. The black-clad elves lifted their heads, pointed ears twitching slightly. The voices drew closer, crying out something in elvish. Whatever they said, it hardened the faces of Fentor's attackers.

Suddenly, those faces became blurry. Fentor blinked to clear his eyes, but his vision wasn't blurred — the elves were. Looking down, he saw that his own body and the clover under his feet were clear. He was standing in something like a giant soap bubble.

The now-hazy elves plunged their weapons through the bubble. The barrier slowed their attacks, and halted some of them completely. Still, Fentor found himself in the center of a rapidly shrinking cage of blades. He parried the spears nearest him. He turned and turned, keeping low, parrying wildly, as more weapons approached from all directions. As he knocked them aside, the bubble enveloped them, then spat them back out.

A spear grazed his thigh, then a sabre nicked him near the elbow. More and more attacks pierced the blurred barrier, too many for him to avoid completely. They cut him, over and over, from all directions.

Some great, indistinct tide of gold and red broke upon his attackers. The shouting reached an urgent peak as some kind of brawl commenced. No more spears reached in to claw at him. The blurred barrier seemed to solidify, becoming almost milky white, as his attackers battled a large group of newcomers.

Fentor, looking down at himself, caught sight of his blood-soaked clothes, and became suddenly dizzy. With a giddy chuckle, he took one step forward before falling, senseless, to the ground.

****

Fentor woke to find Sidarí leaning over him. Hess, Angsley, and Crauford all hovered a few paces away, arms folded and speaking in low voices. As a hoarse groan escaped his damaged throat, Fentor promised himself that he would not lose consciousness the next time he participated in battle. That sort of thing quickly grew tiresome.

"He is awake," Sidarí said softly.

His friends crowded around him at once. Hess took one of his hands, Angsley took the other.

Fentor recognised the poorly-joined timbers of the nearby wall as those of the Crown. He had been bandaged and slathered with a pungent, floral-scented ointment. Raising his head creakily from his oddly stiff pillow, he sniffed his arms with great distaste.

"We're sorry, old boy. We had to let them fix you up," Angsley said. "They did it *their* way."

"This stuff they slathered all over you … you should have seen the way it stopped all the bleeding." Hess cleared her throat. "When you came in, it looked like you were …"

Fentor tried to speak, but his throat only produced an airy wheeze. His neck, too, had been tightly bandaged and salved. While the welt left by the rope ached much less, his vocal cords still burned as though he'd inhaled scalding steam.

"Don't speak, Fenny." Hess stroked his hand.

A teary Angsley stroked his other hand.

Crauford stood at the foot of Fentor's bed, peering at him through his tiny spectacles. His lips moved absently, the way they often did when he was silently solving a calculation. He seemed to be more interested in the bandages than he was in Fentor.

"May I speak with him alone?" Sidarí edged closer to the bed, looking tentatively at Hess and Angsley as though they were wild deer that might startle at any moment.

They shot Sidarí the same hard-browed look. Fentor half-expected them to stamp, snort, and lower their antlers for a charge.

"About what, exactly?" Angsley said.

"The cause of the attack."

"Go ahead and tell him, but we're not moving." Hess' ears became flushed, and her grip on Fentor's hand became painfully tight.

He breathily begged her to let go, but his voice was too faint for her to hear.

"Fentor may not want you to hear what I have to say," Sidarí said, with a wary tilt of her head and a glance at Fentor.

"Hess. Hess! My hand!" Fentor rasped, but again he went unheard.

Hess redoubled her grip as the flush spread across her cheeks. Fentor wheezed with all his might, but he went unheard.

"What do you know about what Fentor wants?" Hess spat.

"At this moment, I think he wants you to loosen your grip," Sidarí said, pointing.

Hess looked at Fentor's reddening fingers and his anguished grimace, and loosened her grip at once. She lifted his hand, kissed it, and then froze. Their eyes met for an instant, after which Fentor found it hard to look in her eyes at all.

"Sorry, Fenny, I didn't realize I was squeezing you like that."

Fentor cleared his throat gruffly and nodded his head. He hoped the cadence of his little coughs clearly said: *Not to worry, Hess, all is forgiven.* New red spots shone on Hess' cheeks, matching the warmth on Fentor's face.

Angsley became intensely interested in a gap in the timbers nearby. Crauford, half-present, continued working on arithmetic only he could see.

"Fentor, do you want your friends to leave?" Sidarí said.

He shook his head.

"Very well. You will be pleased to hear that all of your attackers have been exiled."

Fentor nodded sharply and wheezed his approval.

"The Elarím of Rivumaí have also investigated their origins and methods. It seems these attackers shared no special connection prior to your arrival. They converged on Rivumaí from surrounding clades—villages—united by a desire to subvert the laws of the Common Power. Their goal was to kill you, then Elatea Talentus. As for their methods …" Sidarí's usually morose face briefly fell into a drawn, despairing, and haggard look. Fentor had seen the expression before in a field surgeon's tent. It was worn by nurses who had toiled through the night, lost a slew of patients, only to continue their sleepless work in the morning light. A few moments passed, and Sidarí regained a more neutral bearing.

"They severed their ties to the Common Power. Voluntarily, and with deadly intent. Outside of the protective influence of Crann Arborím, they created their own telethymic bonds. A burning hatred for you and your Lady inspired them. An undercurrent of this feeling has swept through the minds of many other elves. It is growing."

"They're going to attack him again?" Hess said.

"They believe they are protecting their home," Sidarí said, uttering the words as a long sigh. "The hatred of the righteous is not easily extinguished."

"You think these maniacs are righteous?" Angsley growled.

"No. I think they *believe* they are," Sidarí said. "In reality, they are … *Uthuím*. You do not have a comparable word."

"Well what do we do now? Will you give us weapons?" Hess asked.

"That is not permitted."

"How are we supposed to defend ourselves?" Angsley asked.

"We have requested a garrison to help guard Fentor. He'll be watched night and day—whether he likes it or not," Sidarí said, raising a slender, stern eyebrow at him.

In answer, he made a rumbling noise of displeasure.

"Fentor is lucky to be alive," Sidarí said. "Fortunately for him, an alarm call went out across the Common Power before he was overwhelmed. The call had a strange, external character, like an unfamiliar smell drifting into one's home. It must have been one of the attackers experiencing … what is the Madean expression? A change of heart."

"Having doubts at the eleventh hour doesn't make them any less guilty," Angsley rumbled.

"Indeed it does not." Sidarí looked at each of them in turn, nodded, then turned as if to leave.

"Wait. What have you been writing?" Crauford said abruptly in his soft voice.

"Excuse me?" Sidarí asked.

"The ink on your fingers." Crauford pointed at her hands, pushing his spectacles up his nose.

"A long-abandoned work that I recently returned to, *Treatise on the Human Mind*," Sidarí said slowly, narrowing her eyes as though wary of some trap. "Some of my assumptions proved to be misguided. I've been correcting them."

"Do you have a draft I could read? Even rough notes would be welcome," Crauford said.

Sidarí did not reply for some time. Then, shaking her head a little, she said, "I'm afraid I destroyed all my notes. I started fresh."

"Pity," Crauford said, and then turned away from her. His frowning, absent-minded bearing made it look like he had forgotten she existed.

Looking a little bemused, she left.

Once she had left, Crauford squared his shoulders and looked sharply at Fentor. "I need a sample of the unguent," he said briskly.

"A sample of the what?" Angsley said.

"The ointment. Salve. The paste on Fentor's skin. I need to take some away for testing," Crauford said.

"Well …" Hess spread her hands over Fentor's bandaged arms. "The Elarím healers told us not to disturb his bandages."

"Are you going to trust their word over mine?" Crauford said. A stern glint flashed across the lenses of his spectacles, giving him the air of a headmaster.

"I suppose not. Here—just be careful." Hess carefully peeled the gauze from Fentor's forearm, layer by layer, until the milk-white, strong-smelling ointment was exposed.

Crauford took out a small vial and dragged it gently along Fentor's skin, collecting a rippled white lump in the mouth of the vessel. He corked it, stowed it away, then pulled out a folded sheet of paper.

"Fentor, I need clarification," Crauford said, handing him the paper. "Some of these were easy enough to procure, but others will be nearly impossible. The rest of the ingredients and processes are too vague. I need clearer instructions, or at least some hint of what I'm making."

Fentor opened the page, upon which he had scrawled whatever he could remember of the recipe for the Elixir of Power. In his mind, he had handed Crauford a near-perfect set of instructions. All Crauford would need to do was fill in some gaps—or so he had thought.

In reality, based on the dozens of questions and notations Crauford had added, he had not given Crauford a recipe at all. He had given him a vague gesture in the direction of an idea of a recipe:

Soporific matricks? Saporafic?
Ethyl Vitriol – From sapwine
Solvent: It is definitely 'Oil of Something' or 'Acua Vitae' or
'Temlin's Antimony' or something similar to one of those three
Oil of Telium? (Highly unlikely)
Caustic white-ash, or possibly non-caustic red-ash
Something that rhymes with 'Ferret's box eye'
Enriched kryside. Or was it enriched krysite *with a 't'?*

Crauford's compact writing surrounded Fentor's sprawling, looping script like ants marching around rows of feathers. After poring over his friend's many notes, Fentor at last understood what they had, and what was missing.

The saponific matrix and ethyl vitriol narrowed the solvent down to a single possibility — 'Oil of Something.' If, by 'Ferret's box eye' Fentor had meant ferrous oxide, then that meant they needed red-ash. Krysite must be converted to *kryside* to be enriched, which solved that particular point.

Crauford had everything they would need except the saponific matrix, ferrous oxide, and krysite.

"Caustic and non-caustic red-ash have opposite effects," Crauford said. "If you could just tell me what we are making, then —"

Fentor shook his head violently, provoking a sharp twinge in his neck. He cringed, expecting his ears to ring, but they remained quiet.

"You don't have to tell me." Crauford sat on the bed beside him. "Non-caustic red-ash is an agglutinative. A binding agent. Potions made with it will fuse disparate things, you see? Caustic red-ash, on the other hand, is a powerful dissociating agent. It breaks things down into the smallest possible pieces, and scatters them. Which do we need?"

Fentor thought hard for a few minutes. He remembered Galton's tour of the distillery so hazily that there was no hope of recalling such a minor detail. Then, simply thinking of what it *felt* like to drink the Elixir of Power, to see the world splintered into its constituent parts, he thought of the most likely answer.

He showed Crauford the page and pointed at the word 'caustic.'

"Very well. Now, the solvent. It must be an oil. Can you remember which?"

Fentor grimaced, and shook his head. The word teetered on the very tip of his tongue, waiting breathlessly for the slightest push to emerge.

"Oil of antichlor? Oil of vitimus?"

Fentor shook his head.

Crauford cleaned his spectacles on the corner of his scarf, sucking on his teeth. "That leaves only one, which, combined with krysides, forms a potent poison. Oil of telium."

Fentor sat up, and the word leapt hoarsely from his tongue, "Telium!"

As the others pushed him back onto his pillow, they exchanged foreboding glances that clashed with the triumph beaming from him.

"Are you certain?"

Fentor nodded emphatically, and jabbed the word 'telium' on the page repeatedly.

"You're making a poison, then?"

Fentor shook his head, and continued pointing.

"Alright. I trust you. Ferrous oxide—that is common, everyday rust. The only problem is, the elves use just about every metal there is *except* for iron. Rust is exceptionally rare here, but there is a way to derive it from blood."

"Blood?" Hess said, paling. "How much blood?"

"A little from each of us over the course of the next few days."

"Whatever you need, I'll give it now," Angsley said.

"I appreciate it, Angsley, but we all need to keep our strength. Besides, between treatment, filtration, and evaporation, a large sample will spoil before we can use it. We need small, fresh donations at even intervals."

"Oh, sweet Providence. Does it *have* to be blood?" Hess looked down at Fentor, her face so pale that even her freckles had retreated. "I'd run to the sinner's abyss and back for you, Fenny, I would. But ..."

"Why so green, Lancer? Why, you've seen rivers blood at the Gutter Trench," Angsley said gruffly.

"Yes, but not my own! Not in little glass bottles!"

"Take from me, too," Fentor rasped.

Hess and Angsley started to protest, but Crauford waved his hand until they fell silent. "We will take some of Fentor's blood—but no more than his body is already losing. If I am right about this ointment, that may be more than enough."

"What does that mean?" Hess said.

"I have to carry out some tests, first." Crauford held up the sample of ointment he had collected, turning it in the light. Once more, his distracted, owl-eyed manner had returned.

Fentor watched the change come over his friend, and made a note not to read too many books. He didn't want to end up the same way.

As Crauford hurried away to the other corner of the tavern, Angsley and Hess resumed their places beside him.

"Drink?" Fentor wheezed, miming the motion.

"What would you like?" Hess asked.

Fentor gave her a stony look that he intended to mean, *Take your best guess.*

"Wine? You oughtn't have anything harder than tea when you're in a state like this," Hess said with finality.

Seeking to appeal her ruling, Fentor turned wide, pleading eyes to Angsley.

"Well …" he said, pawing at his beard with a large, ruddy hand. Then he produced a bottle of sapwine as if from nowhere. "This elven swill is only a touch stronger than tea. I doubt it could make a cat dizzy."

"How long have you had that on you?" Hess nodded at the sapwine as Angsley took a swig.

"This whole time." Angsley wiped his beard, then offered the bottle to Fentor. "There you go, old boy. You've been through it lately. First a knifing and now this! Wash the memory of those beastly elves away."

Fentor drank from the bottle, grateful for the wine's cool mildness.

Hess took it next, and gulped down far more than either of the others had. "Why must I always try to be the sensible one? I can't even be my *own* voice of reason."

They continued to pass the bottle around. Fentor had come to appreciate the floral taste of the drink, and didn't wince or gag once. Angsley and Hess, however, still made pinched faces whenever they drank. A warm, numbing freshness radiated through Fentor's body, replacing his stiffness and aches.

Crauford returned with a pair of vials in hand. One was filled with a cloudy white liquid, the other with a few clear green drops. "You will only like half of what I have to say."

"Out with it, then," Angsley said.

"I found a way to synthesize Oil of Telium." He tightened his lips, and looked down at Fentor's bandaged body.

Hess gently touched some ointment that had oozed through the layers of gauze. Rubbing it between her fingers, she said, "How much will you need?"

"As much as I can get. Unless Fentor objects."

"Now hold on just a moment, Fentor was leaking like a bucket made of rags before they salved him!" Angsley's beard wagged as he looked from Crauford to Fentor, from the vials to the bandages. "It irks me to say it, but he needs this elvish ointment to get better. You can't just take it!"

"If there is any other way, Fentor, now is the time to tell us," Crauford said.

"Fenny? Do you really have to make *this* potion?" Hess leaned close to him, as a puff of warm, floral air drifted to his nostrils.

Fentor looked from Hess, to Angsley, and finally to Crauford. Taking the nearly-empty bottle, he drained the last few drops, then nodded.

Chapter 30

When Slee had been escorted out of the dungeon to face
Dídac's questioning, the elf had stayed behind for a
minute to make her cellmates an offer. They would be
given freedom in exchange for information. Dídac wanted
to know what Slee was doing, and with whom. As
Horvald told her, all four of them had spat on the elf and
his offer. A new bruise covering Horvald's eye seemed to
confirm this.

Still, they could not risk their plans becoming known.
Slee, Horvald, and Cartín therefore spent the next few
days trying to speak silently across the telethí.

She slept with the geode and Dit-Dit hidden securely in
the pockets of her dress. Soon she was used to the weight
of them, and felt a great absence whenever Dit-Dit left. The
little rat waited for the stillness of night and old Tybalt's
snores before venturing out. She explored the distillery,

finding passages through cracks in the wall, becoming accustomed to its many smells.

The geode began to dominate Slee's thoughts. She guarded it jealously, as a human will guard riches. Often, in the middle of a fitful sleep, she would wake, feeling around for the geode, gripped by the fear that it had been taken. It was always in that same pocket. With all the anxiety and lack of sleep fogging her mind, she could only 'speak' with Horvald and Cartín sporadically and with great concentration.

Aizman, Batha, and Tybalt stared at Slee often, turning away whenever she caught them. When she told Horvald telethymically, he assured her not to think too much of it. She hadn't slept, she was beset by all kinds of worries — her mind was embellishing harmless looks into malicious glares. Regardless, Slee could not help but wonder how much the three men valued their freedom, and how little they valued her.

The calm she needed eluded her. Her task was too great, too urgent to be delayed. Her hand had swollen and turned purple and yellow, but she paid it little mind. Hour after hour, she grappled with the telethí and her fears alike.

Despite Slee's troubles, Cartín was able to report some small changes. The air in the Extraction Chamber seemed somehow charged. The exhausted faces of the Bluefingers looked determined; the Greycoats looked nervous. Cartín continued to reach out with his thoughts, carrying images of the distillery's destruction with him through the dormitories. Potential allies would be more receptive in dreams than awake, as Slee told him.

Meanwhile, Dídac continued to tighten his grip on the distillery. Rations were reduced almost to crumbs, and punishment for small infractions were severe. With Dídac disturbing the mood in the distillery, it was hard to tell whether their efforts with telethymia had any effect.

One afternoon, Slee woke from a restless dream. Aizman, Batha, and Tybalt whispered together, while glancing at Slee. The three men had stretched their chains to the limit, huddling together as much as they could.

They thought their voices were too hushed to hear, but Slee's sensitive hearing made every word clear. They were debating whether they would take Dídac's offer.

"Gentlemen — pray tell, what is so fascinating that it must be whispered?" Horvald said.

They fell silent and looked around. Horvald's affable smile did not falter, even as the others fixed him with stony glares.

"Let them whisper," Slee said. "They've all but made up their minds, anyway."

"About what?"

"Whether they'll give Dídac what he wants."

The stony gaze turned to her.

"I see." Horvald began picking the lock on his shackles. "That's the sort of thing we should discuss out in the open. Wouldn't you agree?"

"We've a right to talk privately," Tybalt said.

"A right to speak is a wonderful thing. The trouble is, it covers wise words and nonsense equally." Horvald unlocked his shackles, and massaged his freed wrists.

"We can judge the wisdom of our own words," Aizman said evenly. "You have no right to barge in on them."

"What could you even have to tell Dídac that he doesn't already know?" Horvald asked.

"We know about the rat. And the rock she's hiding," Tybalt said.

The smile slid from Horvald's face, and he stood up. The other three men slowly drew their limbs in, tensing.

"What are you going to do?" Tybalt said. "Beat an old man over some whispers?"

"Oh, Good Providence, no," Horvald said. "I just wanted a stretch."

"Stretch all you like, but keep it to your side of the dungeon," Aizman said, his dark eyes flashing.

The three of them flexed their fists, rose to a half-crouch, and narrowed their eyes at Horvald. Slee watched them all, just about snorting and dipping their heads like stags in rutting season. Such foolish displays of violence made at least *some* sense in nature. As always, human thought proved itself to be inferior even to that of wild beasts.

"Why must humans always be so *dense*?" Slee broke in.

"Now, Slee, I know you lived alone your whole life, but this is not the way to make friends," Horvald said.

"Watch who you're calling dense, *elf!*" Tybalt spat the last word like a curse.

"You hated Dídac not long ago. Now you want to make a deal with him?" Slee asked.

Her head rattled with all the things she wished to say. Humans changed their minds constantly, in response to everything but reason. She folded her arms and organized her thoughts. Dídac's offer was at the heart of it, she knew.

"We're not settled on the decision. Dídac might not hold true to his word," Batha said.

"What elf does?" Tybalt grumbled.

"Slee keeps her word," Horvald said.

"Of *course* you'd say that," Tybalt said.

"What does that mean?"

"You heard what Dídac said." Tybalt's grey whiskers fanned out as he puckered his cheeks. "You're bewitched!"

A wintry silence followed his words.

"Ridiculous," Horvald said softly into the quiet.

"How would you know? Are you defending her because you want to, or because *she* wants you to?" Aizman said.

"I can defend myself," Slee said.

With a loud rattling of her chains, she rose to her feet. Horvald turned to her, key in hand, and made to unlock her shackles. She waved him away.

"If you want to use me to buy your freedom, then I'm the one you should talk to," she said.

"You'd just lie to save yourself," Batha said. Under Slee's glare, he lowered his gaze. "If – if Dídac is right."

"Then I'll only ask questions. Questions cannot be lies, can they?" Slee said.

She would use a form of the ancient elven art of *dialogh*, from which 'dialogue' was derived. It was believed that when all other reasoning failed, only questions could reveal the truth. Those gifted in the art, like Slee's mother, believed that the right question could change the most stubborn mind.

Unfortunately, compared to Mama, Slee's skill with *dialogh* was nothing.

"Questions cannot be—what sort of nonsense is this?" Tybalt squawked.

"Questions can be misleading." Aizman nodded slowly to Slee.

Batha watched on, eyes wide and shining, but his mouth tightly closed.

"Has Dídac ever misled you?" Slee asked.

Horvald, who had been hovering between Slee and the other prisoners, seemed to perceive something of Slee's intentions. He backed away, giving them a clear view of each other.

The three prisoners looked between themselves.

"Has he?" Slee repeated.

"Just answer her, for Temlin's sake," Horvald groaned.

"Yes, blast it, he has. He lied more than once," Tybalt said.

"How many times have I lied to you?"

"We don't know. All we have is your word," Aizman said.

"Do you all trust each other?" Slee pointed at the three of them.

The men looked at one another.

"Of course we do," Tybalt said.

"As well as I trust anyone else," Aizman said.

"What is the basis for that trust?"

"We risked our necks together and got caught together. I know they'd do it again; that's trust," Batha said.

"Before you sabotaged the animus, how did you build the trust to take such a risk together?"

"Well, we had to. Things couldn't go on like—"

"Wait. Don't answer." Aizman threw up his hands, rattling his chains. "She's trying to trap us."

"Trap us how?" Batha said.

"She wants us to say that since Dídac lied, and she hasn't been caught lying, she's more trustworthy. Then we'll say the three of us trusted each other out of necessity. She'll say that we have to trust *her* now out of necessity. Each question is bait in the trap, and we're falling for it."

"I wouldn't call it a trap, but that's about the shape of it. What's the difference between you three trusting each other before and trusting me now?" Slee said.

"You might not have grown up around mirrors, but I can clearly see two big, pointy differences," Tybalt said, tweaking his ears and pointing at hers.

"I see. Dídac's ears are pointed, too. If you're choosing between me and Dídac, are pointed ears really a factor worth considering?"

"Enough of this." Aizman slapped his thighs for emphasis. "Slee, I have nothing against you, but you must see the reality. No amount of debate or rhetoric can get us out of this. There are three of us — four, if Horvald is counted — and one of you. Surely, as an elf, you realize that our collective needs outweigh yours?"

Slee felt the warmth drain from her face. The dungeon, grey and barren as it was, lost a little more of its color. She sank back to her place and wrapped the blanket around her knees. Another corner of the human mind had been illuminated at last, but it brought her no joy. Some words surfaced — *exchange, barter, trade* — with a new dimension of understanding. Even life could be measured, commodified, and thus traded away.

"I've never heard such baldershite!" Horvald said heatedly. "What kind of thinking is that? Why not let one child starve so the other three can have a bigger supper?

Why not cut off one of your fingers so the others can move more freely?"

"You're raving! Get a hold of yourself, man!" Tybalt said.

"These are desperate times, and we cannot turn away any opportunities. Even distasteful ones," Aizman said.

"Can you really bewitch people?" Batha said softly.

Slee looked up to see his round, youthful eyes watching her with fearful curiosity. He looked at her the way a child looks at a horse, his question reaching out to her like a palmful of oats.

The other men fell silent, though still a little red-faced. Tybalt shot a brief, heated look at the young man.

"What? We never actually asked her," Batha said to the others.

"No. I could not bewitch anyone even if I tried," Slee said.

"But the Common Power—"

"I lived apart from the elves to be free from the Common Power, and even *I* would not call it bewitchment."

"What *can* you do?"

"Connection," she said.

Tybalt huffed air through his moustache and muttered about 'all sorts of poppycock.'

"Can you read my mind?" Batha asked breathlessly.

"No," she said, smiling. A little warmth returned to her face. "For one thing, a mind is no book. For another, a person is more than just a mind."

Batha picked at the red spots on his chin as he thought her answer over.

"Let's all agree to just return to the way things were. When we got along, and we all hated the same things — and the same elves," Horvald said.

"I'll admit I said a few things without thinking," Aizman said. "But circumstances haven't changed."

"I called humans dense," Slee said. Then, fighting through her own stubborn sense of honesty, she managed to add, "I was wrong to say that. I just wish you would have seen that Dídac made you this offer with the specific purpose of dividing us. To me, his motive was clear as day, but to you three —"

"If we end it there, Slee," Horvald said, raising his eyebrows meaningfully. "Your apology will stop just short of turning into another round of insults."

Slee nodded, and dredged up the words, "I'm sorry."

"We won't make any hasty decisions. I just hope it's clear that whatever the outcome ... it's nothing against you," Aizman said, nodding slowly to Slee as he spoke. "You could never weigh one life against another, of course. But one against three..."

Slee's eyes widened, as a new idea rose before her. She would speak to the humans in terms they would understand.

"If you take Dídac's offer ... you're getting a *bad deal*," she said, remembering the phrase from Papa's book on the basics of commerce. She had never purchased a thing in her life, but she understood the concept. "A bad deal, do you see?"

"What do you mean?" Tybalt said.

"You think you'll just be trading the secrets of one person for the freedom of three, but you're wrong. You're giving away more than my secrets. You're trading away any hope of destroying the distillery. Without me and what I can do, you'll be trading the freedom of hundreds of Bluefingers for your own. How do hundreds of lives weigh against three, I wonder?"

None of the men replied.

"You risked your own freedom just days ago, trying to sabotage production. I came here to put a stop to this distillery. We had the same goal, which Dídac couldn't allow. His offer wasn't made from the goodness of his heart—it was out of fear."

"Fear? What could he have to fear? He's got us all chained up, and he's got the Bluefingers too exhausted to resist," Tybalt said. "Everything is exactly as he wants it."

"Is it? If he's so at ease, then why come and interrogate me? Why offer you your freedom for a hint of what I'm doing?"

The three prisoners said nothing.

Then Batha, frowning in concentration, said, "Why hasn't he just killed you?"

"That woman, Elatea, won't let him," Slee said. "She wants me alive."

"So Dídac won't kill you, but only as long as he doesn't want to defy Lady Ironhands?" Aizman said.

"There are worse things than being killed," Slee said. "Those options are still open to him."

"Like what?"

"No orders prevent him from killing any of you," Slee said, looking across the dungeon at Horvald.

"We have two choices, then. Either we turn you in, knowing you won't even be killed, and gain our freedom.

Or, we stay with you and wait for Dídac to kill *us*. Your argument is running rather thin, I'm afraid." Aizman shook his head slowly.

"It's the truth. If my argument couldn't succeed without it, then I wouldn't deserve your trust," Slee said.

"That's a noble stance, Slee, but we aren't talking about high ideals. We're talking about reality, and a harsh one at that," Horvald said. "I wouldn't sell you out for the world. I hate that these three are tempted... but I understand it."

"There is no more to say. The decision is in your hands. If you decide to stay, I hope you will help me tear this place down. If you take Dídac's offer, I hope your freedom is worth the price," Slee said.

No one spoke. A long, heavy silence fell over the dungeon. Aizman, Batha, and Tybalt stared at the ceiling, the walls, and into the dark corners of the dungeon, but never at each other. Every so often, Horvald and Slee exchanged a smile, though they had no warmth.

As gradually as the bars of sunlight creeping across the floor, some deep part of Slee's soul unclenched. Dancing threads of moonlight unfurled from her, wandering farther and farther without her prompting. She touched the edge of Horvald's thoughts, then Cartín's. The three of them acknowledged each other lightly, as if nodding to an acquaintance on the street.

Dit-Dit ventured out long before it was dark. She kept to the shadows and explored cracks in the wall, despite having the prisoners' eyes on her.

Slee sank into a doze, absently knitting telethí and watching the moods that colored her companions. It was as though some knots inside her had become untangled, causing more and more threads to extend. Cartín, Dit-Dit, and Horvald unraveled as well, like spools of silk thread. Together they made a net that spanned the distillery. Though each thread was as fragile as a hair, the tapestry they wove was soon unbreakable.

Dit-Dit flitted in and out of unoccupied rooms, avoiding the scent of humans and the deep rumbling of their feet. She found trinkets, and one by one brought them to Slee. Pins, nuts, feathers, and twigs soon filled Slee's pockets. The little rat shone like a star when Slee stroked her behind the ears, warm with gratitude for the gifts.

Cartín continued to patrol the dormitories and the Extraction Chamber, letting images of Dídac's defeat spill out of him wherever he went. Through his eyes, Slee could see Bluefingers staring at him, wondering, the faintest clouds of murky curiosity rising from them. They could not fully understand what was being said in the language of telethymia, but they could feel it. There was anger simmering, too, a ripening charge of static just waiting for an outlet.

Soon, the distillery echoed with a silent beat and glimmered with invisible visions. Bottles of elixir smashed, the Greycoats disarmed and beaten, the distillery falling in on itself like a shack in a storm. As varied as the particular visions of victory were, they all held in common the burning desire to make it happen.

Slee jerked awake with a loud sniff and found the dungeon had gone dark. Dit-Dit was nestled in her pocket next the geode. Horvald snored gently. How much had been a dream? The telethí criss-crossing the dungeon shone as brightly as ever.

WAR WITH ELVES: FOR PROFIT AND AMUSEMENT

The threads lurched, like a spiderweb struck by a moth. Charcoal-black fear and clotted indigo despair ran down the lines, dripping from it like sickly dew. Somewhere in the distillery, some distress had caused an aura to burst out from a private mind into the open. She checked her bonds — Cartín was safe. Her relief almost stole her breath. That particular mixture of fear and despair, its aroma and texture, usually signalled death.

She reached out as much comfort as she could, but her telethí, winding through the halls, found no purchase. Whoever was in trouble, they couldn't recognise help. At least, not of the kind Slee could offer.

Heavy boots in the hall.

There was no great clamor, no grunts or shouts or beatings. The door opened, waking Horvald and the others. A woman with one leg was led in. In the dark, Slee couldn't recognise the guards, but she knew that Cartín was not among them. Still, they treated the new prisoner gently.

They placed her beside Slee. She brought with her the aura Slee had sensed. Close by, it chilled the air and made Slee's heart ache.

The guards chained her without saying a word, then left.

"Who's that? Is that you, Mary?" Batha whispered.

"No, no. It's me, Charlotte," the new prisoner said. She gasped a few times as though she'd been splashed with icy water. "Oh, I can't believe they put me in here!"

"Oh, dear Charlotte, neither can we," Tybalt said.

Slee caught a wisp of a pulsing, reddish aura. It rose from Tybalt like a cloud at sunset, then faded away before she could be sure of what she'd seen.

"Tybalt, is that you? Oh, Saint's tears, what am I going to do?" Charlotte shrank under a chaotic cloud of colors muted by fear and shock.

"You'll be alright, girl. We're in here together." Tybalt's rumbling voice exuded warmth and comfort. "What did you do to get thrown in here? Something destructive enough to make us proud, I hope?"

"Oh, good Providence, no!" she said. "I could never do anything like that. I have a family back in Madea City — oh, Chandon's mercy, what are they going to do now? Oh, Tybalt, I did my best, I truly did. I just couldn't get out of bed. Dídac brought the Greycoats, made a big fuss … Ordered me to get up and get moving. I asked him just for one day to rest. I just felt *wretched*, I couldn't have made it to the extractors without collapsing. Well, he said, if I wanted a rest I could have it. And they – they hauled me here."

A stinging heat rose off Charlotte, and Slee's neck twinged in sympathy. She was confused for a moment, before she realized that the poor woman was not feeling the heat of anger, but of *shame.*

Humans seemed to constantly get feelings of pride and shame backwards. Those who felt the greatest shame often deserved to feel proud instead. The most prideful humans, without exception, should have been the ones who felt ashamed.

"You did nothing wrong, Charlotte," Slee said, once more reaching out with threads of comfort that Charlotte seemed unable to perceive.

"Oh!" Charlotte shifted to face Slee. "Sorry, I didn't realize someone was there. Are you the…?"

"I'm Slee. The half-elf, if that matters."

"Oh!" Charlotte said. She inched away from Slee,
perhaps without thinking.

"She's alright, Charlotte. She's not one of the enemy — at
least, we don't think," Tybalt said.

"Oh, dear. I'm sorry, Slee. How do you do? Charlotte
Wixler."

"Meeting you is a pleasure, despite the circumstances."

"Likewise."

"Did that pale bastard really lock you up for needing a
day off?" Tybalt said.

"I'm afraid so," Charlotte said, once again radiating
shame.

"You did no wrong. Dídac had no right to do such a
cruel thing," Slee said.

"You're very kind. I just can't help but think — what
about all the people that were depending on me? My
children, my aunt … There'll be no money coming in
before long. I've let them all down."

"Dídac let them down," Horvald said. "You did all the
right things, which is more than I can say."

"If you ask me, it's a wonder nobody else has reached
their limit," Tybalt said. "Day after day in the Extraction
Chamber … it's not healthsome! Dídac simply cannot be
allowed to keep doing this!"

A new aura shivered in the dungeon. It was like the faint
rumbling of large stones, the invigorating chill of
mountain air, and the rosy glow of the dawn. Everyone
present held it in common, though it remained vague, and
skirted around the edges of their minds. It beat with a

regular rhythm, halfway between a battle drum and a beating heart.

"Tybalt, Batha—are you thinking the same as me?" Aizman murmured.

"Providence help me, I think I might just be," Tybalt rumbled.

"Then I say, to the abyss with Dídac and his deal," Aizman said. "Slee was right all along. We can't free ourselves just to leave everyone else at the mercy of Dídac's whims. Even if we perish in the attempt, I say it's better to go out in a blaze of glory. The distillery must be destroyed."

Tybalt gave a subdued cheer of, "Hear, hear!"

"Good Providence! Please don't all go and endanger yourselves on my behalf," Charlotte said.

"In all honesty, I'd almost reached this decision before you arrived," Aizman said. "You just made the commitment easier."

"But how can you hope to fight Dídac with all his potions and weapons and Greycoats and Providence-knows-what else?" Charlotte said.

"Dídac has great fears of our friend Slee. I say we justify them," Horvald said.

The beating, shivering, dawning aura warmed and enveloped the dungeon, as though a spring morning had bloomed between the prisoners. It pulsed with determination, taking errant sparks of anger and channeling them into a disciplined, shared goal.

Slee could hardly believe how strong the shared feeling had grown without any conscious effort. She touched the geode, sensing the thick cords of telethí that clung to it.

The little stone seemed to work best when she put it from her mind, so she withdrew her hand from her pocket.

Aínan, Muanan, Crantarín, Telethían.

Trust, emotions, goals, and threads. These four pillars were all she needed. If she took care of them, the rest would take care of itself.

She looked around the dungeon which was no longer dark. In her eyes, the glowing aura brightened the faces of her new allies. Each of them shone with the same determination, quivered with the same fear. With the common goal decided, the same invigoration flowing in their veins, their trust growing, and the number of telethí multiplying, the foundations of a powerful telethymic web was in place.

Aizman, Batha, Tybalt, and Charlotte had not joined the web yet, but Slee hoped they soon would. If those four could trust telethymia, even a little, then the whole distillery might be united against Dídac.

The pale bastard was nowhere near as safe as he thought.

Chapter 31

Every morning, increasingly perplexed elven healers came to re-apply thicker and thicker layers of ointment to Fentor's wounds. They mostly spoke elvish, but Fentor gleaned that they believed human skin could somehow absorb the salve at an astonishing rate. Before long, small crowds of healers in leaf-green aprons came to see the spectacle. They poked and prodded him with all sorts of cold brass contraptions. None of them seemed able to divine the cause of the missing ointment.

Their reaction almost brought Fentor enough amusement to make up for the pain of having the soothing ointment scraped off his raw, bleeding skin.

The minute the healers left, Crauford would collect the ointment into small glass bottles. He worked with haste and many apologies, but the ordeal still hurt. Most of his cuts reopened fresh each morning, oozing dew-drops of blood along their length. This, too, Crauford collected. Fentor began to feel like the worlds strangest dairy cow.

It was all worth it. He went through it for the mission. For Lady Ironhands. For King and Country. For Temlin's *sake,* did it hurt. But it was all worth it.

He would make sure it was all worth it.

By the time his cuts, abrasions, and sore throat had healed, Crauford declared that he had harvested enough. The Thambrian's time became wholly occupied with transmuting the ointment into Oil of Telium, and their donated blood into rust.

The next phase of Fentor's plan had been percolating throughout his recovery, and was now well-steeped.

Fentor was drenched in both Madean and Norimandian heritage. In mind, heart, body, and soul, he was so thoroughly soaked in humanity that his boots squelched wherever he went. Sidarí could never believe Fentor wanted to join the Elarím. Not when every word that left his lips was a patriotic anthem.

All he needed was to borrow un-Madean words from someone else's lips. Someone who was a true believer. A convert. A spineless, twitchy sort who might easily fall victim to flim-flam.

As was their usual habit, Angsley, Hess, and Fentor drank and played dice while Crauford toiled in the cramped 'alchemy nook.' It was concealed under loose boards under the bench that served as their bar, and filled with all manner of makeshift alembics and beakers. The small space only allowed one occupant, so Crauford worked alone.

Angsley and Hess were contesting the result of a die that had landed on an angle when Fentor cut in.

"Don't you think it's time we assemble all our fellow Madeans here in the Crown and throw a little soiree for them?"

Angsley blinked at him, feathering the tip of his beard with his fingers.

"I'm sorry, did I miss the first half of a conversation?" Hess asked. "Where did that come from?"

"It's just such a marvellous idea that I think it rather burst from me. What do you think?"

"A *soiree*? Who do I look like, Vicomte de Chauverie?" Angsley chuckled at his own wit. "Fetch my powdered wig, won't you?"

"Half the other prisoners here are miserable, the other half are sprouting elf ears," Hess scoffed.

"They're *what*?" Angsley stopped mid-drink, spilling some sapwine in his beard.

"I'm being colorful. It's figurative. Like poetry. They're about to join the Eralim—I mean, the Elarím, ergo, it's metaphorically like they're dying their hair silver and growing pointy ears," Hess said, waving her glass in Angsley's face for emphasis.

"Ah. *Figurative.* I knew that," Angsley said, mopping his beard. "Everyone knows you can't just sprout points on your ears …"

"We should invite them all," Fentor said brightly. "Why, young Thorassa is an Elarím convert, but I still feel like he's a good sort."

Hess and Angsley narrowed their eyes like cats woken by a bright light. They looked at each other, shaking their furrowed faces in shared perplexion.

"Thorassa?" Hess asked. "*That's* who you want to see?"

"Yes, him and all the other Madeans in the area. A reunion ought to be a diverting affair," Fentor said with a jaunty grin.

"Is this part of the …?" Angsley nodded toward Crauford's hidden alchemy operation, then in the general direction of the hill where Elatea was being held.

Fentor let the silence stretch on for a few beats. He certainly couldn't so much as nod his head, or even acknowledge that he understood what Angsley had referred to. He also did nothing to deny Angsley's question.

"So, we're all agreed: we shall invite our fellow Madeans here tonight!" Fentor raised his glass. The others slowly raised theirs, and gently they all clinked together.

A small contingent of brassmail-clad Elarím warriors stood guard around the Crown, gleaming like candlesticks. The bustling elves parted around them like waves around rocks. Fentor gave them all a cheery wave. Let them stand all around him and watch his every move. Pulling victory out from under their noses would be all the sweeter.

The others had insisted that Fentor shouldn't set foot outside the Crown. As a result, Hess and Angsley had played a round of dice to determine who would go to invite their evening guests. Crauford, busy with the reagents, could not be spared.

So it was that a Hess went out into the streets of Rivumaí in search of humans, while Angsley and Fentor stayed behind to make the tavern more festive.

They procured a small number of chairs and tables, and two hundred bottles of sapwine. After spending a few hours trying in vain to fasten the reddish elven lanterns to the ceiling and to the walls, they settled on simply placing a lantern in the center of each table. Angsley picked some wildflowers that were growing nearby, used empty wine bottles as vases, and gave each table its small bouquet. Declaring a job well done, they made an early start on the wine.

Crauford did not join them, but remained crouched in the cavity, swirling vials of liquid and sniffing vials of powder.

"You'll have to stop all that tinkering soon, Crauford." Angsley rapped on the table above Crauford's head. "We can't have any guests seeing what you're up to. Unless … that's the plan?" Angsley addressed the last part to Fentor.

"Crauford's going to be the life of the party. The very beating heart of it. We can't have him alchemizing and transmuting, unless it's to turn this sapwine into a proper Norimandian Cabernet," Fentor said.

"So the guests are not coming here to be 'entertained' by Crauford's dazzling alchemical talents, then?" Angsley said with deliberation.

"Oh no, not at this time."

"Why *are* they coming, then?" Angsley said, finished his glass, then poured a new one.

"We shall see which of them are suitable for future get-togethers. Speak to them, see if a stout Madean heart still beats in their chest. If it does, invite them back." Fentor swirled sapwine on his tongue. A hint of lilac-honey and an earthy note, like smoked cinnamon. And could it be? A bright note, like the clear ringing of trumpets at dawn, a note heralding his victory.

"I see. And at the next soiree?"

"*Then* Crauford shall unveil the fruits of his labor and dazzle our guests."

Crauford paused in his work. His dark eyes darted across Fentor's face, slid unfocused to the middle distance, and then returned. He nodded. "Twenty 'guests' will be sufficient."

"Try to double it." Fentor held his golden drink to the light. "After all, a party with insufficient guests is an impediment to solitude without being a distraction from it."

"If you say so, old boy."

Between them, they finished a bottle and started on a new one. A blinking Crauford emerged from his alchemy crevice like a fox from its den. The three men replaced all the floorboards over the hole, then dragged the largest table directly over them. So long as nobody stood directly on them, the loose floorboards would not be discovered.

"The solution is ready—save for the final, secret ingredients," Crauford said. "We don't have enough reagents to make another. We *must* keep the hiding place secure."

"Not to worry, dear Crauford. With me guarding it, not a soul, whether elf, man, or otherwise shall be able to find it," Angsley said.

Hess returned late in the afternoon, followed by a few humans. They trailed timidly after her like ducklings. Fentor and Angsley greeted them enthusiastically, thrusting a glass of sapwine into every free hand. As more guests arrived, Fentor sidled over to Hess.

"Did you get Thorassa?" he asked.

"He's not in Rivumaí, but I met someone who said they would pass the invitation along. If he's too far away to make it, or doesn't want to come, it won't be my fault."

"Providence willing, he can come. Look how many guests are pouring in! You've done a marvellous job, Hess. Simply marvellous." Standing side-by-side with her, he encircled her shoulders and kissed the top of her head.

A grin struggled—against heavy opposition of her cheek muscles—to glow upon her face. She spoke twice as fast as usual. "Oh, pish posh. Rivumaí is such a dull place. Getting Madeans to come was the easy part. The hard part was explaining to the elves that they *couldn't* come. The concept of a guest list has not yet reached their scholars, apparently."

"They will doubtless appreciate that particular innovation. Now! Let us mingle and ply our guests with drink. Get to know them. I want to know, for example, which of them pine for home, and which are content in Rivumaí. The next guest list will depend upon it." He raised his eyebrows at her, holding her gaze as she nodded slowly in return.

"Why, of course," she said. "It takes a thoroughly Madean spirit to enjoy these occasions, after all."

"My thoughts exactly."

They nodded, then parted to mingle with the guests. For brief moments, Fentor could almost believe he was back in Madea City, drinking at the *real* Crown Upon a Crown. However, the stark differences between his nostalgia for home and his present situation kept intruding upon his fantasy.

For one thing, the guests were dressed all wrong. There was not a proper Bluefinger jacket, tricorne, or moustache to be seen. Instead, they wore long drapery that might have been robes, and thick leggings, patterned scarves, and belts that looked like they were woven from straw. Half of it looked like Norimandian bedclothes, the other half like work attire. Fentor spoke to one man who wore, for example, a buttonless coat with long purple sleeves and trees embroidered onto both breast pockets.

For another thing, each new guest seemed to be the complete opposite of the last. Some were blissfully at ease, while others had chewed their fingernails bloody. Some were open and friendly, others shivered alone in the dark corners. Some drank the sapwine with evident pleasure, others gagged on every sip. Many seemed to behave normally, right up until they excused themselves from conversation to pace around the party's fringes, muttering and twitching.

Obviously, Fentor was after the most nervous of the nervous wrecks, who had the darkest rings around their sleep-deprived eyes. Only those paranoid mutterers had remained loyal to Madea long enough that they had started to crack. Anyone that seemed to be enjoying themselves, he marked as an enemy.

Fentor circled the party like a shark in search of lone swimmers. He whispered in a few ears, shook a few hands, told a few offhand Madean jokes about elves. With each new victim, he tested their reactions. Thus, the exclusive guest list began to grow.

Each time he shook hands with someone, he'd glance down to note the blueness of their fingers. Inky fingertips proved to be a promising sign.

Thorassa's unmistakable face waded among the guests at the door. Fentor, who had been speaking to a young man who sleepily cradled a bottle of sapwine like it was a baby, excused himself. In the next moment, he pounced on Thorassa and shook his hand vigorously. The young man's fingers were unstained. Fentor steered him to the nearest table, and sat him down.

"Thorassa, Thorassa, my dear man! How glad I am that you've come," Fentor said.

"I must admit, your invitation was unexpected," Thorassa said.

"I imagine it must have been. What do you think of my little soiree?" Fentor swept his hands outward.

"Well, I think—"

The door crashed open. A bald elf, as lean and sharp as a knife, stood just outside the doorway. He wore a coat of brassmail armor that glinted angrily in the red lantern light, but appeared unarmed. A hush fell over the party.

"Don't move," Fentor intoned to Thorassa, then sprang toward the intruder.

He emerged from the crowd at the same time as Angsley, shortly followed by Hess.

"Hullo! Can I help you?" Fentor wore a welcoming smile, looking the new arrival up and down.

The elf swept the room with hawkish eyes.

"I'm afraid this is a human-only function," Fentor said.

Hess, Angsley, and Crauford huddled close to Fentor's sides. He tried to shrug them off, but they clung to him.

"What are you all doing in here?" the elf asked. "What reason is there for so many humans to gather?"

"Why, it's a soiree. A party, a celebration, a gala, a get-together, a spot of carousal. It's a popular Madean custom to gather all your friends together and drink."

"Friends?" the elf narrowed his eyes at the eclectic mix of attendants. "All these are your friends?"

"By the end of the night, they will be!"

Two Elarím guards came up behind the bald elf. One touched his shoulder. "Mannoc, come away. We are not welcome to join the humans."

"Of course we are not welcome," the elf called Mannoc said. "Why would they let us see what they are up to?"

" 'Up to?' " Fentor covered his mouth with both hands, as though deeply affronted. "My good sir, I pray you don't think we're doing anything untoward!"

Mannoc's already severe face hardened. "All manner of strange requests have been traced back here. Chemicals, powders, rare flowers and roots. No other humans ever ask for such substances."

"Mannoc, what harm could they do? The Common Power will prevent them from hurting each other or anyone else," the elf at Mannoc's shoulder said. "Leave them in peace."

"In light of the recent attacks, I find myself less certain than you," Mannoc replied.

"You cannot enter their dwelling. Unless Rivumaí agrees otherwise, we must watch their doings from across the road."

"Then rouse the willing for *á Coríthe*. This little clade has ignored reality for too long," Mannoc said.

The elf glowered at Fentor, then turned away with a sweep of his red cloak. The door closed, and the party hung suspended in silence.

Fentor turned to see the entire room staring at him. He drew a large breath and began to sing the first drinking song that came to mind: *Lady Ironhands*.

Hess, Angsley, and Crauford joined him, a little haltingly. They seemed unable to follow his many flourishes with the tune, the timing, and sometimes, the key. Before long, voice after voice took up the song, and the Crown resounded with a song Fentor hadn't heard in far too long.

His eye beaded with a patriotic tear. He'd give anything to be back home in Madea City. The rain on the cobbles, the parades in the streets, Methúsel's endless chiding. The thought made his heart ache. There was no country like Madea. More tears crowded into his eyes. Quite suddenly, his patriotic sighs turned into nationalistic hyperventilation. He loosened his scarf, finished his glass, and attempted to seize control of himself.

"Fenny? Are you alright?" Hess took his arm and looked at him with concern.

"All that singing—I'm not sure my throat was quite ready for it. I'm fine now, really."

Hess let go of him. "If you're sure."

"What was that business about rousing the willing, I wonder?" Fentor said.

"I'm not sure, but it can't be good."

"Help me keep an eye out, will you?"

"Of course."

Fentor gave her arm a brief squeeze, then left. He passed Angsley, who continued to sing *Lady Ironhands* in a boisterous baritone that drowned out half the other voices.

Thorassa was sitting right where Fentor had left him. He had an untouched glass of sapwine sat in front of him, and an uncharacteristically pensive look. Not a single muscle twitched as he rested his clean-shaven chin on interlocked fingers. Even his watery eyes looked sharp and perceptive.

"Pardon the interruption. Where were we?"

Thorassa looked up. "You aren't doing anything 'untoward' in here, are you Fentor?"

"Good Providence, no! Of course not!"

"You're not … brewing something that you shouldn't be?"

Brewing? What did Thorassa know? *How* did he know?

After a pause, Fentor said, "No!"

"Mannoc has a point. You've been asking for odd things."

"Is that against the law?"

Thorassa smiled. "Don't worry, Capilet. I won't report you."

"There's nothing to report."

"Good. I'm curious, Fentor, why did you want to see me in particular?"

"Because I let you down, dear boy. I would like your forgiveness, if I may have it," Fentor said.

"If it means something to you, then you may have it. I forgive you." Thorassa raised his glass, touched it to Fentor's, and the two drank.

"I hardly made my apology, and yet you accepted it! I dare say you've forgiven me with the readiness of a Saint."

"Actually, I am just learning to see things the way the Elarím do."

"They are a forgiving sort, are they?"

"Not quite. They find the whole process irrelevant. When harm is done, it is simply repaired or prevented wherever possible. Compared to taking action, words like 'sorry' are scarcely needed."

"Fascinating!" Fentor lied. "What else have you learned about their ways?"

"You find it fascinating?" Thorassa asked, drumming his fingers on the side of his glass. "Really?"

"Why shouldn't I? I find everything about their whole … enterprise intriguing!"

"Well, what in particular piques your curiosity?"

Fentor asked various questions, from the ways elves produced their food to their history to matters of etiquette. Thorassa answered him with short, guarded responses. Still, Fentor gleaned every little tidbit that might help him sound more convincing to Sidarí. Through it all, he tried to discern what the Elarím had done to win Thorassa's loyalty. No clear answers surfaced.

Once his questions were exhausted, he risked a topic that had been weighing on his mind: the bald elf, Mannoc.

"That last thing Mannoc said before he left, what did that mean? Do you remember? Some elvish phrase that escapes me ..."

"You mean *á Coríthe*? Is your interest in that based on curiosity or self-preservation?" Thorassa said.

The young rabbit-faced man drew his arms closer to his body, leaving his glass where it was. Fentor sensed that he was losing ground. Thorassa was giving him the sort of suspicious look that had been directed at him too often, lately.

Thus, Fentor reached for his most-neglected tactic: the truth.

"You've caught me. I *am* worried. I need to know what they're doing for my own peace of mind," he said.

"Well ..." Thorassa pursed his lips, then drank some sapwine. "It's a kind of vote. Without formal laws, they depend on agreements, standards, that sort of thing. This Coríthe will decide whether human prisoners should have the same private dwelling rights that Elarím citizens have."

"They're voting so they can burst in here and rifle through my things?"

"Essentially, yes."

"That's not fair! I'm entitled to my privacy!"

Thorassa snickered behind his hand like a schoolboy.

"What? You find that amusing, do you?"

"Only *you* could think that the way Elarím treat prisoners is unfair. Can you imagine a Madean prison looking like *this*?" Thorassa gestured at their surroundings.

"How should I know? I've never been in one. I imagine the conditions are … comparable." Fentor glanced around at the red-cheeked revellers. He knew full well that Madean prisons were nightmarish, but admitting that would have helped to make Thorassa's point.

"Remind me, what does the Madean Land Corps do with elven prisoners?"

"They're shot, naturally."

"And yet, you find the idea of this Coríthe unfair?"

"Absolutely!"

"As you drink freely provided wine, surrounded by friends, in a building that they let you build?"

"A building they're just now voting to invade!"

"Such hard luck has befallen you," Thorassa said, shaking his head. "I can only hope you will somehow manage to get by."

"Alright, alright! I will admit that Elarím prison is slightly more agreeable than I might have previously thought," Fentor said. "All the same, I don't want them barging in here and spoiling the mood."

"Is that really your concern? The atmosphere of your party?"

"Yes! It might sound petty to someone like you, who squanders his leisure time reading elvish philosophy, but yes. I miss home. Having everyone here reminds me of Madea City." Yet another, quite unwelcome, patriotic tear leaked from his eye. Some pressurized well of nostalgia and homesickness seemed to have erupted from Fentor momentarily. But rather than spoiling his strategy, it seemed to work in his favor.

Thorassa must have caught a glint of it before Fentor wiped it away, because the young man's face changed. His glare softened, and his little rabbit nose twitched ever so slightly.

"It is hard being away from home," Thorassa said.

"Everything is the opposite of what it should be here," Fentor said. "How can anyone adjust to this place?"

"No one adapts overnight. It takes time. But also, a certain openness."

"How did you manage it?" Fentor looked up at Thorassa with an earnest face. Inside, he glowed with triumph. For some reason, it felt a little like heartburn.

Young Thorassa looked at him with such compassion that Fentor knew he had won. Even with this knowledge, his body felt as though it had been divided right down the middle. One side of him crawled with gooseflesh, all hollowed out and sickly. The other side glowed, fever-hot, anticipating victory over Thorassa's mind. But he had won.

All it had taken was a little performance and a little of his true feelings.

"Sage Nyendí wrote often about the differences between the human and elven minds. Much of it was dense, verbose, dusty stuff. One passage stuck right in the back of my head, though. It went, 'In old Madea, the serfs were chained to their toil for the king; the king was chained to the toil of the serfs. So long as such chains persist, neither are free.' "

Fentor almost scoffed, but he managed to catch it in his throat and turn it into an interested murmur of, "Hmm-mm."

Nyendí had clearly never heard of the protection, inspiration, and leadership a good king provided for his people. Without the king, there *would* be no serfs, nor any land for them to work. Nor would the light of Providence shine upon them, of course. Whatever measure of freedom serfs had had in their simple, grubby little lives, it was all thanks to the king. For Temlin's sake, in all the Norimandian revolts, the peasants brandished pitchforks that their own king had provided to them without a hint of self-awareness!

The serfs weren't chained to their king—they were indebted to him!

"What does it mean?" Fentor asked, feigning deep interest.

Thorassa's answer was cut off by the door slamming open.

Mannoc stood on the threshold.

"The Coríthe has been decided," Mannoc said.

Across the room, Fentor caught Angsley's eye. The loose floorboards were under his feet. They nodded at each other; they could not let the elves find it.

Mannoc stepped inside.

Chapter 32

*A table heaped with bread aplenty rains
crumbs upon us all.*

Saint Temlin.

The pre-dawn hours crackled with frost. The iron bars on
the window grew a thin layer of ice crystals, and the
prisoner's breath bloomed white in the dark. Dit-Dit
sheltered in Slee's hands, which she kept in her pocket.
Her blanket, thin as it was, was better protection than the
other prisoners had.

Charlotte shivered and gasped beside her. Slee peeled
the blanket off despite the stinging cold and passed it to
her. The pale shape of the blanket floated in the gloom as
Charlotte held it in her hands.

"Oh, I can't take this from you. Please." It drifted closer
as she offered it back. Charlotte's breath misted the air
between them.

"You are colder than I."

"But it belongs to you. I'd feel awfully wretched, like I'd stole it off you." Charlotte did not seem able to keep her teeth from chattering as she spoke.

A red bubble of indignation rose up from Dit-Dit, then burst by Slee's ear. The little rat wanted the blanket, too.

"I'd feel worse. My crime would be greater than mere theft," Slee said.

"Your crime?"

"There is a law that cannot be broken: *All life cares for all life*. Your need is greater than mine, and I must see to it."

"Take the blanket, Charlotte. She'll never relent," Horvald said.

"If you insist, then … thank you, Slee. I am greatly in your debt." Charlotte fanned the blanket out, then drew it in about herself until she was a small, pale bundle in the gloom. Her shivering subsided, and she gave a muffled sigh of relief into the fabric.

Slee knew that humans often expressed gratitude in financial terms—*I owe you; I'm in your debt; I'll pay you back*—but it did not sit right with her. Kindness and care should not be tallied on ledgers. A world built on such miserly accounting would collapse in a week!

Slee held her tongue. Charlotte meant well.

The aura that had warmed the chamber earlier had now almost receded entirely. The common goal had briefly united their thoughts, but the cold, sleepless night had driven them all back into themselves. Besides, no true connection had been made. The telethí drifting between Slee and Horvald still passed right through the others as though they weren't there.

"There's no chance anyone else has a spare blanket?" old
Tybalt's chattering voice split the frigid silence.

"If I did, you wouldn't get a thread of it," Batha said.
"Saint's tears, my fingers are about to drop off!"

"Any blankets, rugs, or handkerchiefs should be given
to me. I'm Thambrian, I didn't grow up with ice and cold,"
Aizman said. "It affects me more."

"So, you regret leaving home then, Aizman?"

"These days, every minute."

"We could all be warmer with a little cooperation," Slee
said.

"Are you quite sure they're ready?" Horvald asked.

"That's their decision."

"Hold on just a moment — ready for what?" Tybalt said.

"Telethymia."

They all went silent.

"I'm not *that* cold, yet," Tybalt said. "Ask again when
my nose has fallen off and my toes have turned black.
Maybe then I'll think about pointy-eared witchcraft."

"I don't want to be controlled by something I can't see. I
want my mind to be my own," Batha said.

"Controlled? Where in the world did you get that idea?"
Slee asked. "I *told* you —"

"Slee, they aren't ready. They hardly know what
telethymia even is," Horvald said.

"Then I'll explain it," Slee said.

"No need. I know more than enough," Tybalt grumbled.
"You seem a decent sort, Slee, but I can carry on the way I
always have — alone. I don't need my soul stitched up to
the fellow next to me to care about him."

"What about Dídac and his elixir? We can only fight him if we fight together," Slee said.

"But we *will* be together. I'll be right beside you the whole way," Tybalt said. "I've seen combat more times than you've picked your nose. I don't need to share my head with anyone else to know how to think."

"Slee, listen to me a moment," Horvald said. "You're not arguing with the people sitting here — you're arguing with every song, poster, book, rhyme, joke, report, and lecture about the Common Power they've ever come across. I grew up in Madea. Until I met you, I thought the same."

"Well, I didn't grow up in Madea," Aizman said steadily. "Tybalt, if I try Slee's magic and it warms me up, will you relent?"

"No."

"Will you at least stop grousing so loudly about it?"

"I'll consider it."

"Be careful, Aizman," Batha said. "I'm sure Slee wouldn't do anything that's … well, you never know do you? Just be careful."

"If Slee starts wearing my brain like a glove and making me dance across the room, then I will be sure to tell you," Aizman said, with a drawling, ironic cadence.

"You never know …" Batha repeated, almost under his breath.

"Before we start, Slee, where will this warmth come from?" Aizman asked.

"What do you mean?"

"Are you planning to transfer your body heat to me? Or perhaps, Horvald's? The warmth must come from somewhere," Aizman said.

"If two equally cold people embrace, each body warms
the other. The transfer is mutual, and they are warmer
together than they would be apart. Do you see?"

"Ah … I think so."

"Are you ready?"

"Just hurry up, before I freeze over completely!"

Slee withdrew into the space inside her where threads
of moonlight wandered in starless space. The telethí
waved on invisible currents like river-weeds. Many
silvery cords tethered her to Dit-Dit and Horvald, and
many others reached far across the distillery to Cartín.
Smaller hairs and filaments of silk bound them all to tiny
mosses and motelings and insects too numerous to count.

Across the room, several tentative fibres rose from
Aizman's shoulders. Slee reached out to them in
invitation, with a promise of warmth and comfort as sure
as the sight of a fire at the end of a weary road. Aizman
took the threads easily. His telethí wound around those
Slee had offered, like vines curling around a trellis. A little
warmth passed between them, then a little more.

Slee felt her numb fingers blush with warmth. At the
same time, she felt Aizman's relief as the cold stopped
biting his toes.

"Ah," he breathed.

"Already?" Tybalt asked.

"It can't compare to a Thambrian summer, but I'm
warmer than before. Or rather, I'm less cold."

"And are you … alright?" Batha asked. "Are you, you
know, yourself?"

Tell him you are now my loyal servant, Slee thought to him.
Tell him your will is broken.

Aizman laughed softly, "I am as much myself as I have ever been."

Privately, to Slee, he thought, *Now is not the time for a joke like* that.

"What's it like, then?" Tybalt said. "Are you all reading each other's thoughts?"

"I suppose … I can hear what they have to say to me. Not much else."

There was a long silence. Different auras rose from the prisoners, some like reflections off water, others like the glow of fireflies. Aizman bathed, content, in a small pool of humming yellow light.

"Excuse me, Slee?" Charlotte asked softly. "Do you think I could…?"

"Of course. The more of us join, the warmer we'll all be," Slee said.

"Thank you! It's just so frightfully cold."

Charlotte joined the web of telethí as easily as Aizman had. As they shared their warmth amongst themselves and the new member, the frosty air lost still more of its sting. Soon, Slee wasn't shivering at all. Even Dit-Dit dozed, content and warm, the blanket forgotten.

The geode still funneled the many wandering threads of telethí, wove them together, gave them shape and discipline. With every new addition, they could reach a little farther, soothe a few more aches, beat back the heavy curtains of darkness and despair and solitude.

Cartín, a bright wandering spot at the other end of the distillery, thought, *Be careful Slee, Horvald. There's a chill in the air here that has nothing to do with the weather.*

What do you mean? Horvald asked.

Something about Dídac has changed. I can't explain it. He's looking at people like he's at the markets inspecting bits of meat. The other Greycoats are circling his ankles like dogs waiting for the bones to fall.

We'll be careful, Slee thought.

Stay in your shackles. He might come at any moment, Cartín thought.

Slee silently agreed. She had to learn more about the strange mood.

Slee closed her eyes and drifted along the farthest-reaching telethí. She moved blindly through the corridors and the Extraction Chamber and the dormitories, feeling her way as though the threads were guide-ropes. The distillery shivered. It shivered like a line about to snap. She could almost hear the moan of drawn-out tension pulling on a thousand unseen strings all around her. Human minds creaking and straining with things she could not understand.

Something in the distillery was about to break, but she knew not what.

She wafted past Dídac's office, where the hollow air tasted of metal. His aura repulsed the wandering telethí, sent them curling back on themselves like a long hair singed by a candle. It was a hostile, scorched emptiness, a vessel scoured by acrid soap. He had not lost the part of himself that could connect; he had burnt it off entirely.

With Aizman and Charlotte bolstering the web, Slee could reach farther than she had been able to for some time. She wondered, breathless, if that could mean …

She fanned out in all directions, her inner senses becoming like spokes on a wheel. Around the distillery, the gravel and the shores of the lake murmured and rustled with tiny creatures. Beyond, beleaguered trees groaned under their own weight. Their roots strained to draw life from the soil, but there was little to be had. They were like lost men in the desert, clawing down into the sand in the desperate hope of finding water.

Beneath the trees, where Dit-Dit had found them, they had to be there, somewhere …

Slee felt her way with gossamer fingertips and smelled the breezes that passed through her. She reached as far as she could, pulling every line taut. They were not there. No particle of them got caught on the fibres. No sound of them shook the web. If she could just reach a little farther …

She could remember Slowjaw's mighty presence, the beat of Felheim's stout heart. They were just outside her reach. They had to be.

If they weren't there, just beyond the grasp of the telethí, then that would mean they had already …

She had stretched out like that, holding her breath, for too long. She let the web go slack and returned to the dungeon, to her normal senses.

Mama's words fluttered to her, like moths in starlight. *In this life, some will be beyond your reach. Beyond your help. Even, sometimes, those you love. It does not help anything if you cling to them. There will always be others in your reach.*

The tension in the distillery continued to throb. Some undercurrent burbled beneath, like a low chanting in an unknown language. Something within reach needed her help. She needed help, too.

"Horvald?" she asked.

"Yes?"

"Can you feel anything … unusual?"

The faintest light of the coming dawn outlined him in silver. He tilted his head. "I'm not quite sure. Unusual in what way?"

"Like something out there is coloring your mood, intruding on your thoughts."

"No, nothing like that."

"Why would he feel like that?" Batha asked, hugging his knees tightly. "What's gone wrong?"

"No, the telethí are fine. It's the Bluefingers in the distillery, the dormitories. It is like they are all waking from the same, shapeless dream. Dream, or nightmare—I cannot tell."

"I think I know what you mean," Aizman said. "A little feeling here and there, like a fly darting by my ear."

"What does it mean? What are they feeling?" Slee asked.

"I can't be sure. I suppose they're just tired, overworked, anxious."

"There is something beyond that … a finality. Something approaching a sharp drop into a black pit." Slee frowned, her fingers tracing the telethí nearest her, like a harpist checking her strings.

"I can't feel things through the air the way you can, Slee, but I remember what I felt," Charlotte said. She had drawn the blanket up to her chin, and she had stopped shivering. "I don't know what help I could possibly be …"

"Tell me, please. You might be the only one that can help me understand," Slee said.

"I can't say what anyone else was feeling, mind. Dídac forbade complaining, you see, so nobody spoke at all. We didn't even dare to look at each other with the Greycoats watching… Everyone around me was getting on with things, but I couldn't keep going. I'm a good woman. If I agree to something, I see it through. But day after day, all those hours strapped to the extractors, I was tempted by thoughts of the gravest sin …"

"Which sin is that?" Slee asked. She recalled reading about the human concept of sin—*evil, guilt, immorality, misdeed*—but she could not see how Charlotte could have contemplated the worst of all evils.

"She means the sin of indolence. Laziness," Horvald said.

"*That's* the gravest sin?"

"It was Saint Candade of Rodessia who said: 'Indolence is worst of all sins. A sluggish body rejects the gifts of Providence; an idle mind forsakes its teachings. Look to the alleys and gutters—there dwell the indolent, who spread every other sin like a plague of fleas.' "

Slee almost scoffed aloud, but the others did not share her scorn. Indeed, Charlotte seemed to be glowing softly with reverence after Horvald's recitation. Faith mattered to her. What good could scoffing do? What good had it ever done?

She held in her scoff and her incredulous comments. Instead, she tried to connect with the way Charlotte felt about Saints and sins.

"That must have felt awful," Slee said.

"It was," Charlotte said. "I kept thinking, 'What have I got to complain about? The pay from this job will keep my household ticking over for a while. That's more than a lot of people can say!' I kept praying and praying to the Saints for strength. I've never complained or given up, not once in my life. But I let myself turn into a stranger. A lazy, slothful, pitiful stranger. A sinful woman. I *hated* her. I … I worry that I still do."

Slee listened carefully to every word Charlotte said, and absorbed the strange tides of her aura. Charlotte looked at the world through warped, distorted glass. A lifetime of beliefs smudged the pane, and Slee was on the outside, unable to wipe them off. All Slee could do was offer her own hazy, blemished view. Perhaps that was for the best.

"I don't know much about sinners, but you don't look like one to me. Nor do you feel like one."

"You are too kind," Charlotte said.

"No, I'm perceptive," Slee said. "At least, with some things. And what I see here is not your sin, but Dídac's. Every day, he takes more and more animus from his workers. Your very life essence was being drained away! Feeling sluggish is no fault of yours, it's Dídac's. He makes impossible demands, and chastises those who cannot match them. I'm sure it suits him very well that you all put the blame on yourselves, instead of where it belongs."

"I won't say thoughts like that didn't cross my mind …" Charlotte said. "But I can't blame everything on someone else. After all, *I* signed a contract. They offered pay, and I agreed to work for it."

The silver-dust sky began to blush at the sun's arrival. The distillery began to shuffle and stretch as it woke. Beds creaked and clothes rustled. Slee heard the sounds through Cartín's ears, and felt the tremors through Dit-Dit's whiskers.

Startled, she checked her pockets. Her little friend was not there—she had gone to explore the distillery. Slee cautioned her to be careful, then let her be. Perhaps Dit-Dit would see things that Cartín couldn't.

As Slee allowed Charlotte's nameless mood to wash over her and pool up inside her like rain filling a bucket, the waking distillery rubbed its eyes, and left the night's dreams behind. The air coagulated. Anger that had nowhere to go scabbed over, a hard skin of rock trapping lava. The heat was still there, a simmering resentment that bubbled like rancid tallow. Cartín, Horvald, and Dit-Dit felt it too. Charlotte and Aizman closed up like clams, though they didn't know why.

Slee understood at last. All the Bluefingers smoldered, using themselves as the fuel of a nameless, directionless anger. With nothing else to blame, they blamed themselves. With nothing else to burn, they burned themselves. Dídac sucked most of the life out of them, and whatever they had left, they threw on the flames. Like candles reaching the end of their wicks, the Bluefingers knew that the end was near.

Somehow, none of them smelled the smoke or felt the heat. Each of them carried their rage, turned fully inward, cloaking themselves in such dark smoke they could not see the fire mirrored in their neighbor's eyes. They all, simultaneously, felt uniquely alone.

All they needed was to see.

"It think I understand, now," Slee said. "Charlotte—thank you for explaining everything."

Dit-Dit, wedged in a dark corner, watched dozens of weary feet shuffle by. Her nose twitched at the scent of sweat, heavy despite the cold.

"If there could ever be a day for us, then it is today," Slee said to the room. She sent the words by thought to Cartín and Dit-Dit, too.

"You're sure?" Horvald asked.

"Aínan, Muanan, Crantarín, Telethían … all four are stronger than they ever have been."

"What does that mean?"

"The bonds between us here, the conditions in the distillery, they are ready. If we do not harvest them when they are ripe, then by tomorrow they might wither away. Our chance will be gone," Slee said.

"Right. Just tell us what to do, and we'll do it," Horvald said. "I'll start by getting everyone's shackles off."

"Not yet. If Dídac or Greycoats come in and see us …" Slee said.

"Well, we can hardly do battle in chains. Here's the plan," Tybalt said. "Horvald, unlock us. Then we'll wait in our places, pretend we're still chained up. Then, when they come in with our breakfast, not suspecting a thing: *wham*! Lock up the senseless guards, change into their clothes, and —"

"You could sooner knock out a brick wall," Charlotte said. "The Greycoats are all drinking the elixir."

The air seemed to leak out of Tybalt. "Well, then, what *can* we do?"

"We need to prove to the Bluefingers that they aren't alone," Slee said. "And that Dídac has no power that is not given to him."

469

"And you'll do this by magic?" Tybalt asked.

"It's the only way."

"Your magic is the only way to fight?" Tybalt's throat rumbled quietly for a long time, sounding like some far-off walrus with indigestion.

"What in blazes is that noise you're making?" Horvald asked.

"Tybalt is torn. He never wants to be left out of a fight, but you heard what he said about elven magic," Aizman said coolly.

"Suppose I lend a little brainpower while you spread the word. Then, once the proper, heart-pumping part begins, you release me from the spell?" Tybalt said.

"Join and leave at your own will," Slee said. "There are no oaths or obligations. This is not the Common Power."

"You're not afraid, are you Tybalt? Or are your whiskers just shivering from the cold?" Aizman said with playful, drawling cadence. "Don't tell me *Slee* frightens you?"

"Oh, blast you all to the Abyss—I give in," Tybalt said. "Stitch me up in your little web. Let's give Dídac's nose the bloodying it's been crying out for."

"Batha?" Aizman said, turning to the youth.

"I … well, I—" Batha shifted nervously.

"If old Tybalt can change his ways, then you certainly can."

Batha continued to stammer.

"Leave him be. If he doesn't want to join, he doesn't have to," Horvald said.

"Baldershite, he doesn't! If he doesn't want to risk his pimple-studded behind, then it can stay on the cold stone where it is!" Tybalt crowed. "We'll all break out, and he can stay."

"Tybalt, please," Aizman said.

Tybalt blustered on. "Out with it, Batha! Are you yellow of belly? Eh? Is your belly, or is it not, stained yellow from—"

"I don't want anyone knowing what I've been thinking!" Batha burst out. The whites of his eyes flashed orange in the new dawn light that fell on his face. "It's not exactly something to be proud of."

"It's alright, Batha. We won't know about it, and we don't need to know about it," Horvald said. "But if that won't reassure you, then you don't have to join in. Isn't that right, Tybalt?"

Tybalt blew a puff of air through his moustache, apparently in agreement.

"Well then, is everyone ready?" Slee said.

They murmured in agreement.

"Follow me. Keep your mind on our goal, our anger, and whatever kinship we have together. I will lead the way—you need only support me," Slee said.

Their heartbeats quickened together, rattling along the telethí like marching drums. The dawn burned inside the dungeon, as the soft rising heat of the sun was matched by the fires kindling within them. The frosted iron bars steamed. The warmth, the beat, and the soft pink glow all spread beyond the dungeon door, reaching toward the rest of the distillery.

"Wait!" Batha said. "I don't want to be the only one left out."

"Come on, then, pitch in while we're young!" Tybalt said.

"I was going to take Dídac's offer." A warm, humid fog of shame rolled off Batha's shoulders, shrouding the ground around him. He sagged forward, covering his brow with both hands.

Nobody spoke for a moment. The feeling that had been building in the dungeon contracted and cooled.

"You were going to, but you didn't. That's what matters," Aizman said gently. "We all considered it."

"You don't understand. I was going to do it after we all agreed not to. I had the words right there in my head, I was ready to whisper them to the Greycoat who brought me my food ..." Batha jerked his head one way and another, like a fussy infant. "The Greycoat was there in front of me, but he didn't look at me. I wanted to get his attention, but I froze. I *would* have done it. I would have betrayed you all just to free myself. If I hadn't froze—"

"What good is this doing?" Slee said sharply.

Batha, round-eyed, looked up at her.

"What function does this guilt, this shame serve? You did nothing. There is no harm to undo."

"He feels bad, poor lad," Charlotte said softly. "We forgive you, Batha. We've all taken wrong turns."

The air in the dungeon cooled still more,

Batha drew his arms around himself and stared down at his feet. "I don't deserve forgiveness. I just feel so wretched ... I could have been the reason you all—"

"Enough! You have forgiveness. Self-persecution past that point is self-indulgence. Your feelings are not the only ones that matter, here," Slee said heatedly.

"Saint Temlin says that a wrongful thought is as bad as a deed," Batha said.

"And I say that thoughts are like seeds. They grow and bear their fruit in our actions. You need not plant bad seeds or eat bad fruit. Good fruit carries good seeds, so forget the rest," Slee said. "Do you understand?"

"I - I think I so. I'm sorry Slee, it's just that I can't help but think this way," Batha said.

"Then stop thinking and act. Will you join us?" Slee said.

Batha's pale eyelashes flickered for a moment. Drawing in a long breath, he looked at Aizman, then at Tybalt, both of whom nodded.

Something strange happened then, and Slee seemed to be the only one to notice. The clammy warmth of Batha's shame dissipated like mist vanishing under a rising sun. Even though the young Madean was not connected to their telethymic web, his mood was lifted by theirs. The longer Batha looked at his cellmates, the clearer his aura became. Slee looked down at the geode. Could it be possible that humans had some small, natural gift for telethymia? Or was she making a connection out of nothing?

Whichever was true, the rattling beat of the prisoners' combined aura swelled once more.

"I will," Batha said.

Slee reached out toward Batha with her telethí, slowly, gently. Before she got close, a few shining threads unspooled from Aizman, and then Tybalt. These new threads, consciously or not, converged on the young man. Batha's own telethí snaked timidly outward, then joined the threads of his neighbors.

473

Slee narrowed her eyes. *Could it be?*

Her mind raced with all manner of theories. Without training, humans had never been able to make such connections. Were some rare humans able to? Was the geode capable of more than she had thought?

Then, the prisoners looked expectantly at Slee.

"Well?" Tybalt said.

"Has he joined us yet?" Aizman said.

"You can't tell?" Slee said.

"How would we?" Horvald asked.

Slee looked around at them all. Perhaps she had been mistaken. After all, there were many threads of telethí floating among and between them. Aizman and Tybalt couldn't have added Batha to the web without realizing they had done it.

"He's with us. We're ready," Slee said.

"Well, gentlemen, ladies, whatever happens next, it has been a privilege to share this harrowing ordeal with such fine people," Horvald said. "The accommodations may be lacking in cheer and comfort, they may be colder than the depths of the Sinner's Abyss, but the company has kept me warm and smiling."

"Hmph! Wish I could stay the same. I haven't felt my left buttock since—" Tybalt began.

"Hear, hear! Now let's stop talking and start doing," Aizman said. He turned to Slee. "Lead the way, Slee, before someone else has a heartfelt outpouring."

"Outpouring! Why, I just felt that the occasion called for a few words," Horvald grumbled.

"Words are action, and actions speak like words. We must speak to the Bluefingers, teach them what we know, invite them to join us," Slee said. "Then we will 'speak' to Dídac, in the language of force and resistance."

"What can we say?" Horvald asked.

"Follow me. Close your eyes, hear my words, and add your voices to mine. Let your whispers carry along the telethí. Cartín and Dit-Dit will bring my words to the Extraction Chamber, silently at first. We shall speak to all the Bluefingers the only way we can," Slee said.

"And then what?"

"We wait for their reply."

Slee and the prisoners closed their eyes. In the darkness, she could see the shuffling feet of the Bluefingers as they filed past Dit-Dit. Then she could see them through Cartín, lying down on cots, having spider-leg needles inserted into their foreheads. The other prisoners cringed at the memory of the sickly sensation of needles piercing skin.

You are not alone.

Slee's words trickled along the silvery threads like morning dew on a spider's web. Once they reached Cartín and Dit-Dit, they turned to mist and spread slowly through the air. As mist, the words lost their form, but kept their essence. The message remains. And like fog coats a windowpane and runs down in drops, some of the unseen words condensed upon the Bluefingers' stunted bristles of telethí.

You are not alone.

Some of the Bluefingers paused. They looked around, their eyes narrowed. Mouths hung open, tracing words they weren't sure they could hear.

You are not alone. You are stronger together.

All the soldiers were past Dit-Dit now. She crept along shadowy corners and recesses, drawing closer to the Extraction Chamber.

You are stronger together. You can fight together. You are not alone.

Horvald, then Aizman, then Tybalt and Charlotte and Batha added their voices to Slee's. Soon all the telethí were beaded with the words, dripping with them. As they dispersed, they filled the distillery air with thick clouds of vapor, unseen but not unfelt.

Dit-Dit, sniffing, ducked under a door to an unlit corridor. There was a crack in the wall at the far end, where she would get a better view without being noticed.

You are not alone. You are not alone.

The words found purchase, slowly and subtly. The Bluefingers looked at one another as if for the first time. Nature's law cannot be taught, only remembered. Connection is nature's way, and separation is the human way. To sever, to fence in and wall off, to sophisticate the surface and to forget the deeper truth. As the Bluefingers remembered, their haggard faces shone, long-hidden wisdom breaking like the dawn.

They all halted, which the Greycoats noticed.

Cartín, standing between two other Greycoats, had plunged his hands into his pockets so that none would see them tremble. Clammy sweat ran down his back. He could hardly swallow. Around the room, Greycoats nudged each other. Cartín's neighbors muttered about sloth and disobedience. They began to run their thumbs along the stocks of their Aurinium rifles, inching closer to the triggers, as a seductive hand will drift along a thigh.

Cartín had not drunk the elixir. He never had. Dídac required them to, but Cartín had disposed of every vial he'd been given. He never *would* drink it, having seen the effect the Extraction Chamber had. But now, he found himself between two Greycoats who were strong enough to crush his skull like an egg.

Yet still, he brought Slee's words into the room, praying to all the Saints that his part would be enough to put a stop to Dídac.

We are not alone. Together we can fight, together we will win.

One of the Bluefingers, a black-haired woman, wrenched the spindly extraction needles from her head and threw it to the ground.

"No more!" she cried.

Greycoats raced toward her.

"Not another drop!" she shouted.

Another Bluefinger tore the needles from their forehead, and another. Soon the room was filled with cries of, "No more! Not another drop!"

The timid dawn that had begun in the dungeon now blazed across the whole distillery. All the hidden, inwardly-burning rage erupted, fiercer in the open, hungry for fuel. The Bluefingers no longer fed themselves to the fires of self-loathing and shame. The stone walls trembled with their shouts of defiance. Now that the anger was expressed, now that they had proven that they held it in common, they knew where to lay the blame.

It was working. Despite everything Slee thought she had known, it was working.

"Not another drop! Not another drop! Not another —"

There was a deafening, metallic clang.

A body collapsed under immense force. Telethí dissolved. A pair of eyes dimmed, then went out.

All at once, Slee was back in the dungeon. Somewhere, on some distant world, the Greycoats beat and restrained the Bluefingers. The remaining telethí quivered, disturbed by the violence. She was still connected to Horvald, the other prisoners, and, by longer and thinner threads, to Cartín.

But not to Dit-Dit.

"Slee? Has something gone wrong? Everything feels hazy," Horvald said.

"I – I …" Slee stammered.

She was still tethered to the others, but she felt alone. How could Dit-Dit have vanished all at once? If the little rat was hurt, Slee would have felt the pain. There had been no pain, just a shock, and then a swift fall into total darkness.

The other prisoners urged her to reply. They tugged on her with the telethí, somehow, as though they were ropes. They repeated their questions, loud and insistent. She could not answer.

She looked down, to the pocket where Dit-Dit had often hidden. The geode still wove the telethí like a loom. The Bluefingers still struggled against the Greycoats, but she could only sense it dimly. They needed her. There was still a chance to overcome the enemy. This was their *only* chance. Slee gathered herself up and plunged into the inner, telethymic world.

The dungeon door burst open.

The hazy specter of Dídac radiated into the room, a half-forgotten nightmare, then solidified in Slee's bleary vision.

He stood tall, neatly, wearing a wolf's grin. His presence washed over Slee's skin like pins and needles, grated like sand caught between her teeth.

The elf stood over her. "I knew who, and I knew why. The only riddle left to me was *how*? Telethymia can't be learned by humans — not this fast, and certainly not so far from Crann Arborím. Now, at last, I have my answer."

He threw a small object at Slee's feet. It clattered loudly on the stone. She glanced at it — a rectangle of wood, a spring, a wide metal bar pressing down on a soft, deformed lump — then shut her eyes and looked away. Despite trying not to, she had seen the eyes — the little, lifeless black beads on Dit-Dit's face.

"Oh, sweet Temlin!" Charlotte gasped.

"I'm afraid I've been eavesdropping," Dídac said, then revealed a short necklace with a simple, red jewel. "You see, I keep a piece of home with me wherever I go. I may not be able to use telethymia, but I can *see* it with the help of this fragment I took from Crann Arborím."

Slee trembled, enraged.

"Of course, such a small gem can only reveal the strongest of telethí. Today's events were *exactly* what I needed. Imagine my surprise to discover such strong threads connecting you to a rat … and to another rat, of a different sort," Dídac said.

The pale elf turned. A pair of Greycoats hauled Cartín inside, bound and gagged. They slammed him against the wall. Horvald shot to his feet, shouting, straining to reach them. Cartín's wrists were soon shackled. The guards crossed the room and struck Horvald's stomach, winding him, and threw him to the ground.

"Stand up," Dídac said to Slee.

Without waiting for her answer, he took her by the collar and dragged her upright.

The heavy geode protruded from her pocket. She made to cover it with her hands, but Dídac had already seen it. He snatched it out, and held it up to the light.

Slee's stomach filled with acid. There, through the geode, through Dídac's pale hands, all the woven strands of precious telethí quivered. The sight of such wrongness drove all other thoughts and language from Slee's mind. For a moment, all that remained was a human word, a word she had never before used or understood: *profane.*

If anything was sacred, it was life. To see it coursing through Dídac's cruel hands could only be called profane.

Red mist rolled off Slee's trembling shoulders, sparking and roiling. She longed to throw him to the ground, to smash his head against the hard stone, to feel his throat crushed by her hands. She reached out.

Dídac contracted his fingers as though idly flexing them. With a small crunch, the geode burst into powder.

Stunned, Slee watched with limp arms as Dídac produced a square bottle filled with sapphire-blue liquid, and poured the dust inside. The mixture frothed, almost overflowing, then settled down a second later.

All the telethí that had crowded the dungeon slipped away from her. Severing, dissolving, retracting, and fading away, each thread disconnected from the others. Hope melted away before her eyes. The other prisoners watched on, gaping, their faces as empty as Slee's heart.

"It almost defies belief. A device to bridge the gap between elven and human minds, right here under my nose. I almost doubted myself. I *knew* it had to be you. I knew it from the first whispers of discontent. The nature of humans is to rule or obey the ruler, to strive and compete, to seek advantage by all means. Elven nature is toxic to them. Could you not see how much damage you've done to them? Every one of these prisoners is here because of you. Like a dandelion's feathery seeds, so meek and harmless, your ideas drift on the wind. Had I left you alone, you'd have sprouted out of every crevice, choking the air, strangling throats, robbing the humans of the ability to think for themselves. Thankfully, now that I've destroyed your means of propagation, your corrupting influence is at an end."

Slee, half-conscious, staggered backward to the wall. Dídac closed in on her, lowering his voice, his eyes like icicles seen from below.

"I promised Her Excellency that I would deliver you to her alive. I almost risked her wrath — I was sorely tempted to kill you just to keep you in check, but by the grace of Providence, I triumphed. However, I promised nothing about your friends." Dídac stepped away, then made a slow circuit of the dungeon, looking into each of the prisoner's eyes. "At dawn you will be hanged. I could shoot you all now, I suppose, but others ought to be given the chance to watch, to learn from your mistakes. Besides, I would rather not waste precious gunpowder on any of you."

Dídac left, beckoning the Greycoats to follow him with a lazy flick of his fingers. The door closed with ringing finality.

Slee sank to the ground. Her eyes fell upon Dit-Dit's broken body, and she did not look away. Rumbling, echoing words broke upon her ears, but she heard no meaning in them. She only looked at Dit-Dit's delicate whiskers. Underneath it all was a pounding, pounding, pounding in her head. The knocking of some heavy object against an empty skull.

Something blocked her view of Dit-Dit. Hands took her hands. Someone lifted her chin, and she saw a blond man. A stranger.

"Slee?"

"Horvald," she said, unsure, testing the word.

Horvald spoke rapidly, digging in the locks in her shackles, freeing her hands. She did not move.

"Slee, we have to do something right away. If we work together, we can—"

"No," she said.

"Listen to me! We only have until morning. We can shift the bars, or – or break down the door!"

"There's nothing you can do," Slee said.

She looked around at the others. They were all strangers. Untethered from her and from everything else. As isolated as a small planet turning in the dark, far from then sun. No telethí means no knowledge. No bonds. No hope.

From outside came the sound of felled trees, then of sawing and hammering. Cartín, also free of his shackles, looked through the barred window.

"They're already making a space for the gallows," Cartín said breathlessly. "Temlin's tears … they're working the Bluefingers to death, beating them."

482

"They have the elixir! The bloody Greycoats could effortlessly do it themselves, but of course then they'd miss the chance to kick their inferiors."

"He was right," Slee said.

"What?" Horvald said.

"Dídac was right. I got you all into this. It's my fault," Slee said.

"We all got in this together, and we're going to get each other out. Now get up and help!"

"They are too strong. We have no strength. There is nothing between us," Slee said.

"Baldershite! What would you have us do, then? Just sit here and wait?"

"If you must do something … you could try sleeping to pass the time," Slee said.

Horvald's hands fell to his side, and his face made a strange expression. Slee might have recognized the look he gave her earlier, but now it was written in a language she couldn't read. He turned away from her. Together, the prisoners made noise stamping around, pulling on the door, feeling for cracks between the stones, and testing the strength of the bars in the window.

She curled up, covering her face. In the darkness it felt as though she was falling into a pit of complete darkness. She could not feel the rush of air or touch the sides of the pit, but she knew she was falling by the swoop in her stomach. There was no telling how far it was to the bottom, or whether she would ever stop falling. All she knew was that she would never resurface into the world of light and living things.

Chapter 33

Mannoc led a troupe of brassmail-clad elves into the Crown. They were unarmed, which may have emboldened Fentor's guests. Some openly mocked the elves that passed them. Despite this, the stern-faced Elarím searched, poked, and prodded every inch of the building. They communicated only by nodding at each other.

Fentor hung at the back of the crowd. He watched the search progress with the aloof disinterest of someone who is very concerned with not appearing guilty. He bolstered his thoroughly credible innocence by periodically saying, "I don't know *what* you expect to find!"

Angsley still sat directly over Crauford's hidden laboratory. He looked like he thought his chair was a spring-loaded trap that might catapult him at any moment. Fentor met his bulging eyes. Mannoc and his elves were checking under the tables, shifting bottles, sniffing empty cups, drawing ever closer to Angsley's table.

Angsley mouthed something behind a cupped hand. Fentor squinted, try to read his beard-shrouded lips from across the room.

"Desperate farm?" Fentor breathed.

Angsley mouthed the phrase again, slower and with greater exaggeration.

"District thumb …?"

Angsley pummelled an invisible boxer's speedbag in his frustration. He bared his teeth in his effort to silently enunciate. An elf reached Angsley's table, and leaned under it. Angsley shielded his mouth with both hands, and repeated the soundless plea. The elf appeared to be focusing on a spot under Angsley's feet.

"There's no time to decipher whatever he's saying! I need to distract them!" Fentor said to himself.

Then, he rushed across the room, to the sleeping area, opposite from Angsley. An elf was inspecting Fentor's bedsheets with a wrinkled nose.

"Stop that! You!" Fentor cried in a carrying voice.

The elf looked up, dropping the linen with visible relief.

"Don't look in there! That's private. You can't just look through a person's bedding. Besides, there's nothing worth finding there! Just look somewhere else!" Fentor blustered and pointed and stamped with great nervous energy.

Mannoc and the other elves exchanged knowing, somewhat beleaguered looks. Then, apparently obeying a silent command, some of them converged on Fentor's bed. Fentor continued to bleat about his privacy while more and more elves came over to shake out the blankets and pillows. When nothing was found in the bedding, they pulled at the floorboards and felt along the nearby walls.

The guests chattered, tutting and shaking their heads about the indecency of the elves' search.

The elf near Angsley left his table at last. Fentor dared not look as Angsley left his seat and disappeared under the table.

"I tell you, you won't find anything!" Fentor said.

Across the room, there was a yell and a crash.

Fentor turned. Angsley had fallen, and was now half-in and half-out a nest of splinters. The room gasped as one, and held its breath.

The elves swept across the room like leaves on a brisk autumn wind. Before Angsley could extricate himself from the wreckage, they were upon him. Fentor rushed over, choking on every breath. The elixir … so much work ruined …

A trio of elves pulled Angsley upright. Before Fentor could unstick his tongue from the roof of his mouth, Mannoc swooped into the space under the floorboards. A moment later, he emerged, holding up cracked and broken vials, flasks, and beakers, each filled with traces of various reagents.

"The Coríthe to search this place has been justified. By force of tradition, we have allowed you humans to live freely among us. Until now, the Common Power has ensured neither prisoner nor guard could be harmed," Mannoc held up the broken glassware for all to see. "By bringing this *Uthuín* magic into our land, you have begun to corrode the bonds we depend upon."

"Now listen here, dear boy, what you have there is the remnants of Crauford's pastime," Fentor said with strained geniality. "Unorthodox, I know. Some people play cards and dice … others play with beakers and acids. I know they may *look* harmful. Being an elf, you're simply unable to tell oxidizers from—"

"Oil of Telium," Mannoc said, holding up one of the test tubes. "Caustic red-ash. These are no trifles. I may be an elf, but I know the toxic products of Madean alchemy when I see them."

"What of it?" Fentor spat. "Making them wasn't illegal; you don't even have laws! At least, not anything *normal* folk would call laws. We're already your prisoners. What will you do, build a prison within a prison and throw us inside?"

Mannoc regarded Fentor coolly for a moment. "The next Coríthe will decide whether or not you will be considered enemy combatants."

"*That's* your punishment? To change your term for us?" Fentor asked.

"Prisoners are guaranteed life and shelter," Mannoc said. "Combatants are not."

"I can take care of myself," Fentor scoffed. "I need no guarantees."

"Whoever wishes to harm you will be able to do so." Small muscles in Mannoc's jaw flexed, tightening his expression. "And they *will* harm you. That is a guarantee."

Fentor scowled. "They are welcome to try."

Mannoc glanced briefly at the other elves. The Elarím gathered up all the broken glass left under the floorboards and began to file out the tavern.

487

Fentor maintained a menacing glare as Mannoc and the others left. The moment the last red cape swept out the door, he collapsed, shaking, onto the nearest chair. He pulled a nearby bottle of sapwine to his chest, shook himself, then drank greedily from it.

Hess came to his side and clapped him on the shoulder.

"Chin up, Fenny," Hess said. "We'll find a way. We always do."

Around the tavern, there was a sound of scraping chairs and shuffling feet. Thorassa sidled toward Fentor with a pinched expression.

"I must take my leave. The Coríthe …" Thorassa said, extending his hand for Fentor to shake it. "It wouldn't be appropriate for me to stay."

"Thank you ever so much for the gift of your company," Fentor said with habitual brightness. He took Thorassa's hand and shook it firmly. However, he did these things while staring vacantly, unseeing, at a spot over Thorassa's shoulder. "Do come again."

Thorassa nodded. He and a few other guests left. Nobody else seemed to know what to do. Fentor certainly didn't; why should they?

As Fentor watched, the guests ceased being guests. The party left the room without them, leaving behind lifeless mannequins. They clutched at their wine, but didn't drink. They looked at one another, but didn't speak.

"Well," Fentor said at last. "It's over. Any moment now, my head will split open and you'll see its contents. You'll see …"

"What does that mean?" Hess said.

"It means … all hope is lost. Lady Talentus entrusted me with a mission. To make an Elixir of Power, to free her. To make everything right," Fentor said, every phrase a labored sigh. "I failed. We are now at the darkest hour. My hopes have dimmed to a black so absolute that it dims all other stars. There is no hope for *any* of you, now."

Fentor glared around the room. Privately, he hoped someone would say there *was* still hope, just so he could shout them into silence. Nobody met his eyes, or his challenge. Even *that* catharsis was denied him. With nobody looking at him, he felt especially scrutinized. After all, the only people at parties that nobody looked at were the ones who were making a scene.

Nobody ever looked a spectacle in the eye.

"She spoke right into my mind, you know. Every word was like a needle in the brain. A bee-sting on the eardrum. Any moment now, you'll see. She'll do it again. I'll lose my mind. I was meant to keep it secret. She'll kill me before the elves do, and maybe that's better. I'm not supposed to tell any of you this, but …" Fentor shrugged, then drank until his bottle was empty.

"Why didn't she let you tell us?" Hess asked. "If we had known …"

"It is not my place to question Her Excellency," Fentor said. "It is my place to obey, and in doing so, make myself obscenely wealthy. Or, at least … that *was* my place. I have no place now."

Thick silence hung over the room like a theatre curtain. Every now and then, it was broken by the soft tinkling of glass as Crauford gathered the remains of his broken laboratory in his hands.

Angsley came to Fentor's other side, his face strained and ashen.

"Fentor, I cannot begin to tell you how truly, deeply sorry I am," he murmured.

Fentor looked at his friend's overgrown, scratched, contrite face. Out of habit, Fentor pictured everything he might say to Angsley. He might scream in his face. He might — justifiably — lay all the blame at Angsley's feet. He might insist that Angsley take his place and face Lady Talentus' displeasure and the Elarím death sentence.

Instead, Fentor found himself speaking without thinking. He said, "I don't want you blaming yourself. You performed your duty admirably, and you trusted me all the way through without even knowing what it was all for. You didn't fail. I did. You have my forgiveness."

A fissure of tension split across Angsley's face, breaking his gloomy expression into a half-smirk.

"What is that look for?" Fentor asked.

"What look?" Angsley spoke through his teeth, which he held together forcefully. His whiskers wobbled.

"That look on your face, like you've just seen a cherished enemy sit in pudding," Fentor said.

"Oh, it's nothing," Angsley mumbled. "Nothing at all, dear boy."

With a little trembling, more cracks appeared in Angsley's face, and his façade soon gave way altogether. A hearty grin broke through. For a moment, Fentor *did* want to scream in his face.

Then, with a slow but extravagant flourish, Angsley opened the front of his jacket. Nestled in a bit of scarf was a vial of elixir, whole and unharmed. He offered it to Fentor, shaking with concealed laughter.

Fentor, shaking for a different reason, took the bottle and held it up to the light. It looked real, it felt real, but it could not *be* real.

"You saved it," Fentor said. "You saved *us*."

"I told you — with me guarding it, not a soul will find it."

"You did it! You great, magnificent, lummox, you did it!"

Fentor leapt into the air with a cheer, kissed Angsley on both his whiskery cheeks, and danced about, laughing with the irrepressible glee of a child. Hess danced with him, and Angsley as well, until they were all flushed and doubled over.

Pain shot through his skull. A condor cracked his head open like an egg and pecked his eyes out. A blizzard of broken glass crashed upon him. As he crumbled to pieces on the ground, blind from pain, a familiar voice skewered him from ear to ear like a bayonet.

While you dawdle, the elves are preparing to kill you. You are wasting my remaining power by forcing me to remind you.

Fentor fell to his knees, clawing at his head as though he could dig the pain out.

Find the location of Crann Arborím and free me at once! With or without the help of the others — I care not. Do whatever is necessary. Time has run short.

All at once, the pain ceased. He was back in the tavern, with warm hands holding him.

"Steady, there, old boy," Angsley muttered.

His friends hauled him upright.

The guests, his fellow Madeans, looked at him with a collectively held breath.

"Just a minor headache," Fentor said to the room with a feeble smile.

"What did she say?" Hess whispered.

"She said it's time."

Hess, wide-eyed, looked from him to Angsley, and then to Crauford. The three of them nodded, their expressions grim.

Straightening the front of his clothes, shrugging off Angsley and Hess' hold, he cleared his throat and addressed the room. "Friends. Madeans. My countrymen. The true purpose of this gathering is not revelry, but liberation. Salvation! They say that every man's destiny is forewritten in the ledgers of Providence. Only the boldest and truest Madeans can turn the page to write a new fortune. Tonight, we write the word: 'Freedom.' "

The room was silent. His words seemed to hang in the air, unabsorbed, like drops of oil in water. Some watched him warily, others with concern, and a few with slack-jawed consternation.

"But … you were going on about how all hope was lost just a moment ago …" a red-cheeked man said. "Then you were dancing … then you had a headache …"

"Never mind all that. Forget everything else. Circumstances can change very quickly! Try to keep up, won't you?" Fentor snapped.

The man shut his mouth.

"Good. Her Excellency the Lady Elatea Talentus has stood, encased in crystal, waiting for this very moment. She drank an elixir of such potency that she could have torn all the Rivumaí elves to shreds like tissue paper. But she bode her time. She chose a bigger target: Crann Arborím. The very beating heart of the Elarím. To strike at it, she must be freed, and I need your help to do so."

Fentor paused, giving his words time to soak in. Gradually, faces and postures were shifting. Some looked guarded, with furrowed brows and folded arms. Others brightened and opened up.

"I need true sons and daughters of Madea. I need the stalwart, the loyal, the patriotic. Who among you dares to challenge the might of the enemy? Who is ready to turn the pages of the ledger of Providence and write a passage in the everlasting ink of destiny? Who?"

Slowly, with furtive looks to their neighbors, five or so people raised their hands.

"Is that all?" he barked.

One hand went down.

Stifling a growl of rage, he turned to Hess and whispered, "Get the rest of them to agree. By any means necessary. Angsley, you too."

Angsley leaned in. "What, exactly, are they agreeing to?"

Fentor pulled Crauford closer, knocking his spectacles askew. As he adjusted them, Fentor murmured, "You'll be extracting animus from them, you see? And the krysite we need—it's in their fingers. Bluepowder stains their fingers because of the krysite in it. Tell me you can extract enough for our purposes."

Crauford froze for a moment, except for his darting eyes. "I can do it, but I *must* know what the potion is for.

Otherwise I won't know which transmutations are needed."

"It's called Elixir of Power. It compresses the strength of many men into one vial. The potency of a dose depends on how much animus is put in," Fentor said.

"Ah. I understand, now," Crauford said.

"How strong is the dose Lady Ironhands took?" Hess asked.

"She drank many bottles just before our capture … the animus of two, three thousand soldiers might still be in her."

"Sweet Providence above …"

"Can you carry this out or not? I can't stay," Fentor said.

"Where are you going?" Hess seized his arm.

"I need to find out the location of Crann Arborím. There's only one way to do that," Fentor said.

His three friends watched him, eyes slowly widening as the meaning of his words soaked in. The color drained from Hess' cheeks. In contrast, Angsley's face reddened. Crauford's usually restless eyes stilled.

"No one has ever come back from that," Hess said.

"Have a little faith in my resilience. I'll be the first to come back. After all, dawn is breaking on a new era of 'firsts,' " Fentor said.

"It's not about resilience … the Common Power, it changes you. There's a *reason* no one has ever come back from it," Hess said.

"You're quite sure you have to do this, old boy?" Angsley said.

"The order comes from Lady Ironhands herself," Fentor said. "It's all going as she planned. Trust me."

"Well …" Hess said.

"There's no time. I really must be heading off," Fentor said lightly. He took Hess' hand off his arm with some difficulty. "If time runs out, one of you will have to drink the elixir and free the Lady. I'll see you all again once I learn Crann Arborím's location."

"Fenny …"

"See you soon."

Fentor saluted them, then headed briskly for the exit. If his feelings were able to leak out and infect those around him, his guests would have saluted him while singing the Madean national anthem. He marched for the door the way he marched toward battle, straight-backed, bristling with pent-up energy that yearned for an outlet. This time, he also felt slightly ill. The blank, staring faces of his fellow Madeans got a little disconcerting, but soon, he was past them.

With a smile, he put his hand on the door. An encouraging golden glow was starting to shine around its edges.

****

Fentor, a parade of one, marched along the paths of a darkening Rivumaí. A great crowd of elves, including those who had searched the tavern, were gathered there. They glared at him, but he paid them no heed. They let him go. Why wouldn't they? As far as the Elarím knew, he would never be able to leave Rivumaí. So he went on beyond them without a care, like a gull drifting over a busy dock, untouched by the concerns of those below.

The way to Sidarí's house was filled with elves. Huge, huddled crowds of them watched him go by, bright red lanterns in hand. Their eyes were on him from the threshold of the tavern, past all the vats and work benches of the main village, through the orchards and nut-trees, until at last he reached Sidarí's home.

He walked slowly along the dark, mossy path. It was spongey, perhaps seldom travelled, and it silenced his footsteps. Sidarí's windows were lit by a flickering, orange flame. Now that he was far from the lanterns of the other elves, the darkness seemed to draw in around him. He hurried the rest of the way and knocked on her door.

"Enter."

The unlocked door opened smoothly. Sidarí sat with her back to him, hunched over an open, yellowing book that she read by the light of a few tall candles. The rest of the small room was furnished simply. There was a narrow bed in the far corner, two long tables stacked high with books, and a small cluster of pots, pans, and crockery that Fentor took to be both kitchen and dining area.

Fentor cleared his throat. "I've come to ask you —"

"I know." Sidarí turned a page, slowly and gently. "I know what you've come."

Fentor caught sight of densely written columns of text as the page glowed translucent in the candlelight.

"Well, then, how can I convince you to let me?" Fentor approached slowly, circling around the edge of the candles' flickering orange glow.

Sidarí said nothing. As Fentor drew closer, he spotted a strange, glinting object on Sidarí's cheek, like a tiny bead of dew. She wiped it away, then turned to face him. Fentor suddenly felt like a burst sandbag, limp and empty of contents. Why he felt such a sensation, he did not know. She had always seemed melancholic, perhaps even morbidly so. But she only seemed to be sad in the way a statue or painting was — that was simply how her face had been arranged. Sidarí seemed about as likely to shed tears as an oil portrait was. And yet, there it had been. A little drop. Somehow, it still felt as though it was still falling, and would fall endlessly.

Fentor shook his head vigorously. The sapwine … the Coríthe … the Lady's echoing voice … his thinking had gone wobbly.

"I was just reading some of Sage Nyendí's writings …" Sidarí said. Her voice was clear, but her eyes seemed to have a thin, crystalline coating that reflected all the light that touched them.

"Perhaps you should read cheerier books."

"It's the chapter on justice. These pages contain the reasons we treat captives of war the way we do. The reasons we use the Common Power to keep people from hurting each other. The reasons we have no jails, no jailors, no judges, no executioners, no criminals."

"While this is a highly stimulating topic, my question is rather pressing at the moment."

"The Coríthe is not decided, and won't be for some time. Sit." Sidarí pointed to a nearby chair.

Fentor took his seat. It was a hard wooden chair, yet, by the way it was shaped to contour his body, he found it instantly comfortable. Despite what Sidarí had said, he could almost feel time slipping through his fingers like hourglass sand.

"May I ask which way you are casting your vote?" he asked.

Sidarí flashed him a brief, ironic smile. He took that to be her answer.

"Nyendí wrote that revenge and punishment have no place in justice," she said.

"Without disrespect to your Sage, those things are the *essence* of justice."

"For humans, perhaps." Sidarí traced the page with her finger for a moment, then looked back to him. "Elves, together, are a social organism. It is in our nature to balance the individual and the society in a different way than humans. But you and your Lady may have proven our way to be … mistaken. Inferior."

"How so?"

"Nyendí believed that crime creates criminals. That jails create prisoners. Penalties and punishments do not repair harm, but multiply it. A system of *revenge* propagates wounds, passes them on, in endless cycles. Do you see?"

"What is done with thieves and murderers, then? Without punishment of some kind, you'd be encouraging them to continue."

"Again, perhaps it is so with humans. For elves, the action matters less than the harm it causes. Hanging a killer doubles the harm. Two deaths instead of one. Not all deaths are counted as harms. Killing an attacker in self-defence. Killing an enemy during wartime, which goes with the phrase 'so long as a threat is posed by them.' "

Sidarí paused, then turned away from him, apparently to watch teardrops of wax run down the candles, slowing until they hardened at the base.

Fentor, legs bouncing and fingers drumming, could barely contain his impatience any longer. The Coríthe would not wait while Sidarí prattled about criminological claptrap. The Lady certainly wouldn't wait, either. Was she stalling him deliberately? Did she already know the result of the vote? Was he moments away from victory, or death?

The elf kept her face turned from him. She made no indication that she would speak again. His patience snapped.

He half-rose from his seat, wagging his finger at her. "Now, look here, Sidarí—"

She faced him, and the air in his lungs froze solid. Two more objects twinkled on her face, one on each cheek. Strange crystals, beads of amber, with tails that stretched up to her eyes. He stared, uncomprehending. The candles flickered, and the strange gemstones fell away. Fentor wanted to speak, but he couldn't. Some spell had robbed him of his free will. His heart had become chained to an anchor in an icy sea, plunging down into the dark. He felt wretched. He felt *sad*. Tears stung his eyes. Something was profoundly wrong, he was certain of it, and it wasn't just the fact that the feelings and the tears were not his own.

Ensnared in that strange emotion, feathery thoughts that were not his own brushed against his forehead. They came with faint music, strange notes with alien harmonies.

Ask him. It is better to know than to suffer more doubt. Ask him. You will not forestall the inevitable by avoiding the question.

Fentor almost blurted out: Ask him what? But the faculty of speech had not yet returned.

499

A moment later, the sensations gripping his body ceased. Sidarí wiped her face. The whole process had taken perhaps a few seconds, but it had felt like hours. Fentor was still holding his finger in Sidarí's face, half-crouching above his chair.

"Yes?" she asked.

"I … forgot what I was going to say," he said truthfully. He eased himself back into his chair.

Sidarí tapped her fingers absently on the page. "I wonder if you can grasp the effect your arrival had on us."

"Aside from the attempts on my life, I confess I haven't noticed much of a fuss."

"The battle at the bridge where you were captured claimed so many lives, in a way we had never thought possible. Visions of you and Elatea, soaked in Elarím blood, persist in the nightmares of the survivors. Those that captured you wanted to kill both of you on the spot, but they could not. The Common Power would not allow it."

"Soldiers die by the dozen in any battle. What happened at the bridge was no exception."

"One crucial difference remains. You were weakened, defeated, bound, and captured. From that moment you 'posed no threat.' Elatea became a frozen object, but we sensed a vast store of latent power within her. None could agree: was she still a threat to us? By law, was she a combatant or a captive? Then, you spoke to her, so the question was asked of you. Are *you* a threat?"

Fentor said nothing. A strange, pensive expression crossed Sidarí's face, and the air between them fluttered strangely. A shining, golden premonition came to him, vague, but glorious. He was about to win.

"I have a question for you, and if you answer honestly, I will give you what you want."

"Ask it then," Fentor said, his mouth dry. He leaned toward her with the sound of unseen trumpets ringing in his ears. His moment had arrived at last, and he wanted to savor it.

The small, reedy voice of doubt spoiled the moment. It asked: *Why would she give you what you want so easily? What could she gain?*

He silenced the voice, slit its throat and let it bleed. He had won her over because Providence had made it so. It was his destiny. It wasn't his place to question why's and how's.

"Is this the end of my people?" Sidarí asked in a rush. Her usually steady voice quivered, and another pair of tears fell from her eyes. She held his gaze with trembling effort. Whatever dam had walled in her grief seemed, at last, to be breaking.

Fentor couldn't feel his face. "Is this the...?" he echoed, half-absent.

"This potion, the one you were making, the one that gave Elatea so much power ... more are being made in Madea. Aren't they?"

Fentor's eyelids fluttered. He opened and closed his mouth, tried to moisten his lips with his dry tongue, but he couldn't speak. An overwhelming tide of grief and heartache had swept his words away, grief that poured through the space between them.

"No matter what happens now with the Coríthe, more Madeans like you will come. I always knew that my people would not win this war, and that defeat slouched toward us. I tried so hard to find a way to prevent it. I told myself that I did not hope in vain. But it has all come to nothing, hasn't it? This is the end of the Elarím."

"You want me to answer ... honestly?" Fentor said croakily.

"Before you say anything," Sidarí said, then drew a long, steadying breath. "I will know if you lie."

"Of course. I only ever speak the truth," Fentor said.

All he needed was the location of Crann Arborím. He could tell her the truth, or, just as easily, a comforting lie. The only consideration was which answer would get him what he wanted.

And yet, his queasy stomach seemed less enthused with thought of lying.

"You don't understand. Many Elarím are able to sense honesty, the same way you might feel the heat of an open flame. I *will* know."

"Very well, then," Fentor said. He swallowed.

She watched him in silence, calm and still. Her face held no particular expression. No more tears threatened to spill over onto her cheeks. Despite all that, some vile bewitchment of hers locked him in place, unable to even blink. He marshalled his words, lined them up, prepared to give them the order to advance. He had to tell the truth, it seemed. Doing so proved hard to do.

Not because he feared for the mission. The words were hard to utter because they would be hard for Sidarí to hear.

What was happening to him?

"Is this the end of my people?" Sidarí said.

"I'm afraid I believe it is," Fentor said.

She sagged deeper into her chair. She did not weep, or sigh, or say a word. She only sat, limp and blank-faced, all the strength gone from her. The candle flames bobbed and danced on their wicks, and she watched them, utterly detached.

Fentor had the bizarre urge to say something comforting, to ease the pain of his enemy's defeat. He did not feel anything he had expected to.

Where was the fanfare, the golden sunburst wreathing his triumph? Where were the parades, the crowds cheering in his ears? Where was the giddy euphoria?

Instead, he felt empty, a hollow vessel for cold wind to blow through. The blasted elvish magic may have robbed him of his joy, but it would not rob him of his victory.

"Now that I've answered your question ..." Fentor said softly.

Sidarí remained silent.

Suddenly, he remembered the voice that had brushed his ears not long ago. It had been Sidarí's voice saying, *Ask him. It is better to know than to suffer more doubt.*

Numbly, without thinking, Fentor repeated the words aloud. "Ask him ... it is better to know than to suffer more doubt ..."

Sidarí, eyes wide, looked at him. "What did you say?"

"Never mind. I've answered your question. I'm ready to join the Elarím."

"Very well. You were honest," Sidarí said. "I must honor the exchange we agreed to. The barter, the deal, the trade …"

With great apparent effort, like someone three times her age, she eased herself upright in her chair, and turned to Fentor.

"If the Coríthe judges you to be a threat, joining the Elarím will not shield you. They will eject you as easily as they accept you; that is our way. The most you can do is add your voice to the proceedings. Do you understand?"

"I'm not joining in some cowardly bid to save my skin!" he protested.

"I know. I just thought I should tell you. Now, close your eyes and brace yourself," she said. "There is nothing I can say to prepare you adequately for the plunge you are about to take. Humans tend to find the Common Power disorienting."

Fentor closed his eyes.

Chapter 34

*Some troubles cannot be overcome. Some
problems cannot be solved. Even when we
face such times, the rhythms of life persist.
There comes a time to weep, and a time to
persevere. There comes a time to wonder, to
contemplate, to ask desperate questions.
There may never come a time when we
understand.*
Sage Nyendí

In the darkness behind Fentor's eyelids, a silver ribbon
was dancing. The frayed ends, fainter than threads of
Norimandian silk, fanned out. They looked like tiny
worms, blindly searching in the dark for purchase. He
watched, fascinated.

The ribbon came closer. It turned out to be woven from
many threads, each of them spun from silver starlight. It
fluttered to and fro like a butterfly looking for a perch.

Perhaps it would land on him, if he was quiet and gentle. He reached out.

Instead of raising his hand, he raised a knot of translucent threads. It looked like a snarl of fibres that had been jammed in a loom. The silvery 'hand' brushed against the ribbon. Their frayed ends began to intertwine, curling around each other like the pig-tail tendrils on the ends of grape vines. He was pleased. As he'd expected, it gave him the same hushed feeling he'd once felt as a lad, when a cobalt-blue butterfly chose him for its perch. A breathless feeling of ease, wonder, togetherness. Camaraderie.

Points of light raced along the ribbon, vibrating gently as they reached him. Each one of them, it turned out, was a whispered word.

Good. The voice was Sidarí's. *That was quicker than most humans.*

This is it? The Common Power? His words, too, became points of light. Fentor coaxed his much slower thoughts along the ethereal filaments. It felt like flexing a muscle between his ears that had never been used before.

This is but a small window into the telethí closest to you – mine.

The ribbon grew longer and longer, coiling around more of Fentor's tattered threads. It was warm and firm, as any decent handshake ought to be. The motion certainly *seemed* like some sort of handshake, at least.

Usually, a few volunteers would guide you through this early stage for days, showing you small glimpses of the Common Power at a time, Sidarí thought.

More moonlight ribbons sprang out of the dark. They enveloped him. Embalmed him. Warmth became heat, and the firm hold became constriction. Far away, on some other, unreachable plane, his physical body gasped. He heard the intake of breath through his own ears, and Sidarí's, an instant echo. The ribbons tightened.

Your initiation will be far less gentle, Sidarí thought. Each of her words stung like embers spat from a fire.

What – what are you doing? Fentor — or maybe his spirit, or his mind — flinched.

I am showing you everything. This way, when my people are destroyed, you will know the full weight of what you have done to us.

Her disembodied voice roared in his ears like an open furnace. The shining tendrils held him tightly in place, as unforgiving as shackles and chains. In the outer world, he was unrestrained, but in the inner world, inside his own mind, all the gears stopped turning. With his mind immobilized, his body was trapped. Helpless as a stopped clock, he could only watch as Sidarí lifted the veil from his eyes, and showed him the world beyond the darkness.

Everywhere, saturating everything with ethereal light, countless silver threads spun. A billion fractal deltas, unfurling and connecting, branching and weaving, stitching and coiling. The world was revealed as a self-weaving loom, stitching warp to weft, always in the same branching pattern. Some strings were smaller than a cat's whiskers, others as thick as anchor chains. Fentor watched it flow. Points of light raced in all directions. Branching and branching, weaving and weaving, flowing and flowing.

The Common Power posed a question that had no language. The blood vessels in an eye fork, reach out, dividing into ever smaller strands. The waters of a river delta branch and branch into smaller channels as they reach the sea. Roots reach beneath the soil and branches reach into the air. A thought forks like lightning. His brain was not one thing, but an organ of many cells. Each of them striving to connect to its neighbor, sprouting hairlike filaments until the brain was complete, a web within a web within a web. Connection and understanding; understanding and connection. He trembled with the question, and the telethí, somehow, glowed with the answer he craved. He could not reach it. He could not make the connection. Root and branch, river and sea, question and answer.

You came so close, Sidarí thought. *You almost discovered everything on your own. When you were attacked, it was you who called for help. You reached for the Common Power and called out for connection, and it saved you.*

Fentor did not answer. He had forgotten how to speak, how to think. Everything in his skull had been burned away by the light of the telethí.

Desperation opens the mind. Telethí quake when the direst, most desperate of needs are spoken. Everyone in Rivumaí heard your call for help. But the barrier that saved you was of your making.

No, Fentor thought. He tried to say more, but he could only repeat, *No!*

You began to understand, slowly. Human thoughts began to wither away. A minute ago, you even caught a glimpse of my thoughts. That potion undid everything.

Coiling snakes of telethí tunnelled under his feet, passed through the walls, shot through Fentor's glowing chest. A great cacophony of intense emotions overtook him, and he was thrown from searing anger to hollow despair to giddy joy in the space of a few moments.

Make it stop, he begged. *I can't endure this!*

Not yet. I may be new to using revenge as a tool for justice, but I believe this must continue to my *satisfaction, not yours.*

Fentor felt himself lifted out of the chair — out of himself. Clasped by ropes like prey caught in a hawk's talons, he flew far away from Rivumaí. The world rushed beneath him, a dazzling blur. His body, left behind in the chair, became intensely nauseated.

At last, he came to a halt. Before him was a towering column of silver light, the apex of a tapestry spun from moonlight, the centre of a many-spoked wheel, the eye of a silken storm.

Behold, Crann Arborím. Yours, at last. This is the sight you were craving, is it not?

The pillar of telethí reached up through the clouds, branched and reached beyond — but for what did it reach? Crann Arborím revolved slowly, with the inexorable grace of a planet. As it turned, it spooled and unspooled millions of threads in all directions. It was many immaterial things fractally superimposed — a web, a river delta, roots and branches, flashes of lightning, a tangle of arteries and veins and capillaries. Fentor saw it all simultaneously, from its smallest filaments to its largest limbs. But all he could see was the telethí. The connective tissue. He could not see what it *was*, nor where it stood.

After all his hardship and planning, he was before his quarry at last. He ought to have felt triumphant. Why did he feel sick?

Let us drift a little closer. You ought to experience the wonder of the Ruby-Tree before it is killed.

Fentor's bonds pulled him down toward the silvery skirts of the tower. He resisted, but he felt himself pushed down the way a child forces a kitten to drink. The great searing lights of Crann Arborím enveloped him, and he fell unconscious to himself.

Then he woke up, not as Fentor, but as everyone else.

Líndar turned over, kicking at his sheets. The same dream, again. Would he never sleep?

The Common Power was no balm. It was the intimacy of connection with others that gave the dream its horror, after all. Over and over again, he saw it.

Brother Seras, Sister Maraní, his cousins Teloch and Beranadh, all of them running ahead of him. Líndar was the slower runner. They joined the fighting where it was thickest, raised their bows and added their glowing arrows to the faedós bal.

Then, in the dream, Líndar's feet became stuck. A great trembling roar shook the earth. A star from heaven fell on the heads of his brother, his sister, and his cousins. They were all devoured in the great plume of fire. With each dream of their death, his heartstrings were cut open afresh.

He had not seen them perish on the day it had happened. They had all run ahead, beyond his sight. But not beyond the telethí. In the dream, reliving their deaths night after night, he saw each of their faces. He felt them being wrenched from his embrace.

Líndar turned over again, cursing the humans and their cannon that scorched the earth.

"*Oe Telethí Muanan.* Life continues," Anmúan sighed, wiping machine grease from her hands. "Whatever else may come, as the Sages all say, life continues."

"Yes, but are *you* continuing? Lately you only … persist," Torínen asked. "You are withering away."

Anmúan gave no answer.

Torínen fitted the new lever in place, securing it with gentle taps of her lode-hammer. Tiny bolts turned in response to the moving magnetic field. Anmúan turned the spigot at the base of the well.

"Try it now," she said.

Torínen pulled the lever down, and the spout sputtered thickly. She pumped three more times, and at last the spout released a stream of clear water.

"It's working," Torínen said.

"Good." Anmúan turned to leave.

"Anmúan, wait." Torínen caught her arm. "You have worked enough. Your body must rest."

"It was easy work. I am not weary." Black spots of dishonesty swarmed around her head as she wiped sweat from her brow.

"At least sit down with me until the Coríthe is decided. The matter will be hard to resolve."

"Not for me," Anmúan said.

"What do you mean?"

"I have decided already. If it weren't for that *vicious* human…"

"Anmúan…" Torínen said softly, disbelieving.

"What? Do you disagree that this Fentor is a threat?"

"Many people lost sons and daughters at the bridge. That is not sufficient reason to abandon Nyendíthe. You must sit and reflect on this."

"The time to sit and reflect is over," Anmúan said.

She pulled away from her friend, severing some of the telethí between them.

Young Sidarí looked up at the twinkling rubies in the cavern wall. Like stars, they made constellations, but these ones could only be seen by her. She traced her fingers from point to point. It was a memory game. She could remember her lessons more easily by making a game of the shapes.

The adults didn't approve. Non-branching shapes are abstract. Learning isn't done by abstraction and solitude, they said. Learning is connecting with others, with the knowledge they have. She *was* connecting, she would say, but they never listened.

In any case, no adults were present. For the moment, the cavern walls were a plaything that she did not need to share or hide. She could be as solitary and abstract as she liked.

She traced the isosceles, the equilateral, the scalene, the orthogonal …

Aunt Isendra ran into their midst, her face flushed. Sidarí and the other children got up and crowded around her. Some of the younger ones pulled on her long sleeves.

Usually they would ask a dozen questions each, overlapping each other. To quiet them she would say loudly, "Noise is not useful! If you all speak at once, none can be heard."

That day, Isendra had no need to hush them — the hard look on her face silenced them immediately.

"Young ones, I am afraid I must tell you something awful. Sage Nyendí has perished."

The older children gasped, ears flattening against their heads, and exchanged looks of shock. Some of the youngest ones hardly knew what a Sage even was. Sidarí, neither youngest nor oldest, knew a little about Nyendí. They called some theories 'Nyendíthe' in lessons. Some of the older children talked about human soldiers snatching anyone who misbehaved, 'Like they did to Sage Nyendí.' The death of someone like that was an Important Thing.

"Did the humans kill her?" someone asked.

"We don't know," Aunt Isendra said. "We may never know the full circumstances."

"They *emprisoned* her! They must have killed her, too!"

"It is harmful to say things that aren't established to be true," Aunt Isendra said. "We don't know that she was ever 'imprisoned.' "

"Who else could have taken her?" Sidarí asked.

Isendra fixed her with a steely eye. "Be careful of flawed thinking like that, Sidarí. Eliminating bad answers doesn't yield a good one."

A few more Aunts and Uncles arrived, and lessons resumed as normal. Sidarí sighed to herself, standing apart from the other children. Above her the scarlet gems of the Ruby-Tree, Crann Arborím, twinkled at her, an invitation to play.

Fentor raced along the telethí boughs of Crann Arborím. He was a flash of light, a nerve impulse. At each fork, he caught a glimpse of another life, and another. Thousands of farmers caring for crops, each plant drawing sustenance from millions of threads beneath the soil. Thousands of healers tending the injured and sick with the Common Power. Thousands upon thousands of elves living — mothers, warriors, children, artisans, singers, Sages. Elves digging and sewing and cutting and gluing and stacking and sorting. Everywhere, every life touched the Common Power, and the Common Power touched them.

Fentor could not understand it all, but he understood one thing. Crann Arborím was no weapon. The aegis and the whistlers were the least of what it did. The Ruby-Tree wasn't used by the Elarím — it *was* the Elarím.

Now you see what destroying it will mean, Sidarí said. *I think I've had my fill of revenge.*

His silvery shackles halted his flight across the telethí, then wrenched him across countless leagues in the space of a few heartbeats. The bright, criss-crossing cords darkened as the world rushed beneath him, around him, and through him. They slammed him back into the chair. He felt like a bottle that had been vigorously shaken then set down again — solid on the surface, but swirling inside. His tongue was stung with acid, then he leaned forward and vomited on his shoes.

After the explosions of searing light that had filled his vision, Sidarí's home seemed especially dim. Her face was little more than an orange outline where the candlelight brushed her cheek.

"Now you know," Sidarí said.

Fentor took hold of his head with both hands and pressed hard, as though he could squeeze out all the other lives that had crowded in there. He would never see his cousins again, or his daughter. The thought made his heart ache. But no, they weren't *his* family. The grief of other mourners had lodged inside his skull, supplanting his own thoughts. He squeezed his temples with all his strength.

Gradually, he regained himself, piece by piece. His vision was blurred, and he was shaking uncontrollably. At length, he realized that he had been sobbing. His own voice, wailing softly, came to him as though echoing through a long tunnel. The gossamer ribbons that had held him released him, drifted away, growing fainter until they dissolved into the air completely. His mind and his memories had returned, but they were not unchanged.

The dregs of the Líndar's dream stuck to the back of his eyelids. He saw the faces of his brother, his sister, and his cousins when he closed his eyes. He seethed with remnants of Anmúan's rage—rage that was directed at *him*. He hated himself, with Anmúan's burning hatred and his own self-loathing. What had he done? What could he do?

"The Coríthe is not proceeding in your favor. Did you see it?" Sidarí said softly.

"I don't know what I saw," Fentor croaked. "I saw everything. Then I saw it all again, from every other perspective ..."

"You were like an ant crawling across an open page in a vast library written of the Common Power," Sidarí said. "Did you think I would let you join the Elarím so easily? You are not one of us and you never will be."

Fentor said nothing, if only because he still needed to catch his breath.

Sidarí glared at him with a volatile expression. All the brittle edges of her face quivered like overheated glassware on the verge of exploding.

What did Fentor care? He had won.

Remembering the landmarks, the direction of his flight, he had determined the location of Crann Arborím. All he had to do was return to the Lady, and tell her. All he had to do was rise from his seat, leave the room, and take the path that led up the hill. He tried to move, but he couldn't. Victory was his at last, but he couldn't move a single bloody muscle! He had won, but it felt like a loss.

Triumph rang in his hollowed-out chest, a bell chiming in the dark.

"Sidarí …" he began. He couldn't say the rest, not yet.

"All this time you Madeans have fought for riches and renown," Sidarí said. "We have been fighting for our *lives*."

"Sidarí, listen to me …"

"To think, Nyendí believed humans and elves could one day … that if we just … well, she was wrong!" Sidarí struck the table with her fist. "Decades of my work trying to prove it, thrown out into the mud. A waste of ink—and a waste of lives!"

"I have to tell you—"

"I worked toward an impossible solution. Flawed reasoning! Eradication was the only possible outcome. Do you see? The Madeans had it right all along—humans and elves are eternally, irrevocably, fundamentally different. One must devour the other or perish. We are as opposed as foxes to hens, as spiders to flies. *All life cares for all life …* a fine ideal. But it was never more than a dream. No—it was a lie. It was always a lie!"

Sidarí's flushed face contorted. She grabbed Nyendí's writings by the fistful and tore the pages apart.

He had to tell her. Something had to be done. He just wasn't sure yet what it should be.

"Sidarí!" Fentor shouted.

She looked at him sharply. Shreds of paper fell from her hands.

"Mannoc didn't find everything," he said.

The words had tumbled past his lips, half-dressed and groggy, before Fentor had fully formed a thought. Heat prickled across his neck. As Sidarí's eyes widened and then narrowed, Fentor tried to pull himself together. It was difficult, since the telethí had bent and stretched him in directions he hadn't known were possible. He was hopelessly tangled steel wire—he'd been twisted up in a furnace and now he had hardened in the new shape.

Elatea waited for him. Sidarí stared at him. Between the two was a vast gulf that could not be bridged.

He shook his head. He only had to get up and leave. If he delayed, the Lady would make scrambled eggs of his brains. But if he got up and left, if he told the Lady about Crann Arborím …

517

"Mannoc? What didn't he find?" Sidarí shook her head slowly.

Fentor barely heard her.

The Lady's Great Bombard had robbed Líndar of his brother, sister, and cousins. All Fentor had worried about was killing enough elves to justify the cost of doing so. At the bridge, with the Elixir of Power coursing through his veins, one of the faceless elves he had slaughtered was Anmúan's daughter. But at the time, it was not slaughter. It was fun. Amusement.

Without Crann Arborím, thousands upon thousands of elves would perish. Soldiers and children and innocents alike. He could not begin to comprehend such an extinguishment of life. The weight and size of the concept alone defied the limits of his imagination. He could, however, see Líndar's dream. He could hear Anmúan's voice. He could feel their grief as though it was his own.

With a cold, plunging, nauseous feeling, the golden glow of victory before him turned into a jaundiced stain. He could now see that he was not a glorious, triumphant hero waiting to be Sainted.

He was the villain.

"There's nothing we can do now," Fentor whispered hoarsely.

"What are you talking about?"

"It's already too late. I didn't know what I was really doing ..."

He drifted outside himself, watched himself speaking, heard his own faint words. He could no longer feel his face, or the clothes on his skin, or the chair underneath him.

"Fentor!" Sidarí took his forearms and shook him. "Explain what you mean."

"Mannoc didn't find everything. They're finishing the potion now. This was always the plan, and I played my part. I found out where Crann Arborím is … just in time," he said, lips numb. "Just in time for Elatea to break free."

Sidarí paled. "It's not true."

"She's going to destroy it. The war ends tonight. There's nothing we can do." Fentor felt cold drops running down his cheeks. "But I—I played my part."

"Why are you telling me this?"

"I … don't know," Fentor said honestly.

"Are you going to tell her where it is?" Sidarí said.

Fentor looked at her. He was not sure whether he understood her question. When he didn't answer, her face hardened.

The Coríthe, at that moment, was decided. Fentor was judged to be a threat. An enemy combatant. Somehow, he knew it had happened, as instinctively as if he'd felt an abrupt change in the wind.

"So it's decided, then," Fentor said. His heart rattled like a marching drum, and a sudden flush of blood stung his fingers. He needed to explain himself, but the words and the time to speak them in slipped from his grasp.

Sidarí's eyes darted over his shoulder. Fentor turned. A rack of sabre-spears stood by the door.

Sidarí sprang from her chair and darted past him, and Fentor followed. They collided with the rack at the same time, grappled over the weapons, and then leapt apart. Fentor pulled his sword from its scabbard just as Sidarí drew hers. She stood in the doorway, half-crouched, blade up.

"Let me past," he said.

"No."

"I don't have a choice."

"Neither do I."

She pounced.

While submerged in the Common Power, Fentor had seen how all Elarím are trained in the arts of war from a young age. He expected a fight. Still, the ferocity and fluidity of Sidarí's attacks astonished him. He countered each advance and deflected every thrust. He could hardly keep his feet as she drove him backward, crashing into stack after stack of books.

"Wait!" he cried. "Wait!"

She pelted him with steel, relentless, each new thrust and slash a continuation of the last. She jabbed at his thigh, and he flicked her blade aside. She followed the motion of his parry and whipped her sword up and across his face. He moved his sabre up to meet it, but too slow. The tip grazed him across his cheek, from ear to chin. Peril, thankfully, dulled the vicious sting. He had neither the time nor the breath to spare for a gasp.

Sidarí did not relent. She herded him across the room, as he flung his sword in all directions just to ward her off. She had him pinned against the wall. In desperation, he threw a wild slash with all his weight. Their blades crossed, locked together near the hilt. He threw her sword off to the left and dove to the right. Her counter-thrust missed his ribs by a hair.

He needed to explain himself. He needed a moment to think. He needed air. Sidarí denied him all of them, as though each motion of her blade cut off his every thought, every breath.

The books, strewn all over the floor, made treacherous footing. Fentor backed away from the onslaught, slipping and stumbling. He crashed into the table Sidarí had been sitting at. The candles toppled, igniting the shredded book. Even then, Sidarí didn't stop.

In the light of the blossoming fire, her face shone with unveiled rage. Her sabre flashed silver and orange as it wheeled around his defenses. He was caught between her weapon and the heat of the burning book.

With his strength flagging, he took the hilt in both hands. Even parrying two-handed with all his strength, he could not gain an inch. The flame licked his back, causing it to arch. He acted without thinking.

Aiming the sabre point at Sidarí's heart, he twisted the hilt. The weapon sprang into its full length, the blade leaping toward her like a striking snake.

She leaned to the side, trapped the spear under her arm with the flat of her blade, and wrenched it out of his grip. In the same motion, she threw Fentor to the side, and he tumbled to the ground.

The fall drove his breath from his lungs. Before he could collect himself, a sharp point pressed onto his throat.

"Nyendíthe," he choked.

Sidarí glared down at him. If she cared that the flames had spread across the table to other books, she did not show it. She lifted the tip of her sabre slightly.

"What?"

"If you kill me, it goes against Nyendíthe. Doesn't it?" Fentor said. He had grasped the word at random from his memory, even though he barely understood it.

Sidarí stared at him for a moment, open-mouthed. Then, blinking and panting, she looked around at the spreading flames. Her posture sagged, but the point of her blade wandered up Fentor's throat to his chin.

He looked up at her without saying a word. Perhaps he imagined it, but there seemed to be a silvery gleam in the air between them that had nothing to do with Sidarí's glinting sabre.

She threw her sword down. The blade rang as sweetly as a tuning fork.

"Thank you," Fentor breathed. He addressed the words to Sidarí, to Providence, and maybe even to the Common Power. "Thank you."

"Don't thank me. There are hundreds of elves in Rivumaí. You know how they feel. They'll never spare you."

"But you did."

"What do you know of Nyendíthe?" Sidarí asked. "Of all the words, why did those come to your lips?"

"I - I don't know. I'm still dizzy, I scarcely understood a tenth of what I saw. All I know is that if I understood these things properly before now, I never would have —"

A timber cracked loudly in the heat. The fire had spread up the walls to the ceiling, and was consuming more of Sidarí's home every second.

Sidarí helped Fentor scramble to his feet, and together they rushed outside. Once they were clear of the heat, Sidarí turned to watch the flames.

" 'A violent seed grows to bear violent fruit … means and ends are cycles of one kind,' " she intoned softly. "Is this what my life amounts to, in the end?"

"I might say the same thing, myself …" Fentor said. "Although, perhaps not that first part about seeds."

He watched the flames swell and leap, exhaling a great curtain of black smoke. If Mannoc and his allies were searching for him, at least he'd done them the courtesy of making it easy for them. Sidarí's brightly burning home seemed poetic, in a way.

He hated poetry.

Fentor had always considered himself to be a beacon waiting to shine, with his latent talents stacked up like kindling, ready to dazzle the world. In truth, like the house, Fentor's life and ambition were going up in smoke. In a short while, all of it would be cold ashes. He laughed softly.

His mind was made up. He wouldn't tell Elatea the location of Crann Arborím. Not willingly, at least. She would have to pry the answer from the deepest wrinkles in his brain. If he was lucky, an angry mob of elves would tear him apart before the Lady could. The only thing he could do in the meantime was wait.

"I'm not going to tell her," Fentor said.

Sidarí frowned, and blinked slowly as she turned to him, looking as though she had just woken from a long and vivid dream.

"It might not affect the ultimate outcome, but at the very least I can refuse to participate."

"That's quite a selfless gesture. Could it be that some of the Elarím ways influenced you after all?"

"In spite of all my best efforts," Fentor said, shaking his head. "But too little, and far too late."

"Fenny!" Hess' familiar voice called out from the darkness.

Fentor turned. Oddly, he felt the same way he had when he'd broken Father's Flores y Espadas vase playing with his practise sword. Methúsel had then walked in on Fentor hiding the pieces. At the time, it had been the biggest mistake he'd ever made.

Now, he had broken things that could not be swept under a rug and forgotten. Father would be home soon, and the disappointment on his face would be terrible to behold …

"Fenny!" Hess plunged through the trees toward them, with Angsley close behind her. Their faces flashed orange in the firelight, bobbing through the gloom like a nightwatchman's warning lantern.

"What are you doing here?" he asked.

They thumped along the path and halted right before him. He glanced over his shoulder at Sidarí's burning home, self-conscious. His friends seemed unfazed by the fire.

"Something's gone terribly wrong …" Hess clutched her side, wheezing.

"What happened? Where's Crauford?"

"The volunteers … every one of them," Angsley panted. "Every last one of them …"

"What?"

"They dropped dead."

"Crauford was extracting the animus like you wanted," Hess said. "Half of them refused. Then, out of nowhere, they all fell over, clutching their heads."

Fentor's hands and feet felt ice-cold. Some slowly-stirring part of him struggled to comprehend, to feel, to understand. The rest of him was still numb, wading slowly through a dream.

"I suppose he has all the animus he could ever need, then," Fentor said lightly, as though remarking on sandwiches at a garden party.

"Fentor! Was this part of the plan?" Hess shook him by his collar. "Did you know this would happen?"

Fentor looked into Hess' pretty face, focused on it. Unlike the absurdity of everything around him, she seemed real. That was nice. "As it turns out, I didn't really know anything whatsoever. The plan—the Lady's plan—had always been this, I suppose, but I found out too late. The Lady used me, and I used you and Angsley and Crauford. I used Sidarí, as well. And now the Lady has used all those volunteers. Used them up completely."

"Why? Why would the Lady do this to her own people? We're Madeans!" Hess shouted. "We're not the bloody enemy!"

"The time has passed for asking 'why,' " Fentor said.

"Well, then, what are we going to *do?*"

"There's nothing we can do. Crauford's going through with it," Angsley intoned. "He hesitated when all the volunteers died. But then he got a headache of his own ..."

"What's going to happen when the Lady breaks free?" Hess asked.

"I expect the Elarím, including the innocent, will suffer untold casualties, death and destruction, and possibly witness the end of their people. The moment Her Excellency learns where …" Fentor trailed off as another thought occurred to him. Some of the warmth came back into his fingers.

A daring idea had fallen into his lap. Daring ideas had always come to him that way, like parcels dropped from Providence. In his past life he'd always called them bold, daring, intrepid, audacious.

In reality, this idea was as reckless, foolish, and fraught with danger. His ideas had always been that way, he realized. The difference was that this time, the risk was worth taking.

"Sidarí—is there a way we can get to the Lady without being seen?" Fentor asked.

"I thought you weren't going to tell her," Sidarí said.

"Oh, I'll tell her," Fentor said, voice shaking with a suppressed cackle. "I'll tell her all about Crann Arborím! I'll tell her more than she ever wanted to know!"

"Fenny, are you quite alright?" Hess said, looking up at his face.

"This may sound unlikely to succeed. Impossible, even. But if we were logical about the hopelessness of the present situation, we'd conclude that the impossible must be made possible. By sheer force of will, if necessary."

Fentor paced among them, just about vibrating with fervor. The others stared as his wild gesture and bulging eyes, but they couldn't see what he could see. It was his job to put it into words, to manifest his vision, make it solid.

"What have you done to him?" Angsley asked Sidarí.

"If I did this to him, it was not by design," Sidarí said softly.

"Trust me, friends, I have never been sounder of mind," Fentor said. "You'll see when you hear my plan."

"Let's hear it, then." Hess watched him apprehensively, as though he was waving a loaded gun around.

He didn't blame her. Words could be just as dangerous.

"I'm going to save the day. All I have to do is tell dear old Lady Ironhands a well-crafted mistruth," Fentor said.

The others looked at him as though he had announced a plan to sail to the moon in a one-man sloop.

Chapter 35

Anger is like fire.
Useful when controlled, destructive when
free.

Sage Nyendi.

Between Slee's bare feet, an intrepid little flower quivered in the wind. Its scraggly stem had pushed up through the gravel in its stubborn search for sun. She recognized the flower's yellow pad and short white petals, but she could not recall its name. Papa would have called it a weed. Mama would have called it brave. Slee couldn't decide what to call it.

All life cares for all life, Sílandra. Promise that you will never forget that.

Frigid spray from the lake stung Slee's face, arms, and bare feet. The cold had burned at first, but now she could feel nothing.

Cartín, who stood opposite her, kicked the gravel to get her attention. A large dust cloud rose from the chalky rocks. Like the other prisoners lined up on his left and right, his hands were bound and his mouth gagged. He raised his eyebrows and tilted his head toward the distillery.

Dídac had emerged through the heavy front door, flanked by four Greycoats.

All the Bluefingers had been herded to the shore to watch the hangings, and Slee stood at the front of them, under guard. Some watched the nooses sway. The rest, like Slee, looked down at their feet. Dídac's approach inspired a little ripple of shudders to run through the crowd. Cartín, Horvald, Tybalt, Aizman, Batha, and Charlotte, standing in a row in the shadow of the gallows, shivered as well. The pale elf marched around the crowd toward the gallows with slow, deliberate steps. It seemed as though he enjoyed the effect his entrance had on his audience.

Slee shrugged and looked down again.

The little white flower had chosen to fight a losing battle. The slim gaps between the ash-colored gravel forced its body to grow crooked. The constant wind tossed it in all directions. The water, tainted with so much run-off, must have leeched the very life from the soil. Yet still, the little thing persisted. Whatever wisdom flowers were given, this one clearly had not got its share. The flower should have grown somewhere else, far away from the lake. Some battles are best left unfought.

The sound of boots crunching on gravel drew near. Slee could feel nearby Bluefingers stiffen. She did not lift her eyes.

A little green crab, no larger than her thumb, darted across the ground in front of her. Shortly after, three others followed it. They scrambled between the little crevices with their curious, staccato movements. Slee stared. There was not a single telethí near the lake, and yet life persisted. Life continues.

She heard Mama's voice.

All life cares for all life. Aínan, our word for trust, love, care. Remember, Mama aínar Sílandra. Papa aínar Sílandra. Always.

Dídac reached the gallows and began to climb the steps. The timber planks groaned at his arrival. Slee shut her eyes and filled her ears with Mama's words. Even as a memory, the warmth of her Mama's voice was the only thing that could ward off the cold.

Muanan, a shared feeling, a common emotion, but it translates poorly to Madean. It means that our bond is strongest when we struggle together, persist together. Life continues — Oe Telethí Muanan. Pain unites us.

Dídac reached the middle of the platform and faced the crowd. Six nooses hung behind him, three on each side. Lumpy clouds clotted in the sky behind him. He raised his angular face and looked down his nose at the Bluefingers.

"Every one of you signed a contract," Dídac said. "Every condition, caveat, and contingency were laid out in full, and you agreed to them all. You took on your responsibilities, and in turn, you were promised fair pay.

The *consequences* for breaches of contract were also made clear." The elf turned and waved a hand toward the nooses.

"Scoundrel!" a Bluefinger at the back of the crowd called out.

"Rotten to the core!"

"Saints damn ye, Dídac! Damn ye to the abyss!"

A chorus of voices joined in. The insults became more vulgar and more obscure, until Slee could hardly understand what was being said. She turned to see who was jeering, but the crowd was too thick. Those who called out kept themselves hidden.

Dídac, flushing pink, shouted, "Enough!"

Greycoats plunged into the crowd of Bluefingers, shoving and beating indiscriminately. The outcry became cries of pain. The sharp sounds of fist upon flesh and the discordance of angry and distressed voices stung Slee's sensitive ears. Her pain was almost as real as theirs.

Dídac watched, with deep furrows of loathing engraved across his face.

Cartín, Horvald, and the other prisoners seemed to squirm at the sight of violence. Soon, Slee realized that they were actually struggling to escape their bonds, but struggling in vain. They applied all their strength in the effort, despite having no hope of success. Some instinct had taken hold of them, which they could not help but obey. Slee was reminded of the persistent little flower. Perhaps the same impulse drove them.

Oe telethí Muanan.

At length, the Bluefingers were subdued.

Quiet, but not peace, settled over the crowd. The quiet held tension. It was the same tension as the spring in a loaded rat-trap, the same foreboding as a black, humid sky pregnant with thunder. The Greycoats prowled the perimeter, wolves herding sheep.

A strong gust shook the nooses. Charlotte shivered, bowing her head against the cold. The flower at Slee's feet bowed to the wind, as well. Dídac and the Greycoats remained unmoved. Perhaps they were numb like Slee. Perhaps the wind could not move them because the wind was a part of the living world and they were not.

Crantarín, Common Thought, subtlest of the four pillars. It is the undercurrent which runs between us, felt but not seen. The struggles of life are the same, so our goals are the same. We need only understand them. The strength of Crantarín is in clarity, not force. Seek clarity, understanding.

Years ago, as Mama explained the pillars of telethymia for the last time, Slee had hardly been listening. The lessons were old, but the urgency in Mama's voice was new. All Slee had been able to do was cling to her Mama's hand and watch her bloodless lips move.

Tears clouded Slee's eyes, but did not fall. She blinked until they cleared, but she could not shift the heavy lump in her throat. She should have never come to the distillery. Mama should have never left home that day. All this death could have been avoided.

"If any of you makes another sound, it will earn you a place up here." Dídac pointed at the platform.

The Bluefingers kept quiet.

Dídac continued, pacing, "Be reasonable! This task brings me no pleasure. You all have forced it upon me, but

532

I shall carry out my duty without flinching. Each and every one of us must honor the place Providence has planned for us. The worthy rise to the top; the rest sink. I know my place: it is to remind *you* of yours. To correct the derangement that the half-breed Slee infected you with.

"You all came to this place from wretched, gutter-stained lives. Lady Talentus plucked you from your indigence, from the piss-stained streets and brat-infested tenements where you wallowed, too feckless or drunk or stupid to support yourselves. She gave you the gift of a warm bed, guaranteed meals, and generous pay. Her table is piled so high that you gorged yourselves on the falling crumbs. Clearly, it has fattened you. You've become spoiled children. She reached out her hand and you spat on it.

"You will learn your place. You will obey. Hate me if you wish, I care not. Just know that without people like me, you would all starve, breeding like rats in your hovels, hopeless in your wretched incompetence. You strain the larders of civilization, and you test the generosity of your betters. The least you can do is repay my mercy with obedience."

As Dídac spoke, his fervor built and built until his face and ears flushed deep pink, and every word frothed out of him like a kettle boiling over with venom.

Slee became enraged just listening to the lies, the *Uthuín*. She ground her toes into the sharp gravel and dug her fingernails into her arms. She dug harder the longer Dídac spoke, wishing to inflict pain but strangely also wishing to feel it.

Dídac's anger seemed to became *her* anger as though they were bound by the tightest of telethí. She could not help her reaction. *Oe telethí aínar oen telethían.* Even hatred seeks a connection.

A crimson aureole surrounded Dídac, a storm of pulsing forks and swirling sparks. Cartín, Horvald, and the other prisoners glowed like rubies in the sun. She knew it looked that way because, in her anger, overheated blood filled the small vessels in her eyes. It made everything look red. After all, the redness pounded in time with her heartbeat. Still, it looked just like a telethymic aura of rage.

Dídac continued to speak, but the pounding in Slee's ears drowned him out.

Once more, she was back by her Mama's side, watching her slip away.

Sílandra, listen to me. I have little time remaining. Do not give in to Uthuín, the lies. Uthuín opposes Telethían. The lie of separation, isolation, division, dominance.

Papa had already grown cold. Slee couldn't breathe. Many arrows and bullets had pierced him. He lay on the other bed, still, quiet. All his telethí had dissolved into the air when he died.

Both of them had gone out to help, and got caught between barking guns and shrieking arrows. Papa sheltered Mama as best he could. Afterward, she carried him back to their hidden home, but she had been wounded badly, too.

As the light dimmed from Mama's eyes and her warmth and telethí faded from the world, Slee found herself drowning in the dark.

*Oe telethí aínar oen telethían. It is always true. The truth
persists through everything. Life continues; truth continues.*

*Remember, that Mama aínar Papa, Papa aínar Mama; we love
each other. The hatred between elf and man is not infinite or
everlasting. You are the proof. Teach others the truth. Where
telethí are hidden, make them seen. Where aínan is weak, make
it strong. I do not have the time to explain to you all things, but
some things you must always remember:*

Oe telethí aínar oen telethían.

Oe Elarím telethíar oen Madeaním.

Mama aínar Sílandra.

Always.

Slee watched as the gallows and the curdled sky were
stained red and orange and choked with clouds of black
smoke. Waves of anger broke upon her, waking her
dormant heart. The dead go cold, and the living persist.
Too much had been taken from her already. Her parents,
her home, her animals. She had been bent and broken and
chained up, stuffed underground, made thin and crooked,
but *oe telethí muanan.* Like the stubborn little flower at her
feet, she would keep fighting.

Irrepressible heat bubbled up inside her, and all her
muscles tensed until they trembled. In her eyes, or her
imagination, Dídac was burning up.

If the world was not truly ablaze, she would make it so.

Dídac gave an order. Greycoats pushed Cartín, Horvald,
Charlotte, Tybalt, Aizman and Batha up the timber stairs.
As they began to cinch the nooses around her friend's
necks, Slee swelled up until she felt she would break open
from the pressure.

Life surrounded her in all forms and sizes, from the tiny flower to the massed Bluefingers. She knew they all felt the same as she did, that they shared a common goal. She knew they cared for each other and hated Dídac in equal measure. She could not see a single thread of telethí. She could not sense a thing beyond herself. Yet, if all the pillars of telethymia were there, then an unseen web must link them all. *Oe telethí aínar oen telethían.*

How could she deny reality?

All the torment and rage that had been welling up in her chest burst.

"You are weak!" she shouted.

Dídac turned, his icy eyes narrowed.

"Uthuín!" She spat the word. "Your entire life is *Uthuín!* You pathetic, simpering exile!"

The elf's pink face paled. He seemed to shiver and diminish in stature, but he said nothing. For once, Slee had shut him up.

She bent to pick up a small rock, meaning to throw it at him.

The Greycoats on either side of Slee grabbed her roughly, and she dropped the stone. One covered her mouth with a heavy hand. She kicked and struggled, and they beat her. Her fury was so great that she hardly felt their blows.

Bluefingers cried out insults when Slee could not. Small pebbles began to rain down on Dídac, too small to cause harm, but clear in their intent.

"Coward!"

"Exile!"

"Uthuín! Uthuín!"

Dídac bared his narrow teeth at the crowd, his face so contorted by rage that he resembled a gargoyle. He bellowed back at the jeering crowd, spittle flecking his lips and chin. Still, he could not be heard.

The crowd, by common instinct, began to chant, *"Uthuín! Uthuín!"* They could not have known what it meant, but they saw the rage it inspired in Dídac.

The Greycoats on the gallows gaped at the crowd, nooses and prisoners forgotten. They looked to Dídac as though waiting for orders, but Dídac paid them no attention. The rest of the Greycoats dove into the crowd, swinging their pistols like clubs.

"Greycoats—do not to kill more of them than is necessary!" Dídac shouted over the cacophony. "Dead workers yield no profit!"

Every Bluefinger joined in, chanting, stamping, throwing stones, fending off the advancing Greycoats. The mass of the crowd frothed and roiled, a cauldron of rage about to boil over.

With a mighty effort, Slee wrenched herself away from her guards.

"Uthuín! Uthuín!" she bellowed, her eyes locked to Dídac's. Even when the Greycoats seized her arms again, she did not turn away from the glowering elf.

Dídac turned to the prisoners. He waved the Greycoats away and began securing the nooses of the prisoners one after another.

"You are weak! You are a coward! Your strength comes in a bottle!" Slee shouted. "Without the elixir, you're nothing! *Uthuín!*"

Dídac reached Charlotte and tightened the rope around her neck.

The Bluefingers burst like a river from its banks. The Greycoats retreated, forming columns apart from the frothing crowd. Some of them were bloodied and bruised.

Slee smirked. Dídac, ever the coward, must have given diluted doses of elixir to his cronies. He wouldn't have been able to bear the thought of the Greycoats being as strong as him. As always, his *Uthuín* was its own undoing.

Telethían sustains. *Uthuín* destroys. It destroys all things, even itself.

Slee should have listened to her parents and carried out her Mama's wishes. She had been so consumed with hatred for their killers that she had not honored what they died for. Cartín and Horvald met her eyes, steady and resolute. Even moments from death, they did not shrink or cower.

She did not stop struggling or shouting, even when Dídac had drawn nooses around the necks of each prisoner. He placed his hand on the lever at the end of the platform. The moment he pulled the lever, the trapdoors under the prisoners' feet would open.

Gravel still pelted him, and the Bluefingers still jeered at him.

"May the Saints of Providence speed you back to the gutters, where you belong!" Dídac cried.

A brief, powerful rumbling shook the very bedrock and rattled the gallows. Dídac froze.

The commotion in the crowd stilled. Every head turned in a different direction, in search of the source. Slee's guards let go of her and drew their weapons.

Little regular quakes threw ripples across the lake. It was like the beat of an enormous heart far beneath the ground. The sounds grew louder. The pines quivered. The gravel skipped.

Then, a wild, trumpeting roar sailed on the wind to Slee's ears. She clutched her chest, hardly daring to believe. The call was for her. Her heart swelled until it filled her whole body. Joyful tears wet her eyes. If it hadn't been for the fearful looks on the Greycoats' faces and the muttering in the crowd, she would have thought she had imagined the sound. How else could it be possible that Slowjaw would call out at that very moment?

Dídac snorted, shook his head, then took hold of the lever.

Slee started forward, despite knowing the distance was far too large to cross in time. She reached the bottom of the platform and sprang up.

Dídac pulled the lever.

"No!" Slee crashed into the elf, seized his arms. She tried to wrench them away, but he was like solid iron.

He swatted her away, and she tumbled across the rough timber surface.

As she got up, she saw Horvald, Cartín, Charlotte and the others still standing, the ropes slack around their necks.

"What?" Dídac snapped. He pulled the lever again, and again. The mechanism did nothing. "Sabotage!"

"*Uthuín* brings its own undoing," Slee said.

With a strangled cry, Dídac tore Batha's noose from the frame. The youth kicked and gave muffled cries as the elf dragged him by the rope to the edge of the platform. The noose dug into Batha's neck, turning his face red.

The gallows trembled in a steady rhythm as the source of the tremors drew nearer.

Slee sprang up and dove across the platform.

Dídac caught her by the chin with a hand of cold, polished marble.

"Watch," he commanded.

He dangled Batha by the noose over the edge with one hand, and forced Slee to face him with the other.

The young man's face purpled as he bucked and struggled.

"Watch him die. Know that *you* did this, and now there is nothing you can do."

Slee tried to pull away from Dídac with all her strength, but she could not even move his hand slightly. Batha's cries grew weak, and his kicks became feeble. His eyes looked into hers, desperate, imploring.

Another roar burst from the forest, reverberating across the lake with primal force. Slee's arms tingled with gooseflesh. Slowjaw crashed through the trees. He roared again, showing the fleshy insides of his enormous mouth. A swarm of peaducks shot out from the higher branches, then flew in formation alongside Slowjaw's gigantic shell as he charged.

Her beautiful, beloved animals were alive.

If Slee could have moved her mouth, she would have cheered.

Behind her, many boots pounded across the timbers of the gallows platform. Slee could not turn to see, but she felt, or sensed, or *hoped* that the Bluefingers had come to free her friends.

Dídac snarled, but did not relinquish his grip. The visible parts of Batha's lips had turned blue. He only stirred faintly, his fingers twitching and eyes fluttering. Slee reached out her arms toward him, clawing empty air, trying to help in some way. He was too far away, and Dídac's grip was unyielding.

"Struggle all you want! I'll hold you like this until the lesson sinks in!" Dídac shook Slee's chin, his grip tightening painfully. "Watch what happens when you spread Elarím lies!"

A great, confused clamor of stamping feet and shouting voices crowded in Slee's ears. Somewhere behind her, a rifle went off. Loud as the shot was, Slowjaw's earth-shaking gallop almost drowned it out.

The colossal tortoise threw up great plumes of gravel-dust as he hurtled, half-blinded, toward the gallows. What his lumbering gallop lacked in speed, he more than made up for with ferocity. The movement of such massive bulk at speed was, even to Slee, alarming. It felt like she was in the path of an avalanche.

Dídac turned and coolly watched the beast approach. His grip remained iron.

The distance between them closed rapidly, and Slowjaw showed no sign of slowing. His amber eyes blazed through the dust like little suns.

Slowjaw, don't! Stay away! He'll kill you! Slee sent her thoughts outward, but they just rattled in her own head. There was no way to know whether Slowjaw could hear them. Even if he could, it might have made no difference.

Slee's chin was still caught fast in Dídac's hand when Slowjaw's enormous body skidded across the gravel and into the gallows.

The entire structure toppled in a spray of pebbles, dust, and matchstick splinters. Slee was ripped from Dídac's grasp and thrown onto the hard gravel. Sharp stones scraped across her arms and legs as she tumbled across them. She came to a stop, dizzy and winded.

She gasped and coughed as she squinted through the choking white dust. Ghostly shapes stirred and groaned in the fog, melding into one another before splitting apart. She could not tell friend from foe. If she could just get to Batha, he might not be beyond help. With her breath driven from her, she could do little more than wheeze and drag herself across the ground.

Somewhere in the dust, Slowjaw bellowed. Four rifles fired, faint and tinny under the roar. The brief burst of blue light illuminated a row of Greycoats by the remains of the gallows, and Slowjaw towering over them, one massive leg raised above their heads. Then, there was a sound of screaming, cut short by a large, heavy object stamping on the ground.

Slee crawled on hands and knees across the gravel, feeling a little stronger. All around her people were grappling, hitting each other, shouting, crying out in pain. She hoped that by staying low, she would stay hidden from Dídac and the Greycoats.

At last she reached the splintered remnants of the gallows platform. Beside it lay a lumpy, motionless shape, like a pile of discarded clothing. She scrambled over to it.

She touched an arm, a back, a shoulder. The body lay face down, the rope still around its neck.

The last thing she wanted was to see was Batha's face. She was already certain of what she would see. Despite that, she could not stop her hands from turning him over.

The noose had left an ugly red ring around his neck. Above the line, his neck and face were pale and chalky as the gravel, mottled with faint purple blotches. Below the line, his skin looked healthy, almost flushed with life. To see two pieces of his body, living and dead, joined so crudely at the neck seemed wrong. Profane. Batha still had fuzzy hairs on his chin. He had still been growing, changing, maturing. Now he was gone.

Slee clung to him with both hands, as though he would vanish the moment she let go.

A great flurry of wings and quacks descended around her, and she looked up from Batha. Her peaducks landed all around her, on her shoulders, in her lap, all of them quacking incessantly. She laughed shakily.

"My darlings! My little ones! You came back to me." She stroked their feathers clumsily, feeling overcome. "Felheim! Where's Felheim?"

She looked among them for his colorful crest of feathers, but she could not find them. Gretka, Felheim's mate, marched onto Slee's lap and nibbled her fingers. There was a small tuft of iridescent feathers emerging from Gretka's head. Slee touched them gently, and understood.

In the absence of a peadrake, the dominant female could take on their duties, the same way a hen with no roosters would begin to crow at dawn. Felheim must have succumbed to his wound.

Gretka, as though sensing Slee's distress, nuzzled her head against Slee's hand.

The fighting continued around them. She couldn't stay there long. Dídac could have been lurking anywhere in the dust. The sharp cracking of the rifles around her could have marked the deaths of her friends. Slowjaw's constant stamping shook the ground and threw up thicker and thicker clouds of dust, obscuring everything, putting them all in danger. She had to find him, tell him to stop.

Several people stumbled close by, grappling and shouting. In the murk of the dust cloud, they were no more than vague grey shapes. None of them seemed to notice Slee or the peaducks. She crouched low, sheltering them with her arms. Gretka did the same, spreading her wings like shields.

The strangers shoved each other, getting closer and closer, until one of them fell backward inches from Slee's feet. She shrank away, gently pushing the ducks back, hoping none of them would make a sound.

As the fallen man got back to his feet and lunged back into the fray, she noticed he wore a tattered blue coat. Several Bluefingers seemed to be trying to wrest a rifle from the hands of a Greycoat. The Greycoat was stronger than all the others by far, but they did not relent. A moment later, the group plunged back into the haze and were gone.

She tore off one of the pockets of her dress, scattering some of the seeds she had been saving. She tied the cloth around her face to keep out the choking dust. At once, it was easier to breathe.

"Come on, Gretka. Let's find Slowjaw." When Slee stood up, the peaducks crowded around her feet, and began to scratch at the fallen seeds. She almost laughed. Even in the midst of a battle, they could not be denied a meal.

Gretka swiped at the gravel vigorously with her clawed, webbed feet. She plucked up a thin, shiny object in her bill. Slee took it, despite Gretka's loud quacks of protest. It was a thin gold chain with a small red gem.

"Dídac's necklace." Slee prodded the fragment of Crann Arborím without thinking.

A bright spark leapt from the ruby to her fingertip. She flinched, but it did not hurt. Holding it gingerly at arm's length, checking over her shoulder, she could not decide what to do with it. Elarím magic was not to be trusted. It did not function properly with humans. She should have flung it into the lake where nobody would find it.

But then, after all …

The Common Power was no more than a type of telethymia. Every human she had met had surprised her. Telethymia had connected almost every human in the distillery not long ago. Who was she to say that the Common Power would not work the same?

Oe Elarím telethíar oen Madeaním.

Mama believed that humans and elves were bound together, that they could find peace and harmony. Even as she lay dying of wounds from elvish arrows and human bullets, she still believed. She even thought that even telethymia and alchemy, one day, could be united. One magical form for all to use freely.

All around her, the Bluefingers fought for their lives with empty hands against the guns of the Greycoats, and the immeasurable power Dídac had consumed. If Slee used the Common Power to help them, she would be throwing away all her principles. Even if she tried, painstakingly stitching her allies one telethí at a time, it wouldn't be enough. Faced with the same choice, what would Mama have done?

At that moment, Dídac's piercing voice rose above the noise. "Kill that beast! Fire!"

Just ahead of Slee, half a dozen rifles went off with sharp reports. Slowjaw, lit up by the gunfire, raised his head and gave a drawn-out, whining roar of pain.

"Kill it! Kill it!"

She took hold of the gem and squeezed.

Immediately, the whole world around her was ablaze. Shining cords of telethí as thick as her arms *already* flooded the area. All the peaducks and all the Bluefingers and the birds, the crabs, the little flower, Slee and Slowjaw, all of them had woven a great tapestry of silver light between them. Slee gasped at the enormity of the network. Even the pine trees and hidden motelings in the soil and the water had joined. The Common Power was not that different from the telethymia Mama had taught her. Maybe the difference was never as great as she thought.

They were united by a common, desperate cause. The distillery had to be destroyed.

Though he was veiled by the thick dust, Slowjaw stood out brilliantly, a great beacon of animus, a shining spool of many threads. Facing him stood Dídac, a vast, extinguishing presence. The elf's aura numbed those around him, running in swift currents like black water under ice. He reached out his slender hands blindly, groping through the dust toward Slowjaw. For all his power, he could not even overcome a cloud of fine particles.

Slowjaw, get away! Keep stamping your feet — the dust protects us!

Slowjaw rumbled in agreement, pounding the ground with his pillar-like legs as he backed away. Thick white powder swirled in the air, stinging Slee's eyes. Everyone around her coughed as the choking clouds spread.

Cover your mouths! Close your eyes and feel your way! Slee thought, hoping that the others could hear her.

She closed her own eyes tightly, ruby still in hand, and focused on her telethymic sight. The threads shone clearly through her eyelids. It was enough to see where her enemies and friends were, but not debris strewn on the ground. She felt her way toward Slowjaw as quickly as she could without stumbling.

What now? We can't grope around in the dust forever! Horvald thought.

A surge of relief swept over Slee. Horvald and the other prisoners had been untied and made it safely off the gallows as she had hoped. One by one, she felt the presence of the others. They spoke as easily as if they were back in the dungeon together.

Can you see the telethí if you close your eyes? Slee asked.

I think so, Cartín thought. *They are faint, though…*

I can see them, Aizman said.

Good Providence above, I can hear other people's thoughts! Charlotte thought. *Is everyone safe?*

I can't hear the lad. What happened to Batha? Tybalt thought.

Dídac killed him, Slee thought.

Even through her eyelids, Slee could see red mists of rage coagulate along the telethí. A potent barrage of sorrowful phrases and vows of vengeance shot along the web.

She stumbled over a sharp fragment of the collapsed gallows, cutting her shin. Enmeshed in such potent telethí, though, it hardly hurt at all.

We have to destroy the distillery. Even if we give our lives doing it, it cannot be allowed to continue, Slee thought.

Just tell us what to do, and we'll do it, Horvald said.

Even together, we are not strong enough to fight Dídac head on. Keep him confused. Kick up dust to blind him, call out to him, pelt him with rocks and insults.

Rocks and insults? We ought to pelt him with bullets! Tybalt thought.

His body won't be harmed by normal guns. It's his mind that is fragile. Sensitive. The more powerful he becomes, the less secure he feels. The elixir gives him his power, and the Bluefingers give the elixir its power. Without Bluefingers, he has no power. He knows this, and it terrifies him.

You heard the woman, my friends! Cartín thought.

Follow the telethí. Watch out for each other, Aizman thought.

Let's give that rotten, piss-swilling elf what-for, I say! Tybalt thought.

Fight! Horvald thought.

Her friends, bright bundles of light in the web, converged on Dídac. They kicked up dust and threw handfuls of pebbles, keeping their eyes closed but aiming for the elf's black aura.

"Snake!"

"Worm!"

"Failure! Exile!"

The prisoners hurled insults with great passion. Dídac lumbered blindly toward them, snatching at the air with his hands. They avoided him easily, and laughed when he stumbled. The elf spewed a string of curses, both in Madean and elvish, slipping and sliding across the gravel in his desperation to harm his abusers.

Charlotte had found a discharged rifle that had been dropped in the confusion, which she used as a makeshift cane. Tybalt and Aizman kept close by, helping her get out of the way when Dídac stumbled toward them.

Slee rushed across the remaining distance to Slowjaw. He lowered his enormous body to the ground, bleating with excitement. She ran into the leathery crook of his neck and embraced him. Happy tears ran into the gravel-dust on her face, making a paste that clung to her eyelashes.

"You came back," she said. "You came back to me."

Hurry, Slee! There'll time for reunions later! Horvald thought, as he ducked under Dídac's outstretched arms.

Slee climbed onto Slowjaw's shell, followed by Gretka and her flock.

"Let's finish what we came here do to, eh, Slowjaw?" she said.

Slowjaw trumpeted exuberantly.

"Break the door down!"

The colossal tortoise rushed forward, weaving between the bundles of silver threads that marked the position of a friend. On the way, judging by a panicked shout and thud upon Slowjaw's shell, he ploughed right through at least one Greycoat.

All around them, the Bluefingers surrounded the Greycoats one by one, disarmed them, and pushed them to the ground. The Greycoats fired their rifles at random into the haze, usually missing their targets. Three Bluefingers were hit, though, and one of them fell dead instantly.

The bronze edifice of the distillery loomed ahead of them, like the prow of some bizarre ship sailing through fog. Slee was not entirely sure how she would go about destroying such a large structure of metal and stone. The waves of anger crashing all around her seemed forceful enough to sweep the whole building away, but it would take more than that.

I need all the help I can get to destroy this place! Even Slowjaw is not strong enough. Slee cast the thought in all directions across the telethí, where it split into a multitude of shining dew drops.

Smash all the equipment. Every bottle, every flask, every crate of supplies. The building itself doesn't matter, Aizman thought.

Wait! Don't simply smash everything – there is a better way. A new, urgent voice raced along the telethí. It belonged to someone with strange, crystalline thought patterns, one of numbers and formulae.

The others recognised the new speaker, and Slee understood. It was a man named Galton, who had been the former head alchemist. Dídac had assumed Galton's role and assigned him to mind-numbing, repetitive tasks.

What is the better way? Slee asked.

*The reagents can be made extremely volatile rather easily. I
just need a little time.*

How volatile? Cartín asked.

*Alchemy is the art of transformation. Let's just say we'll be
'transforming' the distillery into a large crater rather rapidly.*

Excellent! Horvald thought.

Give us plenty of warning before you light the fuse, Aizman
thought. *Fireworks are best seen from a distance, after all.*

Of course. I'm already on my way, Galton thought. His
node of telethí hurried toward the distillery. *I just need
some help from your, ah … your tortoise, Slee.*

What do you need?

*Have him bend the run-off pipe. Make it go straight up, so the
liquid waste runs back into the distillery,* Galton thought. *Can
he do that?*

Gladly, Slee thought. *Come on, Slowjaw.*

She nudged Slowjaw's neck, guiding him to the right.
Around the side of the distillery, the dust thinned. The
long metal drainpipe lay just ahead, jutting out from the
building like the probiscis of some insatiable parasite. At
the end, the jewel-blue liquid poured out into the lake,
discoloring the surrounding water. Even the brightest
telethí did not cross over that spot.

"Be careful not to get any of that stuff in your mouth,
Slowjaw," Slee said. She sent the tortoise an image of the
water making him sick.

He crooned softly in agreement. The peppery, metallic
scent of the contaminated water made him want to sneeze.
The smell was faint to Slee, but her nose itched in
sympathy.

Slowjaw planted his feet near the end of the pipe, and he probed it gently with his nose and beak. The pipe was large enough to fit Slee's head, but Slowjaw felt that it was thin and delicate. He clamped his beak on it and pulled.

The pipe began to bend with a piercing squeal. Slowjaw let it go. It now had a slight curve, and the end quivered about a handspan above the gravel. A set of deep dents had been left where Slowjaw had gripped it in his beak. Had they been any deeper, the pipe might have been sliced into pieces.

He groaned with concern. As he looked back at Slee, an aura of dark grey steam surrounded his head. He felt guilty.

I did it wrong, he thought. *Sorry. I'm bad.*

"Don't worry, you're not in trouble!" Slee said. "Here, I'll help you."

She slid down his shell to the ground and stepped over the pipe. Wrapping both arms around it, she pulled hard. It did not budge. Her chances of bending the pipe were as slim as cutting diamonds with her fingernails. Still, Slowjaw's large yellow eyes brightened, and his guilty aura cleared.

Hurry! We can't distract Dídac much longer! Cartín thought.

I'm almost ready, but I need the effluent from that pipe! Galton thought.

This is as fast as we can go! Slee replied to both of them.

"I'll pull, you dig under it!" she said to Slowjaw.

Slowjaw scraped away the gravel noisily with powerful swipes of his leg. Great plumes of dust rose up, until Slee couldn't even see the pipe in her hands.

"Good! When there's room, get under it and help me bend it," Slee shouted.

Wedging his head in the hole he had dug, Slowjaw strained against the pipe with his powerful neck. The pipe shuddered, groaned, and squealed as it started to bend. There was a large crack, and some fluid sprayed out of the pipe where Slowjaw's bite had weakened it.

Carefully, now! Almost there!

Slowjaw pushed steadily, and the pipe creakily curved upward. It slipped out of Slee's hands, and then it was above her. Only a sputtering dribble of liquid came out the end. With a final, mighty heave, Slowjaw bent the pipe until it was curled over itself.

We've done it! Slee told the others.

Galton radiated relief and gratitude along the telethí. The others, however, had been seized by a jolt of panic. The wind had picked up speed, and the great clouds of gravel-dust began to disperse.

Dídac heard the metal bending —

Watch out!

He's headed your way!

Slee turned. A great patch of darkness rushed toward her, blotting out the light of the telethí like ink spilled on a page. Dídac emerged from the haze, dusted all over with white powder. Between that and his smooth, blank expression, he looked like a marble statue from a bygone age.

Slowjaw growled, snorted, and dug at the gravel like a bull about to charge.

"Stay back, Slowjaw. You mustn't put yourself in danger this time. The others need you," Slee said.

Gretka and her flock paced around Slee's feet, opening their wings and giving warning quacks to the elf. Tybalt, Horvald, Cartín and the others followed Dídac, flinging small stones and shouting at him. They insulted his mother's honor, called him a coward, an exile, *Uthuín*. Dídac did not so much as blink at the commotion around him. He saw only Slee.

Are you ready, Galton? Slee asked.

I've done as much as I can, I think. Everyone – get to a safe distance! Galton thought.

He only wants me. I'm staying here. Slee removed the cloth from her face, stood tall, and faced Dídac. *Slowjaw, Gretka, get away. Keep each other safe.*

Don't be stupid! There's still time to get away. Move! Horvald thought.

The elf was seconds away from reaching her. His aura, black and cold as the space between stars, enveloped her, and her friends. The silvery threads that joined them together shone all the brighter for the contrast with the dark.

He reached into his long, grey coat, and drew out a sleek pistol set with golden bands. He was only a few steps away.

Slee felt the air rush out of her body, but her determination did not waver.

Aurilium … Cartín thought. *Slee, one shot from that gun …*

You must not let him fire that gun! The distillery will go up like a keg of powder! Galton thought. *Get away, everybody!*

Listen to him, Slee thought. *Run to safety! There is no time!*

She amplified her thoughts and propelled them in all directions along the telethí with as much force as she could. Fat, silvery beads raced everywhere, urging every animal, every Bluefinger, every one of her friends to leave. If Dídac's shot ignited the distillery, so be it. If the resulting explosion killed, or even weakened him, so much the better.

Dídac halted a few paces away, and aimed his weapon at Slee's head.

She did not flinch, or break eye contact.

Slowjaw, Gretka, and the peaducks remained stubbornly at her side. Despite all her urging, they would not move.

Every cord of telethí hummed with latent power. The whole world, both the inner and outer one, swirled around Slee's head as though she was drunk. Everything seemed to rest on the point of a needle, ready to fall either way. She had to delay Dídac, so that the others would have time to get away.

"Won't your Lady be displeased that you've killed me?" Slee asked.

Dídac's ears flattened against his head. "Her Excellency will be informed that you succumbed to a fever."

Cartín and Horvald hurried forward and stood on either side of Slee.

"And what will you say became of us?" Horvald said.

"You met the same fate. Illness spreads so easily among humans," Dídac said airily.

Tybalt, Charlotte, and Aizman came forward and stood by Slee as well.

Slee could not stop them. She had implored them all to leave with as much urgency as she could, but the Common Power does not allow anyone to give commands. The gleaming mesh of telethí that bound them all was brighter than ever. A decision had been made. The decision was not easy, but it was simple. All they had to do was follow nature's highest law.

Oe telethí aínar oen telethían.

All the Bluefingers hurried forward. As they passed Dídac, he shot horrified, bewildered looks at them.

"Idiots! Get away at once!" he shouted.

Soon every prisoner, every animal, and every Bluefinger stood as one group, facing Dídac. The cords of telethí drew them in tightly, knitted them together. They were not dragged there like dogs on a leash. Rather, the compulsion was overwhelming because it came from within. The wren and the ant knew it by instinct. Humans, with great pain, could be taught.

Slee knew Slowjaw and the peaducks would stand by her through anything. She had never guessed that any human other than Papa would ever do the same. Standing between Horvald and Cartín, with Slowjaw's massive head above and Gretka pacing by her ankles, filled her heart until it overflowed. The warmth of true aínan enfolded her, as though she was back in Mama's arms. Muanan hardened her courage, and crantarín united them all in their common cause. She glowed with a warmth and peace that she had not known since before her parents died.

If she now faced her end, it would be worth it.

Dídac shook his head slowly, and tutted condescendingly. How he could not see the obvious peril before him, Slee would never know. The black, numbing aura blinded him, just like the dust had. Before him stood a group of humans bound by pure telethían, powerful enough to rival even the best-trained Elarím. Dídac, an elf raised by the Common Power, would have seen it if not for the Elixir of Power.

Slee had never thought any of it could be possible. Yet there she stood, an impossible person by birth, with impossible allies, facing an enemy who could not be defeated. Perhaps nobody could ever truly know what was and was not possible. But sometimes, in rare moments, they could make the impossible real.

They only needed to learn how to see.

"If you think this nauseating display of unity will stop me, then you don't know just how disposable you all are," Dídac said coldly, aiming down the pistol's sights. "Frankly, it's cheaper to start fresh."

Slee squeezed the ruby.

Dídac squeezed the trigger.

The pistol spat out a great lance of fire, and all the light of the world was burned away.

Chapter 36

Running through the dark, under the trees, Fentor tried to form a properly detailed plan. It was rather like trying to launch a kite with the string tangled around his knees. He had the outline of the plan: lie to Lady Talentus. Beyond that, he had nothing.

Perhaps he was distracted by the constant smack of leaves in his face, and the endless, toe-stubbing rocks which popped into existence wherever his feet went.

Perhaps it was the fact that the fate of countless innocent lives rested on his shoulders.

Either way was fine. He worked best under pressure.

Angsley ran up beside him, puffing.

"Fentor, I have some questions about this plan of yours," Angsley said.

"Ask away, my good man."

"Well … what *is* the plan?"

"To convince Elatea to change her entire plan."

"What's *her* plan?"

"To destroy Crann Arborím and end the war. But it's not what we thought it was. Many innocent lives depend on the Ruby-Tree — destroying it would be nothing short of massacre."

"Saint's tears …" Angsley breathed. "What are you going to say to her?"

"That part of the plan is in a rather early phase of development."

"You don't have a proper plan?"

Fentor frowned at him. "Proper? At this moment, no … not as such."

"Then why are we running so … bloody … fast?" Angsley demanded between wheezes.

Sidarí, a few paces ahead, led the way through the dense foliage. They emerged from the trees onto a grassy slope, and climbed it together.

"What's gotten into the Lady? How could Lady Ironhands be the one doing such awful things?" Hess asked.

"It's the Elixir of Power," Fentor said. "It changes you. It splits the world to fragments, magnifies and shrinks them. Seeing the world that way changes everything else."

"I see nothing that wasn't within her before," Sidarí said, turning back to look at them. "Each new step she takes follows the same path she has always taken."

"You're looking at it like an elf. You must understand that alchemy is the art of change. She drank a staggering quantity of that potion. She hasn't just changed, she's been *transmuted*."

"The art of change?" Sidarí scoffed. "I suppose refining raw material into its pure form is a type of change. In that way, yes, the Lady has changed."

"She's been transmogrified into a lump of crystal, for Temlin's sake!" Angsley said.

"To mirror the shape and hardness of her heart, I'm sure," Sidarí said.

They reached the top of the slope. Ahead of them, the vast, dark mound of Elatea's hill rose up out of the gloom. All across its face, Elarím lanterns twinkled like little red stars. At the top, Elatea's crystal encasement glittered like a shard from a broken stained-glass window.

The contents of Fentor's skull kept spinning and spinning. Angsley was right: he needed a proper plan before he went charging in. The facts were clear, as was his goal. His efforts to bridge the two, make them whole with a strategy, felt like trying to build a wall out of vapor.

Sidarí, silver in the moonlight, closed her eyes for a moment. "Your friend is on his way to the Lady."

"He'll kill everyone that's guarding her," Fentor said.

"They know that," Sidarí said. "They will face him all the same."

"If we hurry, we could talk some sense into him…" Angsley said.

"You saw what the Lady did to him. She won't allow him to change his mind," Hess said.

"Besides, the Lady *and* Crauford must believe we are all enthusiastically and faithfully serving her," Fentor said. "The plan depends on it."

"The plan, which we don't yet have, depends on it," Angsley said flatly.

"If you would just give me a single bloody moment of silence, I'd—"

"Fentor," Hess said.

He blinked. With that one stern, clipped word, she stilled the pinwheels in his mind.

"I think it's time we had a say in your plans," she said, her voice soft but her cadence certain. "We've seen enough of what happens when you come up with them alone."

The others looked at him. Fentor felt scrutinized, vulnerable, like he'd been stripped bare for inspection. Angsley, Hess, and Sidarí all wore the same severe, searching, slightly exasperated look.

A little voice just behind Fentor's ear whined, *But if I'm not the one who makes the plans, if I'm not the hero, then who would remember me?*

He swatted the back of his neck, as though the voice had come from a little buzzing insect. In reality, a part of him had spoken. It was that part he had meant to squash. Strangely, it seemed to work.

"Very well," he said, then cleared his throat. "Let's plan together. How, exactly, do we do that?"

"First, tell us what you know," Sidarí said.

"Then, listen to us—and *actually* listen," Hess said.

"And give credit where it is due. We love you, dear boy, but there are times when you—"

"Alright, alright! You've made yourselves clear enough." Fentor kneaded the stress from his temples, then shook himself. "What do you need to know?"

They asked him about Elatea and the Elixir of Power, and he answered them. They were so short on time that each point of clarification felt like it took an hour. As he told them about the effects of the potion, and everything relevant that Elatea had said, Crauford climbed higher on the opposite hill. They could tell by the lanterns going out along the path, one by one.

"I still don't quite understand what you said about the feeling the elixir gave you," Hess said.

"I felt *strong*. Utterly invincible and unstoppable. But it was more than that. It was like every part of the world — every particle, every atom — was laid out in front of me, all in perfect order," Fentor said. "I could count the leaves on a tree or the hairs on my head with a glance. My thoughts were all in straight lines. Tangled things gave me a headache. I wanted to pull them apart into pieces, lay them out in perfect rows and columns. I wanted to drink more and more elixir — enough to straighten the whole world out."

"So that's it," Angsley said.

"What is?"

"We simply have to get at Elatea's way of thinking. Straight lines, atoms and such," Angsley said. "Nothing 'tangled.' "

"Could we convince her that her plan to attack Crann Arborím is too … tangled? That it wouldn't be logical?" Hess asked.

"I don't believe we could. She came up with the plan, and that makes it untouchable. Admitting that she is wrong would be tangled, do you see? It's straighter, simpler, for her to believe that she is infallible," Fentor said.

"So she has to believe that *she* came up with a new plan," Hess said.

"That's easy. First, praise her, flatter her. Work the new plan into the flattery somehow," Angsley said.

"I doubt it could be *that* easy," Hess said.

"The Lady is not enthused with attempts at bald flattery," Fentor said. "I recall a threat to cut out my silver tongue …"

"Besides, this is a serious situation. We can't just stroll over there and charm our way through it."

"You're right, Hess. I spoke too hastily," Angsley said, gruff and sheepish. "I felt like a real idiot next to you with your ideas and questions, and I wanted to contribute something."

"Oh, Angsley. It's alright." She patted his shoulder. "You know what? Your idea's not too far off the mark. Maybe we just need to iron out the particulars of what we'd actually say."

"Well, I was thinking … no, it's not good enough. You've got a better grip on this than me, I won't interrupt with my foolish thoughts," Angsley said.

Fentor narrowed his eyes. What was Angsley up to?

"No, go on, let's at least hear it," Hess said.

"Well … Elatea's drank every last drop of elixir that she had. And since Fentor mentioned always wanting to drink more …"

"Angsley, you're a genius!" Hess said. "We'll convince her that she just needs another bottle of elixir. She won't be able to resist!"

Angsley grinned broadly, then nudged Fentor with his elbow. "And there, my friend, is proof of concept. Persuasion through flattery — oldest trick in the book. Self-deprecation, of course, being its younger, subtler cousin."

"Why, you—" Hess shook her fist at Angsley, then let her arm drop. "Well, I suppose I must admit it was effective."

"It *might* work. But if the Lady catches even the *slightest* whiff of out-and-out sycophantery, we'll be finished," Fentor said. "Why, I'm a master of guile, and I can hardly sneak a flattering word past her."

"I fooled Hess, and she *knew* I wanted to try flattery," Angsley said. "Let me handle it."

"Well..." Fentor's neck grew hot. Could it be that his way with words was less than masterful? Was Angsley really better than him, at this of all things? The stakes were too high to deny reality. "Right you are. Angsley, you'll be in charge of fawning, cajoling, and flattering. Now the plan has its basic shape, at least."

"So we send her away to get another drink. What lasting good will that do?" Sidarí said. "She will just come back stronger and finish her task."

"Let's save Crann Arborím and all of elfkind today, and worry about tomorrow's calamities as they come," Fentor said. "We'll buy you time, if nothing else."

Sidarí stiffened, as though startled by a voice only she could hear. "Crauford has reached the hilltop."

The four of them froze and watched the movement of indistinct half-lit bodies. A new breeze stirred, carrying the faint perfume of many flowers, and equally faint screams from the unfolding battle. At one point, Fentor could swear he heard Crauford cackling.

"The time is upon us," Fentor said.

"But we're not ready!" Hess said.

"That's alright. We'll muddle our way through together," Angsley said.

"What will you do, Sidarí?" Fentor asked.

The elf appeared to chew on her tongue for a moment, her eyes still fixed on the battle across from them. "The people of Rivumaí are divided. Some follow Mannoc, some hold to the values of Nyendíthe. I will convince as many as I can to aid you. Beware the rest."

"Thank you. For you to help us, in spite of everything … it takes true greatness," Fentor said.

"I do it not for you, but for my people," Sidarí said. *"Oe telethí aínar oen telethían."*

"What does that mean?" Hess asked.

"Many things. For now, it means … hope." Sidarí looked at each of them under a creased brow. She almost seemed to darken and chill the night air around her. A moment later, she turned and disappeared into the trees.

Looking out at the opposite hill, with the red lanterns darting about, he was, as the Norimandians might say, struck with a sense of *déjà vu*.

He was also, as they might say, *terrifié*.

"I have to say," Fentor said, wiping a dry tongue across his dry lips. Why was it that his palms were drenched, but his mouth couldn't generate a single drop of moisture?

"Yes?" Hess said.

"I, er, have to say," he repeated, clearing his throat. "We may not make it through, so I have to say that the two of you …"

There was a lengthy pause.

"What I mean is that in life, we all encounter certain individuals … and there are certain feelings that one may …" he faltered. He looked at Hess and Angsley.

"It's alright, Fenny," Hess said thickly. "We understand."

"We don't need to hear another word, dear boy," Angsley said. "We feel the same."

"Regardless …" Fentor drew in a large, chest-expanding stream of air. Then, all in a rush, he said, "I care for you both very much. And Crauford, as well."

A curious, tingling upwelling of warmth and affection rose from his chest, up his throat, to the top of his scalp. It felt as though his heart had been uncorked and issued a spray of fine Norimandian champagne. Soft, almost imperceptible golden light suffused his surroundings.

"We know," Hess said.

Angsley grunted and nodded, blinking rapidly.

"Right, then," he said. "Destiny awaits. Let's take the next hill."

****

Standing over the bodies of slain enemies no longer held quite the same sense of triumph as it once had. In fact, Fentor was no longer even sure *who* his enemies really were. All he knew was that it felt wretched to see dozens of dead elves strewn about the hilltop. The sight of so much blood made him feel clammy as a sack of vomit. He smiled through it, regardless.

With Hess and Angsley by his side, he approached Elatea's glowing crystal with the outward confidence of a man leading a grand procession. Inwardly, he felt more like a man headed to an appointment with the noose.

The three of them had rehearsed their lines hastily as they climbed the winding path. Now that they'd reached the top, where everything was washed crystalline blue, every single word had evaporated from Fentor's head. He could only hope Hess and Angsley would be able to help him through the ordeal.

Crauford looked nothing like himself. Not only did he gleam in the bright blue light cast from the crystal beside him, but he had also removed his spectacles. Without something to peer through, it seemed, his whole demeanor had transformed. His habitual mannerisms of gentle contemplation and preoccupation and abstraction were gone. The Thambrian looked at them all with perfectly focused, flat, dead-fish eyes. It looked as though all the floating numbers and formulae that usually clouded his eyes had cleared. In their place, he saw a world of one layer only. A clean world of straight lines, neatly divided.

Fentor remembered the feeling well. But had *his* eyes looked as glazed and inhuman as Crauford's?

Angsley rushed forward and fell before Elatea in an act of genuflection devoid of subtlety. He kissed the grass before her, clasped his hands together, and choked, "Thank Providence! Never in all my days had I dreamed of seeing a Saint with my own eyes!"

Fentor, now a few paces away, wanted to kick him. The whole bloody plan rested on the flattery remaining unnoticed!

Then, Crauford spoke. Or rather, his lips moved, and Lady Talentus' voice issued from them. "Rise, Capilet Angsley. The Church of Providence has not canonized me. Yet. The appropriate time for worship will come soon enough."

"F- forgive me, my Lady," he stammered, straightening up. "I was … overcome."

"Understandable," the Lady said through Crauford. "Fentor. You have what I seek?"

"I do, my Lady."

"Where is it?"

"If I could first explain —"

"Tell me now!" Elatea's voice shot from Crauford's mouth like the snarl of a wolf. It was a bizarre mis-match to see Crauford make such a noise.

Fentor raised his finger and pointed nine degrees east of true north, the true location of Crann Arborím.

"Yes. I knew it must lay that way," Elatea said.

Hess dug her elbow into Fentor's ribs. "You can't just tell her without giving a proper warning!" Hess whispered, loud enough to be heard.

"Girl. What did you say?" Elatea asked.

"Oh, I – I didn't think you would hear me, my Lady," Hess said, bobbing awkwardly in a kind of curtsey. Her face turned a convincing shade of red.

"I may be encased in crystal, but my hearing remains exquisite. Why did you mention a warning?"

"It's nothing, my Lady. A trifle. With all the strength and grace Providence has blessed you with, it could hardly pose a danger," Angsley said.

"I do not doubt it. But I asked a question, and I still await my answer."

"M- my Lady, the Elarím have set a trap," Fentor said, falling to one knee, averting his gaze. "During my vision of Crann Arborím, I discovered it. A net spun from light, like a web meant to catch you, but I cannot be sure. It was beyond my comprehension."

"Of course it was," Elatea said. "You lack the necessary acuity."

"My Lady, I beg you, don't walk into their trap," Hess said.

"Nothing devised by the Elarím could possibly touch the Lady's power!" Angsley scoffed.

"Enough!" Elatea barked. "I shall pass through their snares like a meteor through clouds."

"See? Not even Crann Arborím itself could drain the Lady's power!" Angsley said.

"Drain my power?" Elatea said.

There was a long, tense silence. Crauford's face remained vacant, but his hands trembled. Then, the Lady's crystalline voice rang from his lips, "Yes, I knew it was possible. Dídac gave cryptic but strenuous warnings to this effect. I am not surprised at all. I always knew this eventuality was possible."

"But my Lady, we're so close to a true, lasting victory over the enemy! We can't just go back to the distillery and get more vials of elixir!" Fentor said, in his most sincere and insistent voice.

"Fool! That's exactly what I shall do. How could you not see that I have planned for this contingency since the beginning?" Elatea's tinkling voice shot from Crauford's lips, as sharp as broken glass.

They had her. Fentor wanted to share the blazing fire of triumph in his heart with the others. He was sorely tempted to turn his head and give them the slightest wink, but he kept his eyes forward. The performance was not done, and the curtain had not yet fallen.

They still had to make their escape, and survive the ensuing chaos.

"As you command, my Lady," Fentor said, bowing, an expertly suppressed scowl on his lips.

"Before I emerge from my chrysalis, I require confirmation of the facts."

"Of course," Fentor said. "I give you my word."

A grating, metallic laugh sprang from Crauford's mouth. Fentor nearly jumped out of his skin at the sudden, discordant noise.

"Your word? *Your* word?"

"I know my word is worth little," Fentor said. "But every word was true. I swear it. I know that it is customary to pledge something of high value. Every oath needs collateral, after all. Since I have nothing, I pledge my life. May I drop dead if I have told a lie."

"Good. It may come to that."

Invisible talons tore into Fentor's skull. They peeled back layers of flesh and bone, until his brain lay open to the air. He flung his hands up to ward off the attack, but found the top of his head whole, unscathed. No blood, no gore, no viscera.

The piercing claws may not have been real, but the pain was.

Fentor fell to his knees, head in his hands, as Elatea penetrated the soft tissues in his skull.

Show me what you saw.

She dragged him down into the darkness of his own memories. The further they went, the less he could feel his head being eviscerated.

Show me Crann Arborím.

As much to flee the pain as to obey her, he conjured the image exactly as he had seen it.

Crann Arborím, that gargantuan vortex of light, rose before him. The two of them now stood within Fentor's memory, in a kind of vague, ghostly realm. Lady Talentus stood at his side, translucent, ethereal. Her pale eyes traced the myriad boughs, roots, and tendrils of the Ruby-Tree, following them wherever they led.

There must be a terminus ... a core. A final, definitive point where the beating heart sits in its cage ... she mused.

Fentor, disoriented and confused, watched the Lady's expression shift. As she studied the ceaseless ebb and flow of telethí, her eyes narrowed and her lips parted. She turned, her eyes darting faster and faster, until she was frantic. She whipped around in a tight circle, her silvery cheeks flushed, her teeth bared.

Where does it end? Where does it come from?

When Fentor looked up at Crann Arborím, it was clear to him that her question meant nothing. The Ruby-Tree was made of telethí, of the little strands that connect the Elarím together. Connections like that had no source and no end point. Where does a circle start and where does it end?

Thread after thread, branch after branch, all of them in motion. Power in motion. Moving where? Why? Who is directing them? Where is the power kept, *for Temlin's sake?* she spat.

The questions seemed to enrage, and then terrify Elatea. When a few strands of telethí drifted past her, coiling and branching, she squawked and slapped them away. She made herself small, peering up at the ever-expanding, ever-intertwining galaxy of telethí.

Fentor had an idea.

He imagined Crann Arborím pulsing, and it did. It pulsed like a throbbing heart, and shone a little brighter, just as he imagined it would.

Then, he imagined monstrous clawed branches of telethí sprouting, and they did. He imagined them diving down from high above, reaching for the Lady like snakes, and they did.

She cried out and ran.

Silvery cords sprang from the ground and caught her legs. Fangs and claws and twisting pythons of telethí swarmed into the area, and converged on the Lady. Her ghostly face contorted into an expression of abject, unquenchable terror.

Enough!

Fentor opened his eyes, his feet back on firm ground once more. He tested his forehead with his fingers. It was still intact. Cool, refreshing air filled his lungs. Strong, warm hands pulled him upright. Angsley and Hess looked at him with concern.

"I'm fine," he murmured. "Thank you."

"I have seen enough," Elatea said through Crauford.

"My Lady, what did you see?" Angsley said.

"Silence!"

Angsley bowed his head. He still held onto Fentor's arm, so tightly that his fingertips throbbed. The three of them waited for the Lady to speak.

With a delicate series of cracks, like the breaking of thin pond ice, Elatea's crystal shell began to fracture. Pieces broke off, rolled across the grass, then vanished. Soon all the crystal had fallen away. Only Elatea remained, untouched, unmoving, still holding the same regal pose, still wearing the same placid smile.

At great length, she took a step forward, then turned to look at each of them. Her joints swiveled with well-oiled ease. Every slight movement was a glissade, a demonstration of virtuosity. They waited with the same hushed awe of a theatre audience, or, perhaps, a crowd witnessing a hanging.

Or, perhaps, like a trio *waiting* to be hanged.

As her crystalline smile lit upon Fentor, he felt as though needles of ice had been placed delicately against his skin—not yet piercing him, but threatening to. Her lips drew wider, and wider, until Fentor could no longer call it a smile.

"As I said, I had always planned for this exact outcome," she said. Her voice jangled like a crystal chandelier, delicate but discordant. "We have ventured into the Elarím lands, just as the great Saint Temlin once did. Unlike him, we have succeeded. This is the first of a series of victories. I never intended for our initial sortie to defeat the Elarím. We have what we came for: information. If it had not been for your bumbling harlequinnery, I might have retained enough animus power to wipe out the enemy in one stroke—as I originally planned. But now, instead of continuing on to Crann Arborím, we shall have to double back to Madea. I had always factored in a return to my distillery, of course. Dídac will have elixir waiting, and I shall drink every last vial, if that is what it takes."

Fentor had put his hand on his chin to keep his jaw from dropping. He nodded at everything the Lady said. She had contradicted herself with each new breath. Every word had rung with absolute conviction. Had she forgotten her original plan? Or did she believe two separate things at the same time?

The Lady turned away to face Crauford.

Fentor shared an apprehensive look with Hess and Angsley, and he knew they had thought the same things.

Elatea spoke softly to Crauford, and he nodded.

"Very well," she said. She stepped over the bodies of several elves as she made a small circuit of the hilltop, looking outward into the night. "We shall make for Madean territory, then take carriages to the Bianlock distillery. As it happens, the Gutter Trench lies due south of here, and is the quickest way home."

She glanced at a few clusters of stars overhead, and then pointed southward.

"Do try to keep up. I shall be going my own pace, pausing only to fight the enemy. You will have to hurry along in my wake as best you can. Your survival is your own responsibility."

Baring her teeth in a lupine grin, she took a running start, then leapt off the hill and into the darkness.

Chapter 37

I'm off to meet the hangman,
The crowd, and knotted rope.
If they all fought their foes like me,
Then maybe we'd have hope.

'Fight the Enemy,' Stanza Five

Fentor and his friends took sabre-spears and lanterns from
Elatea's fallen guards, then rushed south after her.

They fled wildly down the winding path, past the
outskirts of Rivumaí, and into the dense vegetation.

"We're going to lose our way! You can't see a single star
through these trees, let alone find south," Angsley
grumbled.

"Elatea will show us the way, if only unintentionally,"
Fentor said. He held the red lantern high and swept about
the surrounding forest. A tree had been smashed to
splinters not far off. "Here!"

They followed Fentor to the shattered remains of the stump. Once they stood upon it, a neat line of destruction marked Elatea's progress. Every last leaf, twig, and stone in Elatea's path had been demolished, as though a five-foot high tornado had torn through the woods.

"When she says she is heading due south, she means it quite literally," Fentor said.

"She's not just strong," Hess said. "She's a force of nature."

"Not quite. She *is* force," Crauford said. "Pure velocity and mass."

"Look!" Angsley said, pointing.

Far down the corridor Elatea had carved, red whistlers flared brightly. A shape that might have been Elatea became visible for a moment. The barrage of arrows converged on the shape, then were extinguished. There was no second volley.

"Quickly, now," Fentor said. "They'll focus on her, but they're not fond of us, either."

"The elixir I drank is spent. We won't survive an ambush, and an ambush is certain," Crauford said rapidly. He stared down the length of the corridor of splinters, his eyes and head looking equally empty. "If we take this path, we'll easily be found. If we go a different way, we'll get lost. The probability of survival has fallen to zero point zero."

"Come now, Crauford," Fentor said, standing in front of him and taking hold of his shoulder. "Mathematics might always be correct, but it's not always true."

"That makes no sense." Crauford still stared ahead, straight through Fentor, as though his optic nerves had been detached and his eyeballs left sightless. "The correct and the true are the same."

"We don't have time for all this jaw-flapping! Let's get moving," Angsley said.

"No," Crauford said.

Fentor pulled on Crauford's arm, but he wrenched it away.

"I'm not moving. It's not rational. Survival has become impossible."

"Crauford, please," Hess said. "You can't possibly know that for certain, but it *will* come true if we dally any longer!"

"What's she done to him?" Angsley said.

"Crauford, we can't just leave you here! We've got to go!" Hess said, pulling fruitlessly on his other arm.

"You want rational? I'll give you—" Fentor paced and mumbled, casting about in his brain for something that might un-break Crauford's broken mind.

In the distance, another volley of whistlers screamed softly.

Fentor's boot hit something that rang like a silver bell. It was one of the curious glass flowers they had drunk sapwine from. Struck with a sudden idea, he bent down and pulled it up, roots and all.

"First premise: all trees have leaves. Correct?" Fentor asked.

"Correct," Crauford said.

"Second premise: this has leaves," Fentor said, pointing at the leaves on the flower's stem.

"Correct."

"Conclusion: this is a tree."

Crauford blinked, shook himself a little, then looked right at Fentor. "False."

"But Crauford, my premises were correct. How could I be wrong?"

Crauford stared at the flower. Fentor waited as the silence dragged on. Ideally, he'd have preferred to tie Crauford up and drag *him* along behind them. Every moment slipping past lowered their already slim chances.

At last, Crauford blinked, and shook himself slightly.

"Ah. I see what you mean now," Crauford said. He peered about myopically, first at his companions, and then down the long, dark path the Lady had cut through the forest. "Let's get moving."

"That worked? How did that work?" Angsley said.

"I have absolutely no idea," Fentor said honestly.

"Come *on!*" Hess said, herding the others with her arms. "Get going!"

They obeyed without another word.

The trail of splinters and crushed stone was well-defined, but narrow. They sped along it single-file, Hess in front, Fentor at the rear. Their lanterns washed everything red, throwing long, crawling shadows around them.

The shrill screams of whistlers and dying elves rang out ahead of them. They were getting closer to the bloodshed.

Time did not pass as it usually did. They were trapped like flies in ruby-red amber, eternally stuck in the same moment. The tunnel of destruction left in Elatea's wake was so uniform that it left little space for thought. Fentor simply placed one foot in front of the other as fast as his body would allow, and listened to the cracking of twigs and splinters under their feet.

"Wait! What's that?" Hess cried out.

They came to a stop behind her. She held her lantern high and peered into the trees. The three men squeezed in close, trying to see.

"What is it?" Fentor breathed.

"Old scout instincts ... someone's ahead, and it's not our distinguished superior," she said.

They all held their sabres ready. The forest was so thick, they had no hope against a coordinated ambush. Indeed, they had no hope against a hasty, poorly executed ambush, either. Fentor just felt better searching the darkness with a weapon in his hand.

"Well, they might have gone ..." Hess whispered.

"We can't go back. We have to go forward, no matter what might be there," Crauford said.

"I might be able to creep ahead, get a better look," Hess said. "If there's a trap, you three might get away."

"Absolutely not! We're going together. I won't have any one of us traipsing off alone in a fit of heroics," Fentor said.

"Well, then," Hess said. "Forward together it is."

They crept forward, tightly huddled. None of them would have room to swing their sabres, but that wasn't Fentor's chief concern. There were other, more essential reasons to keep close.

At any moment, Fentor felt sure that the trees would light up with twinkling red stars, and his life would end in a hail of shrieking arrows. Then he thought that the light cast by the lanterns made spotting any potential attacks unlikely. They shone the same shade of red. Was there a reason for that? He had never asked.

They couldn't stumble about in the dark over all the debris. Since they had no choice but to proceed by the light of the lanterns, Fentor decided it was best to carry on. Whatever would happen would happen.

A dark-haired elf stepped out in front of them.

They cried out in alarm and raised their swords. Sidarí, eyes wide with urgency, raised empty hands.

"They are behind you! Shelter with me, quickly!" she shouted.

With frantic backward glances and stifled shouts of panic, they followed her into the trees. Dozens of red points of light winked into existence around them. They vaulted over gnarled roots and ducked under thick branches, fighting curtains of leaves the whole way. At last, they burst into a cleared area where thirty or so elves waited.

"A trap!" Angsley cried, raising his sabre.

Fentor caught him by the wrist. "No! They aren't here to hurt us. Are they?" he asked Sidarí.

"We may be your only hope," Sidarí said. "Get low to the ground. The Common Power is fractured—the aegis will be limited."

"What are you talking about?" Angsley said, even as Hess and Fentor dragged him into a crouch.

The whistlers flew. All around the clearing, a glowing red dome sprang into existence. Sidarí and the other elves reached into the air, as though they were holding the aegis up. The arrows struck the barrier with a hollow ringing sound. A few pierced through, one of which struck an elf in the shoulder. The shield trembled, then burst like a bubble. A few more arrows spun and clattered, harmless, on the ground. A few elves cried out.

Hess grabbed Fentor's arm, and he pulled her into a hunched embrace.

"Telethían! Aínan! Muanan! Crantarín!" Sidarí shouted. "Restore the barrier! More will come!"

Fentor looked around. The elves, sweating and panting, already looked exhausted. More whistlers lit the darkness like sparks frozen in place. The red dome flickered into existence for a moment, then faded into nothing.

"Sidarí! Let us help!" Fentor said.

"Are you mad?" Angsley roared. "We should be running!"

Sidarí offered her hand. "Hold on tightly. With luck, nature's highest law will preserve us."

Fentor took Sidarí's hand, then held onto Hess' with the other. Crauford and Angsley stared, but did not move.

"How can you even think of doing this?" Angsley said.

"How can *you* even think of refusing?" Fentor bellowed. "Grab on or we'll all be pincushions!"

Scowling, Angsley took Hess' hand, then snatched Crauford. The five of them, humans and elf, crouched together in an awkward chain of linked hands.

"Hold on!" Sidarí shouted. "Telethían! Aínan! Mu—"
Then came the shriek.

The arrows drew red ribbons as they floated through the night. The aegis was still not there.

A terrible thought intruded on Fentor as the arrows were about to strike. He thought of Hess getting hit by them. He imagined, in that brief instant, all five of them lying on their backs, fletching sprouting from their chests like flowers. He imagined Hess' warm hand going limp and cold.

I would feel the sting of every arrow if it kept the others safe. Let them fall on me.

Let the others be protected, while I alone am pierced.

Don't bloody tell me I'm going to have to watch the others die! Saint Temlin above, I'd rather get hit a thousand times before any of them get hit even once!

The cascade of thoughts in that brief instant came from all around him, through him, and also from inside his own mind. A deep rumbling resonated in his chest, through his hands to the others.

The aegis flared brightly above them, only a handspan away. The shrieking of the whistlers built to an impossibly loud crescendo, and then there was silence.

Fentor had squeezed his eyes shut. Everything was black, still, quiet. With a great effort, he peeled his eyes open.

The gleaming tip of an arrow rested in mid-air two finger-widths away from his nose. The aegis had caught it, frozen it in place. He dared a look around him. Hess, Angsley, Crauford, Sidarí, and all the other elves were unhurt. They had stopped every arrow.

Fentor raised his fists to the heavens and cheered.

"I don't believe it! I *don't* believe it!" Angsley hopped about, laughing manically.

"We did it," Hess breathed, looking at all the arrows in a daze.

"Perhaps I thought too little of humans, after all," Sidarí said. "But the danger has not passed yet."

"What do you mean?" Fentor asked. His heart had been fluttering around in his ribcage like a hummingbird stuffed with nectar. Now it fell to the pit of his stomach, like a hummingbird stuffed with sawdust.

"The aegis is stable enough to protect us from their arrows. They will assault us with sabre and spear next," she said.

"Can't we just run?" Angsley said.

"The paths are narrow and twisting. We cannot take the aegis with us, or make a new one without the space to gather together," Sidarí said. "We must face them here."

"The correct strategy would be to surround us, wait us out," Crauford said.

"Not in this case." Sidarí held her sword ready, watching the surrounding trees. "They will rush in and try to kill us. With the Common Power fractured, strategy and patience are out of reach."

"Let them rush in, then," Hess said, brandishing her sword. "We're ready."

"I suppose we have no choice," Angsley said.

The forest around them came alive with the rustling of leaves and harsh elvish voices.

"In life, true choices are rare enough," Sidarí said. "War makes them even less common."

"Well, I choose to fight," Fentor said, and looked around at his friends. "Beside you all, for you all. Never again by myself or for myself. A man needs something worth fighting for."

The others looked at him, faces shining with determination. Hess touched his arm briefly, leaving behind warm fingerprints. His heart swelled.

The enemy elves sprang from the trees and rushed toward them.

Swords and spears flashed red, slicing the air around them. Crimson-faced elves loomed out of the dark, their faces chill with menace. Blade clashed against blade all around the clearing in an ugly metallic rhythm punctuated with cries of pain.

Fentor beat back his attackers, overwhelming them with flurries of his sabre. Other elves pushed in on Crauford and Hess. Fentor turned to them, one after another, creating openings for his friends. He dashed one sword aside, and Crauford lanced the elf in the ribs. He jabbed at an exposed enemy's side. The elf blocked Fentor's sword, but Hess darted in low and cut their thigh.

Sidarí got caught fighting three elves alone. She flicked their weapons aside with perfect technique, but they still forced her into a rapid retreat. Technique alone could not always prevail. Hess and Fentor sprang forward together. Two of the elves darted away from the attack, leaving Sidarí with one. She deftly cut across her opponent's knuckles, then jabbed them in the shoulder. The injured elf dropped their weapon and fled.

They continued to assist one another against the enemy, driving them back, disarming them, and halting their advances. Many times, Fentor saw an opening in an adversary's defences, one that would guarantee a killing blow. However, it seemed that each time, one of his friends needed his help. More than once, an uncommonly aggressive elf would drive Fentor into a retreat, but Hess, Sidarí, Crauford, and Angsley were always there to assist.

More and more of the enemy fell or retreated, until at
last they were routed all together. As they dashed,
stumbled, or carried each other back into the thick forest,
Fentor's first instinct was to run them down and finish
them off. His second instinct, which prevailed, was to stay
and check on his friends.

"Is anyone hurt?" he asked.

"A few bruises and cuts," Hess said.

"Some self-inflicted. These bloody things are too
whippy," Angsley said, wiggling the elvish sabre with
contempt.

"We made it through," Sidarí said.

"I think only six sustained fatal wounds. Four on their
side, two on ours," Crauford said, scanning the area and
counting on his fingers. "Why so few?"

"Death is an outcome of battle, not its purpose," Sidarí
said. "At least, that is the Elarím ideal. Why kill an enemy,
when wounding them will suffice? With the Common
Power fractured, though, the enemy will soon grow more
aggressive."

"But why?" Hess asked, open mouthed, looking at the
remains of the recent battle. "Why would you fight fellow
elves for our sake?"

"Because ..." Sidarí said, wiping her forehead and
leaving a faint smear of blood. "Because we have so few
real choices in times of war. I had to make a choice, and I
made it." Then, Sidarí froze. Her ears twitched slightly,
then she frowned. "They are regrouping. Follow me and
we may stay ahead of them."

"What about everyone else?" Fentor asked, pointing at the elves who remained in the clearing. "Your friends the, er, Nyendíthe believers?"

"Some will stay, others will follow us," Sidarí said. "They will do whatever is needed to help you escape. We hope that the rift will begin to heal once you are all back in Madea."

"Then let's hurry onward," Fentor said.

Angsley shook his shaggy head and rolled his shoulders. "You know, we have run all this way and I don't feel remotely tired."

"As I said, we will do whatever is needed to help you escape," Sidarí said.

Angsley tilted his head in puzzlement, then looked at Fentor, who shrugged.

As Sidarí led through the crowd of elves, Fentor understood. The elves who had recently risked their lives looked drawn, haggard, almost entirely spent. Many of them had collapsed in heaps from their exhaustion. Despite that, they stood and gathered around Fentor and each of his friends, and touched their arms, shoulders, and backs. With each hand that contacted him, Fentor felt a spark of vigor rush into him. Soon, he felt refreshed, strong, capable of anything. The elves smiled faintly.

Fentor wanted to thank them, profusely and deeply, but the words caught in his throat. Instead, he simply smiled back.

Sidarí's way through the Elarím woods seemed as tangled as a discarded fishing net. More than once, Fentor could have sworn they had gone in circles or doubled back. Half of the journey seemed to be spent getting to tunnels, rope bridges, ladders, and hidden slopes which they slid down like seals. Each of these short-cuts bypassed some obstacle that would have taken hours to bypass. The seemingly homogeneous, wild, tangled forest transformed before Fentor's eyes. The density of the forest was not an impediment, but the source of their speed.

Old Bluefinger tales of the elves popping out of the trees without warning suddenly made sense. They probably *had* popped out of the trees.

Hours passed as they ran. Thankfully, Fentor's mind was so occupied with navigation, there was room for little else. There was little space to think of all the innocent lives at stake, the danger Hess, Crauford, Angsley and Sidarí were in. There was little space to think about everything Elatea would be capable of with even greater doses of the Elixir of Power.

So he ran, jumped, climbed, and slid along the hidden path. With great concentration, he managed not to think *too* much about the things he was thinking about.

The sun began to rise in a windless, cloudy sky.

They came to the edge of a wide, sloped clearing. It was like a great dimple in the earth, a neat depression of dirt and dust. They stood at the edge and looked out across the vast, empty space. Fentor was simply glad to have the chance of seeing clearly where he was going. Then some clouds shifted, and the dawn illuminated the clearing.

The clearing was, in fact, a perfectly circular crater, like the impression of a giant bowl pressed on flour. At the lowest point in the center stood a lone figure, a pale statue in a long, grey coat.

"This is one of the places devastated by the Lady's Great Bombard," Sidarí said softly.

"It looks … different from this side of the trenches," Fentor said.

"Many things do."

"That's her, smack in the middle of it. What's she doing?" Angsley asked.

"Let's not find out. We can go around the edges," Hess whispered.

They crept among the trees in a wide circuit around the crater. They passed a quarter of the way around, then continued toward the southern end. Elatea did not move even slightly the entire time.

"What is she doing? If we're in range of the Great Bombard, we must not be far from the Gutter Trench," Angsley said.

"Look!" Sidarí pointed at the opposite edge of the crater.

All along the lip of the depression, red points of light were emerging from the trees.

"They're out of range in the trees …" Sidarí muttered. "They are exposing themselves just to hit her."

Rank after rank of Elarím marched out from the trees and down into the crater. Arrows streamed across the pale dawn sky and fell upon the Lady, but she seemed unaffected. There were three rows of elves, then four, coming mostly from the north. They fanned out across the crater until they had nearly encircled their quarry.

"So many have come … elves from both sides of the divide," Sidarí breathed. "Is this our moment of unity?"

"What does it mean?" Angsley said.

"I … am not sure. They might fight Elatea one moment and turn on each other the next," she said. "Whatever the case, we cannot stay and watch."

"No," a rough voice said from behind them. "No, you cannot."

They turned, swords ready. Mannoc stood before them. His expression was severe, fervent. He was flanked by a dozen elves, who drew a dozen glowing arrows.

"Mannoc," Sidarí said. "It does not have to be this way."

"I know. Otherwise, we would have killed you in silence."

"What do you want?" Fentor said.

"What *I* want is of no—"

A flash of light dazzled them, and the ground beneath their feet trembled violently. Fentor clutched Hess by instinct. A moment later, an immense roar filled the hollow sky, and a bright star ascended overhead.

"They've launched the Bombard," Fentor said. "Sweet Temlin spare us—it's headed this way."

Mannoc and his companions lowered their weapons, and pushed past the stunned humans.

"Quickly, into the crater!" Mannoc barked. He waved urgently for the others to follow.

"So now you want to save us?" Sidarí shouted to be heard over the Bombard.

"If the humans fight Elatea with us, the Coríthe will name them allies. It is their only hope, *and* yours, Sidarí," Mannoc shouted. "Come, before the cannonball falls on your heads."

"No! Don't you understand? Only she can order that weapon to fire," Fentor bellowed, pointing at the meteoric projectile above them. "She wants it to fall right on *her* head! We've got to get *away*!"

"How can you know that?" Sidarí asked.

"I'm sure of it. Trust me."

Mannoc scoffed. "Why would she risk her own life? The safest place to stand is right beside her. Come!"

Mannoc and his companions fled down the slope, firing arrows at Elatea as they ran.

Fentor looked at each of his friends. They nodded, and hurried deeper into the woods. The Great Bombard's cannonball wailed, so loud it sounded like it was already upon them.

"Sidarí, is there anywhere we can shelter?" Fentor asked.

"This way," Sidarí said.

They followed her, dodging left and right between the trees. Every few steps, Fentor checked to see that nobody had fallen behind. The screaming grew louder and louder.

She led them to a steep bank, at the bottom of which was a river of brambles with long, deadly thorns.

"Slide down with straight legs and your arms at your sides. It is best to close your eyes," Sidarí said.

"We'll be impaled!" Angsley yelled.

Sidarí laughed softly, then said, "Impaled? You worry about being impaled? Even if we *do* make it to the bottom, the bomb will probably still kill us."

Sidarí slid down the hillside, along what Fentor realized was a narrow chute cut into the dirt. The moment she disappeared below the brambles, Fentor laughed as well. He launched himself down the hill the way she had gone, followed closely by Hess, Angsley and Crauford. Not wanting his final moment to entail getting thorns in his eyes, he shut them tightly.

At the bottom, they all tumbled in a heap in a cleared spot under a bramble ceiling. Somehow, they were all unscathed.

The earth trembled at the meteor's roaring descent.

They huddled together in their meagre shelter and waited for the end.

Chapter 38

Slee hazily remembered a great plume of fire leaping up. The inferno burned bright red, blotted out the world, then vanished. She remembered that the world had roared from deep in its lungs. The ground tremored with such force that she lost her feet. It rattled her teeth, her skull, her organs. She was sure her bones had been shaken loose from their joints.

Then came a long, hollow, ringing quiet.

She lay on her back and stared up at the red sky.

Often, the mortally wounded would feel no pain. Slee felt nothing at all. She was not even sure if she was breathing. All she could do was lay there and look at the bright red sky.

Clouds of thick black smoke drifted by. They looked low to the ground, close to where Slee lay, but they never quite reached her. It seemed as though some curved surface deflected them up and away.

A trickle of soot and powder and pieces of metal rained down. They, too, met some round barrier and slid down it. Strange. It was like she was under an upturned glass bowl.

"Slee." Her name, spoken by a muffled voice.

She blinked, then took a deep breath, then coughed, and weakly clutched her side. Breathing hurt.

"Slee."

She was lifted up and carried.

A large scaly head passed over her, or perhaps she passed under it. The head sniffed her ponderously, ruffling her hair. Then there was only red sky. There was a flutter of wings, and a weight on her chest. Something with an inquisitive bill nibbled on her chin. The wings fluttered again and the weight lifted.

Her carrier set her down on a soft surface. A number of faces—familiar but nameless faces—leaned over her.

"Slee."

Two men leaned closest to her and held her hands. One was fair, and had a thick beard. The other had olive skin and a dark moustache. Both were familiar.

"Slee, are you hurt?" one of the men asked her.

She mumbled something softly.

"Where?"

She lifted a trembling hand and pointed to the left side of her ribcage.

Over their heads, soot and debris continued to drizzle upon the strange, curved barrier. Slee frowned. The strange rainfall meant something. The smoke and the red sky and the pain in her side meant something, too. She remembered again: the massive ball of fire.

The distillery. Dídac. Her friends.

She tried to sit up, but people pushed her down.

"I'm fine," she said, trying to push herself up again. "I'm fine. Help me up."

"Alright. Carefully!"

The others helped her to sit up, and continued to support her back. Then, she saw the full aftermath for the first time.

They were on an island of white gravel in the middle of a large, charred, smoking crater. The distillery, Dídac, and the Greycoats were nowhere to be seen. The island sat underneath a glowing red aegis, a perfect sphere untouched by the explosion. Slee opened her numb fingers. The crystal shard of Crann Arborím was still there. Bloody half-circles had been cut into her palm by her fingernails. It was as though, by holding on so tightly, she had performed the miracle.

That was not true, though. For one thing, the aegis had taken the combined efforts of every being present. For another, it was no miracle.

Many of their friends had died.

Gretka and six of her peaducks had survived. The rest lay motionless on the ground. Gretka paced among the dead ones, preening their feathers. Slowjaw gently touched his nose to each of them in turn, moaning softly at the pain in his heart.

Tybalt and twenty other Bluefingers had perished. The ashen-faced survivors carried the dead together and lay them in neat rows, then covered them with their jackets.

Slee reached out to those nearest to her. Horvald, Cartín, Charlotte, Aizman—they all looked hurt and exhausted, but they had survived.

"I'm sorry," she said, without knowing why. "I'm sorry. I should have – I didn't mean for things to – I'm sorry!"

"Sorry? Why in the world are you sorry?" Cartín said. He put a firm, comforting hand on her shoulder.

"All this. All of this—look at it! Look what I've done! I'm sorry. It's all my – I'm the one that …"

"Slee. Slee! Look at me." Horvald crouched down in front of her. He and Cartín wiped her cheeks, which had somehow become wet with tears.

With great effort, as though lifting a boulder, she raised her head and met Horvald's eyes.

"You saved us. You have nothing to be sorry for," Horvald said.

Slee heard him, understood his words, but she could only repeat, "I'm sorry. I'm sorry."

"There's nothing to forgive, but here—if it will help, I forgive you," Horvald said.

"We all forgive you, Slee," Cartín said.

Charlotte sat down at Slee's side. She didn't say a word, but rubbed Slee's back with a regular, gentle motion.

"I'm – I'm sorry," Slee said.

"I know. You can be sorry if you want to. Feel whatever way you have to. We'll be here," Horvald said.

"You're still holding that gem, but somehow you're not part of the telethían," Cartín said gently. "Would it help if you tried to re-join us?"

"I don't know," Slee said. She gasped for breath. Grey spots filled her vision. "I don't know."

"That's fine. We'll be here."

Slowjaw, Gretka, and the peaducks approached. Aizman, Horvald, and Cartín moved to clear the way. Charlotte stayed by Slee's side, still rubbing her back.

Slowjaw stepped gently and carefully to Slee's side, then tucked his legs into his shell and sank down onto the gravel. He leaned his large head against her. She was grateful for the contact. Gretka settled into her lap, and the other peaducks nestled by her knees.

All the surviving Bluefingers came to stand in front of her. They looked at her as though expecting something. Some faces had tear-tracks on their dusty cheeks. Others looked flat, despondent. Slee guessed that they were waiting for her to speak.

"I'm sorry for everything that has happened," she said. "I came here for my own reasons. You did not ask me to come. Now, the distillery has been destroyed, but many lives were lost doing it. My life was spared because of others. If I had not come, everyone who died would still be alive. You must hate me. I was *selfish*. I got you all to fight for my own cause, without considering yours. I'm sorry. I regret everything I have done to you all."

"Slee, you are quite mistaken to think that we hate you," Cartín said. "It is the opposite."

"You need to re-join the Common Power, or the telethí, or the web, whatever you'd call it," Horvald said, attempting a jovial smile. "Besides, wasn't it you that said that self-persecution is just self-indulgence?"

A thin, feathery strand of light drifted past Slee's eyes. She traced the telethí back to Slowjaw, who watched her with slowly blinking amber eyes.

Slee found the part deep inside her that had become coiled up and knotted. She stroked Slowjaw's nose and took a deep breath. As she released it, she also released the tangled threads. She opened her heart to the others and began to forgive herself. A slender filament, like a young spider's web drifting in the moonlight, rose out from her heart and took hold of Slowjaw's telethí.

Dazzlingly bright silver threads bloomed all at once, criss-crossing the area under the red dome. Slee covered her face with both hands, overwhelmed. Tears of relief leaked through her fingers, but she did not care. Though she could not see them, she sensed through the telethí that all the others had begun to weep as well.

A warm, golden, almost indescribable aura embraced her. It was like a summer sunset with dragonflies darting through the air, and supper in the pot. It was the glow of Mama's presence, the affection in Papa's voice. It was like the adoration and cheers of an audience of thousands, something she had only ever read about. It was a long, lazy day spent with a true friend, where nothing but quiet is needed to acknowledge the love.

The Bluefingers told her how they felt, and she cried until her eyes ran dry.

I am alive because of you. Thank you, Slee.

We had no chance until you came along. You gave us everything.

I will never look at elves the same way, make no mistake. You're a Saint and nothing less.

Bless you, Slee. Bless you.

It was hopeless under Dídac. I even thought of ending it all. You saved me twice over. How can I ever show enough gratitude for that?

We were all desperate to put a stop to that wretched place, but too scared to stand up to Dídac. You were the first to stand up. You gave us the courage. You showed us the way.

After a long time, Slee caught her breath and wiped her face dry. She looked out at the others and saw their faces shining with admiration.

How could it be? How could humans find telethymia so hard, and yet so easy?

Mama had been right. Humans and elves were not so different. One society develops one way, another develops differently. Madeans and the Elarím diverged starkly, but not irreversibly. *Oe telethí aínar oen telethían.* She understood it now. She understood it properly, the way Mama and Papa always had. She could not translate it into the Madean language yet, and perhaps nobody ever would. Some understanding goes beyond words.

Seeing is understanding, Mama had said. *Words can teach you what to look for, but they cannot open your eyes. Experience can reveal the truth, but some go through life looking the other way. Only those who live with open eyes understand.*

Horvald and Cartín helped Slee and Charlotte stand up. Together, they slowly paced along the rows of dead Bluefingers. Slee looked at each of their faces, slowly cementing them in her memory. She lingered the longest by Tybalt, wishing she'd had time to know him better.

At the end of the row of fallen humans, someone had neatly laid out all the dead peaducks. Their russet feathers had been smoothed, and their eyes closed. Slee knelt and placed a hand on each of them. Her breath kept catching in her chest. They had fought bravely, despite fighting enemies so much larger than them. Just like Felheim, they had earned their rest. With her friends nearby, and her heart enmeshed in telethí, the grief was a little more bearable. Slee felt worse for Gretka, who had lost her mate and many of her children.

Slee smiled, remembering the time the tiny peaducklings had followed Felheim and Gretka to a pond in a neat line. There they learned to swim, to dive, to venture out into the unknown, to seek shelter with their parents when frightened.

Gretka waddled around her motionless children, quacking softly, nibbling their feathers. Her aura was mixed, a swirl of golden pride and wine-dark grief.

"It is time we think of burying them," Aizman said.

"Right you are," Horvald said, stroking his beard. "I, for one, hardly feel ready … but we can't stay here."

"Where?" Cartín asked.

"Far from this smoking pit," Slee said. "How about the shade of the trees on the far side of Bianlock?"

The others nodded.

"We'll have a devilishly tricky time climbing out of this debris-ridden hole," Cartín said, looking around.

The explosion had gouged such a crater that the waters of Bianlock were starting to trickle in. Soon, the ground they stood on would truly be an island.

"Young Batha… we'll have to mark an empty grave for him. His body was …" Aizman said, trailing off as he pointed at the area the gallows had been.

"Do you suppose Dídac's body is down there somewhere?" Horvald said.

"If it is, we're unlikely to find it," Slee said.

"I have another, less pleasant question …" Horvald said, with a slight grimace. "Could Dídac have survived?"

They all exchanged dark looks.

"He must have died. But it doesn't matter, does it?" Charlotte said. "This world is filled with seats like the one Dídac sat in. Even with him gone, there'll just be some other crook waiting to take his place. There's always another Dídac."

"That's an awfully gloomy thought," Cartín said.

"Is it?"

"I don't think it is," Slee said. "It makes the solution clear. Get rid of the seat."

Horvald laughed darkly. "Is it clear? Maybe. Is it possible? No. Seats like that go all the way up to the throne."

"I'm not suggesting we actually do it," Slee said. "I was just stating the fact. That is the solution."

"We might have to move quickly. This crater is about to become a second lake," Cartín said.

"How are we going to get everyone out?" Aizman said. "The gravel is too loose for us to climb, especially loaded down with bodies."

"Slowjaw?" Slee said.

He bugled softly.

"Would you help us dig our way out?"

The tortoise gave a deep chirp of assent. He trundled to the edge of their strange island, and began to dig a downward slope. The others gathered around to watch the massive beast shift the gravel.

"He is a remarkable creature," Aizman said. "Few of his kind remain in the world."

"He may be the last on this entire continent," Slee said.

Aizman nodded pensively.

When Slowjaw had raked the gravel into a slope wide enough, Slee and the Bluefingers started forward to help him dig. Weary, hurt, drained, and grieving, they dug a way down into the crater, then dug a way up and out. Once they were outside the aegis, it vanished. They carried the dead away together with dusty hands. Slowjaw walked sombrely with some of them draped carefully on top of his shell. Slee helped Aizman carry Tybalt.

The grim procession trudged around the shores of Bianlock until, at last, they came to the other side. Under the shade of the pines, whose creaks and groans sounded like the yawns of old men, they dug the graves. Some, like Batha, had left no bodies to bury. They dug those graves, covered them, and marked them all the same.

With their fingernails chipped and raw from clawing through the gravel, they collapsed, exhausted, leaning on each other. Soon, Slowjaw began to snore.

Nobody spoke, because there was nothing left to say. They sat together and watched a flock of blue starlings wheel over the sparkling lake.

Chapter 39

They had gone deeper into the pines north of Bianlock to find a secluded resting place. Once they had found a high hill with a horseshoe-shaped hollow on top, they quickly fell asleep on beds of pine needles. Slee kept dreaming of the heavy dungeon door creaking open, and Dídac staring at her from the threshold. Each time she woke up in terror, but then she smelled the pine needles, felt Gretka's feathers and Slowjaw's leathery cheek. All her unease melted as stroked their chins. She had never felt so safe.

Just before dawn, she spotted a shooting star. It skated just above the horizon, hung suspended for a moment, then fell out of sight. A moment later came a faint rumble of thunder.

The others woke as the dawn slowly ripened.

Everyone was hungry. The gleaming mesh of telethí had grown faint, but remained stable. Slee wondered how much longer it would last. Their hunger united them, perhaps. The telethían calmed their stomachs, so they seemingly clung to the soothing strands without realizing.

Together, they had done the impossible. They had defied the wisdom of every Saint and every Sage, refuted every word written about the vast gulf between human and elven natures. Even if everyone in the world agreed on a fact, that didn't make it so. Telethymia could, in dire need, be just as powerful in human hands. Slee puzzled over it, until she was left with a dizzy head full of questions. The geode, the telethí, humans, elves, the Elarím, Crann Arborím … no answers came to her. More urgent problems soon took their place. Growing hunger pains, for instance.

"Would your peaducks happen to be magically prolific egg layers, by any chance?" Horvald said, sitting stiffly beside her. "Prolific enough to feed everyone here?"

Slee looked around at the hundreds of Bluefingers and smiled. "They are good, but not quite talented enough for this."

"Drat. I suppose we'll have to go looking for our breakfast, then."

"It looks that way."

"Let's see, then. We have no guns for hunting, no lines for fishing, and besides, Bianlock has been poisoned," Horvald said airily. Then he leaned close and said softly, "Many of these people have eaten nothing but rations their entire adult lives. They're getting a little worried about finding enough food out here."

"They shouldn't worry. There's food everywhere," Slee said. "They just need to learn how to look."

They foraged in the surrounding forest with Slee's guidance. What looked to the humans like barren slopes of pines was a larder in Slee's eyes. True, it was sparsely stocked, and much of the food was tasteless or unripe. Still, there was enough.

Slee showed them how to tell the good mushrooms from the bad, how to gather wild grains, how to spot the pines that dropped edible nuts. She showed them how to find wild solan tubers, tanberries, leafy herbs, and onion shoots. They could have learned much quicker if they passed the knowledge around telethymically, but they shied away from the intimacy of speaking mind-to-mind. They preferred to talk and listen out loud, to learn with their eyes and hands.

As they gathered, Slee thought about the plants and the way they grew. Some preferred shade, others full sun. Some grew in standing water, others on dry soil. Each plant craved its own particular home, and withered in the wrong conditions. Yet all of them, from the tallest pines to the smallest clovers, were bound by telethí to their neighbors. The telethí was strongest where the plants were healthy. Madea City and Rodessia and Norimand and all the other human places were one kind of soil, and the lands of the Elarím were another. Maybe it wasn't the humans who were incompatible with telethymia. Maybe it was the places they lived. The soil of their societies.

Slee turned the ruby shard over in her hand, pondering.

At last, they had gathered enough food. They hiked back up to the high dell where they had slept, and Slee taught them to roast, smoke, grind, and crack open their bounty. The mushrooms were plain and chewy, even when roasted. The tanberries were tart and small, since it was not their season. The wild grain, pounded into a meal paste between rocks, served as little more than something to chew on and fill the space in one's stomach. Still, Slee ate every morsel with deep satisfaction. It had been too long since her last meal under the sky.

Slowjaw, fortunately, ate leafy, woody, mossy, and slimy material that nobody else could eat, and that was plentiful. With his stomach almost bursting, he nestled down, blinking slowly and purring deep in his throat.

Cartín and Horvald had eaten in silence next to Slee. Now that they had finished, Horvald leaned against Cartín's chest, humming contentedly as Cartín stroked the edges of his beard. Charlotte shot disconcerted glances at the men, then excused herself and went to sit elsewhere. Slee watched her bizarre behavior. Did Madean women not like to see beards being touched? Or had the sight of affection reminded her of a faraway loved one?

"Don't mind Charlotte," Cartín said, watching Slee's consternated expression.

"She is just being a—" Horvald began.

"A bit *devout*." Cartín met Horvald's eyes sternly. "She prays daily to all the Saints that will listen."

"So, she's having a … *religious* problem?" Slee asked, having to pause to find the correct Madean word.

"You could say that."

"Well, I'm not moving," Horvald said, closing his eyes sleepily. "We've been apart too long as it is."

"Don't worry, Horv. I wasn't going to make you move."

They sat in silence for a while. Slee made neat little piles of pine needles, enjoying her freedom to touch them. Charlotte's religious problem made no sense. She had read her Papa's entire collection of the writings of Saints Temlin, Chandon, Tagustine, and Candade. She couldn't recall any passages relevant to Cartín or Horvald, so she let the question go.

"We're going to miss you, Slee," Cartín said.

"What do you mean?"

"Well, it will be hard for us to drop in for tea once you've grown a new invisible hedge," Cartín said with a faint smile.

"Oh." Slee placed pine needles in straight lines for a while, and didn't look up. She hadn't thought about where she would go to live. There hadn't been time.

"She could always plant something eye-catching right outside the garden. Then we'd know where to look for her," Horvald said.

"Where will you go?" Slee said.

"Cross the border into Norimand? Stow away on a ship to the Isle of Thamber? Dig a series of tunnels and live like moles?" Horvald said, turning to Cartín. "What do you think?"

"I don't like moles," Cartín said.

"And I get awfully sea-sick," Horvald said. "I suppose that just leaves Norimand, at least in the short-term."

"Why so far?" Slee asked.

"We're outlaws. We have no other choice."

"That's not true."

"What do you mean?" Cartín asked.

"Live with me." She had spoken without a thought. Once she had said it aloud, it felt right.

They stared at her.

Horvald sat up straight, eyebrows raised. "Do you really mean it?"

"Of course. Why would I say something I don't mean?"

"Well, we thought you'd be desperate to go back to living alone," Horvald said. "Believe me, if my first experience with humans was getting thrown in Elatea's dungeon, I'd feel the same."

"We couldn't burden you like that," Cartín said.

"I won't let you be a burden. You'll have do your share," Slee said. "The same goes for anyone else we take in."

"Anyone else?" Horvald said. "We were packed in like sardines in your last cottage. How big are you planning on making the next one?"

"As big as we need." Slee brushed aside the pine needles she had been fiddling with and stood up. "Everyone!"

The Bluefingers gathered around her quickly, looking at her with wide eyes. Some had been eating or dozing, but these things were abandoned the moment Slee had spoken. The quick response to her call brought to mind a thoroughly Madean word, *obedience*. Somehow, though, that word didn't seem to fit the breathless gaze of the crowd. A faint, splotchy aura of purple, black, and gold hung around them like steam. Their mood was unreadable.

Slee shuffled her bare feet on the dry pine needles. She had never realized how uncomfortable it could be to be the focus of a large crowd. "We have done a great thing. We all know that. But you come from Madea, where the laws of nature have been overwritten by the laws of property. In Madea's eyes, we are criminals. We cannot go home.

"Many of you have families, children. With the telethí binding us, I can feel some of your anguish. You are torn between despair and the desire to flee. Seeing your loved ones again seems impossible. But we just made the impossible real. I say that if humans can wield telethymia, and survive against all the might Dídac amassed against us, then we can surely find a way back into the homes taken from us.

"Our task now is not to fight or flee, but to build. Each of you may choose as you will, of course. But for all who are willing, I offer you the chance to make a new home. If we work together, we can grow enough to feed ourselves, and hide away from anyone that means us harm. You have taught me so much about the courage and solidarity of the human spirit. Let me teach you how we can use those qualities to forge something new. A different way to live. A way that nobody had ever thought possible … not even me."

Slee swallowed, her throat as dry as the pine needles beneath her toes. She looked out at the crowd, who watched her in silence. Faint strands of telethí wafted among them. No clear aura emerged. One man scratched his ear.

Slee could not tell what anyone was feeling. She reasoned that, most likely, even *they* were not sure what they felt.

"Take all the time you need. My offer will remain open," Slee said.

Exhausted, she sat beside Horvald and Cartín. They reached out and touched her shoulder, smiling. Quiet conversations sprouted here and there on the hilltop. In response to the privacy, the telethí dimmed. Slee saw their faces cast in every mood, from quiet sorrow, to disbelief, to contentment. Some even looked queasy. Each of them felt differently, and through this difference, they were united.

A passage Slee had read long ago came to mind. Humans, it seemed, mistranslated and therefore misunderstood the concept of *muanan*. They took it for its literal meaning, 'same emotion.' They spoke of elves as though they were forced to feel the same emotion at all times, yoked to one unified, oppressive thought. With muanan, the opposite was true. Living things share thought and emotion *because* they are alive. All life drinks water, breathes the air, feels hunger, falls ill. The force of muanan comes out of this commonality. Forcing things to live against this nature is the essence of *Uthuín*. Control something, and it breaks. Own something, and it withers.

Oe telethí aínar oen telethían.

She turned the ruby of Crann Arborím over in her hands sleepily. Slowjaw dozed beside her, and Gretka blinked slowly on her lap.

What was it that made the red gem work? What had really been lost when Dídac had crushed the geode?

No scholar, elf or otherwise, knew how Crann Arborím had been made. The geode was gone forever, and Mama and Papa had never taught her how to make another one.

609

All her books were gone. If the secret had been hidden away in them, she would never find it.

She placed the gem on the ground. All the telethí that had been drifting through the air around her vanished. Despite that, everything felt the same. The scattered glimmers of the Bluefingers' auras still had a kind of tingling pressure on Slee's skin. Too tired to sleep, Slee watched the humans with her eyes half-closed. In moments where she stopped trying to hard to see them, traces of telethí could be seen. In moments where she believed without waiting for proof, her connections to the others felt more solid.

Gentle conversations rose and fell all around her, lapping like waves on sand. Slee could not hear a word, but she sensed that many would agree to stay with her. The Bluefingers helped each other, tended each other's wounds, and consoled those who grieved.

Slee smiled.

Perhaps she understood humans after all.

Chapter 40

The carriage Fentor had the misfortune of riding in seemed to be trundling through lands consisting entirely of cow dung. The wheels squelched thickly and the driver croaked farmer's songs, neither of which were kind to Fentor's pounding head. The seats were awfully scratchy, too.

"Fenny?"

Vowing once more to never drink again, he tried to sit upright. When he did, something incredibly sharp bit into his shoulder and collarbone.

"What in blazes…?" he groaned, squinting through harsh light to see what manner of snake was biting him.

"Easy, there."

Hess and Angsley gently helped him sit up. The feeling of a snake's fangs on his shoulder turned out to be his own broken bones. His arm—his good fencing arm—was bandaged up in a sling. He had been wrong about three other things and, unfortunately, correct about a fourth.

First, he was not in a carriage, but an open wagon. Hess, Angsley, Crauford, and Sidarí rode in it as well. Second, he had not been drinking; he'd been hurt. His head was wrapped in gauze, as was Hess'. Third, the seats weren't scratchy, because there *were* no seats. There were bales of greenish, smelly hay. Looking around, he found that his fourth, correct presumption was that the land *did,* in fact, consist almost entirely of cow dung.

Pawing through his hazy memories of the explosion like a drunk searching a sock drawer in the dark, he frowned at the others and cobbled together a question.

"How did we get from there to here?" he asked.

They passed by a fat cow, which lifted its tail and added its own contribution to the already pungent landscape.

"You were right. The cannonball fell right on the Lady's head," Sidarí said. "The explosion was larger than any others had been. I suspect that she somehow contributed to its intensity. The shockwave caused a landslide and we were partially buried."

"Those brambles hurt, but they saved us," Angsley said. His face, neck, and arms were covered in deep scratches.

"Tem here pulled us out." Hess nodded at the hunched man driving the wagon.

"Tem?" Fentor repeated.

The driver ceased his croaky singing and turned. His face was smooth and youthful, and yet he had the curved spine and profoundly rounded shoulders of a much older man. He wore a lumpy brown hat, which kept his sharp, angular features in shadow.

"Short for Temlin, my Lord. No relation, of course!" Tem laughed coarsely. "Call me Tem, it suits me fine."

"How do you do, Tem?" Fentor glanced at his bandaged arm. "I would offer to shake your hand, but ..."

Tem laughed again, then turned back to the road.

Fentor shifted around on the hay, searching in vain for a more comfortable spot. His foot struck something hard, and he looked down.

Under a thin covering of hay, there were rifles, brass bows, belts, boots, tricornes, and sabre-spears. Most likely, there would be more under the bales they sat on.

"Say, Tem, what manner of work are you employed in?" he asked.

"I'm just an honest farmer, my Lord. As honest as anyone else that needs to earn a living out here." Tem laughed again, sounding like a raven with a head cold.

"Is that right?" Fentor said. He looked at the others with a raised eyebrow, but they only shrugged.

"Sometimes I go looking for treasure, it's true. Only the kind of treasure what won't be missed, if you catch my meaning."

"I fear I do."

"I'm sure none of you good folk will tell anyone about my little treasures and trinkets. It would only hurt me and my poor, hungry family. The king doesn't know it, but he depends on treasure-finders like me. Do you know why?"

"No, Tem, I don't. Why?" Fentor asked.

Hess pulled Fentor close by his good arm, and hissed in his ear. "He already explained it to us as we woke up. He's said all this, word-for-word, three times already!"

Tem ploughed on, as it were, unaware of his restless audience. "Well, the king's good soldiers lose their things in battle, and the elves do too. They can't always send people to recover the dead, or the things the dead carry. Well, the crows get the dead and I get the rest, if you catch my meaning. I sell my findings on to a man I know, a good man, but shady. He sells it to another man with modest fees added, and that man can smuggle the gear into Rodessia. The smuggler knows a blacksmith in the city, so he sells the treasures to him, adding a little fee of his own for the danger of smuggling. The blacksmith bangs his hammer, makes them all good as new, and sells them back to the Madean Land Corps as if they were brand new. I hear Duke Whelleker of Rodessia knows, but looks the other way. It's this flow of treasures from me to him that keeps our Bluefingers armed, after all!"

"How fascinating," Fentor lied in monotone.

"Me and the crows have the same purpose, see? The same job the vulture has. Unpleasant, but much-needed. Without us, these hills would be covered in bones and buttons and belts, wouldn't they?"

"I suppose that's true."

They passed along a road between furrowed squares of land stippled with little green stalks. Half-collapsed wooden fences kept most of the vacant-eyed cows and goats confined to their respective pastures. Here and there, little cottages with neat, colorful gardens nestled cozily in the hills, with cotton-ball smoke rising from their chimneys. After everything Fentor had endured, even those humble dwellings started to look inviting.

Angsley suffered an attack of nigh-continuous yawns. Hess dozed with her chin in her hands. Crauford sat neatly with his hands in his lap, clicking his fingernails in quiet agitation. Only Sidarí seemed interested in their

surroundings. As Fentor's head cleared, he realized that
Tem had brought an elf into Madean territory. He made a
wordless exclamation, pointing at her. The others glared
at him for the sudden noise.

"She can't be here!" Fentor hissed.

"Fenny, calm down."

"What if soldiers come past? They'll shoot her on sight!"
Fentor looked at the others' faces, searching for alarm that
would match his own. Even Sidarí seemed unfazed.

"Worry not, my Lord. I live with good folk who live by
Temlin's wisdom. That's Saint Temlin, mind you, not
Farmer Tem!" He laughed boisterously. "He passed
through these lands all those years ago during his exile,
spoke to the farmers like they were equals. They heard his
prophecy from his own lips, you know. 'One day,
Providence will grace us with a Saint unlike any other. By
their hand alone, the war between man and elf will end,
and it will end forever.' Do you know what I thought
when I saw you all crushed together by that landslide?"

"No, Tem, what did you think?"

"I thought, 'Now, look here! My, my, an elf and four
humans sheltering together. Temlin's foretold Saint can't
be far off!' Anybody else might have passed that spot by,
but I've long had an instinct of knowing where to dig.
Lucky for you, eh?"

"Now hold on, how exactly did you arrive on that
particular thought?" Fentor shuffled past the others to sit
on a block of hay closer to Tem. Up close, the hunched
farmer had a strangely familiar air about him, as though
Fentor might have met his brother somewhere.

"What do you mean?"

"You saw an elf and four humans, and that suddenly brought to mind Temlin's prophecy. Why?"

"Well, my kin didn't just hear the prophecy. Temlin *explained* it to them. He was a great man. Truly the best of the Saints. There's a reason they named me after him, you know. Would you believe they were almost going to name me 'Jonathon?' "

"Yes, yes, that's all riveting, but what did Temlin *actually* explain to you?"

"Why, the Saint will end the war by *uniting* with the elves, not defeating them. That's the only way to have lasting peace, you see?"

"Unite humans and elves? Baldershite," Fentor said.

Tem laughed long and loud. "Most would say the same, and I don't blame you. Folks see it different where I live. After all, there was once a human and an elf that *united*, if you catch my meaning. If they hadn't, I wouldn't be here to tell you about it."

The farmer removed the lumpy, wide-brimmed hat. Under it was a short, velvet crop of silver-blond hair. His sharp, straight jaw, nose, and brow stood out now that they were exposed. Recoiling by instinct, Fentor saw that Tem's ears were topped with ugly, milk-white scars. They seemed to have been crudely cut to appear rounded, more human. He replaced his hat and covered them once more.

"Well," Fentor said, momentarily quite lost for words. Then, he remembered the strange woman at the distillery. "I've met a half-elf before, you know."

"You have?" Tem asked. "And it never occurred to you that elves and humans could get along?"

After what felt like an eternity, evening fell, and Tem pulled the wagon to a stop outside his home. A litter of children spilled from the front door and clung to Tem's legs like limpets. They varied in age, hair color, and—Fentor looked closely—the roundness of their ears. Some looked positively Madean, while others could have been Sidarí's children.

Tem waved for his passengers to come inside. It was a sturdy home of weathered timber, with extra rooms packed together along on its side, as though the house was nursing a litter of little houses. A bright rectangle from the fire inside stretched out from the doorway, like a golden path inviting them forward. The enchanting smell of cooking pulled Fentor inside, eclipsing everything else. Even the grubby children pulling on his hands and clothes didn't bother him.

A short, black-haired woman greeted Tem with a kiss, and offered the guests seats at the long table that dominated the main room. Neither the children nor Tem's wife gave Sidarí, Crauford, Angsley, Hess, or Fentor a second look. It was as though they frequently entertained wounded soldiers from both sides of the war.

Fentor thought that if the situation was reversed, and a troupe of hungry, injured farmers had showed up at his door …

Before he could imagine the end of that scenario, food was placed before him. He devoured it, enthralled.

They ate beef tongue, roasted chicken necks, pigbone soup, toasted turnips, mashed solan pulp, tanberry pie, and drank a mild dandelion cordial. Nothing had ever delighted Fentor's senses quite as much.

Afterward, somehow, Fentor found himself helping Tem wash the dishes in a tub full of rainwater. Then, he protested Tem's offer of a bed, but he was worn down until he accepted. Their hosts wished them good-night and went to sleep in the barn. Fentor, Sidarí, Angsley, Hess, and Crauford lay inside, warm and comfortable, in beds far too small for them.

A moment later, seemingly, it was dawn. The others still slept nearby, except for Hess, whose bed was empty. Fentor got out of bed, still fully clothed except for his boots, and padded around the house in search of her. She was nowhere to be seen.

He pulled on his boots awkwardly with his good hand and crept outside.

Hess stood on a little rise close by, looking out at the rising sun.

Fentor, strangely, became giddy at the chance to be alone with her. He approached, suddenly very concerned that each step should appear sufficiently casual and naturalistic. Apparently, he had forgotten how to walk, and his knees, hips, and feet all needed explicit instructions to cooperate. Hess turned and watched him.

She wore a hand-knitted blanket around her shoulders like a cloak. Her hair was tangled and her throat hoarse from sleep. She looked magnificent.

"What's wrong? Are you hurt?" Hess said.

"Pardon?"

"Your legs. Looks like you're limping."

"Just a bit stiff. Must have been the wagon ride," Fentor lied. What else could he say? *The sight of you made my legs go wobbly?*

Hess smiled and Fentor's insides turned to buttercream. "I know the feeling. I had to come out and stretch my legs."

"This Tem fellow … odd chap, isn't he?"

"Just odd enough to offer supper and beds to oddities like us," Hess said.

Fentor laughed softly. The icy dawn air stung his nose and the tips of his fingers. He wedged his uninjured hand under his armpit, shivering.

"Cold?" Hess asked. She raised one arm, offering the blanket to him like a dove opening its wing. "Here."

The gesture seemed loaded with meaning that Fentor couldn't articulate. He barely thought about it, or envisioned what consequences may come, or imagined what course their future might take. He only felt himself drawn toward her, as if by some unseen force. There under the warmth of her blanket, pressed against her side, he felt at once that it was where he belonged.

If Saint Chandon was to be believed, a force called gravity kept one's feet anchored to the ground.

Fentor looked into Hess' speckled green eyes and felt himself overcome by a far greater force. It pulled him toward her, and her toward him, until they met at the middle. Their cold, dry lips touched, gentle as butterfly wings. They pulled apart a little, stunned perhaps, but then the strange cosmic power drew them back together.

They kissed in earnest. In spite of their aching injuries, and their dandelion-cordial-laden breath, Fentor never wanted it to end. At last, though, they came up for air. Partially due to necessity — the freezing dawn air had stuffed Fentor's nostrils up.

She looked at him with her hand on his cheek, radiating warmth and affection. She looked at him as though he was a fantastic prize she had won. In short, she looked at him in a way that he thoroughly did not deserve.

She looked at him like he was actually worthy of her.

"Hess …" he said. "I haven't been … I'm not the …"

He stumbled on his words and came to a stop. Hess shook her head, shushing gently, but he staggered on.

"The man I *am* and the man I should be are not … There are things I *should* have wanted all along, and I should have known that I should have wanted them, but I … is this making any sense?"

"Not at all, but it's alright, Fenny. You don't need to—"

"Wait! I've got it. I've got it now. Give me a moment." He cleared his throat as Hess wrapped the blanket more tightly around them. "I did everything wrong. I saw a vision of myself becoming this great man … some kind of adored hero. A Saint. I blinded myself following that shining vision, and with all the glare in my eyes I couldn't see real things. Things that were right in front of me. You're real, Hess, and here you are, by some miracle, in my arms. So … there you have it. It's soppy, but at least it's true."

"Oh, Fenny," Hess said. "I wish you saw what I can see. You've always been great. Now, you're on your way to becoming decent."

Fentor laughed drily. "For me, the road to decency will surely be long and arduous."

"Well," Hess said, smiling. "It's easier with company."

Somewhere in the distance, a rooster crowed.

"Now, what in the name of Temlin's best woolen socks are we going to do next?" Fentor said.

"Which Temlin, the Saint or the farmer?"

"Either. Does it matter?"

"I know it's just a saying, but I'll bet farmer Temlin actually *does* have a very nice pair of woolen socks."

Fentor gave her a look, then Hess snickered, and then Fentor laughed. Soon, they laughed together at the mere fact that they were laughing.

"Well, what is the plan, then? Fight Lady Ironhands? Petition the king?" Fentor asked.

"I've no idea, but I'm sure we can come up with something."

"I'm sure we can. I fear Her Excellency's next assault will make the last one look like a spring picnic."

"For now, let's just keep warm, shall we?" Hess said. She nestled her head under his chin.

"A fine plan, indeed."

They watched as the sun peeked from rosy clouds and draped curtains of gold over the farmland below. Vast patches of ploughed dirt and manure began to look like gleaming fields of treasure. Fentor smiled. It had always been in his power to see things differently. It all came down to a simple choice, really. Would he see the manure, the dirt, and the mud? Or would he see the stubble of green stalks, the honeyed sunlight cascading over the landscape?

The paintings hanging in the Madean Academy of Arts held a truth that he could now, at last, understand. They depicted the countryside not as it was, but as it *could* be seen. Such art no longer felt like a lie. It was a translation.

A transmutation. A true artist could see the oft-hidden beauty in rustic, muddy hills, and paint it for others to see. Out of some dark, long-abandoned recess of his mind, an oil painting of a rose-cheeked woman tossing grain for the chickens rose up before him. Only now, in his mind's eye, the painting was of Hess. In a way, it always had been.

So, he stood with Hess on the hill and watched the dawn unfold. The golden glow portended no call of destiny, no glory, no victory for him to snatch. The hills were simply there before them, not to be conquered, just enjoyed. They became, for a glorious hour, immortal. The memory of their kiss lingered on his lips. That was the problem with such rare, delicate moments of intimacy — one is left with an effervescent tingle from that sip of love's champagne. One would always crave more.

He turned to her and pulled her face to his.

Chapter 41

*I am familiar with Madean economics. It is
the sophisticated set of equations and graphs
used to tell the starving that their hunger is,
in fact, good for society.*

Sage Nyendi.

The esteemed Grand Toque Elatea Talentus, Duchess of
Astralan, Countess of Shorovia, and the chief designing
engineer of Talentus Heavy Ordnance emerged from the
pines. She found not one Lake Bianlock, but two. The
second, smaller, more jagged lake lay precisely where her
distillery had been.

That displeased her.

Fentor and the others had fallen far behind the moment
she took her eyes off them. Many hours had passed since
then. Most likely, they had perished. Such a shame. Now

she was burdened by the task of replacing them. She made a note to keep a closer eye on the next lot.

She rounded the main lake at a brisk pace. On the way, she picked up a round pebble large enough to fill her palm. She pressed her thumb down on it, straining hard, but accomplished nothing. Then she ground it hard between both hands, and it broke into pieces. The method of gauging her power was crude, but informative enough. Her strength had diminished almost to the level of ordinary mortals.

Flushed with the unique frustration of one thwarted after long travails, she marched to the bank of the newly-formed, second lake.

Traces of her property were strewn across the shore and in the water. Her distillery, reduced to shards of twisted metal, splinters, and broken glass. It could not be clearer what had happened. Sabotage.

Not a soul was around to witness any loss of composure, but she maintained it with great effort. Just as Father had always said: "Back straight, chin up, elbows in, even when we're alone. We uphold our discipline for ourselves, not for the world to see."

As a girl, she had sat in front of the mirror and stuck pins in her leg until she could keep her face perfectly calm, unflinching. Then she would drop heavier and heavier books on the pins, until at last she mastered facial serenity. She had not done it for nothing.

She would not pout. She would not complain. She would not stamp her foot or gnash her teeth. She would not, she would not.

Despite her best efforts, her frustrations reached their boiling point. Like a kettle pregnant with steam, they gushed forth. After all, nobody was around to see.

"Bollocks," she muttered, hands on her hips.

With her rage thus ejected, she quickly checked her surroundings to be sure no eavesdroppers had caught her swearing like a milkmaid. She took her hands off her hips, as well. She had indulged in that uncouth posture long enough. If she was not careful, she would soon find herself slouching and cursing like a miner.

A few paces away, a strange flower emerged from the gravel. The odd, pale thing grew as she watched, sprouting four fingers, a thumb, and bloody knuckles caked with dust. She shook her head. She must be in dire need of sleep. It was no five-fingered flower, but a hand. A slender, familiar hand.

She went over, took hold of the hand, and pulled.

Dídac popped out of the ground like a turnip, covered in flourlike gravel dust. He gasped for air and coughed all over Elatea's front—without even covering his mouth.

"Oh, my dear, dear Dídac," she said. She took hold of his chin and forced him to look into her eyes. Wet tracks ran from his streaming eyes, nostrils, and lips. It looked as though his face was melting.

"M – My Lady," he wheezed.

"There, there. Hush now, my dear," she said. She pulled his frail, feeble body into an embrace, and whispered in his pale, pointed ear, "When I am through with you, you will wish you had stayed buried in that little grave of yours."

She held him like a nurturing mother. He struggled and fussed, trying to push her off. She cradled him tighter and tighter, until his arms were pinned.

Revenge, so sweet, would soon be hers. One ill deed creates a debt that must be repaid. The ledgers of right and wrong had to be balanced, after all. She would only be doing her Providence-given duty to repay the sins of her enemies. She hummed sweetly in Dídac's dusty ear, dreaming of the blood-soaked fruition of her reprisals.

Revenge may have been her solemn duty, but by Temlin, she could taste the nectar of it on her tongue.

THE END.

Thank you for reading!

Also by Timothy S Currey:

The Isle of Thamber

Amelia & Athers

The Tyranny of Shadows

Death of the Tree Path

The King & Kishar

Find all my books and more at https://timothyscottcurrey.com

Please leave an honest review wherever you can. Every review helps me reach new readers, so it really does help.

Acknowledgements

Special thanks to my wonderful and dedicated beta readers:

Maureen H., Perry S., Steve F., Michael R., Lisa M., Chris B., Calvin K.

And, obviously, Leah.